SEDUCTIVE MOONBEAMS AND DANGEROUS MYSTERY

Jana looked at her handsome companion in shock and dismay. Was he her beloved Varian disguised for some unknown reason as his evil half brother or was he truly who he appeared to be? *What if you really are Ryker? What if Varian did discard and betray me?* She couldn't halt her tears.

"Dreams and hallucinations can seem real, Jana, but they aren't. This is real: you and I in our private world together. Please don't spoil it."

"I don't know what to believe anymore," she whispered.

"You're safe here with me," Ryker promised. "Varian is out of your life forever, and he'll be married to Canissia soon. You belong to me, Jana. See, you're wearing my marriage band."

Jana gazed at the gold bracelet encrusted with precious gems. It was engraved with Ryker Tryloni's name and their marriage date. Was she still Ryker's property and in his control while Varian . . . She felt so confused, so heartbroken.

"I'm your destiny and your protector, Jana of Earth," Ryker vowed.

Be he Varian or Ryker, alien lover or alien husband, her question had to be the same, "But who will protect me from you?"

PINNACLE'S PASSIONATE AUTHOR–

PATRICIA MATTHEWS

EXPERIENCE *LOVE'S* PROMISE

LOVE'S AVENGING HEART (302-1, $3.95/$4.95)
Red-haired Hannah, sold into servitude as an innkeeper's barmaiden, must survive the illicit passions of many men, until love comes to free her questing heart.

LOVE'S BOLD JOURNEY (421-4, $4.50/$5.50)
Innocent Rachel, orphaned after the Civil War, travels out West to start a new life, only to meet three bold men–two she couldn't love and one she couldn't trust.

LOVE'S DARING DREAM (372-2, $4.50/$5.50)
Proud Maggie must overcome the poverty and shame of her family's bleak existence, encountering men of wealth, power, and greed until her impassioned dreams of love are answered.

LOVE'S GOLDEN DESTINY (393-5, $4.50/$5.50)
Lovely Belinda Lee follows her gold-seeking father to the Alaskan Yukon where danger and love are waiting in the wilderness.

LOVE'S MAGIC MOMENT (409-5, $4.50/$5.50)
Sensuous Meredith boldly undertakes her father's lifework to search for a fabled treasure in Mexico, where she must learn to distinguish between the sweet truth of love and the seduction of greed and lust.

Available wherever paperbacks are sold, or order direct from the Publisher. Send cover price plus 50¢ per copy for mailing and handling to Pinnacle Books, Dept. 639, 475 Park Avenue South, New York, N.Y. 10016. Residents of New York and Tennessee must include sales tax. DO NOT SEND CASH. For a free Zebra/ Pinnacle catalog please write to the above address.

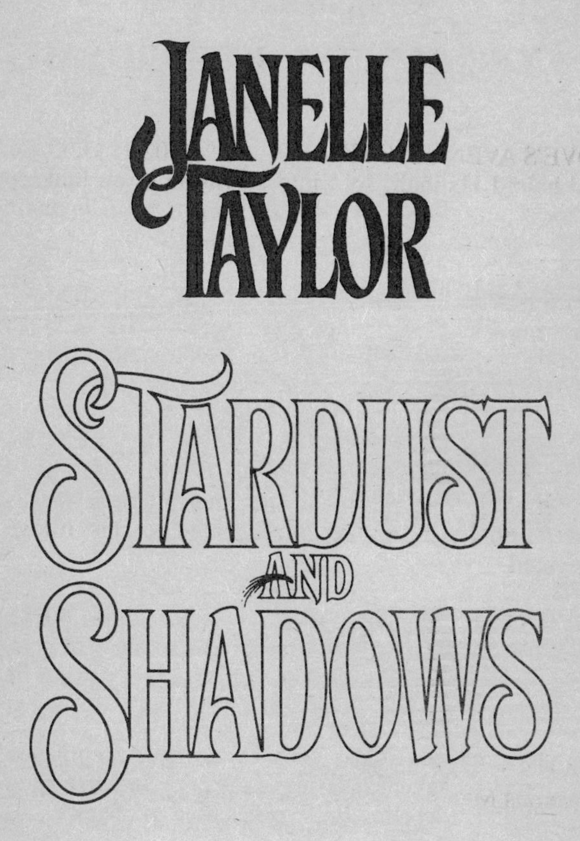

PINNACLE BOOKS
WINDSOR PUBLISHING CORP.

PINNACLE BOOKS

are published by

Windsor Publishing Corp.
475 Park Avenue South
New York, NY 10016

First printing: September, 1992

Printed in the United States of America

Dedicated to:

***Mike Dekle**, a longtime and talented friend who writes and records great music that soothes me when I'm stressed.*

***Kevin Kelly** and **Ken Richman**, in appreciation for your friendship and support over the years.*

***Dr. James Matheny**, who taught me so much about research when I worked with him at the Medical College of Georgia.*

***Walter Zacharius** and the late **Roberta Bender Grossman** who made this book a dream come true.*

Part I
Moondust And Madness

As the playful Gods gather to watch mortals below,
The helpless Fates warns sadly, for only they know:
  Careful of "Moondust" which captures a heart;
  Beware of its "Madness" which tears lovers apart . . .

Chapter One

"You gave me a big scare, Jana of Earth. More than once I feared I was going to lose my new wife forever. I'm glad you're finally awake."

Jana Greyson stared at the blond alien as his gentle fingers stroked her cheek and tawny hair. She realized she was back in the Trilabs Complex on Darkar, but he couldn't be Ryker. "What are we doing here?" she asked.

"You contracted a dangerous disease last week; it was almost fatal to your system. You've been hovering between unconsciousness and delirium for five long and frightening days. I assumed you'd been inoculated for all the ones unknown to your world. As soon as you're well, my ravishing wife, I'll have Varian's oversight taken care of so this won't happen again." He kissed her forehead. "Now that I've found a unique woman who is able to fulfill me, I don't plan to lose her to a mistake on her captor's part. Varian should never have allowed this to happen; you could have died." He continued to caress her pale cheek and to smile. "No woman anywhere is more perfectly suited to Ryker Triloni than you are. Besides being as weak as a newborn, my exquisite bride, how do you feel?"

Jana closed her eyes and shook her head to clear it. This couldn't be her husband, even if that was his face and voice. Prince Ryker Triloni couldn't be stroking her with such gentleness. Nor were the twin green flames in his eyes familiar to her. "Wake up, J. G.," she told herself, "you're only dreaming. Ryker's dead."

"I'm not dead, my beautiful wife. I'm immune to all diseases, so I didn't take ill as you did. When Captain E'los delivered those rare plants from Zandia, he infected you with a powerful germ. You barely survived; for a while, I feared you wouldn't. Thank the fates they dared not take you from me. Don't look so worried," he said soothingly. "The serum and treatment finally worked, but they required a lot of testing and adjusting in my lab. I'm glad you regained consciousness before I had to take drastic steps with an unproven remedy. Never fear, Jana of Earth, you'll be well and strong again soon. I promise."

"This can't be happening," she murmured. "Wake up, J. G." She tried to sit, but the blond-haired man restrained her by the shoulders.

"You mustn't overexert yourself. Your equilibrium isn't normal yet and your circulation slowed while you were confined to bed. You don't want to play havoc with your blood pressure by getting up too quickly or too soon. You need to rest and heal. Give yourself time to regain your strength."

A cold sweat raced over her body; it chilled and dampened her flesh. Her vision and wits weren't totally clear, but it seemed as if she were awake. Her ears had a slight hum that she knew wasn't from the audiotranslator implanted there so she could understand any alien language spoken. Though she'd been abducted from her planet and galaxy months ago, she still had difficulty sometimes with the aural device. When mouths didn't move with the words she was hearing, it was like watching a movie with the audio and video mismatched. Some words, especially slang, lacked accurate interpretations; some translations were even comical or confusing. None of those problems was the trouble today. His words were clear—only the situation itself was inexplicable and alarming.

Jana observed the tall and handsome male as he passed a black boxlike instrument over her head and chest, a medical analyzer that instantly read and recorded vital functions. She noticed the nonterrestrial being used his left hand. Ryker Triloni was right-handed but Varian Saar was left-handed! *Your rescue by Varian was too real. You can't be back in Ryker's evil clutches. You'll wake up soon and discover this is only a bad dream.*

He smiled at the results of the digital readouts. "Much better. You'll return to normal within a few days. Don't worry, my fetching enchantress, there's no hurry to finish redecorating the house. I agree it needs a woman's touch, but we have plenty of time, Jana of Earth—all of our lives. As soon as you're better, we'll get back to where we were. I must admit, I am enjoying the direction of our new journey."

Jana felt almost seared by his fiery gaze. Yet she trembled from a cold premonition. Why was Varian calling her "Jana of Earth" when only Ryker had done so? Why had her love brought her back to this horrid place where she almost died? Why was he still wearing that Ryker disguise? Why was he trying to sound and look like his half brother? "I don't know what you're talking about, Varian. I haven't been ill. Why am I hooked up to these contraptions?"

"You're weak and disoriented, Jana. It's from the medication and *Rahgine's* Fever. That's only natural. You're a doctor, a scientist, a chemist. You know what severe illness and lengthy delirium can do to a person. I'm Ryker. You live here with me now. We're married. Varian no longer owns you or controls your life. Remember?"

"If our captor did one good thing for us on our trek to your galaxy, it was to make certain we were well trained and well prepared for our new lives as enslaved alien mates, *charls*, as you Maffeians call us. Tris is too intelligent to have forgotten vital inoculations. So why this deceit?"

"By Tris, I assume you mean Dr. Tristan Zarcoff, Varian's chief medical officer on the *Wanderlust*. Since you came down with *Rahgine's*, it's obvious Dr. Zarcoff either forgot that inoculation or it didn't take with you. As soon as you're strong enough, I'll have antibodies tests done to see which ones didn't take with your system. Our two cultures are very similar, but I'm sure we have a few biological differences."

"You'll only concoct a test to get results in your favor," she accused. "The reason you faked my auction to Draco was because you needed to hold on to me as a gift to Ryker. You were furious because Draco almost fell in love with me and refused to return me to you. Then, along came Ryker's challenge and my near death at what obviously was bad timing. Did the Supreme Council order you to give me to Ryker that first time? Did they order you to pretend to return me to him and for you to impersonate him? What's the mission this time, Commander Saar? Are you so loyal to the Alliance, *Kadim* Tirol, and Star Fleet that you will do anything they command of you, obey any order, accept any assignment no matter whom it hurts, including yourself? I won't be used again, you space pirate! Take off your disguise, Varian; this wild scheme won't work."

"Disguise? Mission? Varian? I'm *Ryker*, Jana. Don't worry me. I'll summon the best doctor to run a brain scan for possible damage."

"My brain is fine. Why are you doing this? Haven't you tricked me and used me and betrayed me enough times in the past?"

"What I'm trying to do is get you well and convince you we'll be perfect together. I've been near this bed every day and night since you took ill. At times I doubted you were going to survive. I even suspected your inoculations had been skipped on purpose so something like this would snatch you away from me just as I came to want you to stay. Maybe Varian would rather see you dead than with me."

Those words cut Jana like a sharp scalpel. Before she went to sleep, Varian had confessed his love and proposed marriage.

Why this abrupt and vicious change? She stared at the man speaking to her in a seductive tone, a tender expression on his face.

"Odd as it was, Jana of Earth, I found myself praying to the gods, begging them to let you live. I even threatened and bargained for your survival. I told you shortly after your arrival that I had never met a woman like you. I can't explain how you got to me so quickly because I don't understand it myself. For a man of science not to have even a tiny theory to proceed on is scary and frustrating. Maybe you do possess a potent and mysterious alien magic. Maybe realizing that fact frightened Varian into carving you out of his life. Since they accused my mother of bewitching his father with powerful magic, I'm sure the possibility of Varian falling into the same trap was intimidating to him. As for me, my terrestrial enchantress, I find the possibility intriguing. How intoxicating to have my very own angel as my wife."

He spoke with an Androasian inflection that sounded like a southern accent, whereas Varian's had reminded her of Welsh. "I'm getting annoyed with this ruse, Varian," she murmured, "so stop it. You tricked me before, but I'm not stupid. I haven't been struck low by an alien disease; I haven't been delirious or hallucinating. You have five minutes to explain this . . . whatever it is you're doing to me." The way his brows lowered and held taut said he was becoming annoyed. Annoyed, she mused, because he couldn't fool her?

"Maybe I should ask what you're trying to pull on me, Jana of Earth. You're disputing logic and reality. I haven't seen or heard you behave this way before. You said you would marry me and agreed to all my terms. I told you the two things I detest are guile and defiance, so I've tried to be clear and kind with you. I admit I was rough and cold at first, but you know why I acted that way, just as you know I apologized and relented."

Jana stared at him. How could Varian know what had happened between her and Ryker when she had first arrived on his private planetoid, Darkar? Yet, he kept saying things only she and Ryker had known. . . . There were ways, she reasoned: she and Ryker had told Varian the entry code to this impenetrable complex which held all of the secrets of Ryker Triloni and Trilabs; Varian must have read Shara's detailed scientific journals and the evil woman's private diaries. Ryker must have made videotapes of their meetings and Varian had viewed them.

"If you honestly believe I'm Varian Saar, there is a problem here. If it's medical, it can be handled. If it's mental, I hope it can be cured. If it's a cunning trick, we're both in trouble. I'm not a man anyone should try to dupe or betray. I make a powerful and good friend but a dangerous enemy."

Jana saw he was serious, but he didn't appear to be trying to intimidate her. Maybe it was an attempt to caution and silence her, change her position to a defensive one. Yet, she couldn't allow his deception to go unchallenged.

He continued in a mellow tone. "Will it be so disagreeable to live as Princess Jana Triloni, my wife and heir, mother of my children, joint heir to the Androasian throne and Empire? I told you before you became ill that you could resume your research with me in my labs. You agreed. You said you were recovering the pride, confidence, and self-esteem Varian stole from you. You said you wanted to repay his treachery and betrayal by marrying me before he went through with his marriage to Cass. Why have you changed your mind? Why do you think I'm him?"

"Because you're lying to me. Is this an experiment for a new mission? Do you think that if you can dupe me into believing you're Ryker, you can fool anyone? Or perhaps it is a test of my feelings? To learn how I would react if Ryker had survived the attack and I was back with him? You don't have to trick me to get anything. I'm an alien captive. You've proven you have ways to get whatever you desire from me. Why this charade?"

"I'm not deceiving you, Jana. There was no attack. No one, including Varian Saar, would dare attack Darkar. I have sensors all over this planetoid that would detect any ship's presence. I have laser weapons located in every area of Darkar that can blast any ship out of the sky. No one enters my air space without my permission. If anyone managed to get through my security system and defenses and tried to enter this complex, an automatic self-destruct sequence would go into effect; an explosion here would release powerful chemicals into the atmosphere that would destroy life on the nearby planets and contaminate this entire sector of space for thousands of years; everyone is aware of those realities and wisely respects them. I am the only person who knows the entry code."

"*I* know it. So do *you*, Varian. Ryker told you when you two battled to his death. That's how you got us in here. But why this cruel pretense?"

"Varian and I never fought a lethal fight, Jana of Earth, not *yet* anyway, but I'm sure we will one day because that is what he wants. I'm standing here before you and he's on Eire with his grandfather, *Kadim* Tirol. I can prove to you that no one, including you, knows the entry code."

"Then you've changed it since you drugged me. You pulled that trick before—once when you abducted me from Earth and then when you snatched me from Draco's. I want to get up. Call Tris to unhook me from this apparatus or I'll yank myself free. I mean it, Varian; stop it and let me up, now!"

He captured her hands and pinned them to her sides. "Calm down, Jana. You're too weak and disoriented to get out of bed. You still have two hundred cc's of medication to be infused. I can't allow you to endanger yourself."

Jana ceased her struggles. "Then tell me the truth."

"Everything I've told you since you awoke is the truth. I thought you had come to accept me as I've accepted you. These things you're saying didn't happen. Why won't you believe me?"

"You're saying you're Ryker Triloni and not Varian Saar's near twin beneath that disguise of yours?"

"Of course I'm Ryker, and we're half brothers. I explained all of that last week. I was shocked to discover you didn't know we were kin; it's no secret, even if most people dare not speak openly about the grim truth, especially to outsiders. We look alike because that's a normal trait for our race: sons always take their fathers' images. Since Galen Saar was our father, we both favor him. But I did take my mother's blond hair and green eyes because Androasian genes are almost as potent as Maffeian ones."

"I am well acquainted with how advanced your technology is and that your knowledge is far superior to my planet's. I've seen your medical miracles at work, including on *me* after I angered you while trying to escape your clutches on your ship. Have you forgotten how you struck me in reflex when I attacked you and your men? You had my injury healed within a day. Is that how Tris removed the cleft in your chin and added that scar on your right jawline to match the one Ryker possessed before you killed him? Tris is very talented; he even smoothed out some of the smile lines around your mouth and eyes. You're wearing green contact lenses to conceal your blue eyes and your black hair is dyed blond, but I'm not fooled. Have you forgotten I saw you convincingly disguised as him after you rescued me?"

"Look closely into my eyes, Jana. See, no iris covers. They're green. The scar has been left for years to remind my half brother and the others of his temper and hatred. If it troubles you, I'll have it removed today. But I won't change other things to make me look more like him, not even for you."

With his face close to hers, she looked into his emerald eyes. Varian's sapphire ones had glittered with vitality and a fiery passion for life. Ryker's were as dark, impenetrable, and lush as a tropical jungle nearing nightfall. Her gaze studied the scar that appeared old. No sign of recent surgical alterations could be found. He smiled then. Varian possessed a grin that could dispel the darkest gloom of night: quick, easy, radiant, and sexy, one that seemed to flow over her like warmed honey. Ryker smiled with the left side of his mouth: slow, reluctant, but also sexy. Their mannerisms, voices, and expressions weren't the same. Even their colognes were different. He was right, but . . . Varian Saar was known for his cool head, steel nerves, sharp wits, and rigid control. Somehow this was Varian still in his Ryker disguise! She had gone to sleep in his arms after making passionate love to him; she couldn't have dreamed *that*! "It's a trick. But why? To try to get Ryker's secrets and inheritance, just as Shara said you would. Do you need to impersonate him to make certain our marriage is legal so all is not lost to you and Maffei? Do you need time to take what you desire from Trilabs before news of his death is released and you're confronted by *Kadim* Maal's retribution on you and the Alliance?"

"I'm not impersonating Ryker, Jana; I *am* Ryker, your husband. I haven't been killed or harmed, and no one is trying to take anything from us or Trilabs. You're confused, that's all."

Jana shook her head. "I told you Ryker was good to me and we were becoming close friends. You're afraid I fell in love with him, aren't you? You're being vindictive because you think we slept together. Why should that bother you, Varian? You've possessed women from one end of the Tri-Galaxy to the other. You spent months attracting and repelling me like a cruel magnet. After all you've done to me, why would my being drawn to a kind and gentle man like Ryker surprise you and provoke you to such extremes?"

"I don't understand you. Rages of Fate, woman, what happened to you during your illness? How could you have forgotten everything we've said and done?"

"What about the portrait over there that Shara showed to me before she tried to murder me?"

He looked baffled and concerned. "My mother is dead, Jana. She has been for seven years; she murdered Galen and Amaya Saar, then killed herself. Her body lies in state in the Androasian palace of my grandfather, *Kadim* Maal Triloni."

"Shara said that wasn't her body on display. I met her here. She told me all kinds of awful things before she tried to kill me. She told me everything about the past and their future plans."

"You couldn't have seen or spoken with my mother, Jana;

she's long dead. When we visit Grandfather soon, you can see the truth for yourself."

"Then explain the portrait behind that curtain and what's in the safe over there." She motioned over her head to the wall behind her.

"What are you talking about, Jana?"

Jana glanced over her shoulder: they were all gone! "But . . . I don't understand. She showed me a portrait of you without your disguise; you and Varian looked like twins. She said there were journals in a safe she pointed to behind the portrait, diaries she kept since she was a girl. She said that you saved her after she used cryonic chemicals to induce suspended animation to fool everyone into thinking she was dead. She said she was going to slay me and take my identity, that you had left to snare Varian in a lethal trap. I was drugged and couldn't fight her. She said you two . . ." Jana halted the rush of words. Her gaze darted about the room as she sought reality and truth. What if, she fretted, he wasn't Varian?

"It's the illness and fever, Jana. You're suffering from delusions. I showed you Mother's picture and related the past to you just before you became ill. Everything's gotten mixed up. But don't fret—your scientific mind will clear as soon as you've fully recovered. Unless, of course, the medication leaves you with partial amnesia; that happens in certain cases—a side effect on alien systems. I hope not. We made a great deal of progress in our relationship in the past week."

Jana's brain frantically reasoned. If her rescue was real and Varian loved her, why would he do this? Yet, with her medical training, she couldn't argue that what he was telling her was impossible. On Earth, certain types of anesthesia and medication caused short-term memory loss. He looked and talked like Ryker, but she was convinced it was Varian Saar standing before her. She had been drug-dazed during her terrifying confrontation with Shara and she had been emotionally dazed during her passionate lovemaking with Varian after his rescue. But those two episodes *had* occurred . . . hadn't they?

Jana gazed at the area between her breasts where Tris had

used direct cardiac puncture to revive her; no mark was there, not even discoloration or soreness. The same was true of her throat, where Shara had jabbed in a syringe to inject a dose of medication she hoped would be lethal. Her wrists exposed no signs of the straps Shara had used to secure her helpless to the laboratory table. Yet, with their technology and elapsed time, those things could have been removed. If her suspicions were true, that meant they had gone over every inch of her body to remove any clues to her recent trauma, including the hangnail, which was the reason she had come to Ryker's medical lab that fated day. She wished to fetch a tiny scissor for repair of it but instead she had encountered Shara and peril. Hadn't she? With their technology, Varian could have been made to look like Ryker, as he had done when she last saw him. Hadn't he? With his knowledge of his half brother's ways, with the aid of Ryker's videotapes, and with Shara's diaries, Varian could easily impersonate the Androasian prince with perfection. Whatever Varian's scheme was, she wasn't going to fall for it. "How long have I been here?" she asked.

"Almost five weeks. Two as my wife, or rather twelve days."

"That's wrong. Ryker and I married a few days ago. That same day, Ryker said he was leaving on business but he really went to . . ." She watched the way he looked at her, as if warning her she was going too far with her challenge of his honesty. *My God, what if you are Ryker? If none of that happened, Varian* did *discard and betray me*. She couldn't halt the tears from leaving her eyes to flow into her touseled sunny hair. She didn't want to be in this place with this alien. She didn't want to be a captive, a prisoner, forever. She wanted to go home, to Earth, to Texas, to her room, to her bed. She wanted her old life returned. She wanted her friends, especially her best friend, Andrea McKay. She wanted safety and peace. Was this horrible nightmare, she fretted in panic, to be her destiny?

"Dreams and hallucinations can seem real, Jana, but they aren't. This is real: you and me in our private world together.

We were beginning a good life together. Don't spoil it because of your wild and cruel delusions."

Her troubled gaze fused with his imploring one as he wiped away her tears. "I don't know what to think or believe anymore. Every time I make a new beginning, he sneaks into my life and destroys it: on Earth, on his ship, at Draco's, on Eire with his grandfather, then with you. How could it seem so real?"

"The illness and medicine, Jana; they played tricks on your mind. Everything that's happened to you since he captured you got twisted up while you were delirious. You're safe here; I promise. Varian is out of your life forever, and he'll be married to Canissia Garthon soon."

Canissia Garthon! She scoffed at mention of the name of the woman obsessed with Varian, the woman who had tormented her and whom she believed—according to her "delusion"—had kidnapped her and brought her to Darkar to be destroyed by Varian's archrival and fierce enemy.

"At first I accused you of being sent here as Varian's spy and assassin. After I spent time with you, I realized I was wrong. He manipulated you many times and almost destroyed you. I thought it had stopped. Destiny sent you here to fill the voids in my life and heart, and I in yours. We're perfectly matched, Jana. You're my wife as the fates designed. See, you're wearing my marriage band."

Jana gazed at the gold bracelet encrusted with precious gems on the top side, the alien equivalent of a wedding ring. The underside engraving gave Ryker Triloni's name and their marriage date. Was she still Ryker's property and in his control, and Varian . . . She felt weak, confused, afraid, and heartbroken. *Merciful God*, she prayed in trepidation, *can this be real*?

"I'm your destiny and your protector, Jana of Earth," the blond alien vowed.

Be he Varian or Ryker, alien lover or alien husband, the question was the same: "But who will protect me from you? I'm nothing more than an alien captive, a lowly *charl*, a slave; that's all I can ever be in your world."

"You're wrong, Jana of Earth; you're no longer a *charl* and you were never born to be a captive mate in my galaxy or in yours. You're free; you're my wife: that was our bargain, remember? Your freedom in exchange for marrying me. You will remain free as long as you remain my wife. If you run away or break our contract, your right to liberty is revoked by law, a law created to prevent alien women from tricking their owners into freeing them. You signed the agreement; it's legal and will be enforced. But I ask you, don't push me into doing that. I much prefer how things were before you fell ill."

Please, God, let me wake up. Let this be only a nightmare.

"I do hope your mind clears soon and you remember what's happened between us. If not, I'll have to woo you and win your trust once again. My half brother might hate alien enchantresses and reject one for a mate, but I don't feel that way about you. I never believed in *charl* laws and the Androasian Empire has never practiced them. I hear Martella Karsh is trying to have them abolished; I hope she succeeds, for they aren't needed any more for Maffei race survival."

He seemed to be trying to dispel her fears and doubts, but would Ryker behave and feel as this man claimed in this situation? As if she accepted his words, she asked, "Why didn't you, or Varian, or *someone*, tell me you two are half brothers besides being fierce rivals?"

"When I realized you didn't know, Jana, I told you. Don't you remember?"

"No, I don't. I know you hate each other because of the past. When I met Supreme Ruler Jurad Tabriz and his son Prince Taemin on the planet Lynrac during the *charl* auctions . . ." she began, referring to the leaders of the neighboring Pyropean Galaxy Federation, "Jurad first mentioned Shara's name before me. He hinted at a conflict and hatred between himself and the Saars because of her loss as his bride long ago. He wanted to purchase me to become Prince Taemin's wife. Varian was furious. And I couldn't believe he would treat high rulers in such a vile manner. Your name was mentioned briefly as Jurad's ally. At the time, Jurad seemed kind to me; he withdrew his marriage offer to appease Varian's temper."

"How did Varian explain his rash behavior?" the alien asked.

"He didn't. When he ordered Nigel Sanger, his first officer, to get me out, Nigel told me there were long-standing troubles between them that he couldn't tell me about. When I asked questions about Shara and Ryker, I was ordered never to speak the names again. Nigel said it had to do with dark and deadly affairs in the past that brought out the worst in Varian. After witnessing his behavior, I knew that was true. Nigel claimed the Tabrizes only wanted to get their hands on me so they could torture me and slay me as revenge on Varian."

"Is that all you heard about us and our troubles before we met?"

"No. While I was living with Draco," she explained about the Maffeian who was her secret guardian for a short time, "I saw Jurad again at a party. He seemed pleased that Supreme Councilman Procyon had purchased me. When I pressed for information about the past, he mentioned the names of Galen and Amaya, and *Kadim* Maal Triloni. From my studies of the Tri-Galaxy on my way here, I knew *Kadim* Maal was the ruler of the Androas Empire in the next galaxy. He told me you and Varian were fierce enemies and led me to believe Amaya was Varian's lost love, not his mother as I learned later by accident. He said Shara killed Amaya, Galen, and herself seven years ago. Until recently, I thought Galen was Varian's brother. Jurad said he was to marry Shara but she fell under the spell of the Star Fleet officer who was transporting her across the Maffei Galaxy as a sign of truce. He wanted me to believe the Commander Saar he was speaking about was Varian, not his father, Galen. He said you and Shara were of the same royal bloodline but never explained you were mother and son. He said: 'Until all Saar blood is spilled, the conflict between the Trilonis and Saars and the Tabrizes and Saars will not end.' That's all I knew until . . ." She paused a moment.

"I learned the rest of the truth here. As I'm sure you know, none of that personal information was in the books we were given to study. I can understand how Varian would hold Shara to blame for his parents' deaths, but that doesn't explain his fierce hatred of you, *Kadim* Maal, and the Tabrizes. I can also understand your hatred of Galen for his negative effect on your life, but that doesn't explain your fierce hatred of Varian—not to the point of you two, half brothers, wanting to kill each other. Surely there's more to the story than I've been told. Or recall you telling me."

"I don't want Varian's fortune, rank, or his life," he answered calmly. "Our father stained the Saar name with his treachery long ago. As Varian and others would have you and everyone believe, Galen was not innocent in the episode with my mother. She didn't force him to have a love affair with her, not from what she told me and Grandfather long ago. I do admit Mother went mad and destroyed all of them. That was wrong. A person can't force another person to love her, or him. In fairness to my father, perhaps he was briefly overcome by her beauty and charms. Perhaps he couldn't resist her. Some women are irresistible, Jana—women like you."

She tried not to recoil from his touch because she wanted answers. Somewhere in the midst of their hostilities lay clues to the truth she needed.

"Galen's crime wasn't in ending the affair, it was in succumbing to my mother, then accusing her of bewitching him with drugs and spells. Since my mother was skilled in those areas and arts, it was a cunning excuse for him when he came to his senses and realized the treachery he had committed against the Androasian Empire and Pyropean Federation, an intergalactic war-provoking deed. To choose Shara would cost him too much; he would have been compelled to give up everything in Maffei—including Amaya, his unborn first son, and his Star Fleet rank—to live out his days in Androas with my mother and our people. He lied to get out of his self-dug trap. He rejected me even though my face exposed him as my father. He humiliated the Trilonis before the Tri-Galaxy. That's what drove my mother insane. I suppose she assumed the anguish and shame would not end until Galen was dead. After the foul deed, she couldn't accept his loss and, having been denied him in life, she joined him in death. You can't blame Grandfather for hating the Saars; they cost him his only child, heir to the throne. The wound was cut deeper when the Maffei Interplanetary Alliance refused to doubt and punish Galen.''

''Perhaps because he was the *Kadim*'s son-in-law and Supreme Commander of Star Fleet,'' Jana said. ''During my journey here, we captives received excellent training and schooling, so I know about the politics of your world. A *kadim* is the highest and most powerful ruler in a galaxy. In Androas, it's your grandfather, *Kadim* Maal Triloni. Here, it's Varian's grandfather, *Kadim* Tirol Trygue. It would be hard for people who loved and respected men of Galen's and Tirol's ranks to doubt their words.''

''Just as it was impossible for people who loved and respected Shara to doubt hers,'' the blond alien countered. ''The Androasians and Pyropeans didn't doubt her. Yet, galaxies do not go to war without proof of crimes perpetrated against them. The truth died with the only two people who knew it—my mother and father.''

As she listened, Jana Greyson studied him. They had so many similarities and yet so many undeniable differences . . . ''Don't you think it's smart to possess such self-control? So many lives could be lost upon words that can't be proven false or true.''

''Of course I agree. War should never be entered lightly. Sometimes, all one has is another's words upon which to base a decision or action.''

She saw him ruffle his blond hair with his . . . *right hand* as Ryker would. She gazed at his chin where no sexy dent was located. Perhaps she could think clearer if he wasn't so near and enticing . . . ''What if that person lies to you and deceives you?'' she asked huskily.

"I haven't done either to you, Jana of Earth. I am one of the richest, most powerful, most respected, feared, and envied men in the Tri-Galaxy. I own my own world and I am heir to a throne and empire. What do I lack that slaying Varian can bring to me? I have the only thing that I desire from him: you, Jana, no matter his sly motive for sending you to me. Varian lied to you when he claimed I demand to be his rival and foe. It is he who hates and fears *me*. He cannot bear having his father's bastard alive and prosperous. He cannot forget or forgive me for being the son of the killer of his parents."

His emerald gaze roamed her features as he continued. "I don't want to conquer the Maffei Galaxy. I don't want to side with Supreme Ruler Jurad and his son Prince Taemin to war against Maffei. I am the only reason Grandfather hasn't allied himself with the Pyropeans. Yet, my half brother paints me evil and dangerous to the Supreme Council and Alliance Assembly. Ask yourself, Jana, why I would supply powerful drugs, chemicals, and weapons to the Maffeians if they're my enemies. If I were a threat to them, why would they grant me citizenship in their domain? Could they fear one man so much? Don't you see? Without saying it aloud, their actions prove they believe the Trilonis over the Saars. They know I want to live in peace."

That made sense to Jana even in her confused and disheartened state. Both men exuded raw power, immense authority, and primitive sensuality. At various times, her safety and survival were under the control of both men: the very air she breathed, the food she ate. Yet, one difference was noticeable: Varian had been secretive, mysterious, and defensive, whereas Ryker had always been direct, open, and, as far as she knew, honest, even about his flaws and wickedness. When Ryker was cold and cruel, he was straightforward about it. Varian often operated on the sly. When she remained quiet, the extra-terrestrial spoke again.

"It's Varian who won't let the past go. He tried to use you to create another deadly and destructive triangle between a

Saar, Triloni, and alien Goddess. It will never work, not if you side with me, not if you accept the noxious truth about him. Varian let his hatred and jealousy of me change him into a monster who's bent on my destruction. How else could he have used and betrayed you so badly? One day we might learn the real reason he sent you to me. For certain, it was not as a peace token; he doesn't want a truce with me—ever!"

No matter what the handsome and charming alien said, Jana wasn't ready or willing to accept the recent events as either illness or drug-induced delusions. Her suspicions seemed far-fetched and incredible but ownership of Trilabs was an important motive, the only one Varian could have. Perhaps the Maffeians had to make certain her marriage to Ryker was legal and exposed before revealing Ryker's death. But why not include her in on the ruse? She loved Varian Saar and would do almost anything for him. Didn't Varian love *her* enough by now to believe that? No matter what the truth was, she must pretend to go along with the situation at hand until she discovered revealing pieces to this hazardous puzzle.

"You need to rest and recover, Jana. We'll talk again later. Close your eyes and sleep. Things will be clearer when you awaken next time."

The man calling himself Ryker gave her a drug for sleep, lowered the lights, and left. Jana glanced at the ceiling in all directions but sighted no observation monitor. She snuggled under the cover to relax. Nothing was what it seemed and hadn't been since her abduction from Earth. She had finally come to believe in outer space, other worlds, aliens, and the reality of her capture. She had tried to make the best of a difficult and extraordinary predicament because she had no choice. But one incredible situation after another came along to terrify, confuse, and torment her. Had the last episode been only a hallucination from an alien disease and strong medication? It was much easier to believe this was a ruse than to believe Varian's rescue was a dream and he really had given her to Ryker, that Varian didn't love or want her, that he could be so cruel. God knows, she loved, wanted, and needed

Commander Varian Saar. Both men were complex, mercurial, and proud; but which one was she with now?

If this is a devious charade, J. G., something will expose it, she told herself. *You're far from Earth, alone, and perhaps in big trouble. Survival and safety are up to you. Maybe this nightmare will be over when you awaken . . .*

Chapter Two

Jana awoke in a strange but exquisite room. Her wide gaze scanned the mauve, forest-green, sky-blue, and ivory setting of sleek furniture and lovely accessories. Gone were the sterile medical complex, the tubes to her arm, and the blue gown. She was attired in a soft and silky pink garment that accentuated her curves. *Where am I now?* She tossed aside the cover and sat up on the edge of the bed, then waited for her head to clear before attempting to rise. She didn't feel as if she had just been snatched from the jaws of death. She smiled and exhaled in relief. She must be on Altair, Varian's private planetoid. She had only dreamed she was back on Darkar with Ryker. What an awful nightmare, the result, no doubt, of Shara's treachery.

She wanted to rush out, find her love, and shower affection on him. First, however, she should bathe and dress. Her tawny tresses were in disarray and needed shampooing. She walked to the sliding door; it opened from pressure on the floor as she approached it, and she entered a luxurious bathroom. From past experience, she knew how this alien tub worked. She pressed a gold button at one end. Swiftly and instantly, water, at the perfect temperature, filled the oblong area. She stripped off the gown and stepped inside. She pressed another button and a compartment that held soaps, bath oils, and fragrances opened. Pulling a cloth from a rack, she began her bath. A leisurely soak would have felt good, but she was in a hurry to see Varian. She toweled off as the tub automatically emptied and rinsed itself. She dried and brushed her hair, allowing the lengthy waves to flow down her back unbound, then applied cosmetics and perfume to make her look and smell enticing. The exertions had fatigued her, but she reminded herself she had suffered a recent trauma.

Jana went to a walk-in closet and selected a blue jumpsuit. Before donning it, however, she changed her mind and slipped into a flowing caftan-type garment in muted shades of blue, green, and lavender that matched her unusual eyes. She wanted to look appealing and to make what might happen between her and Varian easier to accomplish. The last time they had made love after her rescue had been glorious, but too short, their need for each other so urgent after the long and frightening separation. She was eager to kiss him, touch him, and to fuse her body with his. She wanted to dispel the lingering fears of his identity.

As she looked for Varian or a servant, she smiled at the way the plush carpet—as soft as feathers and inches deep—almost covered her bare feet. The house was large, but its style made finding her way about easy. Beyond the hallway, she found herself in a huge, magnificent living area with sofas, chairs, tables, and decorative accessories. She was going to love living here as Varian's wife. She didn't know how he would disentangle her from her coerced marriage to Ryker, but she knew he would find a way. She was free, in love, and ecstatic. The soft music filling the room seemed to flow through her body and make her feel light-hearted and weightless. The domic ceiling had an enormous skylight that illuminated the peaceful setting, assisted by diffused lighting on the side walls. The controlled environment was just the right temperature. She twirled around and made herself dizzy. She sank to a sofa to rest. Surely her love would join her soon.

As she wondered why the *transascreens*—alien windows—were all closed, she heard sounds behind her. She grinned, deciding it was for privacy on this special morning, and turned. Then she paled and trembled. It was Ine—Ryker's household servant, an android she had seen only twice since her arrival. Jana gaped at the nonhuman being with yellow eyes and short light-brown hair. Other than lacking any facial expression and having been made with eyelids too wide open to be human, Ine looked real.

"What are you doing here? Where am I?" she asked in confusion.

"I am here to serve you, Dr. Triloni. You sit in the living room."

"I meant, where is this house? Who's home is it?"

"This dwelling is on the planetoid Darkar. It belongs to Ryker Triloni. Do you desire your meal served? Do you have a choice of food and drink?"

Jana felt weak and faint. Her heart pounded. "This can't be true."

"What cannot be true, Dr. Triloni? Your words do not compute. Explain, please. I am here to serve you. What is your desire?"

"Where is . . . Ryker?" she asked the monotone android.

"He is working in the complex. His orders are for you to rest, eat, and heal. He will see you tomorrow. Do you desire to eat now?"

"Yes, bring me a regular breakfast." Jana wanted the . . . nonliving creature to be gone so she could think. She searched the room with wide eyes and a desperate urge to locate a *telecom*, a communications system with viewer screen. She saw none, and wouldn't know how to operate it even if she did. How could she call for help or escape? She didn't even see a television or radio with which to get news from outside.

The android summoned her to a dining area to eat.

"Thank you, Ine. That will be all for now," Jana said, then abruptly commanded her to wait.

Ine turned and stared blankly at her. "Do you have another order?"

"How long have I been here? In Earth time."

"You have lived here for five weeks."

"How long have I been married to Ryker?"

"For thirteen days."

Jana's heart thudded forcefully, her breathing quickened, and her mouth seemed overly dry. She was stunned. "Have I been ill?"

"You had *Rahgine*'s Fever for six days."

"When was the shuttle area repaired after Commander Saar's attack?"

"The shuttle area has not been attacked. No one attacks Darkar."

"How do you know the man calling himself Ryker is the real Ryker?"

"Your question does not compute. Explain, please."

"Is it possible that the man who looks like and calls himself Ryker Triloni is an imposter?"

"It is not possible. I am programmed to respond only to his voice commands. To be commanded by another would cause self-destruction."

Jana realized it was futile to question the android, who would only feed her the information she herself had been fed. "That's all, Ine. Thank you."

"You are welcome, Dr. Triloni."

That disturbing conversation began a long and intimidating day. Between meals and rest periods, Jana roamed the sealed house to see what she could learn. The *transascreen* buttons would not respond when she pressed them, a fact she found odd. When she asked Ine to open them, the android said she was ordered to keep them closed and would not explain why. Nor would she tell Jana why the other areas of the house were sealed against her entering them. It seemed she was confined inside, to the living and sleeping areas. She looked at books, unable to read them because they were written in Androasian, Ryker's native language. Though she had been taught Maffeian during and after her trek here, she found nothing around in that alien language. It was frustrating and alarming to be trapped in the *oubliette*; it reminded her of the secret dungeons in old castles with openings at the top, any means of escape far beyond her reach.

While inspecting her private setting, she found the farewell gift Varian had given to her the day of her auction: the gold band with chrysoberyl gems that matched her eyes embedded in the braidwork. He had slipped it on her wedding-ring finger without awareness, he claimed later, of its significance to her culture. She had refused to accept it on the grounds it was too expensive and personal. On Eire, after her return from Draco, she had placed it on her finger. She had been taken from him while wearing it. Or, if this was reality, she had been wearing it when she had been given to Ryker. The dark prince had taken away the golden band when he married her, perhaps because he knew it connected her to his despised half brother. Why had the ring been returned then? Was it the alleged "Ryker"'s way of reminding her she actually belonged to him? Jana tucked the agonizing keepsake back into the velvet tray in the drawer and closed it.

She wandered and reasoned until bedtime when her emotions felt drained and her body exhausted. Not once had "Ryker" come to see her or contacted her. If she had been so ill, why hadn't he checked on her? Was this a scheme to give her time to accept his devious charade? Or did he need more time to study Ryker and Shara's journals and videotapes to prevent slips?

As she got into bed, she realized the insensate android had put something in her drink; she could hardly hold her eyes open.

Jana heard movement in the adjoining room, revealed now that a privacy slide was open; it had gone unnoticed yesterday because it fit flush with the wall when closed. She glanced through an archway into another bedroom which was similar in colors and furnishings to the one she occupied. She didn't see anyone, but heard the noise again. It was coming from around the corner, out of sight from her position. Jana eased from the bed to creep barefoot and soundless toward the entryway to see who was there, praying it was Varian and the delusions would be over.

She took a sharp intake of air and halted one step into the room. She paled and trembled. Her presence and reaction caused the man at the desk to turn her way: Ryker Triloni smiled and came toward her.

"I see you're finally awake, Jana of Earth. I hope you rested well yesterday. Ine was ordered to keep a close watch on you and to summon me if there was a problem. I had delicate formulas in progress and couldn't leave the lab. Did you miss me as much as I missed you?"

Jana stared at him. She didn't know what to say or do.

"Come and sit down. You're still pale. That will pass soon. All of your vital functions and body chemistry were back to normal when I checked you last night. I'll order our breakfast."

Jana let him guide her to a short sofa in his bedroom. She sank to it, in need of its support. "I was drugged by that android," she told him in a shaky voice.

"Medicine to help you sleep and heal, nothing more."

"I didn't know where I was. I . . ."

"Don't let it worry you, Jana. I'm sure everything will come back to you soon. If not, we'll make new memories. I thought you'd be more comfortable in your room, so I moved you back to the house after you finished your last infusion. How do you feel this morning? Better, I hope."

"An instant and miraculous cure for someone at death's door for days," she said sarcastically.

When he didn't respond, she asked, "Why am I in the house now? You always kept me locked in the complex suite."

"You moved in next to me the day I returned from conducting my business. We agreed it would help us get acquainted better. You stayed in there until you became ill. I had to move you to the complex for treatment.''

No, this can't be true. ''I don't remember anything since we married and you left the same day. This is all so confusing and frightening.'' She wanted to flee from him when he sat close to her. He exuded such immense power and raw sensuality. He seemed so masculine, yet surprisingly gentle. His physique was sleek and agile, evinced by his snug dove-gray jumpsuit in body-molding material. His posture and expression displayed confidence and self-control. His body was so like Varian's, as were his strong and arresting features. It must be that familiarity that drew her to him, caused her to doubt his identity.

''You have nothing to fear, Jana,'' he answered her, ''I know the first time we met, you thought I was a monster, but truly I'm not. I'm sorry you can't remember the many days we spent together when I convinced you otherwise.''

''So am I.'' *If so, I'd know if they really took place!* Yet, he had been making notes with his right hand when she spied the blond alien at his desk. If it had been Varian, he would have been using the left, unless he had heard her! ''What did your mistress have to say about me replacing her in there?''

He chuckled and grinned. ''I don't have one now and didn't have one when I made that statement to you. I said it to make you feel more relaxed around me, feel as if any pressure in that direction didn't exist. The fact is, I've craved you since the first moment my eyes and hands touched on you locked inside that cage Cass delivered you in. I believe she said you were a gift that would please me immensely, and you have. 'A gift of golden intrigue and bliss, an exquisite bird to sing you to sleep at night' was how she put it. I should have wrung her neck for subjecting you to such anguish and humiliation, but I didn't know you then. To me, you were only a taunt from my half brother, perhaps a spy sent to steal my secrets or slay me after you'd enchanted me into a sense of false dreams.''

''Canissia Garthon is a vile and hateful creature. How can you be friends with a malicious and conniving witch like her?''

''Never in an eon, Jana of Earth. Cass has no friends. She

has lovers and reluctant allies and people who want things from her, but nothing more. She blames others for her faults and miseries and defeats. She's never done anything worthwhile, as you have. She lives only for physical pleasures. She doesn't care whom she hurts or uses to get her way. She's vain and spoiled. She's always craved Varian because she couldn't win him. She even chased me for a while. She's perverted and sadistic, evil to her black soul, if she has one. In a word, she's repulsive. I merely tolerate her to obtain facts she gleans from her father, Supreme Councilman Segall. She's also a customer for some of my most expensive products. Frankly I can do without her business and her irritating visits but not her valuable information."

"She hated me from the first moment she saw my promotion for the auction," Jana told him. "She was jealous of me when there was no cause to be: one of the richest and most beautiful and powerful women of your world envious of a mere slave who had no rights here; a woman who can come and go as she pleases on her own star cruiser unsettled by a prisoner who would be confined to one place and one man! That's foolish and petty. She took devilish delight in getting me out of her territory. It wasn't her right to transport me here. And it was wrong how the matter was carried out in secret. She dearly enjoyed playing Varian's messages to me about his vile behavior . . . Are they married yet?"

"No, but they will be soon. Word has it they were rushing their plans and had to slow down to make sure they give the best party that's ever been held in this galaxy. I'm sure it will be a great spectacle."

"Am I a prisoner? Will no one ever see me again besides you?"

"Certainly not. Have you changed your mind about attending their signing and celebration? You said you didn't want to accept my offer to go because you didn't want people gaping at you. We do have better things to occupy our time and energy, specifically that long trip beginning next week."

"What trip?"

"We have stops at Caguas, Kudora, Auriga, and Zamarra before we reach Tartarus, capital of my grandfather's empire in Androas. You do still want to come along, don't you? You were looking forward to seeing *Avatars* Faeroe, Saito, Rhoedea, and Suran once more. I've already notified them of our visits. They're eager to see you again. You told me one of your friends from the *Wanderlust* lived on Auriga now. I can arrange for you to see Kathy if you'd like, but we won't have much time there. Our stops will be short—a few hours to overnight—enough time to make deliveries and pay our respects. This will be our first time out in public as newlyweds."

"You're taking me to see the rulers of those four planets?" she asked, as *avatars* were the most powerful men on each of the thirteen planets. They were also members of the Maffei Interplanetary Alliance Assembly of sixteen men, the others being the three-man Supreme Council of which *Kadim* Tirol Trygue—Varian's grandfather—was the high ruler of this galaxy. The other two councilmen were Draco Procyon—her past guardian—and Segall Garthon, Canissia's father. Their word was law and no one dared disobey it openly; to do so meant death or imprisonment for life on an inescapable and savage penal planetoid, as Maffei practiced no pardon system. "Can you show me off in public?" she asked.

"Show you off? I do not understand. Perhaps your question does not translate clearly into my language. What does that mean?"

How could Ryker carry her into public if she had been kidnapped from Varian? He couldn't. Perhaps he would find an excuse to cancel their journey. "I was told a Maffeian citizen couldn't marry his *charl*. Did you have the power to free me and marry me, or is it a lie to manage me better?"

"I swear to you, Jana, you are a free woman, a Maffeian citizen. I swear to you our marriage is legal under Maffeian and Androasian law. *Kadim* Tirol had no choice except to do as I asked, and Varian did not resist the deed."

In her beautiful "dream," Varian had said his grandfather freed her so she could marry him. Had she actually been freed so she could marry Ryker first to get her hands on Trilabs before marrying Varian? How could her love paint himself so black to her while impersonating Ryker? Didn't he realize this ruse could destroy her love for him and her trust in him?

"Do you not want to be seen at my side, Jana? Are you sorry you married me? Have I been so terrible to you?"

"Why did you marry me, Ryker, and make me your heir? Don't you realize how dangerous that is? How can you trust me that much? What if Varian did plant me here to seduce you and steal your secrets? You said something was brewing, remember? What if he's after your life now?"

"It wouldn't do him any good to slay me for you to inherit Trilabs. You can't get into the main complex. My best formulas are safe, alive or dead."

"So, you don't really trust me?"

"That isn't my motive. It keeps us both safe from harm for you to be in a position of being unable to betray me accidentally or by force. Besides the enormous value of my products, in the wrong hands they are deadly and powerful. I, as their creator and seller, have a responsibility to make certain they remain in the *right* hands: mine. Do you understand?"

"Yes, and I agree. As long as you don't confide in me, you'll never view me as a threat. I much prefer it that way. But you didn't answer my question. Why did you marry me, your hated enemy's ex-mistress?"

"You're referring to what I said that first day about Varian knowing how much I would resent following him to your bed. I believe I put it: 'A cunning torment to send me a ravishing creature who boils the blood and troubles the mind.' I explained, but I'll tell you again since you've forgotten: that was only to extract clues about my half brother's motive for sending his prized treasure to his hated enemy. I suspected it was a scheme to get you inside my lab and to win my trust. I told you Varian and the Alliance had tried similar ruses before and they never worked. Using an alien captive as their newest Elite Squad member would be a clever ploy. Since you're a researcher like myself, you would understand my work, and who would suspect an alien slave of bold treachery? I surmised you might be a spy or agent willing to do a mission for them to win Varian or your freedom. There are few men in the Tri-Galaxy who wouldn't lay claim to you if they could. But my spy obtained the true motive for me: Varian wanted to be rid of you before marrying Cass. What better place to send you than to me where he believed you'd never be seen again or tempt him again, sent to a man rumored to have little, if any, feeling and respect for women?"

He captured her hands in his before continuing. "I asked you to help me beat Varian at his evil game, to marry me before his marriage to Cass. I told you I wanted your superior image as my wife. I'm the last of my bloodline, Jana, so I need a son or a daughter. The day will arrive when you'll become the mother of my child, heir to a throne and empire. I've found no woman more suitable to that role than you. Varian doesn't, and never has, loved you. He has only lusted for you. I'm not sure he's capable of loving or trusting any woman, especially an alien temptress. Even if he has deep feelings for you, he hates me more than he loves you. He craves me dead more than he wants you alive and at his side. He used you as the cover for his mission to your world by distracting me and others from it with your rare beauty and superiority. He and the Alliance fear my grandfather and I will ally with the Pyropeans to attack Maffei while their starships are away either saving your planet from that rogue worldlet or Stardust seeding your atmosphere before certain destruction."

Jana didn't want to think about her world's possible grim fate at this moment, especially of the Stardusting that induced coma and death. No doubt she was in just as much peril of destruction as Earth was. Besides, there was nothing she could do to prevent fate's hand from striking at her world. Surely God, in his infinite mercy and wisdom, wouldn't allow it to happen.

"I don't want Maffei; I don't even want to become *Kadim* of Androas. I'm too busy with my work here, and politics doesn't interest me. Don't you understand? Varian used you as bait to lure me away from Darkar to your auction because he had spies here and he hoped they could steal my secrets while I was stalking you. They were slain by my defense system. Of course, he and Star Fleet claimed no knowledge of the men.''

After a brief frown, he said, ''Varian pretended you were important to him to catch my interest. He never anticipated I wouldn't fall for his tricks or that I would crave you for myself after I got to know you. Ever since you were taken from Earth, you've been racing toward an unknown destiny, a true destiny—me. It's ironic that Varian was the one who helped us both fulfill our fates. He and others think I hate women; but they're wrong. I only scorn those who pursue me. You're different; you will want nothing more from me than my love, trust, and loyalty, if I'm fortunate enough to win you. The women I've met—women like Cass—either want me for my wealth, powerful status, looks, drugs, or for all four reasons. Some even desire me because I do favor my older brother, and he is Galen's heir. A few hunger for me because they believe I am dangerous and wicked, and they find that exciting. I've never met one who got to know and want the real me. I hope you will do that one day. It's my dream that you'll want to become more than my wife in name only: other than promising to provide me with an heir one day, that was our bargain, but I am hoping you'll broaden it. Does that possibility frighten and repel you, Jana of Earth?''

Her mouth and eyes were agape. Her heart raced. ''Are you saying . . . you want me to . . . Us to . . . consummate our marriage soon?''

The green-eyed blond alien threw back his head and laughed. His tongue flicked his upper lip as he brought his amusement under control and his eyes twinkled with merriment. ''I'm sorry, Jana, but you reached far for that word to describe what should be a normal act between husband and wife. You're even blushing. For a woman in your position, that surprises me.''

''Because I'm experienced sexually?''

''No, because you're a scientist. Mating is something you're well aware of with your laboratory specimens. I didn't mean for us to race into bed this morning or this week or even *next* week. I was exploring the possibility of a future intimate relationship. Simple sex for reproduction isn't what I have in mind. I want a full life with you, Jana. I want you sooner and for more than the few times it might require to impregnate you with my heir. I know we agreed only to have sex for reproduction; that was before I spent time with you and came to desire you so much. You don't have to worry about me breaking our bargain, but I hope you will give us a chance at a rich and full life together."

When she remained still and silent, he said, "Perhaps something is being lost in the translation from my language to yours. Am I being unclear or crude? I've tried to make this discussion light, but I've never had much of a sense of humor. I'll work on developing one and hope you'll help me succeed."

Are you trying to test me to see if Ryker can entice me into this bed? she questioned him silently. *Why are you saying such horrible things about yourself, about me, about us? How can you go this far in your secret assignment as Ryker?*

"You can't answer now or don't want to answer at all, Jana?"

Play along with his charade, J. G., and see where it leads. "I'm not sure what to say, Ryker. This is as unexpected as your marriage proposal was. All the way to your planetoid, Canissia told me of your mean spirit. I met you while I was half naked in a cage with that witch goading me. You examined me like an exotic specie under a large microscope. You did seem cold and cruel. Then, when Canissia was gone, you were different. You told me you allow people to think evil of you so they'll leave you alone, so they'll fear you. Now, you're hotly romancing me. What am I supposed to think?"

"I said I sometimes play out the role fate seems determined to cast me in, but I also apologized for taking my anger and suspicions out on you."

"Yes, you did. You became kind and gentle. We talked and dined together a few times. Then you proposed, wed me, and left home. The next thing I knew, it's over a week later and you're telling me we've gotten close during days I can't remember. You want to get even closer. It seems too fast and curious."

"Have you ever walked into a store and seen something that you had to have that very minute? Or craved a food you couldn't wait to devour? Or run an experiment that you couldn't wait to succeed? Have you ever wanted something so bad that you would feel painfully denied if you couldn't have it?"

Yes, my first prom dress and horse Apache, brownies with pecans, a cure for leukemia, and Varian Saar. "I understand your meaning, but *why*?"

"That's how you make me feel, Jana of Earth. I've only been denied one thing I wanted during my lifetime, until you came along and made it two. Are you immune to me, Jana Greyson Triloni? Totally unaffected?"

Unaffected by an almost irresistible force, even if he were Ryker? A woman would have to be blind, dumb, and sexless not to desire such a man! Or be in love with another one. "What was the other thing you never won?"

He chuckled again. "It's a clever scientist," he teased, "who turns a revealing test in another direction to fool the competition when a result is close to discovery and needs to be kept secret." He grew serious as he replied, "But I'll answer anyway. My father's love, respect, and acceptance. Can I ever win those things from you, Dr. Jana Greyson Triloni?"

She hadn't expected him to be so direct. Why a sudden rush for a commitment? Was Varian here as his half brother to consummate this marriage to make it legal? Was he going to videotape the union as proof? Surely he wouldn't subject her to such a mortifying and private deed. In some foreign cultures of olden Earth, it was said witnesses were mandatory to prove consummation and virginity, especially in cases of royalty. And Ryker was royalty. Did he and the Maffei Supreme Council believe it was necessary to have evidence to prevent any resistance to her inheritance as Ryker's widow? What better way to gain control of the Androasian Empire than through an heir to the throne, particularly if Varian controlled the child's mother through love and desire? Surely no stakes could be that high or motive that great, not even ownership of Trilabs or intergalactic peace. "You own me, Prince Ryker Triloni. What command that you issue could I refuse to obey and survive?"

"I own your life and body; I want your heart, Jana, of your free will."

"To prove to Varian you can have what he never could? Do you want an heir quickly so you can be rid of me sooner? Why seek my cooperation? I am at your mercy in this impregnable fortress. Who would know what you do with me? Who would care enough to battle you? No one!"

"You'll come to see how wrong you are about me. But enough of this: Let's eat. I'm sure you're as hungry as I am. Let me straighten my papers first."

To come to an accurate conclusion, she required indisputable data that she could not acquire if she kept going in this hostile and defensive direction. This man and her predicament were like unknown chemicals in a vital formula. She must test them with caution and respect. Once she obtained all the information she could gather, she would evaluate it and come up with a neutralizing method. Varian had accused her once of always needing to examine and analyze everything, even emotions. This situation required "further testing." Her path and choice were clear: either she could be submissive or be destroyed. Wasn't earning and keeping Ryker's goodwill more important at this time than foolish, misplaced pride and defiance—dangerous traits she could not afford. She must not become a coward or a weakling, but neither must she appear a threat or enemy to him. It was wise to obey until a path of escape presented itself, if it ever did. There was no turning back or returning home. It was accept and endure or . . . What? she didn't know yet.

She watched him put away papers in a desk drawer and replace books on a nearby shelf. As if he had forgotten her presence, he walked toward the door. Jana rose and headed to join him. "If I offended you, I'm sorry," she said. "I need time."

He faced her and said, "You'll have plenty of it with me, so don't worry. Despite my nefarious reputation, I would never attack my own wife, or *any* woman. If we have a chance at happiness, Jana of Earth, it's up to you."

He went through the door and Jana trailed him. He seemed hurt, and she found that disturbing and baffling. Suddenly he seemed nothing like Varian Saar. Should that make her happy or sad? If Varian was lost to her, could she accept Ryker as his replacement in her life? Was Ryker being honest with her? *You're trapped, J. G., and you'll never escape!*

Ine served their meal with perfection and silence. Jana remembered Ryker telling her that most of his servants and workers were androids and robots. It was like being in a science-fiction movie, but this was reality. How long would it take before such things seemed commonplace? If only she knew how accurately their words were being translated to each other. If only—

"Is the food not to your liking? Would you prefer another dish?"

Jana's head jerked upward and she gaped at him. Those were the exact words Varian had said to her on his ship just before revealing her predicament! She watched him shifting his fork back and forth between his hands. His glass and cup were sitting to the . . . left of his plate!

His gaze followed her line of vision. He chuckled. "Ambidextrous. It's useful for taking notes while I'm dissecting specimens or mixing chemicals with my best hand. Have you acquired that skill, too?"

"Not as well as you have. I mostly use my right."

"So do I, but I'm as good with my left when it's necessary. I'll teach you one day; you might have need of it when we work together."

"How will you do that?" Varian wasn't a scientist! He was a starship commander. That was one area in which he couldn't playact the matchless chemist and researcher, not well enough, at least, to fool a skilled chemist and researcher like herself. At last, a path to exposure of his ruse! "When do we begin work in your lab? I'm eager to get back to research."

"After our return from Grandfather's."

She watched him take a bite of food and follow it with *zim*: coffee. So that was it: fool *Kadim* Maal into thinking Ryker was still alive before Varian left on his mission to the Milky Way Galaxy! To pull it off, he thought even *she* had to believe he was Ryker. "Why not before we leave?"

"I don't want you being exposed to any possible viruses until you're well enough to have your inoculations again. Even animals and plants can be carriers sometimes. Your bloodwork revealed three haven't taken effect. I want you to concentrate on getting well and strong before we leave."

"You want your grandfather and the others to see how happy I am?"

"How happy *we* are. Masculine pride. And you might get caught up in your exuberance and let it become real."

"I think we can both accomplish a good act with a little practice."

"That isn't what I want, Jana. You had enough of pretenses with Varian. Just be yourself. You're beautiful, talented, intelligent, charming, and well bred. You know how to conduct yourself in public."

"How do you know?" She sipped the hot liquid with caution as she eyed him over the rim of the cup.

"I've viewed many of the tapes I had my spies make of you during the auctions. I have also read your complete file. I must admit Varian and his staff did an excellent job of selecting, training, and documenting you. I've heard only good reports about you from those who met you along your journey. You make an excellent impression on everyone."

And I must admit, you're quick, Varian. You cover yourself faster than a flash flood does the Texas desert. "Thank you for the compliment and confidence."

"You don't like talking about the days before you came here, do you?"

Keep up the deceitful probing and you might hear something you wish you hadn't evoked. "Why should I? My life and career were torn apart by that bas—beast. I lost my home, my friends, my job, my possessions, my . . . everything. I was on my way to a party when three men in silvery jumpsuits and impenetrable helmets surrounded me, drugged me, and kidnapped me. I awoke on a starship heading out of my galaxy, destined to become a captive mate to an alien. He destroyed every new beginning I made. As I was recovering my courage, self-esteem, and a measure of happiness, he yanked them from me. First, he did it on Earth. Then, he did it on his ship; those were the only friends and only life I knew for a long time. I was terrified and confused, but people like Martella, Tris, and Nigel made it better for me. Varian and I fought until I didn't have the strength or will to defy him and his plans for me anymore. I wound up in sickbay once for provoking him to strike me during an attempted escape attempt. I quickly learned he was telling the truth about where I was and about there being no escape or rescue for me. It gave him great delight to wield his power over me."

Following a glare of coldness at that memory, she continued. "He duped us into thinking he had let these huge spiders eat one of the girls. Later I saw her sold on Kudora and learned *scarfelli* are trained for terror tactics. Yes, I did have privileges the other captives didn't: nice quarters, clothes, extra training, and special treatment, but he was only grooming me as bait for you and a cover for his mission. He threatened to sell me to a terrible beast if I didn't do whatever he ordered. Later he said he'd been joking to halt my defiance, but I have no doubt he would have carried out his threat if I hadn't complied. Then, he began his romantic assault. He was constantly teasing and taunting me. If I let him kiss me, he was furious and mocking. If I refused, he was furious and vindictive. He swore neither he nor his crew were allowed to touch any of us captives, and

I foolishly believed him. I realized it was safer to be his friend and student than his enemy. My change of behavior seemed to satisfy him for a while. I thought it was foolish not to take advantage of my lessons when I needed everything I could get to help me adjust and survive in an alien environment. After he . . . we . . . You know what I mean. I didn't think he would sell me to another man, not the affectionate way he acted toward me. Heavens, that was the worst experience of my life, standing half naked before a crowd of strange men listening to myself being auctioned to the highest bidder like a piece of merchandise. He led me to believe I was Draco's *charl*. I tried to make a new life there because Draco was so kind and gentle. For the record, Councilman Procyon never touched me."

"I believe you, Jana. What happened next?"

"Just as I settled in, he showed up one night and ripped my new life apart. I was drugged. When I awoke, I was back with him, at his grandfather's on the planet Eire. He even went so far as to say he would keep me forever and I would become his mate. He romanced me at his grandfather's. Even *Kadim* Tirol aided his deceitful ruse by telling me how much Varian wanted me and how he was risking his life to save my world. Then, I was drugged again and awakened to you. He won't stay out of my life. He won't allow me to get settled anywhere and find peace. For some reason, he wants to destroy me. I could have fallen in love with him, but he taught me to hate, mistrust, and pity him."

"Pity? I've never known anyone to pity Varian Saar. Explain."

How could Varian sit there, she fumed, and calmly listen to her say such things without defending himself? How could he hear all those charges against him and still risk creating another one with this foul deception? Did he believe he had her so cleverly duped that she was only safeguarding herself from Ryker's wrath? "Yes, pity him, becaue he has no feelings, no scruples, no conscience, no compassion, no honor. His war with you has made him that way. What is a man without such qualities? I would trade anything to have my innocence and ignorance back. He held me so tightly in his evil clutches and dazzled me with his mind-controlling and spell-binding Moondust that I was too cowardly and blind to defy him. I wish my life could be as it was before he kidnapped me and changed me forever. He lied to me from the start. He said I would be accepted and cherished as a *charl*, and I haven't found that to be true. He said if I was nice to him, I would be fine, and I haven't been. Somehow I antagonized him no matter what I said or did. He was suspicious and angry if I was receptive, but he was the same if I was resistant. He was contradictory and cruel. I could never please him. I won't lie to you, Ryker; I was mesmerized by him for a while. He's very appealing when he turns on his charm. He possessed such enormous power over me, even over the air I breathed, over my fate, my life. I feel as if I've been sprinkled with that mind-dazing Stardust and can't think clearly or engulfed by Shadows and can't find my way back to safety and sanity. Moondust and Stardust—such soft and pretty names for such insidious and lethal chemicals."

"You sound as if you know him well and hate him."

"How could any woman in her right mind love a man like that?"

"Are you in your right mind, Jana of Earth?"

She laughed skeptically. "According to you, Ryker, I've lost part of it, perhaps a good part of it. How much more will I lose here with you? What do you want from me? Can I trust you?"

"Varian's taught you to be distrustful of all men."

"Then prove to me why and how I can trust you."

"I will, Jana, given time and the opportunities."

"I hope so, Ryker, I truly hope so."

As they left the house later, Jana noticed the rondure center of the dwelling was of an unknown beige material. Four smaller semispheres stuck out from it like legs on a fat spider and connected to the largest one via passageways. Reflective *trans-*

ascreens were flush with the smooth surface, and each area possessed a large skylight. She knew three of those minidomes held bedrooms where she now slept, the dining area, and the greatroom for relaxing and entertaining. Others, he had told her after breakfast, consisted of the kitchen and storage locations. The unusual structure sat on a thick base similar to a concrete foundation slab.

As if following her line of thought, the alien said, "It's built on a platform that lowers itself underground in case of an attack. So is my private complex. Each has enough supplies to keep several people alive for a long time. A tunnel connects the two structures."

"If there was an attack, how could anyone last beyond the lengthy contamination that would follow total destruction?" she asked.

"Each area, in case the tunnel collapsed, holds an escape pod, an airtight one with enough power and supplies to get us away from this sector."

"What about your workers? How would they escape?"

"Most of them are robots or androids. They appear human in looks, but you can always tell one by his or her yellow eyes. Human personnel are mainly shuttle pilots. Most stay away on deliveries. Those few caught here during an attack will have time to escape in crafts before the self-destruct sequence completes itself. Survival is one reason I use androids; the other is their total loyalty to me and my work. Any attempt to dismantle them for their memory banks results in instant explosion."

"What if someone found the right command code and ordered them to dump their memories into a computer?"

"They respond only to my voice and code. No matter how good an imposter is, my voice cannot be matched perfectly, not even by computer. Nor does anyone know the right code for extracting information."

She eyed the many structures within sight: warehouses, greenhouses, a stable, huge shuttlebay, and the alien's private complex with many laboratories. Plants and trees and flowers seemed to grow in every available location to create a colorful and breathtaking setting. Walkways connected the buildings in an artistic design based on function as well as looks. "This planetoid is so large and so beautiful," Jana commented. "I don't recall seeing the outside before."

"Beyond your vision capabilities are gardens and animal dwellings, some for raising and feeding specimens and some for human consumption. I saw on your file that you enjoy riding. I have a large stable of *esprees*, our specie of horse. Would you like to do that when you're stronger?"

"Yes. One of the things I lost on Earth was a fine Appaloosa stallion named Apache. You probably know I was raised on a ranch in Texas, which I inherited after my parents were killed in a plane crash. My father was also involved in the oil business. I don't know which he loved more, raising stock or bringing in an oil well."

"Your file said you owned an aeronautical company."

"Yes, Stacy Aerospace Firm. I inherited that from my mother. We design and manufacture equipment and parts for satellites, missiles, shuttles, and spacelabs, at least as we know them at our level: things like flight control systems, radar, sensors, and probes. I really don't know much about all that, but I held on to the firm because of the medical and scientific breakthroughs involved in outer space research. A great deal of knowledge and technology comes from space flights, but of course you know that."

"How did you get into researching cures for terminally ill children?"

"I saw several children of family friends die from incurable diseases. One of them I had babysat for years. I was a volunteer at our local hospital—a Candy-Striper—when I was younger. I saw children on telethons—television programs to raise money—who gripped my heart with their sufferings. I had always loved science. I entered every science fair our school promoted. Once I did a life-support exchange between mother and fetus using a tiny doll inside a plastic bubble, complete with a straw for an umbilical cord, attached to a larger doll as the mother. I had charts with diagrams and information and little jars of mouse fetuses in different stages of development that I had gotten from a researcher friend of my father. The school thought the project was too advanced and detailed for a sixth-grader to have executed alone so I was disqualified. I think it was the subject of my paper and the demonstration that made them uncomfortable."

"I can imagine. Tell me, Jana of Earth, how did you get so far in twenty-four years?"

Jana pushed windblown wisps of her tawny hair with its silvery highlights from her face as she realized she hadn't even told such things to Varian during all their days together. He had never asked or seemed interested, whereas a scientific man like Ryker . . . *Don't confuse yourself about who's standing here with you, J. G.!* "I went to school year round. I loved the work, and I did extra projects. I majored in biochemistry and did graduate work in microbiology and chemistry. I worked at the Baylor Medical Complex until graduation. I went home for a few months to see my friends and to handle my business and personal affairs before relocating to Baltimore to take a research position at Johns Hopkins. I was to start there the day I reached Draco's world, to begin life as a captive *charl* rather than saving children's lives on mine. My will left everything I own to research for terminally ill children. I suppose it's been executed by now. At least something good came from this evil."

"I'm sorry, Jana, those must have been terrible losses for you."

"Along with my freedom and pride."

"But you have those back now."

"Do I, Ryker? Is limited, controlled existence really being free? Does being at the beck and call of another person allow for pride?"

"I hope so, Jana. It can if you allow it. All of this explains why Dr. Zarcoff and Lieutenant Sanger were so interested in you."

"What do you mean? How do you know that?"

"It's no secret both of Varian's officers and good friends

wanted him to keep you. I saw you on tape with Nigel Sanger several times. It was easy to see you two were friends; that's natural between two scientists. It's to my advantage they didn't convince him to keep you. I also recall your file listing *caritrary* as the color of your eyes. I can see why Dr. Zarcoff did so. As with that precious gem found on the planet Caguas, your eyes are a coalescence of blue, green, and violet. I've never seen eyes this shade in our world: a kaleidoscope of magical allure and sweet mystery. Despite the fact you've been mostly inside for months, your skin still appears kissed by an adoring sun. The first time I saw you, I didn't think a female so beautiful and perfect could be real. It's understandable why every man in the Universe would desire you."

"That's an exaggeration, but thank you. Every male alive couldn't find the same female desirable. I know I'm attractive and have certain charms. I have intelligence and strengths and good traits, but I'm not matchless or either a goddess or an angel."

"That's what you told me upon your arrival. As I said that day, you're far too modest, and you're wrong."

"Beauty is in the eye of the beholder, as we say on Earth."

"And everyone who beholds you thinks as I do."

"But doesn't *feel* as you do, whatever that is."

When he chuckled and seared her with his jungle-green gaze, Jana asked, "Why are you talking this way to me? We hardly know each other."

"Isn't this how people get acquainted on your world: chatting and observing? Am I being improper? Am I making you nervous?"

"I find it surprising and unsettling that you're being flirtatious."

He laughed heartily this time. "I've certainly never been accused of being flirtatious before. It must be your potent effect on me."

"You've read my file and questioned me. What more do you need to know? Surely we've covered all this ground before in the past week."

"Yes, but I like hearing about you from your lips and learning more than is recorded about you. Your file said nothing about childhood experiences or why you got involved in research, so I've already learned something about you that no other person here knows. Everything we experience in our lives helps to mold us into the people we are. I want to learn all I can about you, Jana of Earth, even the smallest detail."

"To see what really makes me tick?" He seemed to reason on her words for a time, then grinned when he grasped her meaning—a sexy grin.

"Maybe I'll come to learn and use Earth slang, too. There's always something other people can teach us. I'm also trying to relax your doubts and fears by creating a genial atmosphere between us. There's no need for them, not here, not with me."

"That's your opinion, but I suppose you're always right."

He shrugged and smiled. "I've made a few mistakes in my lifetime, but not many. One bad one was with you the first day we met. I don't want to repeat it or to make another. Wait here a moment while I unlock the complex. We have something important to do in there."

What, the anxious Earthling wondered, *is in store for me next*?

Chapter Three

Jana stayed where she was while the man approached his complex and entered the code to open the door. She joined him when he summoned her and walked beside him down a hallway and into a laboratory. He lifted a set of notes in his language and went into an adjoining room, telling Jana he would only be a minute or two.

While he busied himself, Jana watched him. He seemed to know what he was doing and seemed at ease in the surrounding. He measured several liquids in tall cylindrical tubes and poured them into various plants, then apparently recorded the amounts and types used. She strolled to one exquisite flower in a pot: *Tarkitilae Moosi*. Its lacy petals in shades of pink with vivid dots were lovely, but viewing it brought anguish to her heart.

''Eyes of Kimon, *Tarkitilae Moosi*,'' the man said over her shoulder. ''Kimon is our mythological Goddess of Love and Beauty. In her pictures and statues, you look like her. Perhaps you are her incarnate. That would explain your magic and allure. Would you like to have it for your room? I'm finished with it."

"It's magnificent, but no thank you."

"You can accept a gift from me, Jana."

"It's Varian's favorite, so I don't want it around me."

"I understand."

As he returned to his task, Jana remembered the botanical garden on Varian's ship; perhaps that was where her cunning love learned so much about plants that he could carry off this part so well. She approached an odd-looking one with a huge orchid-type flower. Just as she leaned over to smell it, Ryker seized her around the waist and yanked her backward. Startled, she shrieked and struggled for freedom, and he released her.

"It hides a vicious little creature, Jana. Watch."

He fetched a small chunk of raw meat and held it toward the blossom with long tweezers. The petals opened and a wormlike creature shot out to snatch the meat. It vanished behind the velvety petals once more.

"He can take a nice piece out of your finger or nose; has razor-sharp teeth and a hefty appetite for flesh of any kind. They co-exist, can't survive without something each produces. Beauty and savagery bound as one by mutual needs. This is only one of the reasons you can't work with me until you learn your way around such things. You aren't familiar with our specimens and chemicals. Besides causing a terrible accident, you could get injured or even killed. Once you're trained, you'll be an excellent assistant, can even work on your own projects. Come along."

Jana tagged behind him down the hallway into another laboratory. She watched him pull on thick gloves that reached his elbows and approach a glass case on the floor, which was coated with a deep layer of sand. She inched forward with caution and alert this time. His protected hand searched the dirt until she saw a movement which he pursued with speed and accuracy, grasping the neck of a creature that sprung from its hiding place and struck his glove. She squealed in surprise and hurriedly stepped backward.

Ryker chuckled as he withdrew the squirming snake, without fear or any reaction to its attack. "He's quick and mean, but these gloves are impenetrable. He produces a powerful venom used in medicines."

Jana saw him carry the thrashing creature to a table where he skillfully milked it of venom, a yellow liquid that eased down the beaker interior at a snailish pace. She heard it give off "Pssst" sounds before and after the handling, as if a person trying to gain another's attention. After the alien labeled the vial and stored it, he approached another glass container with limbs covered in a furry moss. Large leeches crawled about, leaving trails of shiny slime. Many suckled on tiny dishes of red. "What are these for?" she asked.

"They feast on the blood of certain animals with special enzymes. At a point, they're transferred to another cage to suck off juices from certain plants. A chemical change takes place within their bodies by catalytic action during digestion. They're killed and drained of the product they make. They act like a living test tube. I add the ingredients needed and they blend them for me. I discovered I could get the right substance only in this manner."

"How clever. Our scientists have never thought of doing it this way. I'm amazed and impressed, Ryker."

He smiled. "I always take one precaution with my work: all of my formulas have a certain chemical added that makes them break down their structures if any attempt is made to analyze them. It's one I created myself so no one can find a way to copy it."

"Now I see why you're so valuable here," she said as he jotted down a few notes. "Can I help?" she offered, wanting a peep at what he wrote.

"I wish you could, but I write in my language—Androasian. I know you were taught Maffeian during your voyage here and at Draco's, but that won't help you in my laboratories. I'll have an android programmed to teach you Androasian. Soon, you'll know all you need to work with me."

When he put down the device he marked upon, she glanced

at it to find the language was unfamiliar. Did Varian know Androasian? Did he know this much about research, plants, and animals to act so natural in this setting? All she knew was that he was a starship commander, and Spacer pilot. But couldn't Tris have taught him enough to dupe her and others?

He observed her curiosity and explained, "It's a portable notetaker. Whatever I record here is sent straight to my main input/acquisition data system. I'll have to teach you how all that works, too. I'm sure you're familiar with computers for analyzing data so it shouldn't be difficult to learn. Of course there are certain areas that are protected from release of information, codes I can't share with anyone, including you. I explained why earlier."

"Your technology and intelligence astound me. Your world is so far advanced above mine. I wish some information could be shared with my people. We have so many diseases and problems on Earth. Your world seems to have solved most of theirs."

"It's against intergalactic treaties to share facts with planets not ready for such knowledge and power. Worlds must be allowed to advance at their own pace or chaos results, if they don't destroy themselves first. From the reports I've seen on your world, it's heading for self-destruction: overpopulation that creates shortages of food, living space, fights over territory, and diseases; deforestation of needed rain forests to supply the air you breathe; holes in your ozone and global warming; pollution, acid rain, and smog; wars, rebellions, strikes, and terrorism; racial and religious conflicts. Need I even continue? Oil spills, medical and chemical wastes, and garbage disposal; nuclear wastes and weapons; drugs and crime and health problems. Your world is destroying the necessary balance of nature required for its survival."

"But we're trying to change, to repair damage, to prevent more. We have the Environmental Protection Agency, U.S. Soil Conservation, World Resources Institute, U.S. National Academy of Sciences, the Clean Air and Clean Water acts, the Endangered Specie Act, and more."

"In your country and a few outside, but not many others comply; they continue to create and broaden problems. Everyone must work together, form an alliance as we have among our planets and among neighboring galaxies. Your people are greedy and primitive, Jana. They won't do much until they're scared. By then, it might be too late. Your people have little respect for the law and need tight controls to battle the severe problems. Those troubles were created by man and can only be solved by man. For the most part, we have peace in the Tri-Galaxy. Bringing another galaxy into our system before it's ready can be lethal to ours."

"Like the vengeful alien scientist who created the plague that made *charl* raids necessary, according to the Maffeians?"

"That's why aliens are watched with mistrust and suspicion, why few are accepted and why few *charls* are ever freed to roam at will. Each woman taken captive is decontaminated to avoid bringing alien strains of diseases to our world. When the Maffeians were struck by the plague he created, only the women were damaged, made sterile. What better way to ensure race extinction than by nonreproduction? On the good side of the practice, women were trained and helped to fit into our society. Most accepted their fates and are happy."

"How can a woman be happy when she's a captive, nothing more than a breeder like an animal, when she can't select her own mate?"

"The process is controlled carefully. Only buyers who are Maffeian, unmarried, and financially secure can bid on a *charl*. But the time has passed for the need of them. Female children born of the first captive mates are fertile; some are even grandmothers by now. From my observations, the balance of reproductive nature has been restored. With Martella Karsh and other powerful people involved in the lobbying to strike down the *charl* law, it should be accomplished within a year or so."

"What will happen to the *charls*? They aren't wed to their owners."

"In our society, children belong to the father, except in certain cases. Owners will be allowed to decide if they wish to marry their mates. I assume mates will be made citizens after they're freed and will also be given the choice of marrying their past owners. I also assume most mothers will choose to remain with their children, whether they love their mates or not. But whatever happens won't affect you, Jana. You're already free and wed. And marriage is far more binding in our world than *charl* ownership. Divorces, as you call them, are hard to obtain and carry a dark stigma. A couple doesn't or shouldn't marry unless they are sure they want a lifetime relationship with each other."

"I suppose that means you're stuck with me until death do us part."

"And you're . . . stuck with me. What strange sayings you Earthlings have." He chuckled. "My work is finished, so let's eat and then you can rest. I don't want to overtire you today."

"When can I begin my Androasian language lessons?"

"Give yourself a few days to convalesce first."

"As you wish."

The man scowled and she shrugged, as the response was one of Varian's that everyone in Maffei and other places had heard often.

As Jana lay in bed that night, she was too aware of the man sleeping in the room close to hers with the slide screen open. Why, she wondered, had he taken her into the complex after telling her she couldn't work there because of the possibility of exposing her to plants and animals that might carry viruses? What about the aforementioned immunity worries? Was it because he knew those specimens were safe from contamination and harm or because his explanation—excuse—was a lie? Such contradictions!

Another thing troubled her. If only Shara hadn't shown her that overlay picture of Varian and Ryker which vividly exposed their strong resemblance when their colorings were matched. If only Varian hadn't been disguised as Ryker the last time she saw him on his ship. *If* those two episodes had really happened.

Right now, she wasn't sure because either the man nearby was Ryker or Varian was impersonating his half brother perfectly.

She had watched for slips and spied none. He always seemed to have a logical and indisputable explanation for anything she found suspicious. She couldn't comprehend why she couldn't persuade herself he wasn't Varian. Even so, there was nothing she could do to stop this charade. If only her doubts and suspicions would stop plaguing her. If something didn't happen soon to end this drama, she would drive herself nuts. *Wait and see, J. G.; that's all you can do for the present.* But was it? she asked herself. There was one way to discover the truth, if she dared take that bold risk.

Jana began her fourth day on Darkar after regaining consciousness with the decision not to allow her captor to seduce her just to glean clues to his identity. Her only sexual experiences had been with Varian Saar, but, if he intentionally altered his techniques in bed, the action would accomplish nothing and would bring changes in their relationship that she wasn't ready to deal with at this time. No, she couldn't take that risk.

She had read and heard a lot about sex but had not surrendered to her longtime boyfriend on Earth, a choice she did not regret. Yet, if she had been involved with Alex and hadn't been a virgin, her abduction would not have taken place. Not that Alex hadn't tried every trick in the book to get her into bed during their two years as a steady couple, but it had never seemed right between them. He had wooed, cajoled, nagged, pleaded, and enticed before resorting to verbal badgering, mind games, and other ruses. She hadn't allowed him to pressure her into bed, not even with a proposal of marriage. True, he had desired her, but he had become angry and persistent and mildly threatening toward the end of their relationship shortly before she vanished from Earth. He had tried to make her feel obligated to surrender to him and told her she was responsible for his torment.

With Varian, it had been different, so very different. She

had desired him wildly. He had made her feel as no man ever had and might never do again. He had caused her emotions and desires to blossom like wildflowers across Texas during the spring. He had taken her to the pinnacle of pleasure every time she joined her body with his. But this cruel deception drew emotional blood, cut through her heart, body, and mind as a laser. He possessed fatal magic and potent allure. She had allowed and encouraged him to charm, disarm, and bind her to him. If the man with her now wasn't Varian, she couldn't allow him to do the same, to get a hold on her that would blind her to the truth before it was too late.

She donned a fuschia romper with a surplice bodice. When the ties were secured behind her, she brushed her hair, sprayed on a mist of perfume, added a trace of cosmetics, and left the emotionally stifling room.

She didn't hear or see anyone in the house, not even the android housekeeper, Ine. She walked to the *transascreen* in the large living area and peeked outside, as it wasn't sealed today. She saw "Ryker" playing *forsha* with a male android, a twin to Ine. As far as she knew, Varian didn't play the alien equivalent of tennis, especially with his right hand . . .

Jana walked into the kitchen and approached the *servo* to press a button for coffee. There had been a similar unit in her golden prison on Varian's ship. There were four recessed spaces, of which three contained units with smoky-glass doors. Two of them resembled microwaves without controls: she knew now that one was for supplying hot foods and one for cold. To the left of the lower one was a small drawer which contained numerous metal objects the size and shape of a credit card. She knew the perforations on them were a computer code for ordering selections. Over the drawer was a narrow slit into which the cards were slipped. A disposal unit was to the right, which automatically separated dishes and garbage, washing and storing one and disposing of the other through disintegration. A niche to one side was an apparatus for dispensing liquids. In a row beside it were buttons for instructions: types of beverage and desired temperature. The automatic food center was a wonder of this alien technology: no cooking, no washing dishes, no preparation, many appliances rolled into one machine. All one had to do was select cards, enter them, and wait for a meal to appear as if by magic. When finished, one placed the dishes inside the final unit to do clean-up chores.

Jana frowned. They were marked in Androasian, and she did not know which word or symbol meant *zim*. She hated feeling helpless and dependent. She could press all buttons and wait for what she wanted to appear beneath the spout, but she hated being wasteful even in an alien world. The man holding her captive had promised her Androasian language lessons; it was clear she needed them, and soon. When the yellow-eyed female android entered, Jana asked the nonhuman to order her breakfast. Not that Jana was hungry, but she needed to do something to use up her frustration. She went to the dining dome and sat down. Why it felt so different and vexing to have a robot serve her over a human maid, she didn't know. Perhaps because it pointed out her predicament.

When Ine brought her meal, Jana gazed at it. Would she, she mused, ever become accustomed to such strange-looking food, not only in color but also in texture? It smelled appealing and she knew the flavor was excellent, but red eggs, blue meat, and orange bread was revolting to someone who loved simple food—not to mention the purple coffee!

She decided she must eat to regain all her strength and to remain keen-witted and healthy. She had work to do, a culprit to unmask, and a puzzle to solve. Like the wildcatters who had worked for her father seeking black gold in Texas fields, she must search for her golden truth and happiness.

The tawny-haired male arrived. His handsome face glistened with moisture and his hair was wet. The snug and damp outfit—similar to biking gear on Earth—left little, if anything, to the imagination. She had seen *forsha*wear on the ship when captives played the game and knew the thin, stretchy material was designed for muscle protection against strains. As he mopped his sweat with a small towel, Jana eyed his physique, which matched Varian Saar's to a T! She had seen Varian both clad and naked so many times and knew those lithe legs, virile body, and strong arms. Didn't she? Even if Varian had any telltale scars or flaws, which he didn't, Tris would have removed them for this cunning charade. If he was Ryker, how could his body match Varian's perfectly in size, shape, and color?

Jana returned his gaze when he looked at her. "It's late, so I assumed you had already eaten," she said. "Should I have waited for you?"

"Certainly not, and I have already eaten, long ago."

She wished her trembling would halt and hoped he wouldn't notice it. From his grin and sparkling eyes, he knew he was affecting her in a pleasing way. "I don't usually stay in bed so long. I apologize for being lazy."

"You need your rest for a complete and swift recovery."

"I think I've made a rather fast one considering how ill I was, don't you, Dr. Triloni? I take it you are the one who's treating me?"

"I was and I am. No one is better qualified in this case. I promise."

"I'll take your word for it." Jana fingered the garment she was wearing and said, "Thank you for the wardrobe. Your taste is excellent. It's nothing like the ones I had on Varian's ship or at Draco's. I'm grateful."

"I would like to take credit for it, but it wasn't my doing. You chose it yourself last week. I had a ship bring choices of everything you might need and you made your own selections. That's why you like them so much."

His impenetrable gaze made her nervous, as did his close and alluring proximity. *Cool down, J. G.* "I don't remember that."

"Doesn't matter. How about joining me for a swim?"

"It's too soon to enter the water after eating, but I will join you at the pool."

Ryker assisted her from her chair and they walked the short distance.

In a glass dome not far from the house, Jana observed with

delight the tropical setting that surrounded a long and wide pool of pale-green water. Garden areas with fountains and waterfalls were located in three spots, complete with sitting arrangements nearby. Lush green vegetation greeted her vision from the ceiling and floor. Soft music and the singing of birds filled her ears. Sunlight sneaked through the reflective covering and danced on the water. The setting gave off a sultry and exotic aura. "It's breathtaking." *And much too romantic and seductive!*

"I'm happy you like it. Come here anytime you wish. With few exceptions, you have freedom to come and go as you please on Darkar. Behind those decorative screens is exercise equipment. A little work on the walkometer might help you recover your strength and muscle tone. Changing rooms are there," he gestured. "I'll return shortly."

He vanished into a small room to don his trunks. Jana removed her shoes, rolled up her pants' legs, and dangled her feet in the water. Ryker returned and dove into the pool. She watched him swim back and forth with agile strokes. Wet flaxen hair clung to his head. Sleek golden shoulders broke the water's surface with ease. He was such a splendid sight. Watching him caused her body to warm with desire. After a time, he swam to where she sat and halted to stand in chest-high water. He smiled, and she almost shyly returned the gesture. If he tried to get romantic, she didn't know what she would do. She yearned to be held, kissed, caressed, and loved—but by Varian. *Please, God, let this be my love and let there be a good reason for his deceit.*

"Feels wonderful, Jana. Ready to come in? I know you can swim."

"Not yet." She remembered all too well what had happened the day she had swum with Draco at his home; *he* had become romantic, almost seductive. She had been on the point of surrendering to her "owner" in order to force an allegedly traitorous Varian from her heart to begin a new life with another man, a kind and gentle—but deceitful—one. She had wondered so many times during her stay on Karnak why Draco didn't possess her. She finally got her answer when she learned he hadn't purchased her; Varian had, and came to reclaim her when she and Draco seemed to be getting too close for his comfort. That time, he had convinced her successfully of his ruse of selling her. Was he duping her again? Why?

The desirous way the emerald-eyed man watched her made Jana tense with panic. Drops rolled down his bronzed torso and arms, muscular arms that evinced great physical strength, arms that could entice a woman to want to slip into his protective embrace. He fingercombed his hair with hands that could be gentle or strong, allowing her a good view of his manly chest and flat abdomen. Every inch of him was appealing and evoked the temptation to touch and explore him. She felt herself being aroused against her will and battled her senses to clear and restrain their unbidden urges. She looked at her toes as she wiggled them in the aquamarine liquid.

"I do believe you're having good thoughts about me, Jana of Earth. Your cheeks are flushing and your gaze is glowing. Your respiration has altered."

"You're teasing me and taunting me, Ryker. Please don't."

"How else can I get my wife to notice me as a man, her husband?"

"Have no doubts I know you are both."

"That worries and alarms you? It shouldn't. We are married."

Jana's apprehensions and suspense mounted. "Please don't pressure me. I'm not ready for . . . that kind of relationship."

"With me or with any man?"

He captured her feet and massaged them. His touch sent tingles over her body. She felt as if she wanted to explode, to rant, to rave, to cry, to beg for the truth. She knew she wouldn't get it from him. She finally locked her troubled gaze with his merry one. "With any man. Before I agreed to become your wife, you promised it wouldn't be an intimate arrangement until long from now when you needed an heir."

"That was before I realized you would be irresistible and a

constant temptation. But calm your fears. Anything worth having is worth waiting for."

"Thank you. I'll change now." She had to put distance between them if only for a short time. She hurried to the dressing room and pulled on a swimsuit with French-cut legs but enough material to cover her shaky body. *I'm going to kill you, Varian Saar, if you don't stop tempting me as Ryker!*

She swam for ten minutes while her owner observed from where he lounged; the waves she created lapped at his body. He was so like Varian in his romantic pursuit of her. He smiled the same way. His eyes blazed the same way. His expression was familiar. His aura was the same. His physique was the same. How could this man not be Varian? How had she not noticed how much the half brothers were alike in appearance? Because she hadn't wanted to see it during her terrifying days with Ryker! Too, their physical differences were sufficient and their character variations more than ample to disguise their strong resemblance enough to be missed by an unsuspecting and distracted stranger. Why should she have thought the Maffeian starship commander and an Androasian prince were related, were half brothers? If only she had known the truth long ago, perhaps she could have helped Varian deal with his tormenting past, a past that had forced a wedge between them.

Jana finally swam toward the steps, where she saw him on the pool edge, his elbows propped on his knees to continue his visual attack on her. She had no choice except to join him.

Jana accepted the outstretched hand that helped her up the steps, but she became panicky when it drew her down beside him, too close. "I was going to dry off and use the walkometer while my muscles were warmed up."

"Afraid to be this near me?" he questioned. "I won't devour you, Jana. Relax."

With her head lowered, her gaze touched on his right side just above his narrow waist. It wasn't there! In their rush, they had forgotten to add a scar to this phony Ryker's body! The day before she married Ryker, he had visited her straight from the pool, clad only in swim trunks and with a towel draped around his neck. There had been a scar from an animal bite at the end of his rib cage. He had explained how he had gotten it from a specimen. She doubted Ryker had removed it since then, though he surely possessed the technology and equipment to do so. Obviously it was an oversight of Varian and Tristan. They assumed she hadn't seen Ryker naked or even half clad and hadn't thought it necessary to include that mark. Her accusing gaze lifted to meet his probing one. She studied him for a minute. Take away the green eyes and blond hair and return his cleft chin and smile creases, and she had the face of Varian Saar. It took all of her self-control not to curse and beat him. No, it was better not to let him know she guessed the truth. Obtaining Trilabs and Maffei's security during his Earth mission must be his motives, as she could think of nothing else so vital. If she blurted out her discovery, he would have a false explanation. When and how would he finally confess his terrible deceit? And could she forgive him?

"Your muscles are getting cold, Jana, and so is your mood."

She stood, grabbed a towel, and said while drying off, "Sorry. I was thinking about my world's fate and my friends trapped there. We often had swim parties at my pool or theirs." She wasn't a good liar, but, at that moment, she didn't care if he knew she wasn't being honest. She walked behind the decorative screen and stepped onto the treadmill. She pressed the start button to try to rid herself of the tension and anger. She resisted the temptation to expose her discovery. How could the betrayer dare to make love to her as Ryker? How could he want her to respond to him as Ryker? Just like Alex, Varian was thinking and feeling with his loins, not with his heart or brain!

Twenty minutes later, the alien shouted, "That's enough exertion for today, Jana. Better do cool down or lactic acid build-up will cause cramps. We'll go to the house to shower and change. I want to run those tests on you before lunch and your rest period."

She fumed at his clever command. She knew if muscles

were used quickly for a lengthy time and given an abrupt stop instead of being allowed to slow down gradually, it would cause cramps.

She followed "Ryker" to the house in silence, swinging her garment in her hand. Each went to their own room to shower and change. As she completed her grooming, she couldn't understand why Varian and Tris hadn't drugged her into compliance and amnesia. That would have been safer, since they obviously didn't trust her to carry out her part of the ruse.

On the way to the complex, Jana eyed the shuttle setting and landing grids nearby. Somehow Varian had gotten it repaired and the debris removed before letting her awaken. She tried to steer the blond alien toward a willing revelation. "How did you know about the real motive for Varian's mission to Earth?" she asked. "I thought it was a big secret. I wouldn't know about it if *Kadim* Tirol hadn't told me while I was visiting him. Why he did, I don't know. It seems odd to give me such information right before sending me here to you with facts you could pass to *Kadim* Maal."

He kept walking with his back to her. "It was and is a big secret, Jana. I can't imagine what *Kadim* Tirol hoped to accomplish by telling you. Perhaps it was a test of my loyalty to Maffei."

She caught up to him and observed his expression. "What do you mean?"

"Perhaps they want to see if I'll pass the information on to Grandfather or the Tabrizes. With so many of their starships away saving Earth, it would be the perfect time for enemies to attack Maffei."

"But that would be stupid and dangerous. Besides, I didn't tell you."

"No, but I have my ways of learning things. Besides information Cass withdraws from her father and passes along to me, I have spies everywhere. I have to keep up with matters that concern me. I became suspicious of something going on when Star Fleet kept ordering so many decontamination chemicals from me, far too many for average use. There are other suppliers for most of them, but they give me a nice percentage of their orders to keep on my good side. I wondered who was receiving so much treatment to prevent spreading germs. I learned it was for the *charl* raids in your star system. You know his ship wasn't the only one to raid Earth? By now, they should have around three thousand of your people on Anais."

Andrea . . . Was she there? Scared out of her wits? Had—

"You know about Anais, don't you?"

"That's the planetoid where they've established the Earth colony to prevent our total extinction. Where is it?" she asked. "How will my people live and be protected?"

"It orbits Zamarra, the outermost planet of the Maffei system. It's an environmental protection location that no one is allowed to visit without permission. Don't worry, they'll be safe there."

"What about my planet? Will it be destroyed by that meteoroid?"

"The latest reports have revealed that it's a rogue worldlet on a collision course with Earth. It's believed the rogue is on an elliptical orbit around your sun, not coming from beyond your star system as first believed. Sometimes bodies take thousands or millions of years to make one orbit. If one of that size strikes your world, the results will be catastrophic. Once it enters the gravitational pull of Earth, its speed will increase. The impact will be devastating, particularly if it hits nuclear facilities or chemical plants. It could release deadly toxins into your atmosphere that air currents could sweep around your globe. Radiation, germs, and chaos. Broken dams to flood areas. Contamination of food and water supplies. The impact itself will destroy everything for thousands of miles. If it falls into the ocean, mammoth tidal waves will result. The force of the explosion will be greater than many nuclear bombs or billions of tons of your TNT. In some cases, it might mimic a nuclear blast and provoke a war among survivors. The explosion could crack Earth's core or shove her out of orbit, making her a similar threat to other planets. Dust clouds can block the sun, killing off plant, animal, and human life. It's a bleak picture, Jana, but an honest one. Maffei hopes, with Project Starguard, to either smash it or safely deflect it."

Horror filled her. "Can it be done?"

"Theoretically it's possible. But . . ."

She tugged on his arm and implored, "But what?"

"It's never been attempted on a rogue worldlet of this size. There are too many variables to judge accurately. From their observation, and by your scientists, it's believed another such object struck your planet millions of years ago and sent up dust clouds that blocked out the sun and killed off most life there. Your dinosaurs vanished because of it. Your people took the remains of that tragedy to make the very fuel which now threatens to wreak havoc on your planet. It could happen again."

"Why can't Earth shatter or divert it with a missile?"

"Your people lack the knowledge and technology to ready and launch one in time and with enough explosive payload to work. How could they locate its stress point in order to aim correctly? Besides, heading straight at them, it will appear a fixed star. They lack the detection capability to realize the threat before it's too late. In your year of 1989, your NASA released news of an asteroid large and swift enough at forty-six thousand miles per hour to wipe out numerous cities if it had plummeted to Earth. They didn't even know of its presence until it was speeding away from your planet. A nuclear explosion of enough firepower would be dangerous to explode near Earth; shock waves could be just as deadly to your planet. The sheer size of the rogue makes it impossible for your people to handle. Even if Star Fleet, with all its power and technology, diverted it, the rogue could bypass Earth, strike a smaller planet, and create an even worse catastrophe. If a lesser one closer to your sun was destroyed, there is no judging the effect on your solar system. Nor to ours from shock waves. A disturbance of that magnitude anywhere in the Universe could be felt by all."

Her heart sank in dismay. "So it's hopeless?"

"Not yet. I think their plan can work. I'll do my part."

When he began heading toward the complex once more, she followed as she questioned, "Your part?"

"I'm supplying the lasers and chemicals needed for their mission, when they get around to ordering them and informing me."

She stopped in her tracks. "You?"

He halted, too. "Yes, me, Jana. Some of them only I possess."

Was that, she wondered, why "Ryker" must be kept alive? "You will cooperate, won't you?"

He sent her a smile of encouragement and promise. "Of course, my frantic wife. I already have everything ready for pickup."

"When will they come for it?"

"In three of your Earth weeks."

"We will be back from our trip by then?"

"Yes, so relax. The rogue is being watched carefully this minute. Star Fleet is ready to move against it if anything changes. As soon as Varian handles his private life, he'll be on his way."

You mean handles Maal and the chemicals, she concluded, but said, "After his marriage to Canissia?"

"Yes."

Canissia and her father—Supreme Councilman Segall Garthon, one of the three most powerful men in the Maffei Alliance—guilty of passing Alliance secrets to Ryker Triloni . . . Varian would deal with that discovery when he completed his current assignment. If she had guessed his motives right, much was at stake. She mustn't do anything to disrupt his crucial task. "How can marrying that bitch from hell be more important than saving a whole planet of people, and possibly the Milky Way Galaxy? You did say shock waves could threaten here, so why wait to attack it? Why are they wasting valuable time?"

"From what I've gathered, they have the mission timed perfectly. They can't begin their assault until it reaches a certain point for safe destruction, between your fifth and sixth planets: Jupiter and Saturn."

"May I ask a favor of you?" She glued her gaze to his. "Can you use your contacts to get your hands on a list of the people on the Anais Colony?"

"I think so. Why do you want to know?"

"Varian promised to rescue my best friend, Andrea McKay. Can you find out if she's there? And if so, is there any way to . . ."

"To what, Jana? Bring her here to live with us?"

"Is that asking too much? We've been best friends since age twelve. I was going to her home when I was captured. She must be worried sick about what happened to me and, if she's there, she must be terrified. Perhaps it's selfish to think of only one person's survival when my entire world is in jeopardy, but I love her. She's like my sister. It would be wonderful to have her close to me. At least, can you arrange for me to visit with her?"

"I can only promise to try, Jana. Anais is off limits to everyone. It was established to safeguard endangered species: plants, animals, and such. No one is supposed to know the Earthlings are there. If your world is saved, they might be returned home. If not, over a period of time and after training, they'll be settled in Maffei. I'm not sure how I can do what you ask without giving away my knowledge and sources, and I can't risk that. But if there's a safe way I can learn anything about her, I will. Perhaps I can get your message to her and her reply back to you. But getting her off Anais won't be easy, if even possible. Then again, I love challenges."

On impulse, she hugged him tightly and thanked him through misty eyes and emotion-strained voice.

He returned the embrace and murmured in a husky tone, "If this is the kind of appreciation I'll receive, I'll do more than my best."

"I know I can depend on you to keep your word."

"I promise to try hard."

Just as you promised the same thing once before, Varian.

Perhaps she's already there and you just refuse to expose yourself by telling me.

Inside the research laboratory, Jana watched him feed the leeches once more. "Why don't you let one of your trained androids do that?"

"Would you want others doing your experiments and research? I think not, Dr. Jana Triloni."

"You're right." When he squirted six cc's of a clear liquid into the dish of blood, she remarked, "Six—my lucky number. Do you have one?"

"I believe a man makes his own good or bad luck."

No slip-up in admitting eight is your lucky number: which is why you paid 8,888,888 katoogas for me through Draco's bid. Try something else, J. G., to trip him up. "What's that drug you're using?"

"*Malophine.*"

"But that's what Tris gave me on the ship to treat my injury."

"Couldn't be. *Malophine* is an anticoagulate for the blood they're drinking. Dr. Zarcoff probably used *Clinitroid* on you. It would be his best choice in that instance. *Clinitroid* extirpates excess fluid and blood from an injury site to reduce swelling and bruising."

"You're right; now I remember. I did several projects with him during my stay on the ship and heard the names of so many unfamiliar chemicals that I forgot its name. I won't make that mistake again. Tris even let me insert a veinal cannula on a sick monkey he was treating."

"Since some of your inoculations didn't take, that was dangerous. You're lucky you stayed well."

"I thought you didn't believe in luck."

"But you do. Would you put this crucible in the sink over there?"

Jana took the container and obeyed. "Do you use a gamma-counter?"

"I don't have much need for radioactive tracers and a counting unit."

"What's the half-life of the explosion you mentioned if Darkar is attacked?" she inquired, referring to the time required for half of the atoms in a certain amount of radioactive substance to disintegrate.

"Two thousand years by Earth's reckoning time. But we're safe no matter what happens. We would simply move to Androas."

His intelligence amazed her. Could Varian have learned such things in a short time span? "Do you have to milk the *keelar* again?" The snake's alien name, as well as other words, had no translation in English or Androasian and came out in Maffeian.

"Not today. It takes him three days to rebuild his supply. *Keelars* are one of the few species I hate to handle. One shot out of my hand not long ago and latched onto my side until my android Gar pried it loose. Emptied his whole load of venom into me and scarred me for a while."

She observed as he rubbed an area above his waist on his side. Had he noticed her reaction at the pool? "When did you get rid of it? I recall seeing it the day before we married."

"The morning of our marriage. Gar handled the *latron* beam for it; I programmed him for skill in that area. You're mighty observant, Dr. Triloni. Maybe I should have this one lasered off, too, one day."

She saw him stroke the right side of his jaw. "If there's no need to keep it and it's so simple to have it removed, you should. But it doesn't detract from your good looks."

He half turned and grinned at her. "Thanks."

"You're fortunate you have an antidote for *keelar* bites."

"If not, you wouldn't have a husband. Untreated, death occurs in two hours. Why don't you go across the hall to med lab and get changed for your tests and check-up? I'll be along shortly. There's a wrap in the closet."

Jana went into the medical laboratory. Once more she had the overwhelming feeling she had almost died in this room at Shara's hand. She walked to the wall where the curtain, holographic type pictures, and safe containing the journals and diaries had been. She examined it closely. There was no sign of recent changes. Still, that didn't mean it hadn't been done. Her gaze touched on a pot of exotic flowers in full bloom. She hurried to investigate. When she had come in here that awful day, they hadn't been anywhere near blooming. It looked like the same pot and plant, so how could it have budded and bloomed so quickly, unless she had been unconscious for a long time—more than a week? Perhaps that much of "Ryker's" story was true; she could have been kept drugged while all the repairs were made and Varian's appearance altered.

She quickly changed into the pale-blue shift to be ready when the man arrived. Upon reaching this planetoid, she had feared he would dissect and study her as an alien specimen. What was he going to do to her today? Did "Ryker" have the medical knowledge and skills to treat her?

"All ready to begin?"

Jana watched him come forward with trepidation. Who was he? She climbed upon the table and lay down. "I'm fine now, honestly."

"Let tests and blood samples determine that for us."

He positioned an apparatus at her side, then placed her arm in a tube which tightened sufficiently to hold it still. He pressed a button and a humming sound came forth. She felt a light and painless prick as blood was drawn. He carried the vial to a machine and placed it inside for testing.

"An automated pathologist and lab technician? How clever. In a few more years, your machines can probably run everything and man won't be needed."

"Machines are nothing without superior intelligence and imagination of their creators: humans. Now let's check your vital signs and functions."

Jana remained still, almost rigid, as he passed the black box over her head and chest. He halted it over her heart as he stared into her eyes. His smoldering gaze melted into her apprehensive one. It drifted to her parted lips and he looked to her as if he were about to lean over and kiss her. His eyes roamed her face and hair with an expression that said he longed to caress and stroke them. Her suspense mounted.

"Looking at you makes my heart pound as fiercely and swiftly as yours is doing, Jana of Earth."

When she attempted to push the medical analyzer away from the telltale area, he halted her and grinned. "Don't do that," she pleaded.

"I'm not finished yet. Lie still or I'll get false readings."

"This isn't fair. I'm in a vulnerable position. I'm nervous. Your readouts won't be accurate."

He glanced at the digital numbers on the instrument and said, "Blood pressure, heart rate, temperature, and chemical balances are fine. Your respiration and pulse are a little fast, but I hope that's because of me."

"Is it?" she parried, then changed the subject. "The flowers over there are beautiful."

"A distracting tactic?" He chuckled. "The new formula I created works far better than the old one. It brought them to maturation within a week. A product that speeds up blooming that much will be worth plenty of money to certain people."

Always an answer to discredit every clue she thought she gleaned! Or was it the truth? She mustn't allow him to manipulate her emotions and actions as he had done so many times before. "I'm sure it will. Congratulations. Tell me something while we await my test results; how did the alien virus cause sterility in Maffeian women?"

"By causing the ovums to shrivel and die inside the ovaries."

"But if the plague was fifty years ago and all Maffeian females were made sterile, how was Canissia born? Is she the child of a *charl*?"

"No, her mother was visiting family in another star system and wasn't affected. Once news of the virus spread, Segall orderd her to remain there for several years until the danger passed. It didn't do her much good because she died giving birth to Cass the year after her return."

"So Canissia is one of the few true-blooded Maffeians her age. That explains part of her arrogance and conceit. What about female children? Did it strike them as well as women of childbearing age?"

"Yes. Any female alive fifty years ago was affected. No baby was conceived of a Maffeian female after that time. The vengeful scientist traveled to every planet in this star system and infected the food supplies. He hoped to go unexposed and to live to see the Maffeian race extinct."

"Why did he hate the Maffeians so much?"

"A Star Fleet ship going at a great speed had radar problems and didn't pick up the small shuttle his wife and daughter were in before crashing into it and killing everyone aboard. He went mad. He blamed all of them. They had taken his wife and child, so he, in his own misguided way, took theirs. When the insidious virus made itself known, it was too late."

"What happened to him?"

"Members of the Praetorian Elite Squad traced the trouble to him and killed him when he refused to surrender."

"What's the Elite Squad?"

"Spies and agents made up mostly of starship commanders, military specialists, and a few scientists," he explained. "It's a small and secret unit. They answer only to the Supreme Council. They're the only group that can go outside the law if necessary to accomplish their missions. Varian, Nigel, and Martella are squad members. That rank gives them a great deal of power, something that causes my half brother to feel larger than his size."

Surely Varian Saar would never tell her such secrets . . . "How do you know such— Of course, you have your ways of learning any and everything. What about my inoculations? When do you repeat them?"

"In a few days when you're completely well again. It has to be before our trip. Otherwise, I couldn't let you go with me and take another risk."

So, that's how you're going to get out of taking me along!

Something, a phony test or fever, will prevent the shots so I can't go and be seen. She glared into his back as he fetched the test results. "Any pathogenic microorganisms in sight?"

"No hungry bugs left. The antigens worked fine. I got them into your bloodstream just in time to stimulate T-lymphocytes to produce the right antibodies needed. The new antibodies have already destroyed the antigens and clung to the cells. You're immune now, at least to *Rahgine*'s Fever."

Jana gaped at him with an open mouth.

"What's wrong? Did my words translate wrong? You're fine, Jana."

He had spit out that medical and accurate knowledge too fast for someone who wasn't a doctor! "You're just so smart that it amazes me."

"A simple process of conferring immunity isn't difficult."

"Do you work with endocrines or endoplasmic reticulum much?"

"Knowing and using the thyroid, adrenal, and pituitary gland hormones are necessary sometimes. So is the communication channel for things passing between a cell nucleus and cell environment."

Again, she feared his correct answers came too quickly and easily. This attempt to expose him wasn't going as she planned! She panicked.

"Are you testing me, Dr. Triloni?"

"Testing you?" she echoed as she stalled for time to think of an excuse for trying to trick him into exposing a lack of medical and chemical knowledge. *My God, you seem to know everything. How?* "I'm interested in your research. Why should I test you?"

"Because you still have doubts about your recent hallucination?"

"If you think that, why not use truth serum on me to see if I'm lying? Varian threatened to do that one time when I refused to answer him."

"He wouldn't have dared use *Thorin* on your delicate system. It's too harsh and dangerous. You possess a strong will, Jana of Earth, so you would resist, probably to the point of cell and organ damage or death."

"I could use . . . *Thorin* on you to see if you're being honest with me."

"It wouldn't work. I created *Thorin*, and I created its counteragent. I'm immune to it. So, thanks to me, are galactic leaders and rulers. *Kadim* Tirol, Segall, Draco, the planetary *avatars* and *zartiffs*, and a few others have been made immune to truth serum, too. Including my half brother."

Jana knew from past studies that *avatars* were planetary rulers and *zartiffs* were regional rulers of planets, just as the *kadim* was the high ruler of this galaxy. She also knew there were no words for correct English translations of those ranks. "Why would you share such powers with them?"

"There are men in certain positions who must not be vulnerable to truth serums of enemies. They are my allies, and some even my friends. Other scientists and researchers have developed their own formulas for truth drugs, but only I possess the immunizing agent. It works on the nervous system in the brain, through the interconnections of neurons—afferent, efferent, and interneurons—which give man his memory, thoughts, and emotions. *Thorin* attacks at the dendrites, the stems of the nerve-cell body through which impulses are conducted. It makes it impossible for a man or woman to lie without enduring agony, even well trained and loyal men. *Rendelar* prevents that reaction."

Jana stared at him once more. Panic flooded her. This man before her had to be . . . Ryker Triloni. It was true: she had suffered from illness and fever-induced delusions. Varian had betrayed her, had given her to him as a truce token. Her heart pounded hard and heavy. Her senses were spinning wildly. She felt cold from head to foot, and shuddered. He—Prince Ryker Triloni—had spoken the truth from the beginning.

"You're getting chilled, Jana. You can get dressed. I'll wait for you in the other lab. You should return to the house and eat. You can read and rest this afternoon. I don't want you overtiring yourself. I've selected several books on plants, animals, and chemistry written in Maffeian since you know that language. You can study them at your leisure. Ine will begin teaching you Androasian in a few days. Then, I'll give you books in my language to study, and some of my research notes. I still have work to do."

As he turned to put away the items and apparatuses he had used, Jana wanted to weep in anguish. She wanted to scream at herself for being so foolish and dreamy-eyed. She must forget the fantasy of Varian Saar and accept the reality of Ryker Triloni. She was his wife, his captive, forever. She was doomed to an unpredictable existence here on Darkar. She had already wept over her other losses: her home, her friends, her world, her career, her identity, and her freedom. Now, her love was lost. Never again would Varian hold her in his arms, call her "Moonbeam," and take her to ecstasy's realm in his arms. Nor could he ever deceive and betray her again. The man nearby seemed to be reaching out to her, if he could be trusted. Perhaps, with luck, Varian's evil motive for using her to spite and defeat his half brother had failed. It was a grave error not to know or to misjudge one's enemies and rivals. Had Varian captured her to complete a cycle of vengeance which Shara and Galen had begun thirty-two years ago with their unbridled lust? How stupid and dangerous for her to have mentioned the hallucination about his hated foe! As he started to leave for her to dress, she called out to him.

He stopped and turned.

Her gaze swept over him as he came to her side and studied her heartsick expression.

"What's wrong, Jana? You look ready to cry."

"I just realized something important. I almost died and I haven't even thanked you for saving my life and for being so kind and patient with me. I'm sorry for how I've behaved. It's scary being unable to remember a week of your life, a very important week. I promise to do my best to please you and to make you proud of me." He smiled as he wiped away her tears, but his gaze appeared troubled to her instead of relieved or victorious. She didn't want to ask or to analyze why; she had done too much erroneous reasoning and testing in the last four days.

"I'm glad to hear this, Jana. Things will be fine now." He leaned over and kissed her, a short, tender kiss, full of emotion and longing. He smiled and told her, "I've been wanting to do that all day, for days, for weeks. You go to the house to rest and I'll see you at dinner."

He left the room as if afraid he'd do more than kiss her if he stayed. Jana gaped at his retreating back. If she didn't know better . . . *Don't do this again, J. G.; he isn't Varian. He can't be Varian.* But the kiss . . . *Stop it*!

The alien sat down at a panel in the private lab and switched on the retrometer for light-beam voice communication. He began a scrambled message to someone far away, a full report to his ruler, the *kadim*.

A voice soon filled the room. "How are things going, Varian?"

"Proceeding as planned, Grandfather. The stars be damned, sir! What in *Gehenna* am I doing to her, to us, with this infernal mission?"

Chapter Four

Kadim Tirol Trygue heard despair in Varian's voice. He knew he was asking a great deal of his beloved and only grandson, his sole heir and kin, but he had no choice. No man was better trained or qualified, and no other man could take Ryker Triloni's place. Varian sounded soul-weary and heart-sick, but Tirol knew he could depend on the young man to do his duty to the Alliance. The fates of two galaxies rested on his grandson's shoulders, a heavy burden. Tirol also realized how dangerous this secret and desperate assignment was and prayed not only for Varian's survival and success, but for Jana's safety, as well. "You're saving her world and safe-guarding ours, Son," the older man reminded, "for the near future and the years ahead."

"I know, Grandfather, but you should have seen the look on her face when I finally had her convinced that I'm Ryker. It nearly ripped my heart from my chest. It took all of my self-control not to confess the truth. She's in so much pain and confusion that it's almost unbearable."

In a gentle tone, Tirol warned, "You can't tell her anything, Varian. You have to stay strong. So much is at stake."

"*Kahala*, sir! Don't you think I know that? I'm sorry, Grandfather, but this tension is working on me day and night. I've finished going over their journals and tapes. Added to what Ryker told me at our deadly showdown, our worst fears and suspicions have been confirmed. Maal is planning to form an alliance with Jurad to attack while we're gone. If we don't go, Jana's world is doomed and ours might be damaged by aftershocks. If we do go, Maffei will be attacked as soon as we're out of defense range, unless I can persuade Maal to hold off his plot when I visit him. The Tabrizes would never attack alone. If I can convince Maal I'm Ryker and that it's to our best interests to postpone the assault, things will go our way. He usually does what Ryker suggests, so I'm hoping and praying he'll agree this time, too. I've already decided what strategies to use with him."

After Varian related his plans, Tirol concurred they sounded clever and feasible. "But fooling Maal will be harder than fooling Jana and getting onto Darkar disguised as Ryker," he pointed out. "Don't take any unnecessary risks in Androas. We'll have an Elite Squad on standby in case a rescue is needed for you and Jana. You said you have her convinced now?"

"Yes, sir. We repaired and cleared away all damages and clues while she was kept drugged. We even constructed a cyborg who looks like Ryker to play *forsha* with his right hand. It helps that I'm ambidextrous because she immediately noticed which hand I used. I've convinced her she's been ill from *Rahgine*'s Fever because some of her inoculations didn't take. She finally believes my rescue was only a delusion and she has partial amnesia. She fought the so-called 'truth,' Grandfather, but I've played my role well. I hope she'll forgive me for tricking her."

As they unscrambled at his end, Tirol heard the bitter and sarcastic tone of Varian's words. "I wish this wasn't necessary, but it is. I'm relieved we discovered their treachery before it was too late for all of us."

"If I hadn't started reading Shara's journals while Jana was asleep, this charade wouldn't exist. Before I realized the potential repercussions, it was already under way with my reluctant agreement. Ryker overestimated his cunning. Our new device imitated his voice perfectly so we could reprogram his androids, especially since I had learned the codes from him and from the journals. We have Jana to thank for telling me about them. I also found a stockpile of videotapes; it seems Ryker and Shara liked to record everything that happened here. Hopefully we have enough evidence to coerce treaties with Jurad and Maal when I return; we dare not risk revealing the truth to them before our ships depart. Their reactions are unpredictable."

Varian sighed deeply. "Even with this evidence, they might not believe Father was innocent all those years ago, not with Ryker and Shara dead—both by another Saar's hand—and unable to argue our word against theirs. There's no guessing how Maal will take his grandson's death by my laser shot. He could go mad like Shara and start a war for revenge. Maal will probably accuse us of stealing Shara's body, substituting the phony one on display there, and trying to trick him. I'm not sure he'll ever believe she didn't die seven years ago, and she could do the wicked things we know she has. The same goes for Jurad. While I'm playing Ryker, maybe I can gather even more proof to help us convince them we're telling the truth."

"What about your crew and ship, Varian? Don't let them be seen."

"Nigel and I finished going through everything before he returned to the ship. He'll command the *Wanderlust* until I'm back aboard. I placed Martella in charge of security after Lieutenant Dykstra was transferred."

"A wise choice; she's excellent. What if you come in contact with Prince Taemin? You said those two had been working together on the sly."

"I'm sure I know enough from Ryker's materials to dupe Maal and Taemin and whoever else might be necessary. I know his mannerisms, secrets, and his conversations with them. It's to our advantage again that Shara loved to keep such detailed entries and to make videos. Besides, Grandfather, Tris did a superb job with his surgical procedures to make me match Ryker perfectly. It was almost perfect."

"What do you mean, Son? Is there something he can't alter?"

"We forgot to add one scar we didn't know Jana had viewed, but I convinced her I'd had it lasered off since the last time she'd seen it. She's very smart and observant, but I've been trained to notice any and every thing. So far, I've managed to cover myself."

"You know that iris dye might not be removable after this mission?"

"Yes, sir. If Tris can't extract it, I'll just have to wear blue lens covers for the rest of my life like Ryker wore green ones and blond hair to conceal his resemblance to me and Father. He desperately wanted his own identity, Grandfather. His hatred for me was so deep and bitter. As much as I detested him and his battles with me, I didn't want to kill him. But he gave me no choice. I tried to reason with him, but he wouldn't listen. Shara filled him with too many lies and too much evil. The crazy thing is, while viewing those videos, I picked up on something incredible: I think he was actually falling for Jana. I think Shara realized it, too, and that's why she tried to kill Jana while Ryker was off stalking me. No matter that Ryker taunted me about killing Jana, I believe, if he had been the one to survive our duel, he might have kept her and gotten rid of Shara. He was trying very hard to woo my woman under the guise of a ruse. That's why I have to behave the same way with Jana. Tris did a good job on her, too, didn't leave a single sign on her to make her think her trauma was real."

"She's a scientist, a researcher. How did you fool her?"

"The mental implants Tris used worked perfectly. I answered every question she asked with speed and ease, almost without thinking, even though I didn't know what I was saying. He gave me plenty of lessons and practice in the lab before we awakened her so I could act natural in here."

"Thank goodness you speak and write other languages. You'll need that skill when you head for Androas. With our men working the shuttles now, neither Jana nor anyone else can learn what's really going on there. When the time comes to expose Ryker's accidental death, we'll make certain you and Jana are nowhere nearby. We don't want Maal and Jurad to have any reason to doubt your innocence or Jana's claim as Ryker's heir."

"Even if they protest letting her inherit, by then, we'll have gathered all his secrets and made Trilabs useless to them. I hope, once their powerful ally is gone, they'll agree to treaties without us having to use those journals and videotapes. Too many of our secrets are discussed on them."

"You said Canissia's to blame for part of it. She's committed treason, kidnapping, and the murders of Moloch and Baruch. Moloch wasn't a big loss, but your former friend and officer was. It's too bad he put himself in the position of being blackmailed and bewitched by her. When she's located and arrested, she'll be sent to the female prison planetoid for life."

"If she isn't already dead, Grandfather. I learned from the last journal that Ryker plotted her death, and no one has seen or heard from her since Jana's disappearance. Supposedly she had an alibi, but it won't work now. It seems likely she's gone, since she hasn't responded to the marriage proposal I made to her to lure her out of hiding. Everyone in the Tri Galaxy knows about our impending wedding except her. Ryker even used it to coerce Jana into marrying him. He'd better be glad he didn't touch her! He had Jana believing he freed her to marry her when I'm the one responsible. I wish I could ease her fears."

"So do I, Son. You know we dared not use *Rendelar* on her to make her immune to *Thorin* in the event of capture and questioning; that would have been suspicious. Canissia's abduction of her proved an enemy can get to her even while she's being protected. She has to believe this is real to play her part with accuracy. As Ryker's wife, with luck and your skills to make her appear happy, she's your protection. Hers, too."

"I want to get this assignment finished, Grandfather, and

get her off Darkar as soon as possible. She deserves peace and happiness. After seeing on videotape how that bastard treated her, I could kill him again if he hadn't already forced me to do it last week. We rescued her just in the nick of time, even if Shara hadn't tried to slay her. Ryker told me he was planning to breed her for an heir, then kill her. Maybe he would have carried out his taunt. *Kahala*, I never realized those two were that evil. I can't imagine a mother and son sharing the same bed and planning to marry. Shara would have never persuaded me she's Jana Greyson, even with surgical alterations to take Jana's face. Now I have to convince her to hate me and to fall in love with him. I've already learned things about her that I didn't know because our time together was too short. When this is over, she'll never understand and forgive me, Grandfather, never."

"You know what's at stake and you must do your duty, Varian."

"But why me? Why her? Why at this fragile time in our relationship? We freed her to marry me, not wed my evil half brother. She's suffered too much because of me and my damned secret assignments."

"You can't tell her now, Son; the scheme is in motion."

"Don't you think I know I can't sacrifice everything to have her? I won't turn away from my duty and loyalty to the Alliance or to you, Grandfather. I've always obeyed our laws and carried out my missions, no matter the cost to me. Don't you think I realize she's actually safer at this time as Ryker Triloni's wife than as Varian Saar's? But that doesn't help. She's my world, Grandfather. I can't lose her. Do you know what it's like to continue Ryker's phony pursuit? To draw her toward me when it's to him I'm pulling her? To compel her to think, feel, and say terrible things about me, if only to protect herself from him? I'm forced to say vile things about Father and myself for her to see me as Ryker. At times I know she was trying to provoke me into a confession. I couldn't make it then and can't do so now, not while our lives and worlds are in peril. I want to hold her and kiss her and I dare not trust myself to do so."

Tirol knew Varian wasn't angry at him, but his tormented grandson needed to purge himself of his fury and tension.

"I almost lost Jana to Shara's evil, just like she stole my parents from me. I was afraid an enemy would harm her if I laid claim to her and my fears and suspicions were right. But I never imagined my worst foe would do his worst damage from his blasted grave. How much does one man have to sacrifice? It isn't fair, sir."

Tirol knew that Varian was not a man prone to self-pity or selfishness, but he had just cause to be angry and defiant on this vital and personal matter. "With you in control of Trilabs, Son, we have the weapons and chemicals we need for Project Starguard. If you succeed in Androas with Maal, that threat will be destroyed. When you return from Earth and make treaties with Maal and Jurad, peace will rule the Tri-Galaxy as in the days before Shara began her evil deeds. As we decided, Segall has been told nothing of your current mission and location. He knows it is against the law and treasonous to tell even his family of Alliance secrets. When the time comes, he will be disgraced and cast aside. But we cannot move against him until after you return and everything is settled concerning your impersonation. If Canissia doesn't return soon, we must fake a wedding with a lookalike cyborg. Everyone must believe you are away on your honeymoon. It will be suspicious for you to simply vanish from sight for so long."

"What about when Jana learns of our alleged marriage, Grandfather?"

"Try to prevent that discovery. If you cannot, you must handle it without exposing yourself to her. You must not forget, Varian, her life will be in great danger if Maal or his allies hold her even partly responsible for his death. Everyone knows about your past relationship with Jana. The day Ryker summoned you to his death challenge, he released the news of her freedom and her marriage to him, claiming you gave her to him as a truce token. He registered the marriage, so it is legal and binding. Jana is his heir. It is as much to her safety and advantage to confirm her union to him in the public's eye as it is to ours. Brec has everything under control at Star Base. Our schedule is perfect. Do not weaken and fail us when we are so close to victory."

Varian thought of Breccia Sard, Supreme Commander of the Alliance Force and Star Fleet and head of the Elite Squad, who had confidence and faith in him. "Contact Brec and tell him I will report for duty in three weeks. Don't worry, Grandfather, I won't let you and the Alliance down."

"I know you won't, Son. I love you, Varian. Stay safe and alert."

"I will, sir, and I love you. To victory and peace, Grandfather," he murmured before signing off. His mind added, *And pray seeking them doesn't cost me everything I hold dear. I love you, Jana Greyson, so please don't turn against me, no matter what I'm forced to do for this mission.*

Jana spent the afternoon reading from books the blond alien had given to her after her check-up in the medical laboratory. Concentration was difficult because she could not get his soul-stirring kiss off of her mind. Perhaps it was possible for two men to kiss and to taste the same way, but it was strange and suspicious. The experience had been much too arousing if he were Ryker Triloni. She was distressed she could be so attracted this fast and deep to the blond if he weren't her ebony-haired lover. He had convinced her he wasn't Varian, hadn't he? He wasn't Varian Saar, was he?

If only there was a strenuous chore to drain her abundance of energy and tension. But everything was spotless in the house. All tasks were done either by the technologically advanced appliances or by the android Ine. When the nonhuman wasn't busy, she stayed in the area which Ryker had told her was for storage, perhaps in a rest mode. Jana didn't know what was in that room because the door opened only for Ine and Ryker. She would have loved to look inside but didn't know how to manage it.

Read, J. G., and stop thinking about such crazy specula-

tions! That command worked until she came to sections she and "Ryker" had discussed; there she learned he had given her almost verbatim textbook responses! She looked up *Thorin* and *Rendelar* and discovered that a person given the truth serum would expose an immunity within moments of the injection. If there was a secret mission in progress and she were captured by the wrong side, if given *Rendelar* to prevent slips, it would be suspicious and dangerous . . . Was that why she couldn't be told, why she had to believe this man was Ryker? A new influx of doubts flooded her.

At dinner, Jana noticed that Ryker was watching her with a strange look in his emerald eyes. When his gaze focused on his food, she studied him. He was strikingly handsome and provocative and magnetic. She cautioned herself to cease her line of thought. "You're awfully quiet tonight, Ryker," she observed. "Did I annoy you with all my questions today?"

He smiled with the left side of his mouth as his half brother would have done. As he finished chewing the meat in his mouth, his gaze roved over her to absorb every detail of this woman he loved and desired. She was so beautiful and perfect. His eyes caressed the satiny texture of her face, its covering firm and smooth and flawless. His gaze traced her high cheekbones and inviting lips. He longed to finger her dainty chin and pleasingly shaped nose. What was it about this particular alien woman that caused him to experience such an upheaval of emotions and brought dangerous thoughts of defiance to duty to his mind? Why had he flaunted this rare and precious jewel before the eyes of greedy and evil men, when he should have hidden her away on Altair until he could defeat his enemies and lay public claim to her?

Jana worried over what was taking him so long to respond. He had finished chewing, then sipped his wine leisurely as if stalling a reply. Once more she felt like a specimen beneath his lens.

"Of course you didn't annoy me, Jana. The only way to

learn is by asking questions. Soon, you'll know everything about me and this place. I have important matters on my mind, that's all."

Was there, she mused, an odd inflection on *everything*? His curious mood and probing stare made her nervous, and too warm. "Is there a problem with your research? Can I do anything to help?"

"Things couldn't be going better in that area," he replied. "But thank you. Soon, everything will be back to normal. Be patient and understanding."

His curious tone and choice of words made her tension increase. She recalled the horrid things Canissia had told her about Ryker Triloni. She recalled how cold, harsh, and forbidding he had been at their first meeting. But she also remembered how he switched from freezing winter night to sultry summer day the moment that hateful woman left Darkar. It was stupid to offend or challenge an unknown force. "Is it me? Have I done something wrong or disappointed you?"

"You could never do anything wrong, Jana, and I'm pleased with you."

He looked as if he truly meant what he said. Yet . . . "I hope so. I'm going to try my best to do what you expect of me."

"I'm sure you will." *I almost lost you to death; now, I'm forced to take a big risk of losing you forever. Once before my duty and mission stood between us and they're doing so again. If only I didn't have to hurt you and use you and deceive you in this despicable manner, for a second time. When this is over, will you understand and forgive me? Will you still love and want me?*

Jana pretended to return her attention to the meal. She sliced through a meat-wrapped vegetable pouch and placed a bite in her mouth. It was tender, juicy, and delicious. She sipped lavender wine and set down her glass before reaching for her bread. She was too aware of the alien's potent gaze. Why was he observing her so intensely? She had the feeling he wanted to discuss something with her and couldn't or wouldn't. An aura of longing and dissatisfaction surrounded him. He was so complex, so mercurial, so unpredictable. Yet, he wasn't cold and harsh; nor was he intimidating or threatening. His spirit seemed to reach out to her, to caress her, to tempt her, to baffle her.

Varian hungered for the five-foot-eight-inch treat dangled before his starved senses. She was a confection of sweetness and temptation—warm, generous, unspoiled, and delightful . . . proud, intelligent, and brave. He adored the coalescence of colors in her eyes: a heavy dash of forest green, a sprinkle of deep blue, and a trace of rich violet—all the shades encased in a band of dark green. Her lashes were thick with curled-up edges. She wore little cosmetics, and none were needed to enhance her natural, bewitching beauty. He yearned to stroke the champagne tresses that flowed over her shoulders. It looked as if a magician had stolen colors from the two moons of Zamarra and painted her hair with the gold-and-silver mixture.

Varian remembered how curls had wrapped themselves around his fingers in days gone by, curls as soft as *Mailiorcan* silk, a sensuous material shot with threads of expensive gold and silver. Her tresses were long and bouncy on the sides and back but shorter and fluffy on the top and around her face. His pulse quickened as his study of her ignited his senses and enflamed his passions. He was relieved he wasn't standing, as the snug sapphire garment would expose his desire for her. Never had he blazed to life so hotly and urgently from simply gazing at a female. No women of his world had ever been able to resist him, but since meeting Jana Greyson, she was the only one he wanted. She was like a beacon set out by the bored gods to lure him into danger to provide them with amusement. If he was not careful, the Moondust those mischievous deities flung in his eyes would blind him to his duty, and all could be lost. Shara had used that mind-controlling, trance-inducing chemical on his father to enslave him to her. Unable to resist its potency, Galen had succumbed to the evil enchantress, until

Dr. Tristan Zarcoff realized what was afoot and gave his father an antidote, along with the awareness of the treachery Maal's daughter had wreaked on him.

The silence grew heavy and stifling to Jana. She sought the first subject that came to mind to break it. "Would you like to play *laius* after dinner?" she asked. Immediately she wanted to bite her tongue to punish it for making that crazy suggestion, but it was too late to withdraw her invitation. He grinned and his verdant eyes sparkled with a familiar expression: Varian's.

He was instantly swept back in time to a heady scene on his starship when a chess wager led to their two-week love affair. The flames returned to his body to heighten his desire. He lost his wits for a moment and said, "That sounds intriguing, especially since you beat me the last time we played."

She stared at him. A slip? she wondered. "I did? When?"

"Last week. You asked for your ring back as your winning prize."

Honesty or quick wits? "You want to play for it again tonight?"

"Why? It's special to you."

Varian had given it to her before her auction, no doubt to serve as a constant reminder of him after their separation. "Why would you think that?"

"You told me so. And it was the only jewelry you were wearing when you arrived here. Did your parents give it to you?"

Why would he ask that last question when there were no *caritrary* gems in her world, only in his? His arms were folded and locked over his chest, implying confidence and an air of contempt for danger. Even so, she suspected he could respond to any threat in an instant. In days past, she had witnessed how alert and quick he was. As he ruffled his tawny hair, she caught a gleam of roguish mischief in his eyes. "No, they didn't, and it isn't special to me. It was a gift from *Kadim* Tirol," she lied, "shortly before I was sent here. It's lovely and valuable, but I can't imagine why I would ask for its return. Perhaps, since we were still strangers at that time, it was the only safe wager I could think of. Why did you take it away when we married?''

''Because I assumed Varian had given it to you.''

''Now you know he didn't. But this was a nice exchange,'' she remarked as she fingered the gem-encrusted gold marriage bracelet.

''I'm happy you think so. How did you learn to play *laius*?''

Why hadn't Ryker asked her that question the last time they played, if they had? ''My father taught me chess when I was nine. Until his death, we kept a running competition. On the *Wanderlust*,'' she continued, not wanting to say Varian's name again, ''Nigel taught me your version. He was the ship champion, but I managed to beat him a few times.'' Varian had been number two. Actually Tesla Rilke, the *Wanderlust*'s navigational and guidance officer, had played with her the first time. In her delusion, Tesla had been killed in a *Spacer* accident while transporting her to the ship to be revived from a state that was close to death. How could she learn if Tesla was still alive?

He chuckled at her saucy grin. Being with Jana again was heaven, and it was hell. She was sunshine: warm, radiant, vital, and life-sustaining. She was moonlight: mysterious, intoxicating, romantic. She had more glittering facets than a precious stone beneath bright light. He had never dared to yield to the emotions called love and commitment, but his love for adventure had lessened since meeting her; now, he wanted to settle down and share a different kind of excitement and satisfaction. She was everything a man could desire in a woman, and she was his. Almost. ''So, you're better than I was led to believe? A trick, my cunning wife, to lure me into another game with higher stakes?''

''If you want to play for stakes again, name one. Anything.'' She noticed the beads of perspiration on his upper lip, the smoldering fire in his eyes, the sudden tautness of his body: she was getting to him!

"I'm tempted to accept your challenge, but I'll have to give it serious thought first. I wouldn't want you to ask for something I cannot provide."

"I wouldn't. I'll let you select what's at stake on your side, and I'll let you select what's at stake on my side. Is that fair enough for you, husband?"

When she stood, his gaze roamed her figure. Her bosom was ample and firm. Her slim waist drifted into a flat stomach between seductively rounded hips. Her shapely legs were lithe and smooth. Her ankles appeared both dainty and strong. Her body was taut and supple. Many men must have been tempted by her magic and allure, yet none of them had possessed her the way he had, and would again! "That's a dangerous offer, Dr. Triloni."

"Is it, Dr. Triloni?" *You're playing with fire, J. G. Remember the trouble you got into last time when you were in a similar situation.* Varian had warned, "As surely as my eyes are blue, we'll both live to regret this night." He had disobeyed direct orders to possess her before any other man could do so. This time, it was an emerald gaze giving her that silent caution.

"What prize of mine do you have in mind?" he asked.

"Can I see my files and the tapes you had made of me?" From his expression, her request had taken him by surprise. And disappointment? What had he expected her to answer? The same way as on his ship?

"That's impossible. I destroyed them after studying them."

"Why?" Had any, she mused, ever existed?

"They had private and revealing things about you on them that no one else should ever see. Besides, it wouldn't be good for you anyway."

How could anyone get their hands on anything here on Darkar? For once, had his wits failed him? "What do you mean? Did I misbehave on them?"

"No, but seeing the ruse Varian forced you to play would bring back bad memories, memories of times best forgotten. You were a slave then."

"You're right. I hadn't thought of it that way. I'm glad

they're gone. I was just curious about what impression I had made on you because of them."

"A good one, the best possible. That's why you're here with me."

"That's very flattering."

"Only the truth." Being with this sunny-haired angel brightened his gloomy heart, but having her so close and yet out of reach increased his agony. He had been lonely before he met and won her, something he hadn't realized until almost losing her.

He stood and summoned Ine to clear the table. The yellow-eyed, monotoned android obeyed.

"I'll set up the board while you take a break," he said.

"I'll return shortly. Don't run scared and change your mind," she teased before leaving the dining dome.

Jana sat at the game table that had been placed near a *transa-screen*. Red pieces were on their appointed squares on her side, and blue on his. The large room suddenly seemed small and cozy, or was it the effect of the soft music and lighting? She glanced out the window into a lush garden. It was almost as if she could smell the flowers growing there, or was a floral scent being pumped into the room? Jana ignored the glass of wine nearby, as she wanted to keep her head clear for the game. The setting was charged with emotions, conducive to romance and seduction, yet her calm appearance concealed the turmoil raging within her, just as Varian's stoic expression denied the turbulent winds storming his mind and body. With each passing minute, the chemistry between them, despite his disguise and alleged identity, heightened.

He tried to lure her into a cunning trap. Instead, she captured one of the vital pieces he had failed to protect. With it out of circulation, she assumed the game would end soon. It did not. Her crafty opponent took the matching one from her. She looked at him and nodded her respect.

"You're a big distraction, woman, but I'm trying hard to

concentrate.'' He wanted her to forget the frightening experiences she had endured. He wanted her to smile and to relax. He needed to savor her company. He needed to see her, smell her, hear her, taste her, feel her.

Jana became edgy from his engulfing stare and seductive mood. She yearned to escape this disquieting atmosphere, this intimidating creature. To accomplish her goal, she let him win.

He threw back his head and filled the room with mocking laughter. ''I never suspected you of being a cheater, Jana of Earth.''

''What do you mean? I lost.''

''I know, on purpose and unfairly. Your thoughts are elsewhere. Or is it that I offer too much distraction for my nervous wife? Besides, we forgot to make our wagers. It's early. We must play another game, a serious one.''

Jana's astonished gaze locked with his challenging and taunting one. She struggled to control the tremors which swept over her body, as his words nearly matched those spoken by Varian months ago. ''I've been very busy today, Ryker. I'm too weary to think clearly.''

''Where are your sporting instincts, Jana of Earth? How can you refuse such a challenge? Don't you have a secret desire?''

A feeling of déjà vu flooded her dazed mind, but it wasn't happening for the first time. Didn't he realize . . . *Go for proof if you dare, J. G.* Months ago, those statements from Varian had enticed a fantasy which evoked her shocking wager. They were almost verbatim. Did twins truly have the capability of reading each other's thoughts, of having the same feelings, of knowing what the other was doing? Yet, Varian and Ryker weren't true twins, no matter how much they looked alike. *Go for it, J. G. Play out his little game.* That fated night in his quarters was burned indelibly into her brain. She repeated herself, too. ''A secret desire? That's quite tempting. What if you win? I have nothing of value to offer you, so what prize can you claim? The only thing I have is this bracelet you gave me.'' She added for the new occasion, ''Considering its meaning, surely you don't want it returned.''

"Having you as my wife is the best prize a man could win," he replied. "I'll think of something."

Jana watched his gaze fill with mystery and amusement. "All right. Shall we shake hands on it to seal our bargain? It's an Earth custom." She wondered if his hand had stretched across the table and grasped her extended one before she had finished her sentence explaining the gesture.

The contact sent sparks of excitement through both of them. Their eyes melded. Their knees rubbed together. Their breathing quickened.

She asked in a near breathless voice, "Tell me, Ryker, what will you do if my prize is painful to honor? What if I have expensive tastes? Or dangerous ones? Are you certain you'll allow me to collect my wager?"

"I am a wealthy man, Jana. I can afford to indulge you. As for being painful, I do hope you aren't considering a brutal beating for revenge."

Once more, matching words! Was he giving her clues to his real identity? On purpose? Was he testing to see if she would challenge him on his claim to be his half brother? Was he leading up to a confession and revelation? Or was it cruel coincidence? "For revenge? For what offense?"

"For my vile behavior upon your arrival here. I am sorry."

"I know you are. Don't you think I saw how you changed after Canissia left? I concluded it was only an act to dupe her. You did tell me you have to live up to your nefarious reputation to maintain power in the Tri-Galaxy. You see, I'm a very understanding, forgiving woman. If you do me wrong with valid motivation, then explain and apologize, I'll accept. Besides," she returned to the past talk again, "I have no intention of marring that handsome face. I warn you, sir: I will try my best to win this next time. I give you a last chance to back down."

"Never. I've lured you into my trap and I won't free you."

The second game began with slowness and caution. Time passed without notice. Pieces were lost and won. Suspense mounted. The room's size seemed to shrink even more. The game traveled at a snail's pace as final moves were chosen and played. It looked headed for a stalemate.

Varian observed her concentration and determination. As before, he wondered what reward she would demand. Should he, again, risk losing the game to make that discovery? Would she dare ask for the same glorious and soul-binding prize? Could she be that reckless, that vindictive?

Jana watched him as he analyzed the board and pondered his next move. Would he . . . Her heart fluttered wildly. *Are you my deceitful love?* Where Varian's eyes were like precious sapphires, this man's were like priceless emeralds. They glittered with mystery, enticement, and vitality. His sensual smile, whenever he glanced up and sent one to her, caused her heart to pound. A flaxen lock fell casually over his left temple. She stared at the stubborn section. Despite a little variety in his hairstyle, that defiance was a noticeable trait of Varian's, not Ryker's, hair. At four inches over six feet, they were the same height and of the same build.

Varian became apprehensive under her keen stare. He realized she was being assailed by doubts and suspicions again; they were as heavy in the air as the floral aromas were becoming. He had been stupid to play this game tonight. He had become so drugged by her that his wits were dulled and his tongue loosened. Time was passing as slowly as the summer sun around Rigel, capital planet of his star system, around which his Altair orbited. With ease and skill, she had woven a web of love around his heart and life. Only for a while and surely for tonight, he must cut those silky strands and free himself from her heady allure. It was safer for his mission if he remained distant. It was his duty to make Jana once more a pawn in his battle for victory, but his heart fiercely resisted that cruelty. He had better end this madness before his false mask burned away beneath the fires of desire burning brightly in her eyes. He cursed the events that made such a deed necessary.

Varian captured her piece that terminated the game in a stalemate. "I hate to do that, Jana of Earth, but I must."

"I would have done the same."

"Perhaps our next game will end differently."

"Perhaps." *You hesitated far too long making your decision for a draw.*

"Does it trouble you that Varian and I favor each other so much?"

"I haven't thought about it. Different hair and eye colors take away some of the resemblance."

"So you don't get us confused?"

"How could I? Your personality and character are so unlike his. So is your voice, and there are other things . . ."

"This scar?" he hinted and rubbed his jawline.

"Not really. I hardly notice it anymore. You do look younger."

"By four months. I don't remind you of him when you look at me?"

"No, Ryker, you don't. The longer I'm around you and the better I get to know you, the more you two differ."

"But any hint of resemblance interferes with you forgetting him."

"How does one forget somebody who had such an enormous impact on her life? He changed the course of my destiny. He almost destroyed me. Nothing can justify such cruelty. You make everything better for me. I never knew or thought about you two being kin or resembling until I saw—"

"Saw what?" he probed, leaning back in his chair.

She faked an embarrassed look as she answered. "Thought I saw your pictures overlaid and colorings matched while I was delirious."

"You did see such a demonstration, but from me, here in this room before you became ill. When you resisted what I was telling you, I proved my story. Come with me and watch."

In confusion and trepidation, she followed him to the other side of the room. He talked into what she thought was a music speaker.

"Doors open."

Jana stared as a panel slid aside to reveal a forty-inch cathode-ray tube.

He gave verbal commands to the computer, pausing between each one. "Screen on. Display images of Varian Saar and Ryker Triloni. Delete scar on right jawline of Ryker. Overlay. Match eye, hair, and skin coloring of Ryker to Varian." He waited long enough for her to study the picture, then completed his point. "Separate images. Correct physical traits on each. See, Jana of Earth; that's what you viewed and recall."

Jana looked at the monitor with astonishment. To the left was Ryker Triloni, as he appeared at their first meeting and in this room tonight. To the right was Commander Varian Saar in his dress uniform of dark wine with a gold sunburst over his left chest: Star Fleet insignia. His eyes were cornflower blue, his hair as dark and shiny as polished jet, his skin deeply tanned, and his teeth, revealed by a broad and sexy smile, white as snow. It was the image and expression of a man who felt he was invincible and savored that rank. His gaze shouted of power and passion. No doubt he could make the heavens tremble with the force of his iron will.

Her eyes shifted to the image of Ryker Triloni, Prince of Androas. How could he not be handsome and just as potent when he so closely matched the other magnificent creature? The blond hair and green eyes were actually flattering to his skin color and strong features. His chiseled jawline bespoke strength of character and body. Unaware of her action, she reached out her hand toward the screen to trace the scar Varian had created long ago. The instant her fingers made contact with the monitor, she heard crackles and felt little shocks tingle her fingertips. "Ouch!" she squealed, and jerked her hand away. She rubbed the tingling digits with the palm of the same hand. "Look but don't touch," she joked with a laugh.

Varian didn't join in because he was miffed that it was Ryker's image that enticed her touch. "Screen off. Doors close," he said in a crisp tone.

Then turned to her. "It's late. You should go to bed. I have a few things to check on in my lab. I'll see you in the morning."

Jana couldn't respond before he stalked from the room. He was playing a game of cat-and-mouse with her! He captured her, toyed with her, and released her to run free to be snared again by his sharp claws. Would he repeat his game over and over until she was worn down or he tired of it and . . . What? And who was this alien predator?

Jana tossed and turned for what seemed like hours. She had not heard the man return to his adjoining room, as the slide wasn't open. Even if he was Varian in disguise, he was using her again as he had so many times in the past. If he loved her, he couldn't behave in this cruel way. She berated herself for acting like a fool. Why did she persist in trying to make Ryker into Varian? Persist in trying to make a clue out of anything and everything he said and did? Hadn't the blond alien proven over and over he was the Androasian prince, matchless chemist, skilled researcher? Couldn't she get it through her thick skull he wasn't Varian? If she continued along this self-destructive path, she would turn Ryker against her. That was insane, for her safety and survival depended upon his goodwill.

She must face the truth of Varian's betrayal and loss. She curled into a ball on her side. The torment she was feeling was almost unbearable. It was as bad as when her parents were killed years ago, because another loved one was the same as dead to her. Worse, he had used, deceived, and discarded her. She had loved him. Now she must pay for her foolishness and ignorance that some would call naïveté. One of the captives on the ship, a vain and hateful bitch, had told her she didn't have the courage and daring to reach out and take what she desired. In a way she had called the girl's bluff, with dire consequences. She had herself to blame for part of her suffering.

Hadn't she been prepared for his dismissal? His last words to her before Canissia took her away were: "I'll have a surprise for you soon, a long trip. At last, we'll both find peace and our lives can be settled." She had overheard *Kadim* Tirol, Brec Sard, and Draco talking the day before she was hauled away into this bondage. ''Are you sure it's safe for Varian to go to Darkar?'' one had asked. ''Yes, it's all been arranged,'' another answered. And the conversation had continued, ''You both know Jana Greyson increases the tension between them. What does Varian plan to exchange for the truth and his help?'' ''Varian's determined. He's willing to do whatever is necessary to end these conflicts.'' On the tape Canissia had delighted in playing for her on the way to Ryker's, Varian had said, ''Jana's a challenge to me. You know how I hate defeat on any level. I have some vital business with Ryker before I leave on my next assignment.'' Varian had laughed when the redhead asked if he would like to marry the Earthling. He had scoffed, ''Are you insane? She won't be my mistress much longer. If all goes as Grandfather and I plan, I intend to make Ryker an offer he can't refuse.'' Then, her alleged friend Nigel had said as he drugged her to be sent here, ''I'm sorry, Jana. Varian's orders. You're to be traded for peace.'' And Ryker, he had told her upon arrival, ''It looks as if he made me a wise offer after all. I must admit Varian's timing and gift are perfect. I shall never forget this birthday.'' How could she argue against so much evidence from so many sources? Varian had not stopped to think Ryker—if the terrible rumors about him were true—might hurt or kill her, if either action by his half brother had mattered to him.

Silent tears rolled from her eyes and were absorbed into her pillow. Before she could get over him, she had to go through the grieving process: pain, denial, anger, acceptance. She wished she had been captured by some horrible creature instead of an irresistible human alien; that way, she wouldn't have succumbed to his charms. If a monster had ripped out her heart, it would have been physical death instead of a living hell. It would have been far better for her if he had truly sold her at the auction. Time and time again he had given her false hopes by lying, with words or actions or expressions, about his feelings for her. He had let her hope and dream and believe, all for naught. It was clear now that no matter what she had said or done, it had always been impossible to win him. She didn't possess the skills and power to hold on to that fiery comet which had blazed across her destiny's sky many times. Yet, how could any man behave and speak as he had without feeling anything? How could any man—even an evil one—totally lack all honor, conscience, and compassion?

Damn you, Varian Saar. I believed you, trusted you, and loved you with all my heart and soul. Now, you're going to marry that bitch who also tormented me. I could slay you both with my bare hands for the way you've treated me. Is this what your father did to Shara? Did Galen use her, betray her, and discard her? Break her heart, drive her insane, and provoke her to murder and suicide? Thank God Ryker is nothing like you and your father. At least I hope he's not tricking me, too. If that's what he thinks he's going to do, he's wrong. This time, I'll beat a man at his own game. I'll make Ryker love me and want me too much to hurt me. I'll be the perfect companion, research assistant, and wife. I'll study hard until I'm exhausted. I'll be obedient, desirable, and fulfilling. To win him, I'll use every wit, skill, and ploy you taught me. Starting tomorrow, Ryker, I'll do and be anything and everything you desire, and to hell with Varian Saar.

Chapter Five

Varian came to see Jana the next morning but she was occupied with her grooming in the bathroom. He sat on her bed to await her, to make certain she was all right after his strange behavior last night. When she had reached out to touch Ryker's image instead of his or neither, a powerful surge of jealousy and fear had shot through him. It was unlike him to feel those emotions. But Jana had changed him, and these blasted secret missions were changing him. For the second time, he had experienced deep and true fear, fear of losing the only woman he would ever love.

He knew it was possible for emotions to make an about-face in the flicker of an eye. Long ago, he had detested Shara Triloni and Ryker. The day the Androasian princess had slain his parents, black and potent hatred and a desire to murder her had consumed him. Following years of pity and remorse over Ryker's dilemma, his feelings for his half brother had also turned to hatred and hostility when Ryker provoked a war between them. His affection for Canissia Garthon had changed to revulsion when he discovered her vile character and behavior.

Varian lifted Jana's pillow to inhale the heady fragrance left there. The first time terror had struck him low had been after learning of her disappearance. His days had been filled with anguish. His nights had been worse, nights when he had dreamed of her. She would visit him like an enchanting spectre and look at him with those kaleidoscopic eyes so full of pleading for him to rescue her. Her champagne hair would surround her shoulders like a cape and would move slightly when she reached out her arms in beckoning. Those dreams had been so real that he would awaken in a cold sweat or engulfed by passion's flames. Never had he felt so helpless and vulnerable.

As if sensing imminent danger, she had begged him not to leave her that last day before she vanished—and peril had befallen both of them. He had been lured into a trap: captured, tortured, and almost killed by Prince Taemin's hirelings as a favor to Ryker. She had been kidnapped by Canissia and delivered into the hands of his malevolent half brother. He had feared all he had left of her were memories and dreams and fierce longings. For weeks he had trekked through *Gehenna*. He had become embittered and hardened. He had cursed fate. He had vowed to never love again because losing love cut too deeply and viciously. He had been tormented when he discovered she, a free woman by his own hand, was wed to Ryker.

Then, his half brother had provoked a death duel, had arrived for it without his disguise. It had been like gazing into a mirror! He had known they favored each other, but not to that extent. It was understandable why *Kadim* Maal and Shara had concealed his Saarian looks. Even if he hadn't slain Ryker, their marriage was legal, and a rescue assault on Darkar was impossible. His evil image had shouted, "Only one of us will leave this place alive. If you slay me, you can marry my widow and inherit all I own." Just as the cunningly wicked prince knew that by slaying his rival he would by law inherit the Saar name and estate. Ryker had taunted, "Look at my face, Varian. She married both of us. Would it ease your suffering to learn she mumbles your name at passion's climactic moment?" After rescuing her, she had explained that the purpose of the coerced marriage was to save her life until he came for her and that it had not been consummated. She had confessed her love. How sweet those words "I love you" had sounded. How beautiful their reunion had been. But much too brief, and by his own doing.

Varian inhaled her lingering scent. His gaze touched on the numerous tear stains that rent his heart. On Eire, he had sworn she would be safe and happy in her new home. He had said, "Trust me, Jana. I won't let anyone or anything hurt you." He had broken that promise, and he was hurting her worst of all. *Kahala*, would the demands and sacrifices never end?

Every time he was near her, he was aroused by love and desire. He could not bring himself to seduce her because he couldn't bear the thought of her feeling compelled to respond to Ryker. Yet, Ryker had been wooing her and it would seem odd if he—as Ryker—did not continue that romantic course. But was he pushing too hard and too fast? He put the pillow back in its place and left the room.

Jana joined the alien in the living area. He was about to leave for his complex. She must put her plan into motion. She must accept her fate. She was in another galaxy, married to one extra-terrestrial and still in love with another. She had to forget Varian, as he wasn't worth her love. Nor could she substitute Ryker for him. "Can I tag along today?"

Varian sensed something afoot. "Why, Jana?"

"I'd like to spend more time with you and getting acquainted with your work. And I feel safer and happier near you. Do you mind my being like a clingy child who needs comfort and security?"

"That sounds tempting and pleasing, but the areas I work in aren't safe for you to enter. But they will be after your inoculations tomorrow. Why don't you relax at the pool this morning. I'll join you for lunch there."

"Thank you, Ryker. I'll await you."

She observed his departure. She paced the large and lovely room. She had to come up with ways to let him know she was receptive, yet not behave wanton or overeager. She was apprehensive about his turning distant and distracted. He seemed reluctant to touch her, as if afraid he might lose control and possess her. But wasn't that what he had said he wanted? Why this contradiction? Since that afternoon in the lab, he seemed quiet, subdued, and preoccupied.

Considering her status as a *charl* and an alien captive, she was lucky. She had a certain amount of freedom, respect, and pride. By marriage, she was a princess, his heir, and soon to be his assistant. She was wed to a handsome, rich, powerful, envied, respected—and feared—man.

She had to get that hallucination out of her head. But that was easier said than done. During her medical and scientific schooling and training, she had learned that some dreams and delusions can seem so real that the person experiencing them could pass a lie-detector test confirming their reality. Too, life was filled with many so-called impossible coincidences which could explain the clues she assumed she had gleaned. For one thing, Varian Saar would never make slips like those during the chess game last night. *Dreams and coincidences, J. G., nothing more!*

She was just so lonely and miserable. She missed Andrea and her other friends. She missed her work. She missed her home, her horse, her possessions, and her daily activities. If only she could speak to her best friend by telephone. If only she could watch TV from Earth to learn what was happening there. Her and her planet's existence looked so bleak. Would both be saved by God's merciful hand?

When Varian entered the glassed dome, he saw Jana resting on her side near the pool with her head propped up on an elbow. She was deep in thought and didn't appear to notice his arrival. Her free hand was buried in tresses wet and curly from her swim. The outfit she was wearing exposed all her stunning curves. She seemed to gaze on a waterfall, a faraway expression on her face. He wondered if she were thinking about the romantic afternoon they had spent near a similar one on the planet Mailiorca. It was in that exotic setting that he had told her that he had always fulfilled his duty, no matter the cost, and he was doing so again. They had talked, shared a picnic, and almost made love. If they hadn't been disturbed by an urgent message from his ship, they would have surrendered to the desires burning within them both.

He shoved the stirring memory from mind. "I'll join you as soon as I change," he said to let his presence be known.

Jana jumped. "I didn't hear you. You startled me."

"Sorry. Mental journeys are attention consuming." He saw her blush and shift her position beneath his intense scrutiny.

His voice washed over her as a breeze on a summer southern night: mellow, lazy, and sultry. When he squatted and pushed a straying lock of hair from her face and caressed her rosy cheek, she trembled at his touch. "I'm glad you could join me."

He noticed his effect on her and withdrew his hand. "So am I," he said, then stood and left to change into his swimming trunks.

Jana watched him approach the pool. His body evinced the same strengths of his features. His torso rippled with well-honed muscles. His chest was covered by a curly mat which narrowed to drift down his waist to disappear into his red trunks. Their shade accentuated his dark tan and their fit displayed his sleek hips, firm buttocks, and ample manhood. She quivered as she admitted her attraction.

Could she learn to love this man? Could she shut off her feelings for Varian to respond to Ryker? From past experience, she knew what love and passion were. She had discovered those emotions the first time she had seen Varian Saar. She had fallen under his potent spell. She had wanted to share a lifetime with him. The night of their first union, she had believed having him, if only for two weeks until her auction, would be worth any price she must pay. She had believed that afterward he would keep her. She had been wrong.

Jana dashed aside her troubling thoughts and joined the alien for a swim. She hoped to frolic in the water and soften him. She was dismayed and disappointed when he kept his distance. He smiled, laughed, was nice, and even a little flirty, but he refused to get close to her body.

When Ine brought their lunch, they ate in one of the sitting areas near the waterfall she had been eyeing while bittersweet memories tormented her. They chatted about her childhood, teenage, and college years. Each time she veered the conversation to him or his work, he derailed the attempt with another question about her. Soon it was evident he didn't want to discuss himself, only learn more about her. She complied.

Jana approached the blond alien in the hall after they had finished their showers and grooming, as the slide between their rooms was closed again today. She walked along with him as she asked, "Are you sure there's nothing I can do to help you?"

He kept moving as he answered, "You can help me by taking care of yourself. I want you well and strong before our trip begins in three days."

In the living area, a call came for Ryker from his security chief and shuttle captain. He replied at the control panel.

"Sir," Kagan informed him, "Canissia Garthon has arrived in the *Moonwind* and requested permission to land in her shuttle to visit you."

Cass, alive? Here? At last, a chance to get his hands around her lying throat! No, he realized, he couldn't risk exposing himself by arresting her in front of Jana. He could give Command Ten to his agent to have her followed, observed, and captured at the right time where there were no witnesses. Until this mission was over, he could not, without providing evidence he must keep concealed for a while, press charges against her for kidnapping Jana and for committing treason. Perhaps he could use her to extract information needed for his impending trip to Maal. "Granted, Kagan. When she departs, carry out Command Ten for me. Let me know when she's on the ground."

"Yes, sir."

Jana noticed he was agitated. "What does that vile creature want?"

"Probably to see how you're faring in my hands. She's in for a big surprise! I'm sure you don't want to see her again, so why don't you go to your room until she's gone."

"That will suit me fine. Call me after she leaves, so I can hear how she took the news of our marriage. I'm certain it will come as a shock to her."

"Do you want news about her wedding?"

"If she mentions it to you, don't tell me about it. Nobody deserves each other more than those two."

Varian forced himself not to frown at her insult. He laughed and said, "Nobody is like Cass, not even my unfortunate half brother. I'll get rid of her as quickly as possible. Spending even a short time with her would be repulsive to me. You'd think she'd come to realize I can't tolerate her."

"Why don't you tell the witch never to come here again?"

"Because I still have use for her information-gathering skills."

"She's a traitor to her world. She would betray you, too, for the right price. I wouldn't trust her. How do you know she isn't the spy for the Alliance that you accused me of being?"

"Because her facts always prove to be accurate, and I know Cass."

"What better way to lure you into her confidence than to feed you truths? Besides, they are probably facts you could learn elsewhere."

"No, they are Supreme Council secrets that come from her father. I'm not a fool, Jana of Earth. I don't trust her. I have her watched all the time."

Then why, Jana mused, *didn't you know of her approach?* "Is there another reason you let her come around?"

"Like what?" Suddenly he chuckled and caressed her cheek. "You aren't jealous of that vile creature, are you?"

She faked a mute *yes* while she said, "Of course not."

He chuckled again and kissed her cheek. "You are the only woman for me, so don't worry about her. I would never—"

"Sir, she's landed and approaching the house," Kagan interrupted over the communication system.

The alien acknowledged, then suggested again she leave the room. He didn't want to subject his love to Cass's hatefulness.

The moment she was gone, Canissia Garthon swept into the room as if she owned it. She was wearing a tight purple jumpsuit that revealed she had nothing on underneath. Her near-perfect figure was as noticeable as the smug expression on her beautiful face. The flaming redhead had death rays firing from her turquoise eyes. She stalked to a plush sofa and sat down with one elbow propped on its low back. Her long hair was smoothed back from her face and secured at her nape with a purple band, accentuating the slender neck that held her head high and straight to glower at him.

Varian absorbed her cocky and vain attitude, and her fury. "Do come in and make yourself comfortable," he joked. He saw her gaze narrow and gleam in warning, her posture stiffen, and her mood chill even more.

"You and I have unfinished business."

He raked his green gaze over her from fiery head to slender ankle. It was apparent she knew Ryker had tried to kill her, but he knew how to get out of the situation, thanks to his half brother's tapes and notes. "Such as?" He sat down across from her and grinned like Ryker.

"You know what I've come to discuss, you treacherous—"

Jana seemed to float into the room. "Ryker, my darling, what's taking you so long to join—" She halted and, as a shocked Canissia stared open-mouthed and wide-eyed at her, clutched the robe opening to the diaphanous negligee she had donned for her ruse. She had hurriedly brushed her hair, perfumed herself, and changed clothes to trick the spiteful woman who had aided Varian's dismissal of her. She faked modesty. "Oh, I didn't realize we have a guest."

Canissia glared at the alien girl in the sheer and sexy garments, the female who had stolen Varian's eye and heart. The delicately hazy outfit left little to the imagination and, if Jana wasn't wearing a matching bra and panties, every perfect attribute would be showing! The redhead glared at Jana through the near-slits of her feral eyes.

"Sorry, my eager angel, but Cass stopped in for a short visit. We'll have to delay our . . ." He paused and chuckled. "*Amusements* for a while."

Canissia tried to embarrass Jana by searing her with hot aqua eyes. She was irritated when her action failed. By now, she had expected and hoped Jana Greyson would be destroyed or broken and abused. "What do we have here, Ryker, my sweet? A compliant slave? My, you do work fast. What's your secret?"

Varian allowed his emerald gaze to adore Jana. "It seems my bride is hungry for my company elsewhere. You did drop by at a most inopportune moment, Cass. Perhaps you can send advance notice next time."

"Bride? Did you say, bride? Surely my audiotranslator is broken."

His heart pounded wildly when Jana came to sit on the edge of his chair and placed her arm across his shoulders. Her fragrance filled his nostrils and teased his senses. The sheer covering gave him a view of the exquisite territory he had explored well in days past. "You heard me correctly. Jana and I are married, *very* married," he murmured in a husky tone to annoy the flabbergasted redhead who was gaping at them and sending off rays of hostility.

"You're *what*? Surely you jest?"

"Married. Sixteen days ago to be precise." He felt his body flame as Jana ignited his passions by ruffling his hair and stroking his chest, all the while devouring him with her multi-colored gaze of liquid *caritrary*.

Jana allowed her hand to halt over his heart to test her effect on him. It was pounding swift and hard. As she trailed her fingers up his neck, she found his pulse point throbbing there. He appeared amused by her wanton behavior. She traced her fingers over his lips and admired him with her eyes. "You're keeping my husband from some very important and enjoyable business. Will your visit take long?"

"I can't believe you would do something so stupid, Ryker. How could you marry this . . . this *alien*?"

"By freeing her first. She's no longer a *charl*, Cass. She's my wife, an Androasian princess, my heir, the future mother of my children. Careful how you speak about her. She now possesses far more wealth and status than you do, and more power. In addition, if anything happened to me, she inherits Trilabs, your supplier. If I were you, I'd be nice to her."

"Be nice . . . to her? *You* freed her?"

"How else could I marry her? I twisted Tirol's arm and he couldn't refuse me my request. I am irreplaceable to him and the Alliance. Jana adores me and does anything I desire. If you care to check, our marriage has already been registered and announced. I'm surprised you haven't heard that news by now; the Tri-Galaxy must be humming with it. I suppose you had important business to handle. I hope you got it accomplished."

Canissia caught the clues in his words. "Yes, I did, no thanks to you. Shall we talk in private? Or does your new wife know all of your secrets?"

"We'll go outside. I need fresh air anyway so I can think. Jana is most attention consuming." To Jana he said, "I'll return shortly, my love."

"I'll await you in our suite, my darling."

Canissia glared at the Earthling as she said, "Well, I guess you have more bewitching power than I imagined. It seems we both got what we wanted. But I'll have the last laugh; I always do."

"Don't count on it this time," Jana replied. "And you're right: with Ryker, I do have everything I could possibly want. I'm sure you hoped otherwise, and I'm happy to disappoint you." Jana refused to mention or congratulate Canissia on her approaching marriage to Varian.

Outside and away from the house, Canissia whirled on him and demanded, "How could you do that to me?"

"Marry a beautiful and delightful slave who obeys my every command? Thanks to my brother, she was free to wed me. You aren't in any trouble over her abduction. Everyone believes you helped Jana escape Varian to come to me. Before she goes out in public, I'll tell her the whole story. By then, it will be too late for her to say or do anything about it. I'll make certain she's carrying my child. Jana would never give up her baby to have a man. And Varian would never want her back with a Triloni in her belly."

"That isn't what I meant. I don't care about you and that piece of cheap flesh cozying up in bed. I'm talking about you trying to kill me. Your little scheme didn't work. Oh, it killed Zan all right, but you missed me."

"What are you talking about, woman?"

"I don't trust anybody, Ryker, especially a man like you. I had Zan go to the planet for the Zenufian water and mix it with the *Myozenic* acid there. It exploded and killed him. If I had done it on my ship . . ."

He feigned surprise. "Exploded? He must have mixed it incorrectly. Did you give him my instructions? Did he follow them?"

"Of course!" She repeated verbatim what Ryker had told her.

"What about the salt, Cass? Didn't you tell him to add one cup to the water to balance and stabilize the contents before adding the acid?"

"You never mentioned that part."

"Surely I did," Varian argued with the glowering female.

"You did not. Instead of dissolving every inch of him and pouring his remains into the soil, it blasted him to pieces we had to collect and bury. I'm lucky no one was around to witness and question the bloody incident."

"Don't be stupid, Cass. You're far too intelligent to think I would try to kill you. You're too valuable to me alive. You supply me with too much information and do too many favors to get rid of you. Where else would I get a direct link to the Supreme Council and their secrets? I need you." He watched her fume and reason on his words, then relax and smile.

"I suppose you're right, but it was suspicious and scary."

"I'm sure it was, but don't let your imagination run wild. We've been allies for too long to let a misunderstanding come between us. What about your crew? What did they say about the explosion? Can they be trusted to keep their mouths shut? We can't afford trouble."

"I convinced them it was a terrible accident, and they believed me. Why shouldn't they? I pay them enough for their loyalty and services. If any of them starts to doubt me, I'll arrange for the *Moonwind*'s destruction with all of them aboard. If so, I'll expect you to replace my starcruiser. Its loss and the accident will be your fault, not mine."

He grinned and teased, "If I omitted part of the instructions, then you're to blame. You did distract me that day with your gift of Jana and news of her daring abduction. Don't unsettle yourself again; I'll replace your ship if it goes that far to protect us. Speaking of favors, tell me, Cass, how did you get rid of our problem, Lieutenant Baruch?" A noise behind him caused him to turn to check it out and he missed her reaction. It was only an android doing gardening work. He turned and smiled at her. "I'm surprised you haven't boasted of your cunning to me about such a daring and dangerous feat. You made him vanish forever right under Varian's nose, no clues or witnesses, none that Zan is out of the way now. How did you do it?"

Canissia stroked the man's chest as she purred, "Poor Zan, I hated to get rid of him. He was very good in bed. Out of it, he followed my orders without question or hesitation. But he loved me, and that's dangerous. A lover can be forced to do anything to save his heart's desire. I couldn't let that happen.'' Canissia explained, for a second time.

Varian allowed her to continue caressing him while he probed for clues. ''That was very risky and very clever. I'm pleased with you and your precautions. What about Moloch? How did you do away with him?''

On guard now, the suspicious redhead explained, then listened to his praise of her talents, again for the second time. She knew something was wrong. He acted and looked like Ryker, but Ryker already knew the things he was questioning her about with such eagerness for details. She knew Ryker used a disguise to conceal his close resemblance to his half brother, as genetic law determined. Of course, most people thought Ryker truly had blond hair and green eyes. Wouldn't it be just as easy for Varian to—

''I suppose Moloch's sister won't suffer too much over his loss. She's always craved his position as the eleventh richest person in Maffei.''

She concealed her tension and doubts from him. ''Yes, she has. I'm sure she's in *Kahala* about now,'' Canissia murmured, knowing Ryker Triloni had been told on her last visit not only about the deaths of the two spies but also the necessary one of Moloch's sister who had surprised her while carrying out one of those deeds.

The evil redhead smiled and licked her lips in a seductive manner as she concluded she was with Varian. How far would he go to conceal his ruse? ''Why don't we go to your complex to sneak in a few hours of fun? You know I have skills that little alien doesn't. I can please you far more in thirty minutes than she can in her lifetime.''

''Settle down and cool off, Cass. You know we never get that close. Not because you haven't tried and tempted me on every visit, but I never mix business and pleasure. I gave you enough *Jacanate* and Moondust on your last visit to keep yourself amused elsewhere for a long time. Surely you haven't used it up already? Where have you been?''

The cunning female realized the man before her knew what

had happened inside the complex but not during their talk outside before her last departure. She guessed how. "After that accident with Zan, I stayed out of Maffei for a while. You do know the Androasian and Pyropean boundaries are being heavily patrolled now?"

"Because of that Milky Way mission you told me about. I'm sure the Alliance doesn't want any of their spies getting through to warn their leaders about the imminent departures of so many starships. I hope you aren't angry with me over that misunderstanding?"

"Of course not. But I *am* miffed by your stinging rejections. I would have been the perfect lover or wife for you, Ryker."

"Except you crave Varian more and you don't trust me completely."

"You wouldn't dare harm me. I have evidence incriminating you in some of my past activities. Some of it ties you to Taemin. And my crew is prepared to send an emergency message to Star Base if you attempt to betray me or kill me, today or any day, my sexy genius."

"Cass, Cass," he admonished. "We're allies and friends. I wouldn't harm you. There's no need for such threats between us."

"I hope not, Ryker, because I'll take you down with me if I go. Your little bride doesn't know anything about your business affairs, does she?"

"Nothing, and it will remain that way. Jana is for exquisite display, motherhood, and pleasure alone. She'll do wonders to brighten my dark image. And, flaunting her as my submissive and adoring possession will torment my half brother. Unless you get Varian's mind off her."

"Is she as good in bed as Varian's lack of self-control implied she was? Do you drug her with *Jacanate* to get rid of all inhibitions, drug to force her to obey your every command?"

"I don't discuss my sex life with others. But I will say, she's pleasing."

"Then why don't you bring her with you to my party next week. It will give you the perfect opportunity to show her off to everyone. I'm sure, if you work hard and long, you can have her bred and enthralled to you by next Friday. You two can stay with me and Father after you arrive on Mailiorca."

"If I had known how to reach you, I could have told you I'll have to cancel out on your party. Jana and I are leaving Tuesday to visit with Grandfather. He hasn't met her. That takes priority over a social occasion."

"How exciting for you both. I'm sure a visit to *Kadim* Maal is important to you at this time. If you change your mind, let me know." *Then I can plan a real party, you fake. You won't get a chance to arrest me, you bastard. If I suffer, so will you and plenty of others. While you play your little game, I will have time to escape and to plan my revenge.*

"You look pensive. Was there something else, Cass?"

"Nothing. I'll be on my way so you can amuse yourself with your obviously compliant and mesmerized slave. I'm sure you're eager to climb atop her and slip inside that lovely body. I bet you drive her wild with your skills. I'm envious; I wish it was me being probed by you and this treasure."

Varian grasped her hand and moved it away from his manhood. Her crudity revolted him, as did her touch. He hoped Jana wasn't watching them through the reflective *transa-screens*. "Behave yourself before I have to explain this to my wife. Guard that evidence against me well, woman. If it falls into the wrong hands, I will kill you. I don't like threats."

"Nor do I, Ryker, you handsome devil. As soon as I'm convinced that explosion was an accident, I'll destroy all the files."

"How will you make that discovery?"

"After I make certain I'm not in trouble for kidnapping Jana Greyson. If you did cover me, I'll cover you."

"Fair enough."

Varian watched the woman leave. An Elite Squad member would be trailing her the moment she left orbit. He needed to tell him to confiscate the evidence against Ryker following her arrest. He smiled and whistled, happy about his accomplishment.

Canissia boarded her shuttle to return to her cruiser. She

observed the blond from a window, grinning in what he assumed was a victory. *You fool. I know you'll have me followed, but you underestimate my cunning. Before this day ends, I'll elude your spy. Soon, my unattainable rake, you and that alien bitch who stole you from me will be dead. I know the perfect way and person to help me carry out my revenge.*

"I'm sorry for my misbehavior, Ryker, but I couldn't help myself. I couldn't resist playing a trick on her after what she's done to me. I'm not usually a vindictive or spiteful person, honestly. I only wanted her to see that she hadn't delivered me into the jaws of death or destruction."

"You really put her down, Jana. I've been wanting us to do that for a long time."

A long time? "We did a beautiful job. Thank you for letting me help. I was afraid you'd be angry and embarrassed and call me down in front of her. I'm glad you didn't. Besides, you said she had the hots for you."

"Hots for me?"

"That she lusts for you," Jana clarified the English slang.

He chuckled. "I'm not upset or displeased. I suppose you saw her trying to entice me again?"

"No, I was changing clothes," she lied, as she *had* witnessed the vexing scene. "You should have summoned me to break her fingers and claw out her eyes in defense of my private property."

"She was so flustered that she left without mentioning her upcoming marriage or even why she came here."

Why did he have to keep reminding her of that event? "I hope she doesn't remember and return."

"She won't. I gave Kagan Command Ten; that means she's not allowed to pull into orbit around us again without prior consent to visit."

Something in his expression and tone said he wasn't telling the truth about what had sounded like a military order. "I'm glad to hear that."

"I should get busy. I'll see you at dinner."

"I shall eagerly await your return." Though he took no action on them, she saw how her mood and suggestive words excited him.

Jana snuggled on the sofa with the books he had given to her. She felt that the more she learned and the quicker, the sooner she could get into his labs with him and the easier her task of conquest would be. If she failed to make herself pleasing and indispensable, her life could be in jeopardy. In this world so far from her own, there were far worse fates than being this elite alien's wife and research assistant: death or being sent to another—horrible—owner. At present, she was a free woman, but that could change, by his laws. He could divorce her, take away her freedom, and sell or give her to a terrible stranger. She possessed the status and wealth that she needed for survival; and she mustn't risk losing them. She also wanted to prove to Varian and Canissia that she could survive by her wits and courage, that she could rise above the lowly station in life to which they had condemned her.

Jana learned from one book that no *charl* reproduction had been tried with test-tube babies to avoid a physical mating with other races. Nor had the alien captives become simply breeders to men who had other wives, as in concubine or harem customs on Earth. Since the Maffeian females lacked ovums, nor could the captives be used as surrogates. The practice had created families, and that was good. Yet, after fifty years of inbreeding, their current generations were made up mostly of cross-bred people. The *charl* practice had ceased to be needed and would soon not exist at all. How could the Maffeians logically and emotionally resist freeing their mates? How could they look down on *charls* as unworthy of being wives when their children carried the blood and genes of those aliens? With Martella Karsh and others lobbying for changes in the law, surely it would be a reality soon.

Jana flipped to the section on truth serums and brain functions. She found Ryker Triloni's name and his products mentioned many times. Again, she noticed the rote responses he had given her. It was the same with other sections she perused. She couldn't help but wonder why a genius like Ryker would explain those things with quotations from a *book* to another scientist. She searched for any passage on post-hypnotic suggestion or mind-doping and found none listed. If athletes on Earth could blood-dope or carbo-dope for sports competitions, why couldn't someone mind-dope with information? In a way, students did it when they crammed for tests. Glutting the brain for an exam was like pulling out a cork in the head to pour in facts needed for retention for only a brief time. Was mind-doping possible on this grand scale?

There were medical and research labs with specimens and a botanical garden aboard the *Wanderlust*, with ample opportunities for any person to observe and learn, as if by osmosis. Two scientists were in residence: Dr. Tristan Zarcoff and Lieutenant Commander and First Officer Nigel Sanger. In addition, perhaps these aliens' schooling was more—

Stop it, J. G., you're letting your imagination run wild again. If it were possible for you to glean clues from these books, he wouldn't have given them to you and told you to study them.

Jana tossed the books aside and walked to the *telecom*. She wanted to see if it would respond to her voice command, see if she could catch a news program to learn anything valuable. She repeated the verbal orders the alien had given to the system. As expected, it did not respond. So much for his "wife" of two weeks and a "free" woman being allowed communication or viewing of the world beyond the confining Darkar! She returned to the sofa to continue her research.

It was late and Jana couldn't sleep. She was antsy from tossing and turning from a mind that wouldn't shut down. She rose from bed to fetch a glass of wine to relax her. Ine had shown her how to use the Androasian *servo*. She glanced at the slide separating her suite from the alien's, and saw that it was closed. She walked down the hallway from the minidome to the larger one, her feet moving silently across the lush carpet. Just before entering the room, she heard something shocking that caused her to halt. "Perdition! She's getting away from me," he had said, using a familiar expletive from days long ago and in Varian Saar's voice.

Jana stared at the back of the man's blond head. He was sitting slump-shouldered on the sofa and sipping a drink, probably a strong one from his mood. Was she wide-awake and had she heard him correctly? She waited a few minutes, then approached him. "Can't sleep, either?" she asked.

He jumped and twisted his body to look up at her. "I thought you were lost to the world by now."

She smiled and shook her head. "No, my mind keeps racing with all that's happening. I thought a glass of wine would relax me. Would you like me to fetch you another drink?"

"No, I've had enough for one night, but thank you."

"Perhaps this will help," she suggested as she began to massage the stiff cords on the back of his neck and shoulders. She kneaded the taut muscles with gentleness while humming to him like a child at bedtime. She felt him relax beneath her ministering hands as he allowed his tension and anger to flow out of his body and mind. "I did a great deal of reading today and yesterday. I came across your name and Trilabs many times. My husband is a renowned and intelligent man. I'm impressed."

"Where did you learn such magic tricks with your fingers?"

She noticed that he changed the subject. With fingers lightly curled on his throat, her thumbs drifted up and down the trapezius area of the neck with just the right amount of pressure. "I did this for my father many times. He took a bad spill from a horse that hurt his neck and back. Massages helped ease the stiffness." She shifted the point of her efforts to the tense location a few inches away.

"You're a wonder, Jana Greyson, a sheer delight. The

smartest thing I ever did was lay claim to you; the dumbest was to start off our relationship in such a bad way. I'm happy you don't hold that against me."

Jana was relieved her hands did not halt their movements and expose her reaction to those familiar words. The situation, the actions, the mood changes, and the conversation was reminiscent of—

He captured her hands and stopped their work, but didn't release them or speak. He tilted his head and gazed at her, a long and searching look. He was tempted to pull her over the sofa and into his lap so he could cover her with kisses and caresses. He wanted to take possession of this goddess who was driving him mad with hunger. He was surprised he didn't moan aloud as flames licked without mercy at his loins. At the last moment for keeping a clear head and before yielding to his cravings, he was jolted to his senses. He let go of her hands, lowered his head, and mopped away beads of perspiration from his brow and upper lip. He tried to calm his rapid respiration. He could not permit his desires to run wild, not tonight and not soon, if at all during this ruse. Her touch burned like fire. Her gaze was almost hypnotic. Her feminine allure was powerful and enticing. He leaned out of her reach.

"Does that feel better?" Jana asked, noticing that he had broken their contact with swift abruptness. *Do you hear the quavering in my voice? Do you feel the trembling in my hands and body? Do you read the desire in my eyes? Do you realize how you affect me, Varian?*

He admonished his loss of control. She was too distracting. He must keep a tighter leash on his desires. He blamed his mood and weakness on the bad news he had received before leaving the complex. Canissia had eluded his man with a cloaking device and escaped. The ship following her had no choice except to return to its base on Cagaus nearby, from which Elite Squad member Kagan had summoned it earlier today. He wondered where Canissia had gotten the sophisticated, noncivilian equipment and from whom. From Prince Taemin or from

Kadim Maal? Had he done or said something during her visit to expose himself? Was the redhead on her way to Maal's this minute to betray him in exchange for sanctuary? Should he cancel his trip there? Tell his grandfather about this possible kink in their plans? No, that would worry Tirol. He had to risk going to Androas to try to delay Maal's attack during Project Starguard. He had called Brec Sard and asked for security patrols to be increased along the galaxy's boundary. He had put out an alert on Canissia to Star Fleet commanders to have her observed and followed if she was sighted. That was all he could do at this time.

"Does that feel better?" Jana inquired once more.

Varian stood and flexed his neck. He drew in and exhaled several deep breaths, then smiled at her. "Wonderful. You'd better turn in. It's very late."

"I will. You should, too, Ryker. You must be exhausted."

"I am. Shut off the lights after you get your wine."

Before he could rush away from her, she told him, "I can't. Nothing responds to my voice commands."

He halted and turned. "Since when?"

"Either since I arrived on Darkar or awakened from my illness. None of the voice-activated mechanisms respond to me."

"There must be a glitch in the system. I'll have Griep repair it in the morning. You didn't have any trouble last week. I wonder what's wrong."

"I wouldn't know. I'm not proficient in computers and equipment."

"It will be functional tomorrow. Good night, Jana of Earth."

"Good night, Ryker."

By the next night, Jana had been given her inoculations again. That or placebos, she deduced. She tried to scold herself for having doubts again, but her chiding failed to make her dismiss them. Maybe she had not fallen for the charade at all, only told herself she had during rough moments. Besides the vividness of the hallucination, there were too many clues pointing to a ruse. Instead of trying to unmask Varian, she must attempt to discover the purpose of this crucial assignment.

After dinner, Jana strolled around the living area. She pretended to listen and move to the soft music from concealed speakers. The alien who sat on the sofa with a glass of wine in his grasp watched her. She went to him and, while laughing merrily, took the glass from his hand and set it on a side table. She pulled him to his feet and suggested that they dance. "Please, Ryker," she coaxed when he seemed reluctant. "Come on. We should practice before we have to dance in public during our trip. We should see how compatible we are in all areas. Right?"

She had such an easy way of disarming and captivating him. She was in a capricious mood tonight. Her tone was seductive. Her eyes held hints of mystery and promise. "As you wish, my mischievous wife."

"Thank you, kind sir." She slipped into his arms and nestled close.

They moved in fluid unison in the romantic setting. One tune and dance drifted into another and another while neither spoke. With each one, their bodies gravitated closer and closer. His cheek rested against her fragrant hair with hers against his chest. Their eyes were shut and they allowed their senses to be consumed by the other's nearness.

Varian's fingers trailed to and fro across her back. They traveled upward to caress the soft skin of her neck. His fingers roamed through her radiant mane of wavy hair as golden as the sun. He longed to taste her sweet lips. He craved to possess her.

Jana swayed against his firm body. She flowed with him and the music. She gradually climbed a blissfully torturous spiral, as she had done long ago on his ship in the Stardust Room. It seemed as if her entire body was responding to his erotic messages. She floated between fantasy and reality, between ecstasy and torment. She wanted him so much.

Varian was aflame with burning desire. Jana's nearness unleashed the emotions he had been holding under tight restraint. His body could not help but react to her enticing signals. She was cuddled close to him and was happy, as she should be, as she shouldn't be . . .

Jana smiled to herself. She knew she was getting to him, as she had planned. Obviously he avoided physical contact because he feared she would use her feminine weapons to penetrate the force shield around him. He was reluctant to kiss her, hold her, and make love to her in fear of exposing himself and his charade. But she knew this man was her love; she felt it with every fiber of her being. She must kiss him and prove it was true.

Jana lifted her head and leaned back a little to look at him. His gaze fused with hers. She smiled as her right hand left his so her fingers could touch his sensual lips. She let them trace the angle of his jawline and strong chin. She missed the cleft in it that added such character and a roguish touch to his handsome face. His eye color was different, but she read the expression of desire in those emerald depths. Both hands grasped his head and, rising on her tiptoes, she sealed their mouths.

The kiss was tender and leisure. It explored and pleaded. It melted into one that became swift, passionate, and urgent. Their dancing ceased. Their arms encircled each other and clung tightly and fiercely. His hands shifted to cup her face between them as his mouth worked hungrily at hers.

Varian scooped her up in his arms and without parting their lips, carried her to her bed. As he lay her down, he saw a questioning look in her eyes as they settled on his face and then one of resignation to surrender to . . . Ryker, her husband. He realized they had gotten carried away, that hopefully she had forgotten whom she was with. He captured the hands that reached to pull him to her. He spread kisses over them before saying, "Not tonight, Jana. This isn't the time."

"Is it me, Ryker? Do I displease or repulse you?"

"*Kahala*, no. I desire you more than I've ever desired any woman. In truth, you're the only woman I've ever craved. I knew that the first moment I saw you. I just don't want to rush what will be a very special part of our relationship. We need to get better acquainted first, that's all. When everything is right, we'll share our first night together." *Since weeks ago.*

"I'm sorry for being wanton. I do want everything to be right for us."

"It will be soon, I promise. Good night, Jana."

"Good night, Ryker." *Good night, Varian. No one could kiss like you. No one could dance like you.*

Far away on the *Moonwind*, Canissia Garthon was trying to sort the truth from all the information she had been fed. She had contacted her father, who had related the incredible news of her imminent marriage to Varian Saar. Segall had sworn it was not a trick or a joke, and was in fact public knowledge. He had said Varian was looking for her so they could marry before he left on his next mission. Segall believed Varian desired the marriage to halt any gossip about his feelings for Jana Triloni. It was a known fact that a freed Jana had fled Tirol's keeping and married Ryker Triloni over two weeks past. To prevent further gossip and humiliation, Varian wanted to prove he didn't care by marrying her, and fast. Segall had entreated her to hurry home to plan the ceremony.

"If only you were here, Zan, to help me cull the truth. You and Father are the only two people who love me and trust me. I owe no loyalty to *Kadim* Tirol or the Alliance. They've done nothing for me and view me as debris to be jettisoned. If not for my wealth and Father's rank, they wouldn't be nice or even civil to me. If only Varian and Ryker weren't immune to *Thorin*, I would force the truth from them."

But she didn't know what the truth was. That could have been, she reasoned, Ryker on Darkar. He could have been faking ignorance to make her confess her deeds for a concealed recorder as she had done with others, collecting evidence to keep her mouth shut. Varian was a proud man and wouldn't want to be the butt of jokes and gossip. They had been lovers in the distant past, and their marriage would be a perfect match. If only that alien witch hadn't come into her life and territory and spoiled everything! If Varian and Ryker were no longer available because of Jana, there was only one other choice for a husband and ally: a powerful protector who could provide sanctuary. With her immense value to him and her erotic skills, he would delight in having her. Should she test Varian's honesty and motives or call his bluff on charges against her? Should she return home and see if he would appear, and if he would marry her? Varian could not be impersonating Ryker without the Supreme Council's order or permission, and her father—a member—would tell her of such a matter.

She jumped up to pace her luxurious suite. There couldn't be any real evidence or witnesses against her to endanger her and prevent her from returning home to study this situation. If it was a trick, she could always claim that Ryker extracted his information from her through use of his powerful drugs. She could claim, if necessary, that Ryker had used mind controlling chemicals to force her to slay those men who were his cohorts. But there was the matter of her now-exposed alibi for Jana's abduction. She had claimed *Zartiff* Dukamcea was in bed with her. Drugged, he had confirmed her lie when they were both questioned. Even if she changed her story to say Jana asked for and received her help with escape, could they prove she was lying again? Would Jana challenge her word?

How dare you make me dependent upon you, you alien bitch! I should have slit your throat instead of taking you to Ryker. How did you convince him to marry you? How did you make Varian fall for your charms? Is my love finished with you now that Ryker's screwed you? Who else would Varian turn to except me? It must be true. If you're laying a trap for me, my handsome commander, you'll be sorry. I have ways of learning the truth. Soon, it will be mine. Then, either you'll be in ecstasy between my thighs or rotting in a grave somewhere beside Jana. Yes, that's what I'll do: go to the only person who can unmask a phony Ryker.

Jana and her love were packed to leave on their journey tomorrow. She was frightened and apprehensive. She knew she would locate the truth during the trek to Maal's. She was actually going to be shown off in public as Ryker's wife. Unless something happened to prevent the trip or her going along with him. Could Varian parade her around the galaxy as Jana Triloni? If the stakes were high enough, yes. Would Maal slay Commander Saar if he was exposed? Yes. Would the Androasian *kadim* kill her for being a part of it? Yes.

Her feet and hands felt like ice under the bedcovers. She shivered and trembled as if she were naked outside in the middle of winter. She was heading into . . . only God knew what peril. *Please don't let him be Ryker and please keep us safe.* She began to cry in fear and panic.

The alien sat on her bed and pulled her into his arms to comfort her. "Don't cry, my love. Everything will be fine soon. You have nothing to fear."

Jana sought, found, and fused their mouths. She clung to him. He responded. They kissed and caressed, and passions flamed. As he sank to the bed with her, she knew he would not refuse her tonight . . .

Chapter Six

Varian needed to have Jana completely and, he decided on impulse, the intrusive assignment be damned for a while! This was one mission he could not abort, as an irresistible rendezvous awaited him. If anything went wrong in Androas, this could be his last chance to have her. He kissed away her tears and warmed her body with his heat. He could not let her suffer tonight, nor himself. He needed to be as close to her as possible, to be beside her, to be within her, to unite their souls and bodies as no other action except lovemaking could accomplish. He could say with his actions what his mouth could not at this point. His kisses were deep and hungry, exposing the depths of his emotions. When she clung to him and responded in like kind, his intense yearnings increased. She had captured him as no other force could do. For a time, duty didn't exist, nor anything beyond this room, this moment, this woman. For a time, he was entrapped in a spinning universe of heady desire with the Earthling he loved at its center. Passion's fury blazed within his body and eternal love within his heart. His tongue explored the tasty recess of her mouth. His teeth teased at her moist lips. He felt her tremble with a mutual longing. She had woven her spell around him, and this bond, this union, this night were meant to be.

Jana clasped his head between her hands and held it while she almost ravished his mouth. A near desperation flooded her as she, too, realized this might be the last time she would have him, at least in the near future. It was exciting and stimulating to be in his arms and to have his full attention again. He was tantalizing and tempting her beyond reality, and she did not care. She quivered when his lips seared hot messages over her ear and she answered them with eagerness. She was a greedy sponge absorbing his touch, collecting memories for dry days ahead when her soul, heart, and body were athirst. Her arms slipped around his naked body, as he slept nude and his robe had been discarded.

Varian's mouth brushed over the shoulder he had bared to his questing lips. It traveled to the hollow of her neck and nibbled there. His hands wandered through her cascading tawny hair as they adored the silky texture. Her responses ignited the long-smoldering coals that roared into a blaze of urgency and formed an all-consuming force. He used long and deliberate kisses to tease, tempt, and heighten her desire, as if that was necessary. His mouth branded her face, neck, and satiny shoulders. A feverish mood ensnared them both. Love's deepest desire threatened to burst into instant full bloom and he tried his best to postpone its blossoming until the last moment.

Jana's fingers teased over his body of silk-covered steel. She loved every inch of him. She caressed familiar planes and curves. She journeyed over rippling muscles and hairy meadows. She curled the locks at his nape around her fingers. She was lost in the wonders of love and Varian Saar. He had captured more than her body that night on Earth. He had stolen more than her life there. He had won more than her submission. He owned her heart, soul, and body, forever.

Varian's mouth halted its trek down her throat to feel the throbbing of her pulse point against it. He kissed the line of her collarbone. Her breasts against him felt hot and firm, and he had to touch them, to taste them, to arouse their excitement even more. He moved down her cleft at a snail's pace as if he had a lifetime to journey through the beckoning valley. His stubbled cheek ever so lightly rubbed over her protruding peaks, and he heard her moan with delight and desire. With intoxicating leisure, he kissed every inch of each breast as his fingertips stroked up and down her sleek inner thighs, coming closer and closer to her most private region.

Jana quivered with anticipation and pleasure. A heat hotter than any she had experienced before burned at the core of her being. She quivered and tingled and coaxed him for more. As her love caressed her most sensitive secrets, she kissed and caressed him eagerly. She had long awaited this heady episode. He would not walk away from her tonight, and perhaps never again. Surely after this fusion of their beings, he would confess the truth. She would be understanding and forgiving, and would assist his mission. Afterward, the beautiful life together he had promised her on his starship two weeks ago would begin. For now, all she wanted was to join her body and spirit with his, so she abandoned everything to his rapturous conquest.

She reveled in his firm, bronzed physique. Her hands found his flat belly, virile chest, and broad shoulders. Her palms roamed those stirring areas. Every part of her was sensitive and responsive, as every part of him seemed to be. Her nails gently raked over his torso, careful, even in her aroused state, not to scratch him. Her tongue danced over his ear, and slid down his jawline to savor his taste. She was charged with intense emotion. She was spinning carefree through outerspace. She was aglow with need, as fiery as a blue star that was a thousand times brighter than the sun. A feeling of primitive wildness overtook her. She wanted, she needed, she must have him. She squirmed. She writhed. She groaned. She sighed. She pleaded without words. She took and she gave. With instinct and without words, she encouraged him to do as he pleased with her; and everything he did, pleased her. Only total fulfillment could be sweeter than this prelude.

Varian's breathing quickened. Her touch was as light and gentle as a summer breeze. Her kisses were delicious, some long and soft, and some short and almost savage. She trailed velvety lips over his face, throat, and shoulders. She snuggled against his stalwart frame. Forgotten were any reasons not to take what was his by right of conquest, by right of willing surrender. The sensations she sent coursing through his body and mind drove him wild. He had never possessed any woman to the limits of love and satisfaction until Jana. He had never shared himself fully with any woman except Jana. He had never attained such heights of pleasure except with Jana.

They were locked so tightly together that not even air could get between them. Fires raced through them and consumed any inhibition, reluctance, or denial. As if by cue, their bodies united as one. Uncontrollable fires leapt and burned, becoming brighter and hotter by the minute and with each thrust. Their faces touched and nuzzled. They reveled in their contact, in their shared passion, in their enthralling love. His darting tongue was met by hers. His questing hands found and claimed treasures, as did hers.

Their tongues mated in an erotic dance that matched the one their bodies swayed to. As she arched to meet his motions, passions soared to explosive levels, and still they labored with speed and skill. They felt weightless and free. Their velocity increased as they approached the boundary into bliss. Wits and self-control were things lost during their journey toward ecstasy's pinnacle. Their embraces tightened until they could wait no longer for their ultimate pleasure.

Afterward, they lay drowsy and entwined without speaking, only touching and feeling and sharing. They were together again and nothing else mattered. The agonizing weeks of denial and loneliness had vanished. No matter what the cruel future had in store for them, they had tonight; they had peace and each other, for a while.

When Jana was asleep, Varian eased from the bed. He stood over her, gazing at her, adoring her with his eyes, branding her his, memorizing every detail of her face for the thousandth time, as if he could ever forget any feature or inch of the exquisite Earthling! He was confused, vexed, and hurt that she hadn't whispered his name during the throes of her climax. It was him she had made love to, not Ryker, wasn't it? Though he had convinced her of the delusion, didn't she at least suspect she had been stolen from him? Didn't she know he would never give her away? Didn't she know he loved her and wanted her? Did she think him that cruel?

He knew for a fact that she had been coerced into marrying Ryker and had never slept with his treacherous and evil half brother. But he had awakened her passions long ago, and he had aroused them again tonight. How could she have resisted such skills and desires? She had confessed her love that last time on his ship. Surely this was too fast for true and powerful love to die. Many times he had been forced to risk slaying her love for him, but he hadn't. Always she had retained those emotions. Always she had believed him and forgiven him. But his crimes against her were mounting: his resistance after her capture, the many difficult and demanding times along their route home, the humiliating auction he had put her through for her protection and that of his mission, and now this dark and dangerous ruse. Was it drawing her closer to his dead half brother? Was his ruse working too well? Was he slaying precious love and hurting her beyond repair?

You fool. This deed only makes things worse for her and for you. If you don't carry out the ruse, everything will be destroyed, including her. Even if you and the fleet remain here and allow Earth to be devastated, Maal and Taemin will still attack. An intergalactic war will cost too many lives. You have the power to make peace within your reach. The only price might be releasing Jana from your hand long enough to grasp it. Can you not risk sacrificing one love to save so many lives and worlds? Can you think about anybody except yourself and her? What kind of man would give up his honor and duty and allow such devastation only to have the woman he loves? Yet, what kind of man takes his love into the gaping jaws of death with him?

* * *

Jana stretched and yawned. She felt mellow and happy. She felt relaxed and calmed. She almost whooped with joy as she tossed the covers aside to greet this glorious morning. She looked up as the yellow-eyed android entered her suite. "Good morning, Ine. I feel wonderful today."

"Greetings. I was commanded to awaken you. You must bathe, dress, and eat. You must be ready to depart in three hours."

"Thank you, Ine. That's all. I'll be ready on time."

The monotoned and expressionless android left the room. Jana danced around her suite before grooming herself. There was no way, she told herself, that "Ryker" could convince her he wasn't Varian, not after murmuring "Moonbeam" in her ear last night. No doubt, in his ardor, he didn't even know it, but she had heard the favorite endearment. "That wasn't a delusion, Jana." *But did Varian say it*? her mind retorted; *he isn't the only man who knows that word and murmurs it.*

Jana sat in the living area to await departure time in one hour. Her love was busy with last-minute loading of deliveries to several planets along their route. A bundle of nerves and energy, she got up and approached the *telecom*, as it had been programmed by another android named Griep to respond to her voice commands. After obtaining what she wanted, she returned to her seat to view the news. Fifteen minutes later, she bolted up and went to stand within inches of the large viewing screen. It was Varian being interviewed "live" about his approaching marriage to Canissia.

"It was delayed because my fiancée hasn't found the wedding gown she wants," he answered the reporter. "She's been to every shop on every planet in the galaxy and has just returned. With or without her gown, the date is in two weeks."

"I'm sure it will be a grand occasion," the reporter said.

"No. Cass and I decided to make it small and intimate, just

family and a few close friends. It's to take place at Grandfather's estate on Eire."

"What about Ryker and Jana Triloni? Will they be attending?"

Varian shook his sable head. "They were invited but turned down our invitation because of previous plans. Of course, they're newlyweds, too, so I imagine they are busy elsewhere."

"What about the recent reward and search for Dr. Greyson?"

"After she vanished, I thought she was in danger because so many men were eager to get their hands on that treasure, legal or otherwise. I felt it was my duty to look for her and to post a reward for her return. We all know now that she eloped with the Androasian prince. You can't blame Ryker and Jana for wanting to get her out of the limelight; she did cause quite a commotion after coming here. From what Ryker told me, they're happily wed. I congratulate Dr. Jana Greyson on her good fortune of becoming his wife and joint heir to the Androasian Empire."

"How could Dr. Greyson elope with Prince Triloni? A *charl* has no right to go anywhere without her owner's permission. That was you."

"*Was* me; that's the key word. Grandfather freed her after she saved our lives during an assassination attempt on Eire by a Captain Koch. She risked her life to save ours, so Grandfather rewarded her with her freedom. She had every legal right to leave without notice and to marry Ryker. If they hadn't been out of contact and had heard about the investigation into her disappearance, I would have been notified of her plans. In fact, she did send a departure message which I received when I returned home to Altair, so I called off the search. . . . Ah, here comes my fiancée now."

The camera panned to a smiling and radiant Canissia who waved at them and halted to speak with friends while they finished the interview.

"I suppose you two will be taking a long and romantic honeymoon?"

"Yes, we will. We—"

"Screen off!" Jana shouted, and was obeyed instantly by the system. How, she fretted, was this possible? Was it too coincidental? The first time she watches the *telecom*, she views *this*! As soon as they made love and she was certain of his identity, this was used to change her mind! Yet, he couldn't have known she would watch the unit this morning.

The blond alien entered the room. He walked to her, smiling. As he caressed her cheek, he murmured, "I hope you slept as well as I did. It's a new beginning for us, Jana of Earth, one that will work."

Qualms, doubts, and fears assailed her. "I . . ."

His green gaze searched hers for a while until she lowered her lashes in guilt and confusion. "I know it was unexpected, but give it time. When it's right again, it will happen. Don't push yourself toward me until you're ready. At least we know one thing: we're very attracted to each other."

Was it a pretaped performance or live interview? "Ryker, I—"

He silenced her with his fingertips to her lips. He knew she was upset by the phony interview he had loaded into the system. If she had watched it yesterday, she wouldn't have surrendered to him last night. The signal on his remote communicator had informed him it was in use, no matter which station she had sought. He hated to do this to her, but a honeymoon would explain his lengthy absence to others. First, he had to get his hands on Cass and get her out of sight. "There's no need to say anything, Jana: no explanations, excuses, or promises. Let's leave it in the test tube and see what develops. It might become a priceless formula."

They were going out in public as a happy couple. Their marriage was legal. But was she Ryker's wife, or his widow and heir? "I just saw Varian on the *telecom*. He was congratulating us on our marriage and talking about his own big event in two weeks.'' She repeated what had been said. ''I thought you freed me. Isn't that what you told me?''

''Yes, and I did free you, *we* freed you. The *kadim* or the Supreme Council are the only ones who can grant freedom. Such an action must be the result of unique service or courage that benefits Maffei: saving the ruler's life certainly fits into that category.''

''But I didn't save their lives from Captain Koch. In fact, I almost botched a trap they had set for him. I got . . . one of his men killed.''

''You did try to save Varian's unworthy hide; he told me about it, so it made a good story to cover the truth.''

''The truth!'' she sneered from frayed nerves. ''Is it legal, even for the *kadim* and an Elite Squad member, to deceive the citizens of this galaxy? Perhaps I should tell them about the perils of Watergate and Iran-Contra affairs to show them how dangerous government lying can be. Why didn't Tirol and Varian tell everyone the real truth, that an insignificant alien slave saved all of them by being sacrificed to their worst enemy?''

''Do you want me to say it again, woman?'' he almost shouted.

Provoked and hurt, she asked, ''Say what?''

He captured her flushed face between his hands and stared into her glittering eyes. ''That you're the only possession Varian owned that would be of value to either of us. Do you like hearing he wanted you and despised giving you to me? Does that make him less of a monster in your eyes?''

Jana ignored the way he forced those words from between clenched teeth. ''He didn't want me. Nothing could have forced him to give me away if I meant anything to him. The same is true of you, Ryker Triloni. Neither of you fear anything or anyone. It must run in the blood you two share.''

''Are you saying we're more alike than in looks?''

This time, Jana noticed the chilly look in his eyes and in the tone of his voice. He was angry and challenging, and she was acting stupid. ''I'm sorry. I didn't mean to sound so cold and cruel. Of course you're nothing like him in personality and character, thank goodness."

She flattened her palms against his chest and gazed into his eyes. "How would you feel if you were passed around like some unfeeling object, if you had no control or say over your life? Don't you see, Ryker, it doesn't matter to me if he wanted me as a possession? It doesn't matter to me that he didn't want to part with a pleasing slave so soon. It doesn't even matter that he considered me so valuable that I could be used as his peace token, his *only* peace token. What matters is that I was kidnapped and turned into a slave. That my freedom, pride, and life were taken away. That I was so unimportant, I was handed over to a foe who might torture or kill me. I made friends with them, Ryker: Varian, Tris, Nigel, Martella, Tirol, Draco. I trusted them. I obeyed them. I worked hard and learned everything they tried to teach me. I finally accepted my fate as a *charl*. I bent, yielded, and surrendered like a coward or weakling. For what? To be betrayed? Even if I'm only an alien captive, they owed me more than that. I thought it would be different, better, here with you. Now, *you've* lied to me."

"How so, Jana?" he asked calmly.

"You said you freed me."

The tape had been a grave mistake. He had no choice now except to lie. "I am responsible. After you were given to me and I decided to marry you, I requested your liberation. They used that incident with Koch as a reason the public would understand and accept. It would serve no good purpose for the citizens to hear the truth, and you don't want anyone to know how you got here. If Cass had kidnapped you, Jana, she wouldn't be floating around the galaxy a free woman; she would be a hunted criminal. Everyone knows you're married to me and you're living here. If a crime was involved, we would be under attack for your rescue and my punishment."

Why mention her delusion about Canissia's abduction? "No one would dare attack here or harm you, even if you *had* kidnapped me."

''That's true, but I didn't. On the other hand, I couldn't leave my stronghold if it would risk my capture, could I? Away from Darkar's defenses, I'm as vulnerable as any other man.''

''That's true,'' she agreed, but didn't believe it. ''I shouldn't have gotten so upset. I turned on the *telecom* to try to pick up some interesting bits of information to use in conversation along our journey. I never expected to see that snake and his slithering companion congratulating my good fortune. I'm sure they would be delighted if you destroyed me for them.''

''You have to put them out of your mind, Jana. Don't let them hurt you or embarrass you again. Remember who you are now.''

''I will, Ryker, and I am truly sorry for behaving so badly.''

''It's forgotten.''

''Thank you, and it won't happen again.''

''I'm sure it won't. We're ready to leave anytime you are. After you visit Caguas, Kudora, Auriga, and Zamarra, you'll see I'm in no trouble and all your doubts will vanish. But there is one thing left.''

''What?''

''Varian sent you a video message after we married. I didn't think you were ready to view it until now. If you'd like, I'll call it up.''

Jana panicked. ''What does it say? I'm sure you've seen it.''

''He wished you well in your new life as a peace token. He asked for your forgiveness and understanding for deceiving you. He said you're doing the Alliance a great service by providing a truce between us. He even promises you'll be safe and happy here. Do you want me to call it up?''

''No. In fact, erase it, please. I'd rather not see his mocking face or hear his lying voice again. I'm ready to leave now.''

They walked to the landing grid and entered the shuttle. She let Ryker buckle her seat harness, then watched him attach his own. He smiled at her before issuing the command to lift off. The vehicle took flight, and later docked inside his orbiting starship. Jana was guided to the control room and shown where to sit. This time, seat belts weren't needed. The large ship left orbit around the planetoid as easily as a feather gliding on a gentle air current. It wasn't as big as the *Wanderlust* his half brother commanded, but it was still enormous. She recognized only two of the crew at the controls: Captain Kagan and the android, Griep. Two other androids sat at panels, and two human strangers relaxed nearby. At starlight speed, as Ryker called their swift pace, they would reach Caguas within hours.

Jana watched the clouds rush past the wide span of clear material. Space . . . Starships . . . Shuttles . . . Starlight speed . . . NASA and the astronauts on Earth, she decided, would love to possess such knowledge and technology. And SETI, the Search For Extra-Terrestrial Intelligence, would turn cartwheels over meeting just one of these superior beings. So many people in her world believed there was life elsewhere in the galaxy or universe, but never would they imagine to find it on this scale. With their weapons and advantages, the Maffei Interplanetary Alliance, or Androasian Empire, or Pyropean Federation could conquer Earth with ease in one day. It was a relief to know that none of them seemed interested in doing so.

Jana looked at the moon rounding the right side of the planet before their craft. When Ryker sat down beside her, she asked in a tone that couldn't be overheard by the men, "Are you ever afraid the Caguas moon will crash into Darkar like the rogue body heading toward my planet?"

He glanced at the pale object of her attention. "We're on different orbits, so there's no chance of that ever occurring. Even so, there's no threat of explosion. If my sensors detected a natural disaster in the making, my complex would automatically lower itself far below ground."

"That would leave your warehouses open to destruction. What about the chemicals and other things inside them? Would they present a hazard?"

"Only contamination to Darkar's air and soil. Everything that could endanger this sector is kept within my complex."

Jana's eyes widened. "What about a malfunction with a computer or something like that? Why would you keep such powerful threats so close to you? If anything went wrong, you could be killed.'' *I could be killed.*

''Or glow in the dark for thousands of years,'' he whispered in her ear. He grinned and chuckled as he attempted to calm her fears.

Jana frowned at him. ''It's no joking matter. I'm serious. I live there, too, and I'll be working inside the complex as soon as you permit it.''

''Don't worry, my beautiful wife, the self-destruct weapon cannot be started except by my voice command, which can't be matched.'' He wished he could tell her that threat had already been disarmed by him and Nigel.

''What if something happened to you? A big threat is left behind.''

Varian lazed nonchalantly in his seat. ''Not really. Grandfather has the disarm code. He would use it after he collects my secrets and my wife.''

''But he's an enemy, a rival empire.''

''Not mine. Not yours, either. You are, as you Earthlings put it, his daughter-in-law, wife of his sole heir. Grandfather will make certain you're safe after I'm gone. If anything happens to me, go with him and do what he says. You wouldn't be safe here without my protection; everyone would try to gain control of Trilabs by getting to you. After we return home, I'll have to take precautions along that line for your protection until Grandfather can reach you.'' He stroked her tawny tresses. ''But don't worry, my golden moonbeam, the self-destruct system gives Maffeians and others a good reason to keep me alive and well.''

Keeping him alive was important to her for another reason. ''You said Maffei needed you for the mission to my planet. What did you mean?''

''They intend to use the most powerful chemical lasers in existence to blast the rogue into fragments small enough to be further reduced or disintegrated by photon fire.'' At her look of confusion, he explained, ''Photons are quantums of electromagnetic radiation that are harnessed and sent out in a wide beam similar to laser fire. It's a very powerful and destructive weapon, but its range and target area are limited. To do any damage to something as enormous as that rogue worldlet, the ships would have to get too close and risk being hit and crippled by large chunks of debris traveling at high speed following an explosion; being that far from Star Base and repairs, it would be foolish and detrimental, and could cost the lives of many crew members."

"I still don't understand what that has to do with you and Trilabs."

"One of the chemicals they need for the Triloni Laser is *Barine*, produced from *Tremolite*. It happens that I own the rights to the only three mines where it's found, here and in Androas."

"You own the *Tremolite*, *Barine*, and most powerful laser?"

"That's right, Jana of Earth." *And, you own Trilabs, the truth serum immunity process, and many other priceless secrets . . .*

She sent him a fake radiant smile and remarked, "I'm impressed again. It seems my husband gets more and more important every day."

"Important? How so?"

"You'll be responsible for saving my world, everything I know and love. How can I ever show my gratitude for such genius?"

"By not making those your only loves," he answered too quickly.

This time, her phony smile was seductive. "I promise you, they won't be. Tell me all about Caguas and your mines there."

"We'll be landing soon and you can see them for yourself. I'm going to enjoy showing you around this galaxy and mine. It won't all be work."

"I hope not."

"So do I. If you'll excuse me, I have work to do at this time."

She watched him go to Captain Kagan and order him to send a message to *Avatar* Faeroe, the sixth richest man in this star system, to tell the planetary ruler they would join him for dinner as soon as he completed his inspection at his mine. He sat down with the two strangers who had not been introduced to her and began talking in a tone she couldn't overhear.

They eased into parking orbit around the large planet and went to the shuttle to go below. They were met in a tube-shaped land rover with an impenetrable clear bubble on the sides and top. Taken along a well-used road, the ride was smooth. An android drove the vehicle to the location Ryker gave it. They halted at a force shield and waited for it to be lowered for them to enter the area. Security was heavy and well armed. She heard Ryker tell the top guard that he was going to do a complete inspection and was assigning two new men to head up security of the main location: the two strangers traveling with them.

Once inside, the four got onto a tramlike vehicle that whisked them deep into the dark recess, where tunnels were lighted by rows of lights on either side. When it halted, Ryker assisted her from her seat to tag along. The two strangers followed her owner's lead, and she trailed behind them.

Jana's eyes darted in all directions. She felt trapped in the loud and dusty site. Giant fans pulled out much of the smoke and dust, and filled the area with a livable amount of fresh air. Machinery for digging and collecting ore, drones for transporting it, and laboring androids sent forth whirs, grinds, whines, and buzzes. The mine was huge, busy, and undoubtedly profitable. Certain locations had voice-activated doors that swished open and thudded shut as they passed through them. They visited every section—some by foot and some by tram—and finished their tour in the control room. There, the two strangers took charge and were left behind, after curious whispering.

Jana had the oddest feeling he was looking at the site for the first time and was seeking something in particular. She also experienced tuggings of suspicions about two new men being assigned as heads of security and at this date so close to her delusion. As she and the blond alien departed, she asked,

"What would happen if someone tried to take over this mine? Are the force shield and number of security men strong enough to defend it?"

"Any attempt to break through the force shield sets off a reaction that leads to explosion. Once *Tremolite* starts burning, it either burns forever or until all of the ore is consumed, making it worthless to them."

"What about the men trapped inside?"

"There are ample escape time and routes for the humans."

"That's good. But it would be a big loss to you."

"To them, too, because they need to buy *Barine* for their lasers. To destroy my supply, destroys theirs. It's actually the best protection policy the mine could have."

"I continue to be amazed by you."

They returned to the shuttle, lifted off, and traveled toward a range of mountains and cliffs nearby where she saw thousands of small and large *transascreens* that exposed rooms and suites carved from their interiors. The shuttle halted on a landing grid atop the largest one. She was guided to an entrance that swished open to allow them to go inside.

Avatar Faeroe greeted them with a broad smile and wearing a flowing robe in many colors. "Welcome, Prince Ryker; it is good to see you. And you," he continued as he faced her. "Princess Jana, it is a pleasure to see you again. I had no doubt you would find the perfect match here in our world. Ryker's choice for a mate could not have been better."

"I am the fortunate one, sir, but thank you."

"Come, I have refreshments ready."

That meeting began what was a delightful evening and delicious dinner in luxurious surroundings and good company. Everyone was fooled by Jana's charade of bliss and affection, and perhaps by that of the man with her.

The huge ship left orbit and moved through the vast ocean of space as easily as a fish in water. Their journey was under way again.

Jana sat reading in the plush quarters she had been given. It had been strange and difficult to sleep with "her husband" last night without speaking or touching. He had told her it was a necessary but not to be considered intimidating action. Perhaps it wasn't for him, but it was for her, especially in her undecided state of mind.

She dropped the book across her lap and stared into space. Was this trip designed to establish credibility of her marriage to Ryker? After she was accepted as "Princess Jana," would he somehow fake Ryker's death to make her the chemist's heir? What then? Was Varian supposed to woo and wed the widow? Would he also try to convince her of Ryker's fake death? Was he going to let her believe this charade forever, that she had shared this time period with Ryker and not a disguised Varian? Was that how her treacherous love planned to get out of duping her? Did he hope to convince her that she had been kidnapped, but that he had been powerless to rescue her against such a potent force, and been forced to play along with Ryker's desires while he suffered over her loss? Did that space pirate who had abducted her like booty believe his power over her and his countless charms were so great that he could win her again?

The object and desire of his secret mission had to be Trilabs. If that was his plan, he was in for a shock when he discovered his pursuit and lies wouldn't work. If he thought that, he had overlooked the fact that once Jana became Ryker's widow, she would be rich and powerful herself. She was also a free woman. Unless she was forgiving and agreeable, there was no way that Ryker's holdings and secrets could be taken from her. She could always move Trilabs and herself to Androas where *Kadim* Maal would be their protection, and get her out of Commander Varian Saar's reach. He couldn't keep using her and discarding her, then expecting her to take him back. There would always be a next time for him to take the same or a similar course of action for a mission. There had to be a point when treachery and sacrifice and duty were too great a price to pay.

Are you relaxed because you think I fell for that phony videotape, your lies, your tricks? You bastard! With the two men you left behind on Caguas, you're now in charge of a vital resource. You have Trilabs in your possession, and everyone there is your man or under your control. You have the journals, complex, and all of the Trilonis's secrets. Now, you're going after your final treat: Kadim *Maal for Maffei's defense. It's imperative to your charade that I believe you're Ryker, so imperative that you'll sacrifice our love and maybe our lives. Well, you heartless space demon, I'll play your little game and see how you like a taste of deception. We'll see how you like watching me come to hate you and to love your enemy. It's your time to squirm and suffer anguish, and to beg to confess all to me. If you think I did a good acting job with* Avatar *Faeroe, you haven't seen anything yet. Prepare yourself for a tormenting siege, Rogue Saar!*

Chapter Seven

For three days, they played chess without wagers, exercised in the rec room, talked about their pasts, laughed and gravitated closer, enjoyed meals alone or with Captain Kagan while androids ran the ship, danced to romantic music, and shared a bed without making love. All the while, they played their deceitful roles without flaws and with charm.

"Why isn't a security team needed on this big ship?" she asked at dinner one night. "We have only one man and a few androids to protect us."

His eyes roamed her face as he replied, "Because of our weapons and whose ship this is, no one would dare attack me or it, here or anywhere."

He seemed arrogant and overly self-confident; no doubt he was trying to portray Ryker's traits. But, they were his, too.

* * *

With each passing day, Jana found ways to let him know she was receptive to another intimate encounter with him and even encouraged it. Why not? She enjoyed making love with the virile and handsome male. Besides, it might strengthen her hold on him, and would remind him of what they had shared and could have shared if he hadn't betrayed her again.

One morning, she awoke cuddled in his embrace. He was lying on his back with her curled to her side, her head and one arm resting on his broad chest. Her right leg was over his and nestled between his parted knees. She heard the steady thudding of his heart. She absorbed his warmth and manly smell. It felt wonderful, exciting, and arousing. She snuggled closer, took a long and dreamy sigh of contentment, and stroked his bare chest with her fingertips. He still slept with no pajama top but now used satiny bottoms to conceal his ample assets, the sensuous material feeling sexy against the flesh of her legs where her gown was hiked up.

She glanced up at his face, then returned her head to his shoulder. Jana knew he was awake, though he didn't speak or move or open his eyes. The tension in his muscles revealed that fact, as well as the pattern of his breathing. Her playful fingertips drew light circles and designs on his bronzed flesh. She flattened her hand to move her palm over the firm terrain: across his chest, over the joint of his shoulder, and down his strong arm. She lifted his left hand, carried it to her lips, and pressed several kisses to it, then used her bare foot to stroke his leg. She sighed once more and ceased her actions.

Jana lay still in the confines of his arms, though she knew from the increased beating of his heart that she was affecting him. She longed to feel his strong and skilled hands caressing her body. She craved to fuse their mouths in heady kisses. She yearned to mate with him again: to seek, find, conquer passion's pinnacle, and to bask in the sunny afterglow of that victory. She was tempted to seduce him with the skills he had taught her long ago, but she didn't want to be the one to initiate their next union and, in an uncontrollable way, she wanted to torture him with what might have been. She wanted to provoke him into taking the first step toward their next bout of intimacy, enchant him into being unable to resist taking her. When he made no move to respond or to take the lead, she rose from the bed and entered the bathroom to shower and dress. She was miffed and surprised that he didn't take what he obviously wanted.

They reached orbit of Kudora: a strange planet of ice, snow, and cold winds; modern cities beneath gigantic clear bubbles that kept out the harsh elements of nature. She asked her companion how that could be possible when planets farther out were warm and green with abundant life.

"Kudora orbits our sun faster than Therraccus before her. With Therraccus always between her and our solar source, Kudora is forever shadowed from our sun's warming rays. They stay in alignment, one of the great mysteries of our star system. If Therraccus or Kudora ever changed their pace and position, the ice and snow would melt and flood the entire planet. Some call this wintry world Nature's way of offering a variety of scenery and providing challenges for man to conquer."

Our? her mind echoed. "It is amazing and beautiful in its wildness."

Varian's gaze drifted over her stunning profile and the tawny tresses that tumbled down her back. He stared at the multicolored eyes of green, blue, and violet that were wide with wonder at the setting before them. He gazed at her golden skin, unmarred and slick as glass. "Yes, it is. One reason we can make this voyage so swiftly is because most of the outer planets are in full alignment this one time of year. All of our four stops are in a direct path toward Androas, or will be by the time we reach them."

She turned and smiled at him. "This trip is fun, not like . . ." She halted and lowered her lashes, then her head, as if she had made an error.

He raised his hand to lift her chin and caress her cheek. He locked his gaze with hers. "It's all right, Jana. You don't have to guard every word you say to me. I'm happy you're enjoying yourself. I know the last time you visited these places it was under terrible conditions. I don't expect you to forget those humiliating days. I much prefer you speak your mind so I'll know what you're thinking and feeling. How else can I get to know you better?"

You really mean, dupe *you better!* She put aside her anger to do her own duping. "I'm sure you don't find it pleasant to hear about my past with him. I wish it didn't exist, Ryker. I wish I were seeing all of this for the first time with you. But in a way, I am. Last time, it was short, horrible, and as a slave. This time . . ." She paused to laugh. "It's still short, but it's fun and I'm free." It was crazy and unexpected, but her eyes teared at her lies and sad mood. She took advantage of the ridiculous happening. "You don't know how much you've done for me and how much you mean to me. Thank you."

Varian wished she hadn't said such stirring things to "Ryker" or slipped into "Ryker's" arms for comfort and appreciation. Yet, he held her tightly, pressed kisses to her silky hair, and said, "I do know, Jana, I do."

His embrace wasn't lengthy, and she knew why: he was becoming physically—and emotionally?—aroused. She let him escape to "departure tasks" for now, pleased with her own ruse and victory.

The shuttle reached the planet surface and parked in a protective hangar. They were met by *Avatar* Saito, who smiled and welcomed them as if they were long-awaited best friends. Again, a delicious meal and evening—this time with musical entertainment—was enjoyed by all.

Afterward, Jana stood at the large *transascreen* in the plush suite provided by their host, Kudora's ruler. Suddenly she wondered if the thirteen *avatars* in the Alliance Assembly were in on this secret assignment as they had been on the Earth mission, or if only the three-man ruling body—the Supreme

Council of Tirol, Draco, and Segall Garthon—were in the know. If more than *Kadim* Tirol and Varian were involved in the ruse, had Canissia wheedled that information from her loose-lipped father? If that bitch knew or learned the shocking truth, that Jana was with a disguised Varian—the object of Canissia's lust—what would the spoiled and spiteful vixen do about it? What could Canissia do without exposing herself?

Jana shuddered at the thought of the elite men she was meeting being aware of her predicament and ignorance. How humiliating!

Varian stepped up behind her. "Is it too cool in here for you?"

"No, it's perfect. I was looking at all that ice and snow and thinking about how cold it must be out there. I'd bet that if you went outside in that temperature or this window broke, you'd never get warm or thaw out again."

He moved his hands up and down her bare arms to chase away the goosebumps showing there. "It's warm and safe in here, so relax."

She turned to face him. "Are all of the *avatars* rich men?"

"It is a high-paying position because of the responsibility for an entire planet's welfare, but most of them have holdings that provide wealth. *Avatar* Suran of Zamarra is the richest man in Maffei. His family, his ancestors, are the ones who created the underwater cities. Everyone who moved there had to pay them, so they amassed a great fortune. Why do you ask?"

She leaned against him and buried her face on his chest so no expression would be revealed. She wrapped her arms around his waist and snuggled close. "I was just wondering; they all seemed so rich and powerful when I met them on my first trip. We'll be visiting Suran soon."

Varian's fingers toyed with the tawny curls that cascaded over his hands. "After *Avatar* Rhoedea on Auriga. Do they make you nervous? They shouldn't. They all like you, Jana of Earth."

She stiffened a moment and wished he'd stop calling her that.

Assuming she was merely tense about meetings with men of such high status, he kissed her forehead and said, "That's no pretense. You were rich on your planet and you know how to conduct yourself around such people. No one is more well bred or well mannered than you are. What's the real problem?" She didn't answer. "You seem tense and distracted."

Varian wished he could be distracted from her potent allure. He should never have placed this sexy gown in her wardrobe. He was stunned that she was wearing it tonight, especially without its matching robe. The deep fuchsia sleepware had an almost see-through lace bodice. Its gathered bottom hiked up on both sides to the hips to expose a view of sleek legs. The front was cut low to the swell of her breasts, and the back dipped in a V to the waist where crisscrossing silk bands held the sides and shoulders in place. Around that lengthy and seductive neckline were frilly ruffles of lace, which his fingers played with. His hands shifted and found bare flesh between the slender strips. She was so soft and smooth, but still firm from a well-kept body. As if the stretchy X's were negative signs of warning, he released her, stepped back, and smiled. "Feeling better now?" he asked.

"Yes, thank you."

"Why don't you go to bed while I finish my business here? We leave early in the morning to avoid the later congestion of supply shuttle traffic." He had to get out of there and away from her pull!

Jana sensed his motive but kept from smiling at another victory. She stretched out on the large bed to see if she could sleep, as she was also aroused from their contact. If this play for "Ryker" was tormenting and punishing Varian, it was because he deserved it. The trouble was, it was doing the same thing to her, and she didn't deserve it. She couldn't help but recall that one of Varian's terrible tricks on her and the other captives was exposed on this very planet. He had pretended to feed a hostile and foul-mouthed disrupter to large spiders called *scarfelli*. At the auction here, the Uranian girl had been taken from solitary confinement and sold. She remembered how that discovery had softened her heart and pulled her toward Varian. Now, another trick was in motion and was hardening her heart anew.

She also remembered that Varian and Ryker were tied as the fifth richest men in Maffei. As Ryker's widow, that spot on the list belonged to her. If Ryker had survived to inherit from his grandfather, *Kadim* Maal, he would have yielded riches and powers beyond counting. If Varian never halted his Ryker charade, he could take over Androas as Maal's heir.

That's crazy, J. G.! Varian Saar would never give up his identity forever, not even for such wealth and power, not even for intergalactic peace which a phony Ryker could control.

Jana shoved the wild thought from her mind by thinking of all the good she could do on Earth with so much money and so many secrets. After Ryker's death was exposed, what or who could stop her? If she moved to Androas and was under her father-in-law's protection, no one. She would have a starship. She would have medical and scientific wonders within her grasp. She would be her own boss, come and go as she pleased. Then, she realized she would inherit alien money that would be useless on Earth; but the technology she could take there would be priceless; it would mean miracle cures for ailing humans, an ailing economy, an ailing defense system. Was it possible to return home after this charade ended?

She gave the idea serious study. How would she explain her long and mysterious disappearance, then her return with such advanced knowledge? The media and gossipmongers would have a field day with wild speculations. She would become a worldwide name. She would have no privacy, peace, or safety from those who craved possession of her valuable secrets. It was too risky to return to Earth, but there might be another way she could help her world battle its problems. First, she had to conquer her own.

* * *

Enroute to Auriga, Jana tried to coax the alien into a game of *forsha*, but he curiously refused and sidetracked her. After watching how well he had played their form of tennis on Darkar, it struck her as being odd.

Varian mistakenly thought he took Jana's mind off the sport he didn't like and could not play well, a fact she would notice and suspect. He couldn't let the Ryker-cyborg that was concealed in a cleverly hidden compartment stand in for him as before. Nor could the other cyborg be seen until it was needed.

Two nights before they would reach their next destination, desires blazed too high and fast to be doused. As they lay in the bed with only the light of a small lamp casting a soft glow in the room, Jana rolled to her side facing him. His head was turned her way, and their gazes met, locked, and searched. She ignored the fact his eyes were green, for she only saw the look—a familiar one—in them, one that matched what she was feeling. Each took in the other's expression of need and desire. The stare seemed to last forever as it wove a spell around them, as if neither could move nor speak. Their hearts pounded. Their passions flamed. Their endless hunger could not be hidden or denied. A silent message passed between their spirits, causing them to reach out and embrace, to seal their mouths. They belonged to each other; they belonged together. If only cruel fate or mischievous gods would leave them in peace.

Varian rolled Jana to her back and lay half atop her. He kissed her mouth, her nose, her forehead, her cheeks, her chin, and her mouth once more. Her hands clasped the back of his head and, with fingers buried in blond depths, held it with possessiveness against hers. Their bodies rubbed against each other, kindling their desires to a higher flame.

Jana's hands roved his broad back and reveled in the feel of his flesh next to them. She trailed them up and down the hard terrain, slow and light at first, then with swiftness and pressure. A tingling glow suffused her. She was captivated by him and his actions. Her senses reeled as if she were racing with the wind across her ranch on Apache's back. Her elusive lover was taking her to paradise, and she was more than eager and willing to go.

Varian was intoxicated by Jana's urgent need for him and her unbridled responses. With gentleness, his mouth ravished hers, then worked its way down her neck to feast on her taut peaks. His tongue circled the rosy-brown tips. He was feverish to obtain the only thing that could cool his temperature: all of her. There was no place on her that didn't beg to be cherished by him and he complied.

Jana was oblivious to anything except Varian and the sensations he created with his skillful lips and hands. She was a shooting star blazing across love's heaven. She wanted a resolution to the bittersweet torment assailing her, but not too fast. She wanted to enjoy every instant of their union. Her kisses waxed bold and deep when his mouth returned to hers like a fiery comet that came, went, then repeated its cycle.

Varian yielded to her magnetic pull. He moaned and his hips writhed as his manroot grew in size. He felt it tremble with longing and plead for entrance to *Kahala*. He fought to restrain his ardor, to make this moment last forever. His adventurous fingers aroused the sensitive areas of her body and soon his lips covered the same terrain. His craving for her was tremendous. Breathing was difficult as he inhaled and exhaled erratically to slow his runaway heartbeat. He cupped one breast, rolled it beneath his hand, and teased the taut bud between his forefinger and thumb. He smelled her hair, her neck, her skin, to find that fragrance that was hers alone. He kissed her in every way imaginable, one dissolving into another and another.

Jana's fingers dipped into the shallow valley along his spine and trekked up his back tiny hump by tiny hump along it. Her breathing became swift and shallow. Surely everyone could hear the thundering of her heart. This was heaven, what he called *Kahala*. His compelling physique had the power to crush her body, yet it felt wonderful resting upon hers. So many impressions and images flooded her enraptured mind, and all of them heightened her desires. His hot breath in her ear made her squirm. His hand tracing over her abdomen made her tense. When it entered the cottony-soft maidenhair, she arched her back, groaned, parted her thighs, and welcomed its visit. The longer he caressed her there, the more pleasure she received, yet the stimulation also increased her tension. "I need you now," she murmured without notice.

Varian's darting tongue was met and joined by hers. Their bodies fused as one. It was a sensation of sheer bliss. He altered between slow and deliberate strokes and swift and urgent ones. He shifted his groin from side to side to caress and tantalize the straining bud. The way she pulled him closer to her and meshed her mouth to his told him she was engulfed by the same fiery furnace in which he was held captive.

Jana curled her hands around his hips and dug her fingers into his straining buttocks. Her legs draped over his and held on to him for the erotic ride. He was swift and forceful, but he wasn't being rough. Her delights increased. She tried to match his movements. Her mouth clung to his lips, and her flesh seemingly did the same to his body.

He nibbled at her breasts, then the hollows of her throat. He teethed her earlobes. Then he made a terrible mistake: "Love me, Jana of Earth, love me," he murmured in her ear.

Pain seared through her heart more fiercely than desire did across her body. She read passion smoldering in his . . . emerald, not sapphire, eyes. She saw his . . . blond, not sable, head towering over her face. As he twisted his head to press kisses along her shoulders, she saw the scar along his jawline. *Damn you, damn you, damn you*. She cursed him for not having the visage of her truelove at this special moment. Her reply was out of her mouth before she could stop herself, "I do, Ryker, I do. Take me now. I need you. I want you so much."

Those words ripped out his heart and wits for a time. He thrust into her with an urgent force, needing to drive Ryker from her mind and body. Over and over he sent mighty strokes into her, movements she accepted with pleasure. He rode her like a wild man on a wild *espree* to vent himself of his pain, yet never hurt her in his rush and confusion.

Jana tossed aside her anguish and urged him onward and upward as a sweet and urgent signal came from deep within her womanhood. Its intensity mounted and teased, then sent charges over her entire frame from head to foot. She writhed and moaned and claimed her reward.

This woman was his heart, his soul, his world. He could not lose her to any man or force, especially to a ghost. She was unique, totally consuming. She was his, by *Kahala*, she was *his*! As she abandoned herself to taste the sweetness of release, so did he. It would be agony of mind and body to stall the inevitable any longer. His body shuddered, and he groaned as potent spasms poured his life force into her receptive portal. As passion's flood began to subside, he caught himself before saying, *I love you, Jana Greyson, I love you*, aloud.

He refused to release her afterward. He switched off the light and cradled her against his dampness. As his body settled down, he suddenly realized what he had murmured earlier. Then he grasped the reason for her expression and response, her striking back at him. *You know it's me, don't you, Jana, my love? May you and* Kahala *forgive me for what I must do soon to convince you it is not. And forgive me, my love, for being too weak to resist you and taking you while wearing his evil face.*

Varian decided that before he took rash action, he should make certain she wasn't convinced of his ruse. He observed and listened as they approached their next stop. He would turn to find her watching him with a glare of anger and accusation, which she concealed quickly. The moment their eyes touched, she would paste a fake smile on her face. As he feared, she doubted him and his explanation. He had no choice but to use his last resort before reaching Maal's, one that couldn't fail him.

On Auriga, Jana was almost relieved that *Avatar* Rhoedea had taken ill and couldn't join them for dinner. The reason was that the ruler's daughter was an old flame of Varian's, and it was just as well she didn't have to spend the evening conversing with an alien woman who might embarrass her with nosy questions or insensitive comments about her past owner.

As promised, she was allowed to have lunch with an old friend and ex-captive from the ship. Kathy had become the *charl* of Ferris Laus, the Security Control and Weapons' Chief on Varian's ship. Varian had even provided most of the money for Kathy's price, as a gift to them. But Kathy had a surprise for her: Heather was visiting and had come along. The other friend was *charl* to Spala Rilke—brother to the navigational and guidance officer on Varian's ship. Was, *J. G., because Tesla Rilke died in that* Spacer *accident while saving your life after Shara's treachery*. How would Varian explain away that death when she confronted him with it? If he had known Heather was here, he would never have permitted this kind gesture! Both females were smiling and bubbling, apparently happy. Jana was determined to enjoy herself before she sought proof of the truth.

"I can't believe we're all together again," Kathy said. "Ferris told me about you being freed and marrying a prince. That's so exciting, Jana. I wish my love could have come today; he's on leave while Commander Saar is planning his wedding with—" The female blushed and said, "I'm sorry, Jana; that was thoughtless of me."

With feigned innocence, Jana asked, "Why? It's big news."

"Because everyone, crew and captives alike, thought he would keep you for himself. The way he treated you and looked at you, I can't believe he didn't. I've heard awful tales about that woman he's going to marry. Commander Saar is too good for a hussy like that. If not for him, I don't know what would have happened to me and Ferris.''

''Commander Saar is very good and loyal to his friends,'' Jana conceded. ''I suppose he thinks he and Canissia are a perfect match or he wouldn't marry her. The same is true for me and Ryker; we're a perfect match. We're both scientists and we both needed a mate. I guess I'm lucky he chose me.'' That was as far as Jana was willing to go to delude the women.

''Everybody knows who your husband is,'' Heather said. ''I heard you eloped without telling anyone. I guess you had a good reason. Tesla told us Commander Saar was furious and worried when you vanished. He searched for you and offered a large reward for your return. When he heard you had run away to marry Prince Triloni, he said he was happy for you, but Tesla doesn't believe him. Tesla thinks he's hopping into marriage with that woman to pretend he isn't hurt over losing you. I'd bet he still wants you, Jana.''

''I'm sure Jana doesn't want to hear about his new romance and upcoming marriage,'' Kathy chided Heather in a soft tone, ''especially since it's over between her and Commander Saar and she's married to someone else.''

Jana sent Kathy a smile of gratitude for her compassion. She knew Heather—not the brightest of females but a kind one—wasn't being hurtful on purpose. It was the girl's simple and honest traits that had enticed Jana to take her under her wing like a younger sister during the voyage to Maffei. ''Tell me about you and Spala.'' She watched dreamy lights fill the girl's eyes.

''He's wonderful, Jana, wonderful. I was so scared on that spaceship coming here. If it hadn't been for you, it would have been awful. I told Spala everything you did for me and he wants to meet you one day and thank you himself. I love him and he loves me. Isn't that the wildest thing? Kathy has Ferris. I have Spala. You have Ryker. We've all made good lives here.''

The three women laughed, chatted, and exchanged stories of their alien romances. Yet Jana left out much of hers and lightly glossed over her surprising marriage to Ryker. "I'm so happy for you two. It's good that everything turned out so well." She changed the disquieting subject. "I love the way you're wearing your hair, Kathy, part of it swirled up and the rest hanging free. It suits your face and personality."

"Ferris likes it this way. I do everything I can to please him. I'm so lucky, Jana. I'm carrying his child, a boy, the doctor said. His family treats me so well. I'm amazed by how much I love it here. I would never go home. I can't imagine my life without Ferris. He's too marvelous for words."

"Don't either of you breathe a word to anyone about what I'm going to tell you. I think the *charl* laws will be abolished soon and you two can marry your men." Jana saw both women glow with excitement and joy.

They chatted again, then Jana asked Heather, "How is that brother-in-law of yours? I miss his grinning face and sparkling personality."

In her childlike manner, Heather answered, "He's doing great. We heard from him two days ago. He's off to some big assignment soon. Of course he never tells us much. Spala says he can't or he'll be punished."

That wasn't the answer Jana had expected. If Tesla was alive . . . He couldn't be; the Rilkes just hadn't been informed of his death! The recent message had been faked or was an old one! He couldn't be alive!

"Have you seen Tesla in the last three weeks?"

Without realizing she was in error, the scatterbrained girl responded, "Yes, he came home for three days two weeks ago."

Jana was so stunned and confused that she had a hard time paying attention to her friends during the remainder of their visit.

Jana paced the hotel suite, that distressing news plaguing her. Even if Varian had known Heather would be visiting this planet and would join them for lunch, he couldn't have put those words in her mouth. And dear, sweet, simple Heather would not lie to her, not to the person she had looked upon as a big sister during their long voyage here. If Tesla had contacted his family since the accident she believed lethal, it couldn't have happened. If that didn't happen, then . . .

It didn't help Jana's tormented mind that this was the planet where she had surrendered to Varian Saar for the first time. Or rather, she had coerced and blackmailed him into seducing her, all because of a stupid chess wager. So many things during this trip reminded her of her bittersweet days with him. If she hadn't been so drawn to Varian, and if she hadn't been afraid of never knowing real love and passion if she were sold to a terrible owner, and if she hadn't been terrified of going to some alien monster as a virgin . . .

Jana halted and leaned against the wall-sized *transascreen* and stared into the lovely garden below. Her gaze widened and her mouth dropped open. She drew in a sharp breath of air and as the spent air rushed out of her lungs and past dry lips, her respiration altered to a rapid, shallow pace. She stared at the scene taking place two stories below her suite. She saw . . . Ryker Triloni and . . . Varian Saar talking, or more like *arguing* from their expressions and movements. She pressed her palms and forehead against the window. She stared in disbelief, alarm, and confusion.

When Ryker motioned toward the hotel, Jana jumped backward to get out of sight. She remembered that the reflective windows were visually impenetrable from the outside. She took her place again and watched her world come apart as her illusions dissolved and her heart was broken. In a near daze, she observed the agonizing episode.

The two aliens talked, with only a few feet separating them. Their rigid stances and glaring expressions exposed anger and disagreement. At one point, the blond alien shook his finger—on his right hand—at Varian. The prince's feet were planted apart and the left arm at his side held a balled fist. Varian stood in a similar position, but with arms akimbo. Neither man showed fear of the other or made any attempt to turn their verbal conflict into a physical one. They appeared to settle down for a while and to speak calmly.

No, this can't be happening! It's a lie, a trick! He knows I don't believe him and his charade and he's doing this to convince me.

Jana wondered if it was a video being played against the wall for her benefit, or a perfected holographic imagery show. She had seen three-dimensional holography on Earth that must be hundreds of levels inferior to what this advanced society possessed. Combined with their laser beam capabilities, it would be a snap for them. She watched the shadowing on the wall and on their bodies, and could find no fault with it. She saw Varian withdraw a small box from his pocket and hold it out to Ryker. She watched Ryker stiffen, glare, and knock it from the ebony-haired man's grasp.

Jana thought she would faint when the box struck a garden bush, shook it, and disturbed a group of butterflies feasting on its blossoms. Her panicked gaze watched the colorful insects take flight, traveling beyond what could be the range of a trick picture. She saw a slender cloud move overhead and witnessed how it shaded the two conversing men for a moment.

My God, what's happening to me? Have I gone insane? How could she deny the vivid truth before her eyes? Her attempted murder and rescue had been an hallucination. Everything she thought Varian had told her afterward wasn't real. Tesla hadn't been killed in a Spacer accident. She hadn't been kidnapped by Canissia and had not left Darkar since her arrival, until now. She had been so terribly ill and must have partial amnesia as the man claimed. The Androasian prince had told her the truth all along. She was married to . . . and living with Ryker Triloni. She had slept with . . .

Oh, Lord, what have I done? She answered herself: *You've enticed and made love to your husband and tried to make him into Varian.*

The two men were speaking calmly after the incident with the box, which she hadn't seen Varian recover from the bushes. No doubt they were discussing her, and perhaps the box contained a gift for her as one had at Draco's: her refusal of the object then had provoked Varian into snatching her away from her new home and life on Karnak.

She was shocked again when the half brothers clasped wrists, spoke, and nodded. *A truce*, she wondered, *with me as the provider? Damn you! Damn you both to hell and back! How dare you turn me into an object to be passed or traded about! How dare you lie to me and betray me?* Commander Varian Saar—that irresistible space pirate—had done so, but Prince Ryker Triloni—her husband—had not seemed to. Not yet, anyway.

Jana saw the two aliens head in separate directions. She saw Varian halt, turn, stare at his half brother's back, then gaze up at the hotel tower. He shook his head and left without, she realized, retrieving the box. She watched Ryker round the wall of the garden. He was probably headed for their suite. She raced into the bathroom, stripped, and submerged herself in a bubble bath. However would she extricate herself from this self-made trap? How could she be a wife to Ryker in more than name only as agreed?

You've already been a wife to him! Twice, you fool! And you've flaunted yourself before him like a cheap slut and enticed him in every way possible! But I was mistaken. And I didn't choose Ryker as my sweetheart or husband or lover, not of my own free will. How can I betray Varian and our love with another man? . . . Betray him? He betrayed me! But that has nothing to do with this mess. How can I make love to him again? He's almost a stranger to me.

The door swished open and the handsome blond alien entered the room. He came forward smiling, and squatted beside the tub. His gaze fastened to her face. Jana eased lower into the concealing bubbles. Her face pinkened so much that the rosy color splashed down her neck and onto her wet chest. Varian knew he had won, because she wouldn't be modest with him in this stirring situation. What he had just done to her was difficult. Was the cyborg ruse worth its motive, even if it hastened and ensured his mission? "Did you have a good time with your friend?" he asked.

The quivering Earthling tried to act calm. "Yes, it was wonderful. Heather, the other captive I told you about from my country, joined us. She's here visiting while her husband handles business matters. She's the one who looks and sounds like a teenager."

Varian knew he didn't need to be alarmed, as Tesla's death had not been revealed to his family. In fact, the Rilkes were led to believe he was still alive because the location and cause of his death could not be released yet. And, before going on leave, Ferris Laus had been given a mind-block to prevent him from sharing the carefully guarded events on Darkar with his wife Kathy or others. "I remember your mention of her. She was the one you were so worried about because she's so child-like. Do you still have reason to worry? Did you get your quota of gossip and good stories?"

Jana nodded. "Excellent food, too. Your choice of restaurants was perfect. It was lovely and quiet and private, just what we needed for a visit. It was so good seeing them again. They're both very happy. It seems they made perfect matches. Oh, yes, Kathy and Ferris are expecting a baby."

"We make a perfect match, too, Jana of Earth. I hope you agree."

Afraid her expression might expose her feelings, she looked at and toyed with bubbles as she responded, "Of course I do . . . I thought I'd take a long and lazy bath, then rest this afternoon. You said we're going dancing and sightseeing tonight, so I want to gather lots of energy. I wasn't expecting you back until early evening."

"I finished one meeting and I have another this afternoon. I'll return in time to have our own fun. I'll see you later." He kissed her forehead before leaving, and left the concealed listening device where it was—the miniature dot that had told him when to begin his last ruse. That, along with the signal that had buzzed when she approached the window and broke the beam between two sensors.

I wish you hadn't forced me to use that lookalike cyborg, Moonbeam. I was desperate for you to believe I'm Ryker before we reach Androas and Maal. One slip and our lives could be lost. Our worlds could be lost. If there was any other way to accomplish something this crucial, I would do it and not involve you. I'll keep you safe from harm. Hold on for just a while longer, my love, just a while longer.

Jana looked in all directions as she sneaked from the room to slip into the garden below their window. Fortunately no one was around to see or to halt her. And fortunately Ryker had not asked her to return the electrocard for operating their suite door. She walked to the bush, glanced around, and tried to nonchalantly retrieve the box while pretending to smell the blossoms. She strolled to the wall, leaned against it, and stared at the item in her shaky hand. Should she open it? Should she put it back?

She lifted the lid and looked inside. Anguish knifed her heart, sliced to her very soul. The box contained the gold bracelet Varian had snapped onto her wrist for her birthday, following a terrible quarrel when he mistakenly believed she had been defiant. In a way, it had been a truce token, as she herself now was. The attraction between them had become powerful and both had been doing their best to resist it. Their nerves had been raw, and the tension almost unbearable. She recalled his words:

"For both of our sakes, Jana, never yield to me, never. If you do, I swear I'll place you at the top of my list of adversaries. I'm truly sorry that friendship has been so difficult between us. From now on, I'll try my damnedest to control my temper. Beware of me, Jana; I can hurt you deeply without meaning to do so." He had kissed her with hunger and left.

How would she ever get Varian out of her life? *By cutting him out as he had cut her out of his.* She walked to the trash receptacle, disposed of the misleading gift, and returned to her room.

Not once during Jana's misadventure did she sight the blond alien who was watching her with troubled green eyes. Perhaps he should be comforted by the fact she truly thought she had been making love to him instead of Ryker, but somehow even that realization did not assuage his anguish. More than ever before, he perceived his great fear of losing her forever. Even if that horror came true, at least she would be alive and safe. Without a truce with Androas and Maal, she wouldn't be either one, nor would Maffei. He took a deep breath, grimaced, and went to fulfill his self-destructive duty.

Jana made it through the dinner and dancing with Ryker. To make certain she was exhausted enough to sleep undisturbed by memories, she suggested they walk back to the tower where they were staying. She almost suggested they take the shuttle and return to his ship because she wanted to leave this planet where Varian had won her heart months ago, then broken it today. She was glad they hadn't run into him and hoped they wouldn't before departure.

Ryker held her hand as they strolled along. He pointed out sites and smiled and spoke to people, who couldn't conceal their astonishment at his genial manner. Most of them looked at the exquisite Earthling at his side with an obvious respect and admiration for her good effect on this powerful and dangerous male who must remain their ally.

"I seem to be the object of great curiosity and disbelief this evening," he quipped. "You would think these people have never seen me smile before." He chuckled and squeezed her hand. "I suppose they're right. You're good medicine for me, Jana of Earth."

"Why would you need healing? You seem perfect to me."

"Then you, my generous wife, are as blinded by our match as I am."

"Perhaps there are times and occasions when a lack of clear vision is wise and rewarding," she said as if jesting, then smiled at him.

"True. Did I tell you how beautiful you look? I'm very proud of you."

"Yes, you did, several times, and thank you again."

His emerald-eyed gaze moved over her glowing features. Her tawny hair was captured within an unnoticeable blond net that had precious gems attached. The clear jewels sparkled and shimmered when light touched them as if she had numerous tiny and twinkling stars settled there. Her outer garment in a striking fusion of blues, greens, and purples was sheer and flowing from neck to ankle, with a silk slip dress in blue underneath. The colors almost matched her eyes and certainly enhanced them. She was radiant and bewitching. She was trying very hard to behave as his happy and lucky wife. No doubt she had everyone fooled by her attempt except him.

"Let's stroll through the park and stop entertaining everyone we pass." He guided her into a quiet, softly lit, and romantic area.

Jana's heel suddenly caught in a crack in the walkway. She almost pitched forward to the ground as it held her captive. With quick reflexes, Ryker caught her and prevented a fall.

As he knelt to free her, Jana rested her hand on his shoulder and slipped out of the shoe. She wobbled slightly on the other heel as she held the bare foot off the ground. She watched Ryker use his strength to unwedge it, then hold her ankle to replace the shoe. His head lifted and he fused his gaze to hers, then rose slowly without breaking the visual bond.

"I can be a lot of trouble," she teased to ease the tension.

"But you're worth every particle of it."

"Only because you have all it takes to handle me. I doubt there is anything you can't do."

"Your confidence pleases me." He plucked a lacy flower, smelled it, and handed it to her. "No where in the galaxy does beauty exist more than in your face and being, Jana Greyson," he said.

She wondered if it was love and not just desire that she saw in his eyes and heard in his voice. Was it possible? So fast? Yes, she knew from experience that love at first sight was a fact. But a man like Ryker wouldn't be as impulsive and foolish as she had been. On the other hand, one did not always pick the person who captured one's heart. Her eyes roved his striking visage. His hair was the color of wheat at various stages of ripening: three-fourths dark and one-fourth light. It had waves that reminded her of the gentle lapping of water on the beach at low tide and was swept back from his face but allowed to remain full and soft before it drifted into near curls at his nape. His skin was like cream sherry, the most expensive brand. His features were bold and arresting: high cheekbones, the perfect-size nose, thick, dark brows, and a jawline that squared at his chin. His eyes were as green and dark as leaves on her magnolia trees. His mouth was full and inviting. It was as if she were looking at him, really looking at him and seeing *him* for the first time.

Her bold study continued down his throat to a virile physique. The off-white outfit made his tan seem darker and sexier. Muscles bulged in his arms and the snug top of the garment evinced his broad shoulders, trim waist, and flat abdomen. Its fitted pants did the same for narrow hips and sleek thighs. He was indeed magnetic and breathtaking.

Her gaze returned to his mouth with its wide and full lower lip. Her fingertips traced over it with provocative leisure, then did the same with his jawline without even pausing at the scar Varian had put there long ago. "I can say the same of you, Ryker Triloni, and I do. You look especially handsome tonight." As her hands moved over his chest, she murmured, "This color is your best one."

He couldn't help but cup her face and hold it while he lowered his head and lips to kiss her. He felt her arms band his body and they kissed several times as their passions heightened.

Soon, in self-defense, he released her. "We'd better get back to our suite. This is dangerous sport in public."

Jana laughed and nodded. "You're right, as usual, my husband."

As they strolled away with arms at each other's waist and snuggled close, a reporter snapped his last picture of what he assumed was a loving couple who could not resist each other. This would make interesting and surprising news across the Tri-Galaxy, and a nice profit for him.

At the hotel, "Ryker" was handed a message sent by a prearranged signal to his man. "It's from Captain Kagan," he told Jana. "He's been trying to reach me for hours. There's a problem I'll have to check on right now. Go on to bed. I'll probably be very late. We leave in the morning." He had to avoid a terrible decision on her part. He couldn't allow his love to test her ability to surrender to Ryker. He also had to prevent tempting himself beyond control to take advantage of what appeared responsiveness in her following his cruel ruse this afternoon. If they went to the suite together and he didn't make love to her after whetting their sensual appetites earlier, she would get suspicious again.

Jana sent him a feigned smile of disappointment. "I understand. I'll see you in the morning for departure. Good night, Ryker. It was a wonderful evening. I come to enjoy your company more each day."

"As I do yours, Jana of Earth. Good night, my enchanting wife."

At starlight speed and with the planet's current alignment and close proximity to their last stop, they reached Zamarra late the next day. It, she recalled, was the first alien world and *charl* auction she had experienced following her capture from Earth. It was where Varian, after their torrid two-week love affair, exposed her as his "reluctant and helpless" mistress to "spare her any repercussions from her future owner." She didn't want to think about those difficult and bittersweet episodes, and dismissed them.

Zamarra was an undersea world that amazed and enthralled her. The shuttlecraft landed on a clear surface above the turquoise water. Another craft surfaced and docked at the edge of the sturdy landing pad. They took their seats in the bullet-shaped seacraft of clear material. As soon as the interior conditions were at correct life-support level, the craft submerged in the watery domain. As before, Jana watched unusual plants, colorful fish, and aquatic creatures pass or be passed by them.

The ride was fast, smooth, and quiet. No one spoke during this almost dreamy part of the journey. A massive city enclosed in various-size clear domes with offshoots spreading in several directions appeared below and left of them. The largest was the planet's business and shopping core. Smaller ones contained residential and recreational areas that were connected to the center via above-floor surface tunnels. The seacraft approached the biggest dome. It skimmed along the outer edge of the main complex, then entered a docking area. The vehicle's door was attached to a portal which opened to allow their entrance to the undersea wonder. Also, as before, Jana stared at the greenish-blue water above them and bearing down with tremendous pressure. She could imagine the terror and destruction if those walls ever cracked or shattered, but she could not imagine living beneath the ocean every day of her life.

As they headed for their accommodations, they walked through a setting in shades of mostly white and green. Walkways and buildings were constructed of ivory stone. Sweeping green plants decorated the landscape and provided a tropical and exotic aura. Every time she glanced upward, she was reminded that the blue "sky" overhead was composed of water, with a man-made sun and clever lighting to fake daytime. Even wispy white clouds had been added for a beautiful and realistic effect. At the proper hour, as she recalled, a man-made moon and stars did the same to supply a romantic illusion. Beyond the water's surface, however, two moons—one appearing gold and the other silver—orbited this last planet in the Maffei star system.

Jana knew a long evening of dinner, dancing, and entertainment was planned with *Avatar* Suran. She had selected her best gown for this special occasion, and she was looking forward to visiting as an elite guest, not a lowly captive slave.

* * *

As the huge starship left Zamarra behind, Jana eyed the strange world of concealed wonders. She sighed and said, "I've had my most fun here. The food was delicious, the dance wonderful, the entertainment enjoyable, and the company and conversation superb. *Avatar* Suran is a rare gentleman and excellent host. I liked him the first time we met and he didn't change my good opinion of him last night. I'm glad you had to make this stop."

"I was happy to see that you didn't let the fact he's the richest man in Maffei intimidate you. You're the perfect guest and companion, Jana of Earth. You made me very proud of you last night. And speaking of Earth, that's Anais on the horizon, the temporary colony for Earthlings." Varian thought of his friends working there for a while: Nigel, Tristan, and Martella. He grinned as he remembered the way his best friend Nigel had spoken of Jana's best friend from Earth during their last communication.

Jana's gaze followed the direction in which his finger was pointed; it located the small and dark planetoid. Suspense, sadness, and anticipation filled her at being close to her race and perhaps Andrea. "I wish we could visit there. It would be heaven to see some of my own people."

He spoke part of the truth first. "I'm sorry, love, but that can't be arranged, and I haven't found a way to smuggle a secret note in or out yet. But I've done the second best thing for you: Andrea McKay from Texas is there, safe and calm. She was told the truth about you, so she knows you're safe and fine." Then, of necessity, he lied. "When Captain Kagan called me away from you last night, it was to retrieve information about your best friend. Cass extracted it for me from a supply shuttle captain. I won't give you the vulgar details of how that lusty vixen worked her task."

His sexual implication was clear, and Jana was revolted by an engaged woman's conduct. "How did you get her to do such a risky favor for you?"

He sent her a roguish grin that caused his green eyes to twinkle. "When I asked nicely for the favor, she refused, so I resorted to blackmail. I threatened to expose her traitorous activities if she didn't comply."

Jana was astonished. "I'll bet she's furious with you. And with me, too. Nothing would make her angrier than to do something kind for me."

"You could say she's miffed with me at this time," he jested.

"I'm sure 'miffed' is a mild word for what she's feeling."

"Something could be lost in the translation with our ear devices," he joked again. "The clever apparatus searches for the correct word in meaning and, if it doesn't locate one in its memory bank, it uses the closest one or leaves it in the user's language."

User's language? On past occasions, untranslatable words had come out in . . . That meant, Ryker was speaking to her in Maffeian, not his native Androasian. Since he lived here, she guessed that wasn't so odd, however. "Why would you risk losing that valuable source of information to do this kind gesture for me? It can cost you a priceless spy and ally."

"I did it to please you and win your affection. I suddenly find that you're more important to me than her stolen secrets. With our new truce, things have settled down, so I don't have to keep a close watch on their doings. Besides, Cass is so vain that she needs my boasting on her skills to stroke her enormous ego. And she needs certain products that I make."

"This is so exciting, Andrea, here, safe, and . . . happy of sorts." She hugged him and thanked him several times, then kissed him.

To cool his ignited passions, the disguised Varian laughed and changed the subject. "We'll reach the boundary in two days, then be at Grandfather's two days later."

Four days . . . The Androasian Empire . . . *Kadim* Maal . . . Her father-in-law . . . What, Jana fretted, would she see, feel, think, and experience in her second alien galaxy?

Part II
Stardust And Shadows

As the playful Gods gather to watch mortals below,
The helpless Fates warns sadly, for only they know:
Casting out ''Stardust'' demands love and life;
Fleeing its ''Shadows'' creates bitter strife . . .

Chapter Eight

"You were unusually quiet last night and this morning," Varian observed the following afternoon. "Is something troubling you, Jana?" After having been so warm and responsive, she was now distant and reserved. He worried over this new mood.

She glanced at him with a look of remorse. "I can't get Andrea off my mind. She's so close and yet so far away. If I could just see her and talk with her for five minutes, I'd feel better. I've missed her. I'm sure she's scared after being kidnapped, hauled to another galaxy on a spaceship, and placed on an alien colony. I know you said she was told the truth about me and the plight of Earth, but seeing each other would help both of us."

He realized she was telling the truth, and he was relieved. "That isn't possible at this time, and I can't promise it will be even possible later. If Project Starguard succeeds, the Earthlings may be returned home afterward. Hadn't you rather that happen than her to be relocated here?"

"Of course!" she replied in a rush. "She has family there. I didn't," she explained to soften the scornful tone of her voice. "But knowing she's near makes me homesick and sad. It reminds me of all that was taken from me because of my capture. We're closer than most sisters, have been best friends since we were twelve years old. We shared everything. I want to see her, hug her, and talk with her, if only for five minutes."

"I can only imagine how you're feeling and I'm sorry that news of Andrea has made you sad instead of happy."

"I am relieved she's there. If Earth isn't saved . . ."

He clasped her hands in his for comfort. "I know. But don't worry, I'm sure it will be. After our return home, write your message to her and give it to me. I'll do my best to find a way to get it to her after Cass settles down and is willing to do me another favor."

"That bitch would only read it, laugh, and tear it up! I don't trust her and I don't want her knowing anything about my feelings."

"Are you suffering so much, Jana love? Are you so miserable with me? Your life here could be far worse. I'm doing my best to help you."

Their troubled gazes fused. "I didn't mean it the way it sounded. I meant loneliness for Andrea and my possessions, for my other friends, my horse, my home, my servants, the ranch hands, my job, all those things and people I lost. But you're wonderful. I wouldn't want to live anywhere or with anyone here except with you."

The apparent honesty of her last two sentences tormented Varian. "Your home and future are with me, Jana; I hope you believe that."

"I do. Please forgive this sorry mood I'm in today."

"I understand, so there is no need to apologize or make yourself feel worse." He could make her feel worse if he told her that Tristan, Martella, and Nigel had been assigned to Anais now because of the outbreak of a disease and a secret attack by men from a neighboring galaxy. The story he had told her about one of her inoculations not taking had happened to the Earthlings on the colony. A medical technician had failed to include one of the serums during decontamination and inoculation processes. Illness had spread rapidly among the unprotected aliens. Fortunately, none had died and all were almost well now, thanks to Dr. Tristan Zarcoff's skills. In addition, there was that military security problem with a ship of Zenufian slavers who had gotten wind of their presence, no doubt from Canissia Garthon. The criminals, thanks to Nigel, had been thwarted and captured. An elite security team was enroute to the colony to safeguard it after Nigel, Tris, and Martella left on the mission to the Milky Way Galaxy. Nigel was to serve as commander and Tris as doctor on one of the other starships, with Martella in charge of security on the *Wanderlust*. It was obvious from his best friend's words that Nigel wanted to remain on Anais for as long as possible, getting to know Andrea McKay. Varian wished he could tell Jana that new friendship—and possibly romance—was why Andrea was so happy in her strange surroundings.

"Do you mind if I ask?" Jana inquired when he did not respond.

"Ask what?" he replied when she caught his strayed attention.

"What happened during that week I can't remember?"

Varian came to alert and thought quickly. "We played *laius* several times, once for your ring, swam, took a tour of Darkar and the research complex, rode *esprees* twice, talked about our pasts and a great many other things of interest, made plans for our future, spoke of eventually having children, and . . ."

"And what? Why did you halt? Please continue. I need to know."

"We agreed to take our relationship slowly while we got to know each other. We decided it would help if we didn't rush things. Since your illness and recovery, we've gotten carried away because we both needed affection, reassurance, and hope. It might be wise to slow down again so we'll have a better chance of getting closer without the pressure of intimacy. Besides, we don't have to make love every time we hug or kiss. We need to be friends first, Jana."

She warmed to his kindness and patience. She smiled. "The old strategy of appreciating and wanting something more if one has to wait and work hard for it?"

"That's an excellent description and a good theory. It probably works."

She laughed and suggested, "By all means, Ryker, let's try it as an experiment. Think of the new experiences and fun we'll have pursuing each other."

Varian assumed she was behaving this lighthearted way because she was relieved to have any sexual pressure taken off her. He warmed and relaxed, too. "So, I have a stimulating adventuress for a wife."

Jana fluffed his blond hair and grinned. "Why not? Before coming here, most of my time was spent in classes, on long hours of studying to become the best researcher possible, and working in labs with specimens, usually alone. All that solitary time got me into a bad habit of talking to the animals and to myself. Perhaps I did it to hear a human voice in so much silence or to impress facts into my head. I remember one of my grammar school teachers telling us that saying things aloud helped us learn faster and better than just reading silently. Many friends and co-workers have teased me about that weird habit. I have another bad flaw, which is analyzing things to death. I think I'd be better off if I accepted things and people at face value rather than delving too deeply into the whys and wherefores of everything."

"Those aren't flaws, Jana; they're results of having a scientific and probing mind. I do the same, but we aren't crazy or . . . weird, wasn't it?"

They shared laughter as each recalled how many times she had been overheard on the *Wanderlust* monitor in her captive's quarters while talking to herself. Jana even remembered telling *Mon Spectre*, as she called the security control officer, that she must break the habit. And she had done so, except during stressful situations when the weakness resurfaced. "I got us off our subject with idle chatter. Where was I? Oh, yes. It's past time for me to get out and taste life, to pick a few forbidden fruits and sample them. I haven't taken many risks or faced awesome challenges."

"I didn't mean for us to live life on the edge of a slippery cliff."

"If I fall, I'll have you there to pick me up, dust me off, and put me on the precipice again. You wouldn't let me get hurt. What force or person would dare threaten the wife of Prince Ryker Triloni?"

"I'm only a man, Jana, one man."

"You are far more than 'only a man,' my modest husband, far more."

"I'm not invincible or immortal. There will always be someone who's fool enough to challenge any power and rank, even mine."

"Only Varian Saar is that big of a fool, and you have a truce with him. No matter how brave he acted, he always feared you. He envied you, too. When he realized he could never defeat you, he came up with the scheme to make you believe he was giving you his most prized treasure for peace."

Varian winced inside. "You are my most prized treasure."

"That's the best part of his failure."

"His failure?"

"He never expected you to fall—" She blushed at her boldness.

"Fall in love with my peace token, his great sacrifice?"

"That was presumptuous and premature talking. I'm sorry."

"Don't be, Jana, it's probably true, or will be soon. Never thought I'd hear myself admit such a thing. Or even feel and think this way. It's scary, so be patient with me."

Jana felt as if she were trembling from head to toe at his confession. So many times—too many times—when she stared into his eyes, she ignored their color and let herself be swept back in time and to another man. That had to cease. "I will be. It might make you feel better to know I'm coming to feel the same way and it scares me. No one wants to feel totally open and vulnerable to the whims of another person or risk having a heart broken if love isn't returned. A big risk of self-inflicted injury is taken when one unleashes emotions to run wild and free, to let someone else take the reins and to control their feelings and lives. I never expected this to happen, not after the way we met. I wish I could remember that lost week because it was a growing time for us and our relationship."

"Then, we plant our seeds again and watch them sprout and blossom."

"Do you have any of that magical maturation formula for emotions?"

"No, and I wouldn't want to rush something so special."

"Nor would I. How about dinner now? I'm ravenous."

The next morning, Jana stood at the *transascreen* in the rec room. The vastness before her was awesome and intimidating. She leaned against it and gazed at the strange sky beyond her. The flesh-colored clouds of long, separate streaks reminded her of a monster's fingers with sharp claws. It was almost as if thousands of planes had zoomed across the heavens and left their jetstreams in lengthy rows that hadn't started to dissipate. She had asked Ryker yesterday why the outer Maffei planets weren't frozen wastelands, as they were so far from solar warmth. Unlike her Milky Way system, he said, this one was in a tighter cluster and most of them had internal sources of heat.

Yesterday, they had been halted by the Alliance Force patrolling the intergalactic boundary. After a few minutes of talk, they had been given permission to cross it into the Androasian Empire, as if any Maffeian would dare halt Prince Ryker Triloni from doing or going as he pleased! She didn't know what awaited her on Tartarus with his people and ruler.

From her habit of talking to herself or specimens in the lab, Jana didn't realize she was speaking aloud. Nor did she know the man in her words was listening, purely by accident this time, and wished he weren't.

"You've made a hard decision, J. G., and you have to stick with it: it's going to take time, heartache, effort, and determination to get over Varian Saar and what he's done to you, but you're winning the battle. It'll require courage and wisdom to let go of the feelings he evoked, the fantasies he inspired, the memories he created. You have to concentrate on a new existence and the man in it. You can't risk losing both—everything—again."

She lifted one hand and stared at it. "Varian is gone like water through your fingers because you couldn't hold on to him. Ryker is your husband, your future. How will you ever know if this marriage can succeed if you don't give it your best shot to make it work? Ryker is who you need, not a traitorous bastard like Varian Saar. You can't help but respond to him. So what does that make you? A passionate woman who wants love from a man who adores you and makes you feel important to him, who lets you be free and proud. And happy, too, if you dare reach for what he's dangling before you."

It sounded so simple, but it wasn't. Besides, if she changed her recent behavior and resisted him, he would suspect something was wrong, and she certainly couldn't use the truth to explain, that she'd believed he was Varian. Her fate was in her own hands for a change. From this moment forth, her actions would determine if she were fortunate wife or unlucky captive. There was only one direction she could take—toward Ryker. She took a deep breath, released it, and left the room to shower and dress.

At his half brother's desk, Varian grimaced and switched off the intercom. He had been searching for Jana to tell her it was almost dinnertime. He feared the flames of their love and passion were burning low. If he waited too long to fan and rekindle those dwindling coals, Jana was lost forever. This assignment was becoming harder and more painful by the day. If he weren't so close to victory, he would . . . Bitterness and resentment took vicious bites from him. He wanted to believe Jana would never stop loving him and wanting him. He wanted to believe she would understand and accept what he had done for this critical mission. He could no longer convince himself of that fantasy, and it hurt him more than anything ever had in his life.

They lay in Ryker's bed, in Ryker's quarters, on Ryker's starship, and beneath Ryker's dark shadow. Both wished they were sprinkled by brain-dazing Stardust so their torment wouldn't be so painful. They were soon cuddled together in search of comfort. Their hands began to move of their own volition, stroking, caressing, fondling. Their lips could not resist fusing in an urgent hunt for peace and distraction. Their garments were discarded without notice. Hands moved over bare flesh. Needs heightened. Passions soared. Desires blazed out of control.

Varian had a desperate need to possess her before they reached Maal tomorrow. He refused to listen to his mind's protests, only to the pleas of his aching heart and throbbing body. He was so hungry for Jana he almost ravished her with his lips and hands. Unable to stop himself, he entered her and rode her with wildness and delight.

In the dark, it was easy for Jana to lie back and enjoy the pleasures she was receiving. It was easy to respond to such intoxicating sensations. It was easy to pretend he was Varian. She was powerless to do anything other than receive and give sensual titillation. She had vowed to test herself to see if she could surrender to him, but that choice had been snatched from her grasp. She wanted to hold back. She wanted to be in control. She wanted to remember he was Ryker, her husband. But her body had needs of its own. Her heart had a mind of its own. A desperate craving uncurled in the core of her womanhood and demanded to be fed.

God help her, in the dark, it was Varian Saar's image that she envisioned! It was his lips, hands, and body stimulating and pleasuring her. He was the one she was making love to. He was the one she wanted and needed. No matter how hard she tried to remember she was with Ryker, it didn't work. His lovemaking was too like his half brother's. His taste and touch were the same. In despair, she prayed that she wouldn't call her husband by his archrival's name. Even in the stirring throes of stunning release, Jana murmured nothing more than, "Love me, love me, love me."

And Varian did, in more than a physical manner. His voice was husky and almost breathless as he whispered, "You're mine, Jana, mine forever."

Time and reality did not exist for a while as they succumbed to the intensity of a love which had reached beyond the planets and stars to unite them as one, to entwine their destinies. For now, they only wanted and needed each other. They were unaware of the forces of evil and treachery that were plotting against them.

Canissia Garthon left her shuttle to join the man awaiting her, a smile upon his face. He was powerful, rich, and elite, ruler in a galaxy. He was the tool with which she would exact her vengeance against Varian and Jana. The ploy racing around inside her head was so clever that she was positive they would never suspect a thing until it was too late to escape, too late to be rescued, too late to survive.

Soon, her evil mind schemed, the loving couple would pay for hurting and humiliating her, pay with their lives and their blood, after hours, or perhaps days, of torture and sadistic pleasures. Her perverted mind could think of so many erotic and wicked things to do to them both. She knew Varian was immune to *Thorin*, but he wasn't resistant to *Jacanate*. She would force the potent aphrodisiac into him and let Jana watch the wild and hungry beast sate the redhead in every way possible. She would not halt the frenzied feeding of her twisted urges until he was exhausted, raw, and unable to service her further.

She would wait until Varian recovered his wits before letting him observe a drugged Jana while several of her crewmen struggled to appease the desires unleashed in the alien witch who had stolen her dreams. With the *Jacanate* coursing through Jana's veins and other similar chemical creams rubbed onto sensitive areas of her alien body, no matter how much she wanted to rebel, Jana would be unable to do anything other than take anything and everything her crewman pushed inside her or did to her and beg for more.

She had just enough of the powerful chemical to punish them both for at least a day. Her body flamed at the vision of the amusements that awaited her at the couple's expense. Before she finished with them, she would force Ryker's complex combination from their lips in order to restock her supply of that and other drugs needed for sexual enslavement and mind control, including *Rendelar*. Cass pushed the last mental picture from her mind, one of Jana being lashed unmercifully with her favorite whip while Varian cringed in empathy. She would shred her past lover's virile body and handsome face as Jana witnessed his agony. She licked her lips in anticipation of having them as her helpless and obedient slaves.

As the ruler stepped forward to greet her, Canissia smiled. "I have valuable news for you today," she said, "more valuable than your empire."

Jana sat in the shuttle as the planet Tartarus loomed closer and closer like a threat she did not understand. She was apprehensive and frightened. Her hands were like ice. She felt shaky and weak. Her heart pounded and her pulse raced. Her mouth and throat were dry. She had the same eerie feeling of impending peril she had experienced that night in Andrea's garden when thugs had attacked her. She had felt it again when three men in silvery jumpsuits with reflective vizards had appeared from nowhere, disintegrated the hoodlums, and captured her. It had assailed her when she saw Varian for the last time on Eire before being sent to Ryker. She had felt it a last time when she had awakened after her hallucination. The sensation of impending doom grew stronger as the craft moved through wispy clouds toward a landing grid. She shuddered.

"Cold?" Varian asked as he placed his arm around her shoulders.

"Just nervous," she lied, and forced out a weak smile. How could she tell him his world made her feel as if she were about to face a firing squad? How could she explain her sudden, inexplicable terror?

"There's no need to be afraid, love. Grandfather will adore you, as I do. We'll only be here for three days. Relax and enjoy yourself."

Relax? She was trying hard and failing to do so.

The same was true of Varian. He could be walking into the jaws of torture and death if Maal saw through his disguise. Or if that vindictive and desperate redhead had warned the *Kadim* of his treachery. At least Jana was convinced of his fake identity and would pass any drug questioning she would endure if he was exposed. As Ryker's wife and truly believing she was with her husband, she would be safe from all harm. It would be obvious she was not *Rendelar*-immune to *Thorin* so any suspicions of complicity would be dispelled. Only because he was certain she was safe could he allow her to come along and to play a vital role in this daring ruse.

The shuttle flew over tall round and square towers of what appeared to Jana to be made of some unfamiliar metal and glass. As their speed slowed almost to hover level and their altitude was nearly ground-zero, she saw moving sidewalks, trams, and tube cars bustling with people who sent out an impression of somberness. She noticed how few were smiling and laughing; most were reserved and formal, businesslike. She saw minishuttles transporting people from place to place, whizzing here and there like giant insects who could not find a place to light and feast on this arid area. The city in sight was almost stark in its ultramodern design without greenery or various colors to soften its bleak gray facade. Everything looked man-made, with nothing of nature: no trees, no bushes, no flowers, no weeds. What vacuous person, she wondered, had laid out such a verdureless landscape? It was a crowded and busy location, but its sterile and unfriendly feel was apparent even before she stepped into the oppressive setting.

They landed and exited to walk to the huge building ahead. Jana was aware of the military-style androids who had awaited their deboarding and were now escorting them to *Kadim* Maal: big, powerful, silent nonhumans unlike the softer and smaller counterparts on Darkar—Griep, Gar, and Ine—except for their standard yellow eyes and hatless brown hair. Their uniforms were stygian black, and weapons were suspended from belts around their waists. The unit had androids positioned on all four sides, encasing them in a moving box. The unsettling quiet and expressionless mechanisms made her tension increase. She wondered why Maal had not come out to greet them, why he had sent emotionless soldiers to do so. She wanted to turn and run, to escape the foreboding sensation in her gut. Instead, she held her head high, shoulders straight, and complied.

The main door swished open. They stepped into a large entry area that lacked furnishings and decorations. The door behind them thudded shut, almost causing Jana to jump at the loudness in the quiet area. A door before them opened and her husband guided her inside. The soldiers' metal shoes clicked on the marble floor as they led the couple along a lengthy, almost barren hall and into an enormous room. Once inside, doors closed behind them and they were alone.

The interior of the ruler's dwelling was much different from the stark entrance and sterile world beyond the palatial setting. It was opulent and luxurious, and imbued with vivid colors. The plush construction of the furnishings implied comfort and invitation. Paintings, vases with fresh flowers, various-size trees in pots, unusual adornments, and *objets d'art* hung or sat in strategic locations. Plants provided greenery, flowers and accessories offered color, exotic birds and fish supplied beauty, along with music from the winged creatures. Jana wanted to scream to break her tension. She glanced at her smiling husband, and her gaze followed his line of vision to an elderly man, also smiling, who had entered via another door and was coming toward them.

The stranger halted, let his gaze roam the younger man, and smiled again. "Ryker, cherished flame of my soul, it is good to have you home."

As he had viewed on the secret Darkar tapes, Varian used his right hand to clasp the man's left shoulder to gently shake it as if the action was a familiar, affectionate gesture. He smiled. "It's good to be home, Grandfather." Varian had been to this residence and city on official visits. That, in addition to detailed surveillance reports, gave him complete knowledge of the location.

As the two men greeted each other, Jana studied the silver-haired one with faded green eyes that revealed astonishing gentleness, as did his voice and expression. This almost frail looking man was *Kadim* Maal Triloni himself. Since her arrival months ago, she had read and heard a lot about him but had never seen his picture. He was alleged to be cold and calculating and vengeful, but those descriptions did not seem to fit the alien nearby. This mild-mannered and tranquil gentleman, she mused, was the terrifying threat that Maffei feared so much? How so, when he appeared the kind, easygoing, and warm-hearted image of a perfect grandfather? Yet, she mustn't forget he was a very powerful and elite person, a galactic ruler, leader of the Androasian Empire. She must remember that if the Maffeians feared him so much, there had to be a reason, one she might discover during this short visit.

"We have many important things to discuss, but they can wait until later. You have brought a long-awaited treasure for me to meet." Maal faced her and smiled as his pale eyes roved Jana's face. He embraced her. "Welcome to Tartarus and Androas, Princess Jana Triloni. I could hardly wait to meet the woman who has stolen my grandson's eye and heart."

Jana bent slightly from her waist and lowered her gaze for a moment in a show of respect as she had been taught. "It is a great honor and pleasure to meet you, sir. Ryker refused to tell me much about you. He wants me to form my own opinion of you and his homeland."

One gray brow lifted in intrigue, then he grinned in good humor. "What are your opinions of them, Jana?"

"It's too soon to have any, sir. No one should make snap decisions and judgments. But I am sure they will be favorable ones."

The old man grinned again and his green eyes livened with pleasure and amusement. He was attired in an expensive tailored suit that matched his silver hair. His features were aristocratic and his bearing was noble, as befitting his high rank. Jana was most impressed, pleased, and relieved.

Maal looked at Ryker and said, "I see that she has as much wisdom and intelligence as she has great beauty and charm."

The disguised starship commander placed his arm around her waist and drew her close to his body. "She's all of that and more, Grandfather."

Jana watched and listened as the two men laughed and chatted about Ryker's excellent selection of wife and joint ruler. Grandchildren, heirs, and the continuation of their bloodline was mentioned. She perceived an immense mutual pride, affection, and respect between the two men, an easy and undeniable rapport. If she had doubted this blond alien was Ryker Triloni, she could never do so again after witnessing this episode. No matter how skilled Varian was at playing his half brother, he could not fool his own grandfather. Any lingering doubt vanished.

People she would meet, places she would be shown, and things she would do were related briefly to her. Rather, they were spoken of *before* her because it seemed more like they were talking about someone who wasn't present. She told herself they weren't intentionally ignoring her, simply a slip in their excitement. Her husband seemed to prove it when he smiled and drew her close again.

"No female is better qualified to take a place at our sides than she is. She will perform her new duties and responsibilities with perfection, Grandfather, because she *is* perfect. If I had searched the entire Universe, I could not have found a woman to suit me better. Jana is totally satisfying and utterly enchanting. Soon you'll see for yourself."

Maal chuckled and teased, "I need not be told or shown she has woven a spell around my grandson because it is obvious even to these old eyes and aging senses. The fact you chose her and married her reveals her matchless value and superior traits. Before your arrival, I had already seen her potent effect on you, cherished flame of my soul."

As he made his last statement, Maal walked to a nearby table and lifted several pictures. "A hidden reporter took these and sent them to any source who would pay for copies to display across the Tri-Galaxy. It appears to be a private moment in a romantic garden late at night."

The blond alien eyed the pictures and frowned for effect. Yet he was delighted by the unplanned aid to his daring ruse and wished he had thought of it himself. "It was a special moment for us, Grandfather. Have I no privacy anywhere in their galaxy?" He teased Jana, "If my exquisite wife had not distracted me, I would have heard or sensed his brazen presence."

"You must stay on alert at all times when you are away from Androas and Darkar," Maal reminded him. "Never trust them, cherished flame of my soul. They will betray you and try to destroy you before we destroy them. If they had no use for you and what you supply, they would have you slain or expelled. They are blind, stupid fools. One day, those flaws will provide their punishment and destruction. Then I will be happy and vindicated."

"I'm safe, Grandfather. Don't worry about me."

"I cannot help but worry, cherished flame of my soul. You are the last of our bloodline. They humiliated and tormented my only child. They killed her. If they dare harm you, Maffei will be destroyed: every person, every animal, every tree, every insect, every living thing. If all is taken from me, all will be taken from them. Any person or thing that survives my vengeance will become my slave and possession. The Maffeians have grown bold and lax; it would be simple and quick to conquer them. When the right moment arrives, it will be done and victory will be ours."

As Maal spoke, Jana witnessed a startling change in the older man: an intensity and deep-rooted bitterness and hatred. Maal had not forgiven or forgotten the transgressions committed against him thirty-two years and seven years ago, no matter who was to blame for both incidents, be it Shara or Galen or both. In the blink of an eye, she glimpsed another side—a dark and deadly one—of this man. His frail and mild appearance had belied an inner strength of body and mind. All soft and serene lines had become sharp and hostile edges. A violent and savage aura now surrounded him that chilled her to the bone.

Maal was harsh, cold, and forbidding, as Ryker had been at their first meeting. The incident was shocking and disturbing because her husband was not only close kin to this mercurial man, but he also had been reared by this unpredictable and suddenly frightening force, and by his crazed daughter. Jana worried that Ryker might be more like his family than he had revealed to her. She hoped and prayed he wasn't. But that initial scene—the barely clad prisoner in a birdcage in his complex after Canissia had delivered her—stayed foremost in her mind to torment and worry her. Perhaps, she fretted in alarm, this new existence was not as safe as she had led herself—or been led by Ryker—to believe. It caused her to wonder if Ryker had been playacting during the past weeks since her recovery. She couldn't surmise why he would go to such lengths to dupe her when she was under his complete control, actually at his mercy. It could have been to evoke her best behavior during this journey, mainly before the *avatars* and Maffeians. It could have been to stroke his male ego or to taunt Varian.

Jana couldn't prevent a stunning suspicion from storming her mind: as Heather had pointed out, almost everyone had expected Varian to keep her. Ryker had admitted he demanded her in payment for a truce, even called her Varian's "prized treasure." He had said *Kadim* Tirol "had no choice except to do as I asked." Varian had disobeyed orders by taking possession of a *charl*. Had his punishment been to sacrifice her to Ryker to prevent Maffei from being cut off by Trilabs or attacked by Androas? Did Varian secretly love and want— *Stop this, J. G.! Listen to them.*

"Let's not speak of such distressing things on our first day here, Grandfather. We have time to discuss them later, in private."

Jana saw the silencing nod that Ryker directed to the old man to signal a stop to the revealing talk. Maal grasped his meaning and complied. She watched Maal's other, gentle, side returned in a blink.

"This should be a happy occasion. Will you have a servant show Jana to our suite so she can settle in before tonight's activities?"

"It will be done, cherished flame of my soul." He looked at Jana. "You are free to go where you wish inside the palace," he told her. "But if you desire to venture outside, you must take guards with you as escorts and protection. We would not want anything to happen to our finest treasure."

Jana feigned a smile. "You are kind and thoughtful, sir. I will obey you." But she was surprised by the caution. She wondered if Maal was plagued by malcontents, rebels, or spies. Here, in the *kadim*'s stronghold? She also wondered how closely her aural device was translating their Androasian words into her English language.

"You must rest and settle in, my new daughter. I have planned a busy evening. There will be a grand reception honoring the marriage of my cherished grandson and future heir, and the first visit of our beloved Jana. We have a special guest tonight, Ryker, one who will surprise you."

Varian looked at the ruler who had called him by name for the first time. "Who is it, Grandfather?"

Maal grinned and winked. "Wait and see."

Varian hoped his sudden apprehension and alarm didn't show. He prayed that Canissia hadn't sneaked here and was waiting to pounce on him and expose him at the party tonight. But if that she-creature had stolen across the boundary and was hiding in the palace, she hadn't revealed his ruse to Maal yet, because the ruler had not made any slips. On the other hand, Maal could be very proficient at acting.

The starship commander also hoped the surprise guest wasn't an old or close friend of Ryker who would talk about things of which he was ignorant. Nor did he want to put himself in the position of having a medical or scientific discussion in which his mental implants might not be able to provide in-depth knowledge and accurate responses.

If only he knew what was in store for him, for them, tonight.

Chapter Nine

Jana stared into the large mirror as her husband fastened a gem-filled necklace at her throat that matched the royal circlet around her head. *The crown jewels?* she wondered. He handed her matching earrings to don. As she did so, she thought about how simple and efficient it was to create a marriage in this alien society. To become Ryker's wife, all she had done was accept his matrimonial bracelet and sign a document agreeing to become his spouse. The only witness had been a video camera to prove both parties were joining of their own free wills. After he signed the form and it along with the video was registered, their union was legal, almost unbreakable as in the word wed*lock*. Because of who Ryker was, they had signed two documents and made two tapes. One set had been presented to Maffei for their records and one to Androas, so their marriage was exposed and recognized in both galaxies. After she was presented tonight to his people, it would be official. Jana mused: no ceremony, no vows, no flowers, no attendants, no romance, no gay nuptials. Yet, if they desired, couples could have their friends and family present for the signing and banding and for partying. Still, it seemed to Jana too much like a business proposition, a merger, a deed they had gotten down to a cold science.

She looked at the expensive golden gown that Ryker told her had been ordered by Maal and made for her and tonight's special event. The snug bodice with flowing bottom was heavy. The garment had a neckline that was off-shouldered and low cut but not immodest. As she moved, it glittered from reflections of light and made a rustling sound like satin did on Earth. Her tawny tresses had been swept up and placed in leafy curls by a female servant, with the circlet passing through them and across her forehead. Her cosmetics were perfect in colors and amounts, again the work of the reserved alien who had carried out Maal's orders and departed minutes ago. Even a heady perfume had been sprayed in strategic locations on her body, a scent Jana found pleasing. As she studied herself in the large mirror, she admitted the makeup, costly gown, and hairstyle were flattering to her. Without a doubt, she looked regal. She was relieved, because this occasion was so important to her and the two men.

Varian pressed kisses on her nape, bared by her uplifted hairdo, and across shoulders exposed by the gown's design. Her skin was soft and enticing. He could not resist tasting it or touching her. In a husky voice, he murmured, "You are breath- and wit-stealing tonight, Jana of Earth, totally enchanting. Every man present will envy and congratulate me, and every woman will be jealous. You look like a queen instead of a princess. Even the goddess Kimon would envy you, my bewitching angel."

Jana wondered about their ranks. Why did her title and Ryker's translate to "Prince" and "Princess" when Maal's remained *Kadim* instead of King. And why were *kadim*s' first names used after their titles instead of last ones, as with political leaders on her planet? Yet, she reminded herself, English and other royalty used first names, like King Richard or Prince John or Queen Elizabeth or Princess Di.

Before she could query Ryker about those matters, a servant arrived to tell them it was time to make their grand entrance. Jana's apprehensive gaze locked with Ryker's encouraging and comforting one in the mirror. He was magnificent, sexy, virile, and enormously handsome in his matching gold garments that fit like a leather glove. His accessories included a gem-encrusted medallion with symbols unknown to her and a solid gold circlet. "You are the one who is breath- and wit-stealing, my husband," she said, her voice quivering.

"Just be yourself, Jana, and they will love you, as I do."

She turned to face him and search his intense emerald gaze. "I'm scared. I feel as if I'm trembling from head to toe. My hands are like ice."

Varian grasped them, rubbed them with his warm ones, and smiled. He noticed she did not respond to his rash confession, and he was glad. "I promise everything will be fine. Come, everyone is waiting to see my wife, joint ruler of their empire one day. You have nothing and no one to fear."

As they walked down the long hallway, she inquired as a distraction, "Why does *Kadim* Maal call you 'cherished flame of my soul?' "

From notes in Shara's diary, Varian explained, "Because I am the sole reason for his existence. I am the flame in his heart, the blaze that keeps him alive and vital. It is what he called my mother before she died years ago. Afterward, he passed the endearment along to me. I don't care for the name, but it gives him great pleasure, so I say nothing to stop it."

"It's good and kind not to steal joy from others, especially loved ones."

They approached large double doors. He smiled, caressed her rosy cheek, and almost whispered, "Remember, you are my wife, not my *charl* or captive. You are a doctor, a scientist. You are intelligent and well bred. You come from a life of riches and elite status. You are a princess, a future queen, their future *kadimess*. No one will say or do anything to frighten or displease you."

Those words and descriptions did not dispel her anxiety, but she smiled as if they had worked magic upon her fears and tension. Maal joined them via another door. His faded green eyes widened briefly in astonishment. He studied her from head to foot, smiling.

"She is indeed exquisite and perfect, cherished flame of my soul."

"Thank you, Grandfather. I was certain you would be as pleased with her as I am. Are you ready?" he asked Jana, who nodded.

Maal entered the huge ballroom first, easing through a narrow opening that prevented any guest from getting an advance peek at them. The music halted, as did voices and laughter.

The blond alien whispered, "You have filled the last void in my life and heart, Jana of Earth. I do love you, woman."

Jana stared at him. It looked as if he were telling the truth! Before she could think of the right response, she heard Maal's voice.

"Friends, loyal citizens of Tartarus and Androas, my grandson and future *effecta* of our glorious empire, Prince Ryker Triloni, and his bride, my new daughter, Princess Jana Triloni, future *effectass* at his side."

The doors were pulled open by two black-uniformed guards, human ones this time, she noticed. Instruments akin to trumpets filled the area with a royal or state herald. Mouths and eyes went agape and everyone seemed to stare at the Earthling in . . . disbelief and amazement.

Jana's right hand accepted Maal's extended one and let him guide her into the crowded and silent room, all without releasing her grip on her husband's with the left one. She felt Ryker's light squeeze of reassurance, and she returned the gesture. She saw people lean close to whisper an exchange of opinions. She saw men eye her with admiration and desire. She saw women appraising her appearance and no doubt reasoning how a captive had snared the royal treasure from beneath the noses of local seekers. She gathered and returned smiles and nods. She even felt a pinch of jealousy as females raked her husband from head to toe with desirous glances.

In a whirlwind of activity that lasted for almost two hours, Jana was introduced to countless people whose names rushed past her in the flurry of excitement. She received congratulations and best wishes from everyone, as did a beaming Ryker. As he had vowed, no one offended or displeased her by word, expression, or action. The tension and fears quickly left her. This time, she was on display as a richly adorned and beloved princess and wife, not on an auction block as a captive and future *charl*. She was looked upon and treated with respect, admiration, and affection.

Jana could not help but enjoy herself. The heady wine in her grasp and many toasts helped calm her and rose her cheeks. She was grateful her breeding and training on Earth, on the *Wanderlust*, and at Draco's had prepared her for such occasions. She noted with pleasure and delight that the same was true for her handsome husband.

At last, Maal led the couple to a slightly raised dais at the far end of the room. He seated Jana between them. The signal given, everyone took their seats and a fabulous feast was served, accompanied by more wine.

The clever Varian made certain Maal and the Androasians saw how much "Ryker" was in love with his bride by his enamored gazes, possessive touches, undeniably evident words, and other little actions like feeding her bites of food and giving her sips of wine from his glass.

Jana was ensnared in the fantasy world and her wits were dulled by wine and exuberation. It was evident the *kadim* and Androasians liked her and were more than satisfied with Ryker's selection of a wife. He was being so attentive and loving tonight. She presumed he, too, was caught up in the wonder of the special occasion. It was easy to be responsive and adoring in return. She realized they presented the image of a couple deeply in love, and it didn't matter to her if everyone was wrong about her feelings.

"Are you going to let me starve or will you share your treats with me?" he teased to evoke her unknowing assistance with the romantic ruse.

Jana pushed a tiny piece of fruit into her lover's mouth. He captured and kissed each of her fingertips while his smoldering gaze clung to hers. She liked this sunny side of Ryker Triloni, and it warmed her to the core. Whatever she had to do to keep any dark side at bay, she must. She laughed and teased, "Careful, my husband, you are playing with fire and there are no extinguishers around to douse your flames in public."

"How can I help but stay on a slow burn for you?"

"Exile me from sight and release yourself from consuming temptation."

"Never. I want you at my side forever."

"I will remain there as long as you desire it, my love."

"Until the Universe ceases to exist. Is that too long?"

"Eternity is not too long," she replied, a twinge of guilt gnawing at her for deceiving him. If only Ryker didn't make it so easy for her to dupe or want to dupe him. It wasn't fair to him to pretend when she still—God, help her—wanted another man. *Stop it, Jana. This past is over.*

Pictures were taken all evening, some posed and some spontaneous. After dinner, the three went into a room where Jana's hair and cosmetics were freshened by the Androasian woman who had done so earlier. Official portraits were taken: hers, Ryker's, the couple together, and one with the newlyweds and aging ruler.

As she paid a visit to the ladies' room before returning to a dance in progress, Jana told herself their marriage was legal and consummated. Her position as Ryker's wife was exposed and firmly established. *If you could see me now, Andrea, what would you think? Jana Greyson, your best friend, wife to an alien, princess of Androas, future . . .* effectass? She assumed that was the word for queen.

When she left the lavatory, Maal was waiting. She was told Ryker was speaking with old friends and would join them soon. "What is an *effectass* and *effecta*?" she asked, as they hadn't translated to king and queen.

"What the Maffeians call *kadim* and *kadimess*," he replied. "You are not a *prutay* here, Jana. I am sorry you were captured to become one in Maffei. It is a role and destiny beneath you. Your humiliation at their hands is unforgivable and cruel. If Androas suffered a similar plague and problem, if our men could not use their charms to win a mate, they would have none. And would deserve to have none."

"Is a *prutay* the same as a *charl*, a slave mate?"

"Yes, *charl* is what Maffeians call their captive breeders. Come, let us join the celebration. We should not speak of troubled times tonight. You have made my grandson happy. For that, I thank you and love you. It is good to have a ray of sunshine here again."

"I am most grateful for my generous reception by you and your people. I will do my best to make all of you proud of me. Soon, my study of your language will begin and I won't offend your ears with Maffeian words."

Maal smiled. "Do not worry over a problem that does not exist. It is good to know the language, customs, and laws of rivals and enemies."

As Maal led her back into the ballroom, Jana wondered why Ryker had spoken in Maffeian to her earlier. Why hadn't he used the Androasian words for *kadim* and *charl—effecta* and *prutay*—words untranslatable by the aural device into English? She guessed it was because time for explanations didn't exist and he knew she was familiar with those Maffeian words.

Seated at their head table, Jana's probing gaze located her husband. As she eyed the two conversing men, Maal revealed the identity of the one with brown hair and a short beard.

"That is the other special guest this evening, the one I mentioned to Ryker this afternoon: Dakin Agular."

"Are they old friends?"

"Only acquaintances. Agular presses me almost daily to make peace with the Maffei Alliance. Our old truce has expired and the Supreme Council has offered us another one. I have not accepted or signed the papers. I must keep a close watch on him. If things do not go as he wishes, I suspect he might inspire a rebellion against me. Agular and his faction are slow to challenge my rule and decisions because they will not go against me rashly because of Ryker's powers. I am certain he is trying to convince my grandson to persuade me to sign the treaty. I invited him so Ryker could study his threat to us and to confuse Agular with our friendliness."

Jana studied the fiftyish-looking man who was clad in sapphire. This was perhaps why Maal had said she needed guards if she left the palace, to avoid being taken captive by rebels, by his political rival, perhaps his enemy. If Androas and Maffei clashed, with their starships and advanced weapons, it would be a massive battle. "War is a terrible and costly conflict. No one should enter it lightly. If one can obtain peace with honor, one should do so. On my planet, we have had many rebellions and coups d'état. They resulted in great losses of life and destruction of property. Wars are cruel to families, *Effecta* Maal; please try to prevent an intergalactic one."

"You spoke the important word: honor. Maffei has attacked our honor in the past and must never do so again. Remember what they did to you."

"That was before Ryker and I met. If it hadn't been for the Maffeians, we would never have met; I would not be here tonight. My father taught me there is always something good, however small, hidden in bad things. All one has to do is look for it and draw it out. If everything was good and successful, life would become boring. Bad things and defeats give us our challenges, make us stronger and wiser, make us appreciate the good more. If people ignore and resist the values and powers of love and peace, many suffer because of such blindness and actions."

"You speak and think as my beloved Shara did before the Maffeians shamed and killed her. It is good to dream, Jana, but it is not reality."

Jana saw the man's pale eyes chill with bitter memories. She realized his dark side would surface soon if she didn't change the subject. "Will you ask the servant to refill my glass?" she asked. "My throat is dry. As soon as it's refreshed, shall we dance, sir?" She was relieved the ploy worked.

* * *

Agular urged the man he thought was Ryker, "You must convince *Effecta* Maal to sign the treaty. We have not known war in our galaxy for a long time. Our people want to keep it that way, Prince Ryker. Many think your grandfather is still too consumed by hatred for the last remaining Saar and the Alliance to think clearly, to rule at his best, and to keep them safe from harm. He must let the past die; to continue his personal rivalry and hatred is dangerous to the Empire. If we are forced into a war with the Alliance, the bloodshed and destruction will be catastrophic. If we ally ourselves with the Pyropean Federation, we could not trust them. They would use us to defeat Maffei, then attack us. You are the only one he will listen to. He closes his ears to his advisers and even to his friends. Persuade him to stop this madness before it is too late."

Varian was tempted to use this political rival to provoke a rebellion in Androas to keep it busy while he and their starships were away. He knew it was wrong to endanger innocent lives for a personal motive and he realized the man before him was the perfect replacement for Maal. The question was how he could get Agular into power and Maal out without inspiring a rebellion here. With caution, he replied as Ryker would or should, "I am not ready to commit to assisting you at this time, Agular. Yet, I believe what you say and it sounds wise to me. I don't want to begin an impulsive war with the Alliance. I will ask Grandfather to reconsider his plans and to sign the treaty. If nothing more, I might convince him to delay them."

Agular's gray eyes filled with amazement. "You've changed since your marriage, Prince Ryker. You were always in favor of war when the right time came. I am glad you've changed your mind."

"My wife is responsible. She has me thinking of home, family, and peace these days. We have a good life on Darkar, so I'm more inclined to keep it that way than to disrupt it.

Besides, your arguments are valid: war costs many lives and much damage. I don't want that for my people."

"Your new wisdom and compassion please me, Prince Ryker. Your grandfather is getting old and must step aside soon. A strong and prosperous empire needs a strong and clear-headed ruler."

"Like you, Dakin Agular."

The older man looked alarmed. "I did not mean—"

Varian interrupted. "It was not a question; it was a statement. You would be a perfect replacement. You know more of our needs and politics than I do. I have been away for a long time. Grandfather does not know I prefer being who and what I am over becoming a galactic ruler. When the time comes to confess that truth to him, I will back you as the next *effecta*. That is, if you are interested and willing." From surveillance reports, Varian decided, this Androasian was the best man to take over the Empire.

Agular was astonished and relieved. "I am honored by your words, Prince Ryker. Perhaps we can meet tomorrow and discuss this further?"

Plans were made for a rendezvous the next afternoon.

Jana danced with many men and chatted with many women. Finally she excused herself once more to freshen up and catch her breath. She was having a good time, but it was late and the golden gown was getting heavier by the minute. The music was nice, but she would love to hear some of her favorite songs and singers from Earth: Barbra Streisand, Lionel Richey, Neil Diamond, and Kenny Rogers. She would love to dance just once to an old Bee Gees tune. She would love to strip off her clothes and shoes, climb onto her bed with a Classic Coke and popcorn, and watch a videotaped movie from Earth. It would be nice if some had been stolen along with her to provide a comforting link to her lost world. She recalled a favorite movie from her personal collection: *Starman* with Jeff Bridges and Karen Allen. It was the story of an Earthling and alien visitor who met and fell in love and shared dangerous adventures. Their love had been bittersweet and ill-fated from the beginning and had ended with the heroine losing the hero forever, as had her own torrid love affair with an extra-terrestrial. She loved science-fiction novels and movies, but had never imagined she would step into the pages or onto the live set of one. She had never imagined meeting a single alien, much less thousands of them.

That reminded Jana she should return to her duties in the ballroom. When she did, the blond alien swept her into his arms and around the dance floor. They moved as one, flowing like a glider in a serene sky. They talked, laughed, and smiled. He pulled her closer and she nestled against his stalwart body. She rested her head against his chest. His hands released her arms so they could band her body. She moved hers to the areas between his shoulders and neck. As one song and dance drifted into another, no one dared to interrupt the dreamy couple until three dances later when Maal approached them and said it was time to end the evening's festivities. Usually no guest departed before an elite host left the room, which was the signal that gave permission for them to do so. Jana, Ryker, and Maal walked to the double doors. They turned for a moment to smile and wave their farewells, then entered the hallway.

Varian grinned and teased, "See, you returned in one piece."

Jana sent him a radiant smile. "It was wonderful, but I'm exhausted. This gown weighs a ton by now."

"Then, by all means, let's get you to our room and out of it."

Jana blushed. "Ryker!" she scolded, but couldn't halt her grin. It was pleasing and flattering that he seemed so proud of her.

Maal chuckled and said, "Do not worry, Jana. I am only pleased that he has controlled his desire for you long enough to do his duty tonight. I will see you at lunch. I am sure you will wish to sleep late tomorrow. Good night, cherished flame of my soul. Good night, daughter."

In their suite, Ryker helped Jana out of the gown and jewels. He laid them over a chair for a servant to tend tomorrow. As he began to undress for bed, Jana said, "I'm going to take a quick shower and brush my hair. I'll sleep better that way."

"Sounds like a good idea," he murmured and continued his task.

Jana went into the bathroom, and the door swished shut behind her. She took a quick and thorough shower, dried off, and donned a nightgown. She removed the pins from her hair and brushed it free of curls. She washed the cosmetics from her face and rubbed lotion into her bare skin. As a last act, she sprayed on a little more of the perfume. She suspected Ryker would make love to her. When she entered the bedroom, only one lamp was on, and Ryker was asleep. Jana was surprised but not disappointed. She was fatigued, ready for slumber. She eased into the bed, switched off the light, and settled down to seek it. Her final thought before slumber was: *It's done; it's legal; I'm Jana Triloni forever.*

On his side and facing away from her, Varian grimaced in self-denial. She was tired and it was late, too late to begin a bout of lovemaking. Besides, she had prepared herself to join bodies and share passions with Ryker, not with him, and that nipped at his male ego and tormented him. Yet, it had been a good day. They had played their roles with perfection tonight and he was tranquilized by success. He had known of Agular's existence and position but hadn't expected it to work in his and Maffei's favor, not this soon. Tomorrow, "Ryker" would strengthen his bond with that valuable ally. From the way things looked, his ruse was working and his mission here was headed for a quick victory. When it and Project Starguard were finished, he could claim the woman at his side. That glorious and joyful moment could not come fast enough to suit him.

Jana awakened, yawned, and stretched as she glanced at the empty spot beside her. She waited a few minutes before rising to see if Ryker was in the bathroom, as she didn't want to walk in on him at a private moment. She was surprised he had fallen asleep last night after being so romantic all evening. Perhaps while awaiting her return he had been lulled into slumber by the fatiguing activities of the evening and an excess of wine.

After she bathed and dressed, she went in search of him. A servant told her the two men had gone out earlier and would return for lunch. She ate alone, then began a tour of the palace, after querying about any spots to avoid. The palace was enormous and lovely and she took a leisurely stroll through it. When she reached one particular room, she stared inside before entering, then, with reluctance, she approached the glass tomb where Princess Shara Triloni lay resting for all eternity. She leaned forward for a good view of the woman who had almost provoked an intergalactic war over an ill-fated love affair with Commander Galen Saar of the Maffei Alliance Star Fleet. Jana's curious gaze slowly studied the alien female who looked forever young and beautiful.

The woman's features were exquisite and flawless. Her skin was shaded like warm honey, as was her long hair. Her perfect mouth was painted with mauve lipstick, her high cheekbones ever so lightly brushed with soft pink. Her lashes were long and thick and lay like tiny black feathers against her flesh. The shadowing above her eyes was in emerald green and had to match those closed orbs. Her hands were crossed at the wrists—small and dainty ones—over her lifeless heart. Nails were polished in mauve like her lips. She was clad in a fitted green gown that evinced a stunning figure that had probably driven many men wild with lust, but only one that Jana knew of had possessed her. Shara looked so tranquil, so ladylike, so regal. She was the embodiment of innocence and purity.

Jana realized they did have the same coloring and body size, but they didn't favor each other as she'd been told several times. She was nothing like this alien, sly enchantress and would never become remotely like her. At that insulting thought, she reminded herself that her bad opinion of Shara Triloni stemmed from a delusion and from the alien's crimes years ago. Shara had not tried to murder her and had not been her son's mistress. The evil and cruel woman she had met during her hallucination did not exist.

Jana wondered what Shara had been like and how Galen's loss and perhaps treachery had affected her, besides provoking the princess to a double murder and suicide. While talking with Maal last night, his eyes had become dewy and he had told her she was speaking and thinking like his daughter. That had to have been before this ravishing creature went insane. Crimes of passion had been exposed in American papers and television with frequency, so it wasn't only an alien flaw. Yet, Jana could not imagine slaying in cold blood someone you had loved and had bonded with in bed. Despite her many charges against Varian, she could never murder him.

Shara looked peaceful and radiant to Jana, as if only asleep. She wondered if Varian's father had fallen in love with the princess in his charge, or simply sought an illicit and brief affair, or had been drug enslaved by her as was his defense. Had Galen used and betrayed Shara's love long ago as his son had done to her recently? A Saar had taken possession of the last and the current Androasian princesses . . .

Jana turned to leave the haunting place. Her gaze found a portrait on the wall. Stunned by what she saw, she approached it and gaped in disbelief. Anger and suspicion soon joined her initial emotion. In the portrait, Shara was wearing the same golden gown and jewels she herself had worn last night, or replicas of them! No wonder everyone had stared when she appeared, like a ghost from their past.

Jana vowed between clenched teeth that she would not become a replacement for Shara to Ryker, to Maal, or to the Androasians. She was upset that her husband would allow her to dress and be adorned as his mother had been long ago. She would demand an explanation later.

Jana stalked down the hallway and was halted by the sounds of birds. She entered a large room filled with cages, some fashioned in glass and some in wire. She looked at the exotic birds, the unusual fish, and other familiar creatures, then stopped at the *scarfelli*'s dwelling. She bent over and stared at the hairy spiders as large as cats. She remembered the terror tactics well from the *Wanderlust*.

"You shouldn't be staring at them, Jana. You told me they frighten you. I remember how you said Varian used them on his ship."

Jana glanced at her husband as he came forward with a smile. "Do they ever capture and devour people?"

"No, *scarfelli* are vegetarians. See," he said, and pointed to their feeding area at one end of the cage where fruits and vegetables were piled.

"It gives me the creeps to think of one of them crawling over me. To be attacked by a group of them, encased in a cocoon, and hauled into their den must have been sheer terror for Sylva. That was so cruel of Varian."

He winced inside. "You said the defiant Uranian gave him no choice, and he didn't really have her killed."

"We always have choices in what we do, Ryker," Jana refuted. "He could have confined her to the brig as he did in secret without terrifying her and the rest of us with his sadistic demonstration."

"It worked, didn't it? No one else disobeyed or rebelled. Afterward, every captive did her best to become her best. Isn't that what you said?"

She had told him the details of that scary incident. "Yes, but . . ."

He didn't like her remembering such rash times. "But what?"

"That doesn't excuse his cruelty. He kidnapped us and was forcing us to train to become breeders to aliens in another world. How did he expect us to feel? I would bet my life neither he nor you would accept captivity without a fight or an attempt to escape."

"That's true. But there comes a time when wisdom must overshadow pride and make us do whatever is necessary to survive."

She almost shrieked at him for seeming to defend his half brother's wicked actions. "Survival at any price, is that what you're saying?"

"Survival to battle an enemy another day, Jana, that's different."

"Some enemies can't ever be battled again."

"There are ways to defeat or punish a foe besides killing him—"

"Ah, there you two are," Maal interrupted as he entered the room. "Ryker, go and tell the cook to serve lunch. I will escort Jana to the dining room myself."

The blond alien nodded and left them alone. "I see you found my collection," Maal said. "Do you like it? The *urikeah* are fierce looking but very gentle." He lifted a lid and stroked several of the hairy spiders.

Jana was intrigued. "What did you call them?"

"*Urikeah*."

"There were some on the *Wanderlust* called *scarfelli*."

"That is what the Maffeians call them. Come, lunch is ready."

Jana took his arm and let him guide her to the dining room. Again, she wondered why Ryker had spoken to her in Maffeian.

In their suite later, Jana summoned the courage to ask about the gown and jewels she had worn last night and revealed her motive for the question.

Even without having read Shara's diary, Varian knew the correct answer. "Of course they were like Mother's; that is the traditional wedding garment of the Trilonis and those are the royal jewels. If you had made your way to the ancestral gallery in the other wing, you would have seen that all Triloni brides were attired in replicas of the 'Golden Dream.' The portrait hanging near her tomb was taken before she left to marry Supreme Ruler Jurad Tabriz of Pyropea. Mother never wore it again because she never made it to her wedding there. It was not her gown you wore last night; it was *yours*. I'm sorry I didn't think to explain it. The portrait of you made last night will be hung with the rest in the gallery. I'll show them to you tomorrow." He grasped her hands and vowed, "I did not choose you to take Shara Triloni's place in our lives; you are nothing like her, Jana of Earth."

"I'm the one who should apologize, Ryker. It's just that so many people gossiped about me replacing her that when I saw the portrait . . ."

He pulled her into his embrace. "I understand. Don't let it trouble you further. Besides, you need a clear head for a challenging task. I told Grandfather how good you are at *laius* and he wants to play with you this afternoon while I visit friends. Are you game, Jana?"

"Yes, that sounds like a pleasant diversion."

As Jana took her place at the table, Maal smiled and said, "I am happy you accepted my invitation to play *breeli* while Ryker is gone."

"*Breeli*? I thought we were playing *laius*."

"We are."

Jana concluded she must tell her husband to start speaking to her in Androasian instead of Maffeian so she would know what everyone was talking about when they used words that did not translate into English.

At dinner, Jana looked at Maal and grinned. "Your grandfather told me all about you while we played *breeli*," she teased Ryker.

"Everything?" he hinted with a mirthful tone. He was in a good mood because his meeting with Dakin Agular had gone well. And they only had one more day to spend with Maal. He was more than ready to leave and end this constant and draining state of alert.

"Almost everything. He said his grandmother knew ancient

secrets of plants and animals, that she passed them to his mother, who passed them to his daughter, who passed them to her son. He said he gave you the best teachers and books in all known worlds. He said you were smart and studied all the time. That must be why you're so intelligent, my husband.''

''When my grandson moved to Maffei, I was pained by his loss.''

''You haven't lost me, Grandfather. I visit you often.''

''Now that you are married, you must visit more often and stay longer. I am getting old and weak, cherished flame of my soul. Soon you will take my place and rule Androas for us, with my new daughter at your side. With all you know and possess, we will be all-powerful, invincible.''

''Do not speak of such things, Grandfather; you have many years ahead to serve our Empire. And I have much work to do elsewhere.''

Jana perceived an unspoken message passing between the two men. She suspected something was afoot. Would they tell her about it? When?

The next day, the disguised Varian related startling news to *Kadim* Maal Triloni. He knew from a tape of the older man's last visit to Ryker on Darkar and from notes in Shara's journal that Maal had been informed of the first mission to Earth and of an impending second one. He knew from those sources that an attempted conquest of Maffei was to coincide with the absence of many powerful starships during that future voyage. He told Maal about the misidentification and miscalculation in timing of the rogue worldlet on an elliptical orbit around Jana's sun which placed the rogue on a crash course with Earth in less than six weeks. ''It isn't coming from deep space as they believed, Grandfather, and its speed has changed. They were too rushed and didn't study the threat closely enough. The team of scientists and remote probes they sent out after Varian's return found their errors. They plan to strike at it between the fifth and sixth planets of that solar system. We have known about this situation before the time I met Jana, not when they communicated their order to me this morning. Varian was to lead the attack on it, but I am taking charge of Project Starguard. A success will prove my friendship to Maffei and will eat at my brother's gut."

Maal focused a pale-green gaze of confusion on his grandson. "When did you come up with this wild idea and make this bold decision?"

"The idea has been whirling around inside my head for two weeks. I didn't make my decision until I was speaking with Breccia Sard earlier. When the Supreme Commander made his request, I pretended to know nothing more than Jana knew and had told me. I accused him of wanting the weapons and chemicals to attack Androas. Of course, Sard denied that provoking lie and was coerced into telling me why he needed them. Naturally he wanted me to believe the lasers would be mounted on shuttles or converted supply ships, not on Star Fleet ships. I told him that was foolish and self-defeating, that only starships have the power and skill to bombard something of that size. I even suggested creating a gravity field to mock a Black Hole between their target and Earth to conceal their presence; with such a field in place, not even a ray of light, much less a laser beam, could pass through it and be seen by the Earthlings. Sard asked why I wanted his starships out of range for so long. After I made my demand to assume control of the mission, I pointed out that Maffei would be safe against any threat from Androas since I would be on one of those starships and could be captured and used to stop any aggression back home. Sard had to discuss it with *Effecta* Tirol and the Council; that's why I didn't reveal it to you after our first communication. When he got back to me in a short time, as expected, they had agreed. They had no choice, if they want the best weapons and only laser chemicals to use."

Maal shook his head of silver hair. "It is too dangerous, cherished flame of my soul. You will be placing your life in their hands. What if they did capture you while you are on their starship?"

Varian chuckled as he had seen his half brother do many times. "They're not total fools, Grandfather. They need Trilabs. *I am* Trilabs. Without me, it is useless to anyone, and a peril to them. I won't be harmed, and there is great value in my going as leader. By taking command of the project, I can glean Maffei's vital military secrets and strategies. I can discover their firepower, witness their battle tactics, see how their starships work together, and observe the skills of their commanders. I can learn of any new or improved weapons, and how much of a stockpile of existing ones they have. Besides, Grandfather, it's Jana's world and people; think how happy it will make my new wife for her beloved husband to save them rather than her despised captor and tormentor. I can humiliate and anger my rival by stealing his place. For me to take charge of this grand mission will annoy and anger Varian and the Alliance. I have taken Jana from Varian; now, I can have my final revenge on him."

"Why did you really take Jana Greyson from Varian?"

Dark-green eyes fused with pale-green ones. *Remember, respond as Ryker might.* "Because my brother loved her and wanted to keep her."

"The rumors of his enchantment by her were true after all, as you suspected. After meeting her, I understand how that could occur. Does your wife know the truth of the matter?"

"No, and she will never be told of his love and reluctance while I am alive. Jana hates him and believes he used and discarded her under the guise of obtaining a private truce with me to end our personal war. Since that is the story my brother was forced to relate, she accepts it as truth. Too, she is aware that he is marrying Cass soon. Jana must never know I demanded her in exchange for peace and supplies for his world, not for a truce with an archrival and foe I can defeat with my bare hands at any time I choose. You have been told the public story of how she was allegedly freed for saving *Effecta* Tirol's life, ran away, then met and married me."

"Why did she agree to marry you, cherished flame of my soul?"

Varian used the reasons he had witnessed on the secret videotape of the conversation in which Ryker had convinced Jana to wed him. "But we quickly realized neither of us wanted a marriage in name only. We realized how well matched we are. As the weeks passed, Grandfather, we were drawn together as metal to magnet, as water to sponge. She is my destiny and I am hers. We both realized and accepted that truth." Varian feigned an expression that came easy for him in its verity. "The first time we kissed, we flamed with passion. The first time we made love was the most glorious experience either of us had ever known. When she looks into my eyes, I know without a single doubt or word spoken that she loves, desires, and needs me. When we unite our bodies, she shares in a special way only a woman who loves me beyond question could do. I feel the same way about her. At first, it was scary to love her and want her so much, but now, it is exciting and fulfilling. How incredible and unexpected it was to find such powerful and rewarding and perfect love. It is even stranger that I have my half brother to thank for bringing her into my life."

"What if Varian feels and thinks the same way about her, cherished flame of my soul? What if he wants her returned? What if he changes his mind and breaks his promise about telling her the truth?"

"He won't, Grandfather. He loves her enough to spare her that pain, because true love is unselfish. Until Jana, I never realized someone else's happiness and survival, besides that of family, could be more important to me than my own. Even though he loves her and may have grasped his great mistake by now, he would never accept her back after I've possessed her."

"Why not? It did not bother you to take her after he had, did it?"

Varian frowned, then grimaced. "At first, but no longer. In the beginning, I told myself I had to have her as pain and punishment to Varian. When I made him my offer, he couldn't refuse because he wanted peace for his world and thought he was making a supreme and unselfish sacrifice for it. He and the Council knew I would refuse them my products in the future and probably provoke you to move against them if I was refused Jana. It did not take long after she was in my possession for me to comprehend why I truly wanted her. Besides, Grandfather, my half brother couldn't accept the fact he loved an alien *prutay*. He resists believing he can't live without her. He is going to be shocked to learn, if he hasn't already, that it's impossible to forget Jana Greyson once she's in your blood. That's probably why he's rushing into this marriage with Cass, to convince himself and others that Jana means nothing to him. He'll fail, but it's too late."

"Are you certain he will not slay you to get her back?"

"I am certain, Grandfather, for three reasons: One, he knows Maffei needs Trilabs products desperately. Two, he wouldn't risk provoking you to war with Maffei to avenge my death. And three, Varian could never bring himself to enter a paradise I have visited so frequently. He has too much pride, too much hatred of Trilonis, and too much obedience and love for the Alliance to risk destroying them over a woman. Yes, I am certain."

"What will he do when you break your truce with him? When we attack Maffei while their starships are gone, if he doesn't go with them, he will be there to plan and lead their defenses. He will strike at Darkar and capture your wife, and the crew of the ship you command will capture you. How can I fight with my only two loved ones in peril?"

Now that Varian was assured of Jana's safety against Maal's retaliation and of her future ownership of Ryker's powerful estate, it was time to see if his daring plan would work to keep Maffei safe. "Grandfather, I want you to postpone any attack against Maffei while I'm gone, and I don't want you to form an alliance with the Pyropean Federation." He witnessed Maal's stunned expression. "The Tabrizes cannot be trusted. Prince Taemin's dream is to conquer and rule the Tri-Galaxy, all of it, Grandfather, including our Empire. They want us to fight the main battles for them. When the war is over and while we are recovering and vulnerable, Pyropea will attack us. I have obtained this information from spies planted there, so I know it is true. I say, let the Pyropeans challenge and battle Maffei for us. As long as the Alliance is punished, since that is your wish, it should not matter to you who does the fighting. The battle will weaken the Pyropeans enough to prevent any threat to us from them."

"What do you mean by, it is *my* wish? It is yours, too."

Varian summoned the courage to refute. "No, Grandfather, it is not. I say that a real truce and peace with Maffei is in Androas's best interest, for now anyway. War is a serious and dangerous matter; it must not be rushed into while we are ignorant of their strengths. A wise man would not attack a foe in the dark and while he, himself, is vulnerable. I have come to realize that personal revenge and intergalactic war are two different matters. If you do not change your mind, at least let them have their treaty while I glean their secrets and Androas grows stronger."

"You mean, *cancel* the attack, not delay it?" Maal almost shouted.

"We must think of what is best for the Empire, Grandfather, not of sating our private hungers. I have discovered that Maffei is much stronger than we realized. A victory would not come quickly or easily, and a defeat could be ours. Have you forgotten the rebellion threat here? Our people do not want war, Grandfather, especially over a personal matter from the distant past. They could refuse to fight and could depose you for ordering the battle. Is your hatred and hunger for revenge so great you would risk everything to appease them? Have they not been amply fed to date? Galen Saar was punished by death for his crimes against us; Tirol was punished with the losses of his daughter and law-son for his refusal to discredit and exile my father. Maffei has suffered because of those deaths and scandal. Even Varian has been tormented by Mother's murderous deed. The Alliance has been cowered by their need and acceptance of Galen's bastard. I took from my half brother—Galen's heir—the possession he loved and desired most. He must agonize every day and night knowing I have Jana. We have drawn heart's blood from those responsible for Mother's shame and death. We must not use the innocent blood of our people to extract more torment from our enemies and their heirs."

"You no longer wish to conquer and destroy them?" he asked in confusion. "You are the one who kept the dream of revenge alive."

"I know, Grandfather, but things have changed for me; *I* have changed. When I was trying to figure out the best way to reveal our plans to Jana, I realized an assault on Maffei and the subsequent provoking of an intergalactic war sounded drastic, cruel, and irrational as a way to settle an old score. Jana has a tender heart and gentle spirit, Grandfather; she would never understand our manner of seeking vengeance for an old crime against us. Many of the women—*prutays*—living in Maffei are from her world. Many of their present civilization were not present when this conflict began long ago. Too many innocents would die along with the guilty. We have lived only for future revenge for too long. It is time to end it."

"So you told Jana nothing of our plot?"

"No, Grandfather, I could not tell her. Before I met Jana, families and taking risks meant little or nothing to me, only the wrong done to the Trilonis. I wanted to make Galen's son suffer as Mother and I had suffered, and I have succeeded over the years. They took Mother from us, and I have taken Jana from them, though it is not the reason I crave her and married her. Tirol will experience more anguish as he watches his beloved grandson and only heir suffer. Every Maffeian knows I won Jana from Varian, and all *prutay* owners know they freed her to marry me. Since *they* cannot get their mates freed, it will breed resentment and dissension. How can we justify hurting our people to further torment Maffeians? Have we become so blinded and consumed by hatred that we would commit such a grave wrong against our friends? You have been a great ruler, Grandfather; do not end your reign this name-darkening way. Do not force yourself to be remembered and despised as a man who destroyed his people and empire for selfish or irrational reasons. Our people want peace." As a result of his secret meeting with Agular today, Varian knew that was true for most of these people. Yet he also knew that too many Androasians would follow Maal into hell no matter how they felt.

"I had not thought of the matter in such light, cherished flame of my soul. To force Varian to turn his ship and mission over to you will vex him greatly. For you to lead the other ships will humiliate their commanders, crews, the Council, and Star Fleet. It is a cunning idea. If we decided to invade Maffei later, with the information you gather, we will be better prepared to win our challenge. It shall be done as you advise."

Varian tried not to give a sigh of relief. He smiled at the elderly man. "You are wise, Grandfather. Now, I must tell my wife."

Jana was summoned by a servant to the room where the blond alien related his astonishing news.

"You're going to do *what*, Ryker? Surely I didn't hear you right."

"Yes, my love, you did. I am going to take charge of Project Starguard and the *Wanderlust*. I and my weapons are going to save your world and people for you, not that beast who captured you from them. You said you were no sacrifice to Varian, but taking his place, his ship, his glory, and his assignment will sting his pride. It will repay him for what he did to you and others of your race. All he cares about are his duty, mission, rank, and pride. This is the only way I can take them away from him; though it will be for a short time, it will long be remembered."

"*Kadim* Tirol, the Supreme Council, and Star Fleet will never agree."

"They already have, Jana; I gave them no choice in the matter. I told them it was me, my weapons, and my chemicals, or nothing."

She gaped at him. "What if they had canceled Project Starguard rather than allow you to blackmail them into such a humiliating corner?"

"If they had refused, I would have used Androasian ships and crews to carry out the mission. I would not allow your world to be destroyed."

"When did you throw down your gauntlet?"

He waited for her to explain her meaning before he answered. "They contacted me this morning about the weapons and supplies they need. I told them I wanted to lead the mission to save my wife's world."

"How will they explain you as the leader?"

"As the perfect technical adviser required to use my lasers and chemicals correctly. And Varian has the perfect excuse for staying behind: his marriage and honeymoon."

Jana winced inside at that cruel reminder but kept her expression from revealing it. "He's not going at all, not even on one of the other ships?" She watched a grin spread over his handsome face.

"No, because he would never stand behind me and take my orders. There is one thing I know for certain about my half brother: he always follows orders and does his duty. He'll cooperate."

"A man like Varian Saar won't take this slap in the face lying down. I hate to see more bad blood develop between you two because of me. He'll probably think I put you up to this scheme for revenge."

"Will that matter to you?"

"No, not really. In fact, it will be perfect retribution," she lied.

"I promise you, this will settle the matter between us forever."

"How can it when you're challenging and taking all he loves?"

"Any retaliatory threat from him is slim to none, Jana. I promise you." He caressed her flushed cheek and murmured, "Besides, taking Varian's mission will provide a stimulating and exciting adventure, something new and different from anything I've done in the past." He sent her a roguish grin. "You said for us to do the unpredictable, to take risks, to confront challenges. You said you wanted to become an adventuress. Well, woman, here's your opportunity. In addition, my worried wife, something very important to you is at stake and you should witness it."

Witness a possible collision of the rogue with her world if Earth couldn't be saved? Watch the impact and explosion, the total destruction? Observe the Stardusting as a euthanasia process?

Varian saw how concerned she was. "I promise you that no one is more qualified to deal with this threat to your world than I am. We leave in the morning to head straight for Star Base on Rigel. We'll pick up the *Wanderlust* there and depart for your solar system."

"*We*? You mean I am going, too?"

He smiled and stroked her hair. "Of course. You don't think I would leave my prized possession behind and alone, do you? I couldn't endure so many weeks away from my new wife, and she deserves to observe and share this adventure. And, in case Varian does decide to try something foolish in retaliation, you wouldn't be left here alone to handle him."

"He wouldn't dare harm your wife, an Androasian princess."

"His father dared to do so long ago," Maal said in a steel-edged voice. "What is to say Varian is not like Galen was?"

"Galen did not have and need Trilabs as Varian and Maffei do. He can not afford to offend or challenge my husband. Tirol would not permit it."

"My wife is correct, Grandfather." Varian gazed at her and asked, "Does that mean you do not wish to come along, Jana?"

"Certainly not, and I do want to go with you. I would be lonely and afraid alone on Darkar." She smiled and touched his lips. "I would miss you too much to stay behind. I always want to be at your side."

Jana listened as the blond alien chatted with his grandfather. She did not believe or accept what he had told her were his prime reasons. She had a suspicion his motive was to spite his half brother, to taunt Varian by taking his ship and mission after taking his . . . mistress. To make it worse for the Maffeian Commander, Varian would have his hands tied and be unable to do anything about Ryker's bold confiscations. Yet Varian had asked for this trouble by giving her to Ryker, as it had been her traitorous lover's idea and choice. Or had the Supreme Council or *Kadim* Tirol—or both—she mused, compelled him to do so for peace? One point she never doubted: Varian would do his duty and obey orders at any cost. But did she know the real reason behind her being with Ryker now? She couldn't help but suspect there was more to the matter than she'd been told or would ever be told as Princess Jana Triloni.

"I wish you would leave Jana here with me," Maal said.

"I can't, Grandfather. We've only been wed for a short time and I'll be gone for weeks. I want her with me. How could I think clearly with her so far away from me?"

"I understand; the flame of desire burns hot and high at this time. May it do so forever, my cherished children."

"It will, Grandfather, it will. She has touched me as no other woman has or ever will. I trust her with my heart, my life, and all I own. If anything ever happened to me, I have left everything to Jana and our children. She is a scientist like myself; Trilabs will be safe and profitable in her control. See that no one takes anything of mine from her and them. Love and protect my family, Grandfather, as you would do the same for me."

"Children? Is there a secret I should know?"

"Not yet, Grandfather, but we are trying our best to have my heir as quickly as possible. Jana wants our first son to carry your name, a second Maal Triloni to one day replace the first."

Jana had not said or even thought such a thing but assumed Ryker was saying she had to win favor with his grandfather. She let it pass and took the praise and gratitude the ruler showered on her.

Maal was beside himself with joy and pleasure. "You have my word of honor, cherished flame of my soul; no harm shall ever come to her or to my great-grandchildren."

* * *

After breakfast the following morning, embraces, best wishes, and farewells were shared before Jana and Varian departed. Jana assumed they would visit again upon their return from the Milky Way Galaxy. Varian knew it was the last time Maal would see ''Ryker'' alive, or so he planned.

On the Trilabs starship, Varian, elated by his many successes and by having his love nearby, gave the desired coordinates to Captain Kagan who laid in their speed and course for Rigel.

Jana gazed out the *transascreen* and wondered what lay ahead for her on Rigel when she confronted her betrayers for the first time, faced them as Princess Jana Triloni and at Ryker's side. Then, it was off toward her world to see if Earth could be saved. She hoped and prayed it could be. Just as she hoped and prayed Varian and Canissia would not be on Rigel.

Here I come, you deadly rattlesnakes; I can hardly wait to see what you think of me and how you treat me now!

Chapter Ten

It had been four days since they left Tartarus, Maal, and Androas at starlight speed to make it to Rigel late the next night. Jana could not surmise the real reason why she and Ryker were going on this mission in Varian's place and ship. For all she knew, her husband was telling the truth, again.

Jana finished her bath and entered the sleeping area of their quarters. Clad only in a silky robe, she sat on the bed to relax a moment before dressing for dinner. The past few days had been confusing for her. Ryker, after being so romantic and attentive at his grandfather's, had not done more than give her quick pecks on her cheek or forehead since their departure. He couldn't have lost interest in her that quickly if he really—

The door swished open and the blond alien entered. Jana smiled at him as he approached and knelt before her. He kissed a knee bared when she shifted her leg. His fingers trailed over her calf and he used his cheek to nuzzle her silky thigh. He inhaled and smiled. ''You smell wonderful. You feel wonderful. May *Kahala* protect me, you are a totally enslaving woman."

The way he was looking at her, stroking her, and speaking caused Jana to warm and tingle. "You've been so busy that I've hardly seen you since we left Maal's. I thought you had forgotten all about me, so I've had to entertain myself."

He brushed more kisses on her knee as both hands roamed up the outer sides of her thighs. "I'm sorry if it seems as if I've deserted you. I could never do that, Jana, nor forget you. I needed to get my report and suggestions ready for our meeting at Star Base. I don't want it to take long. I want to get in, handle the situation, and get out fast."

Jana wondered if he was afraid they would confront Varian. No, that she would *see* Varian and have mixed feelings about her ex-lover. Perhaps he needed reassurance of her commitment to him. His next words seemed to confirm those thoughts.

Varian eased into the space his body created between her legs, cupped Jana's face near her jawline, and gazed into her eyes. "No matter what happens in the near future, Jana, remember at all times that I do love you. I hope you won't ever let anything that you see or hear cause you to doubt that truth or to mistrust me. You are the only woman I have ever loved or *will* ever love, the only woman I want and need. Always believe that. Promise?"

Jana ran her fingers through his touseled tawny hair and smiled. "I promise. I love you, too, Ryker, and I need you." In some crazy way, she wasn't lying! And unless she was mistaken, he was being honest. Perhaps because Varian had lied and misled her, she had feared to trust Ryker without reservation. She couldn't keep doing that. This man was her husband, forever. He was the center of her new world.

Varian sealed their mouths. When their lips parted, he murmured, "Sometimes it seems as if we have so little time together." What he couldn't say was, so little time *left* together. When they reached his starship, things could change. "You have captured my heart, body, and soul, Jana Greyson. When

I'm not with you, I think of you. When I'm with you, I want you." He yearned to chase any thought except of him from her mind and from his own. Tomorrow would begin a new phase in their destiny. As soon as it was completed, he could confess the truth, plead for her understanding and forgiveness, and hopefully carry her off to his home on Altair to live forever as man and wife.

He spread kisses over her flawless face and down her satiny throat. As he nibbled at her neck, he unbelted the robe and pushed it aside. He covered her chest with a blanket of hot kisses, one woven just for her. His lips and teeth teased at her taut breasts, his fiery tongue lavishing moisture upon their blossoms. His hands wandered up and down her body, flesh as soft as silk. He sent a set of seeking fingers snaking up the smooth inner surface of one leg until they reached the heart of her desire.

Jana's senses whirled and flamed beneath his loving quest. He was highly skilled, and sensitive to a woman's needs. Her fingers moved over his broad shoulders and she wished the shirt were gone so they could make contact with his supple flesh. Her respiration quickened as desire coursed through her. Suspense and anticipation flooded her entire being. His actions had stolen her wits and control. Nothing seemed to matter, not even who or what he was, except dousing the fires of passion he had ignited. He tantalized her beyond reality or resistance. His mouth feasted at her breasts. His deft fingers explored and pleasured her feminine core. She was consumed by achingly sweet sensations and wanted this loving siege to last forever.

Varian used one hand and his lips to capture both taut brown nipples at the same time. Moistened fingers made sensuous circular trips around one point while his tongue did the same around the other. He realized she was burning hot with desire for him. Her eyes were closed as her body swayed from side to side with unbridled passion, emotions he had unleashed. She sent him unspoken messages to continue his conquest, signals he caught and obeyed with eagerness. He gently squeezed her pleading breasts and tantalized the thrusting peaks that exposed her height of yearning. He guided her to her back as he made a trail of kisses down the valley between her breasts, over her abdomen, between her hipbones, and to her upper thighs. He slipped one finger into her beckoning portal to find it moist and eager for him. He bent his head and began his feast on the fruit of paradise.

Jana could not help but give him free rein over her body and will. As his fingers and tongue stimulated her very essence, she experienced exquisite and astonishing pleasure. She groaned as her head thrashed on the bed. Tension built within her. She wanted to relax, but she couldn't; the blissful attack on her senses wouldn't allow it. Her stomach muscles tightened and calmed in rapid and recurrent session. The peak of her womanhood throbbed and pulsed under his stirring attention.

Varian's tongue flicked and circled, sometimes slow and sometimes fast. His finger within her matched that same course and pace. Dreamy moans escaped her throat, and her hips undulated to the pattern and speed he set. He increased his endeavors to give her supreme satisfaction on their voyage to the heavens tonight. He carried her to the brink of love's universe, and brought her home again. He stripped off his garments and moved atop her, overjoyed when her arms reached for him and drew him tightly and swiftly to her. Shuddering with hunger, he thrust into her receptive core to feed his own needs and hopefully hers again. He felt her legs overlap his and grip him tightly. He drove into her over and over, rotating his hips to shower her with delicious sensations. He wanted to find victory, but he wanted her to find a second one first.

Their tongues touched, savored, and titillated. Their hands stroked, caressed, fondled, and explored.

Jana felt almost drugged by him. He was an intoxicating combination of strength and gentleness, tender and forceful, giving and demanding. Wild and wonderful feelings washed over her as she found herself aroused again. She quivered when he groaned his deep need for her. She trailed her hands over his rippling muscles. Each time he plunged into her receptive body, his kisses went urgent from blissful torment. Soon, her body was again calling out for appeasement. The intensity built to a level that was almost unbearable. She buried her fingers in his hair and kept his mouth fused to hers. As if she had gone wild, she ravished and plundered his tasty recess.

Their urgency increased as they drove each other wild. The moment he realized she was approaching the summit of ecstasy, he increased the pace and strength of his thrusts. His intensity mounted higher and higher. She was reaching for the stars, as was he. When she arched her back, clung to him, and trembled with release, he joined her with a cry of joy.

With passion and energy spent for a while, Varian rolled to his back. He pulled her along to rest across his damp chest; he had to continue touching her. Knowing he could give Jana such enormous pleasure made him happy and proud. He closed his eyes as he let his heartbeat return to normal. As he did so, his fingers took a slow journey over her arms and back. When that trek halted, his arms embraced her, tightly for a moment. The afterglow of the golden moment was so warm and soothing that he was evoked to say, "I do love you, Jana. You're like a magical moonbeam that lights up my life and heart. I never thought the day would come when I felt like this about a woman. May the stars fall down if that isn't the truth."

Jana lifted her head and gazed into his verdant eyes. How could she disbelieve what she saw there? She wiggled her body to bring their mouths into contact for a soul-stirring kiss. When it ended, she propped on one elbow and looked at him. "I love you, too, Ryker. You are as powerful and life-giving as the sun. I hope I never lose you because I could not endure such agony. If my love and obedience and loyalty aren't enough, ask anything of me to make certain that never happens."

"I swear by all I am and know, that will never happen." Varian's heart flooded with love and happiness . . . until Jana continued her compliments, and he was forced to conceal his pain and reaction.

"You are a talented lover, my husband. And so handsome and virile that I can't think clearly when I look at you. Your eyes are like expensive emeralds, so green and full of sparkling vitality. Your hair is like the mane of a lion, king of the jungle on Earth, as you are the king of my world. I want to run my hands and mouth all over you. I want you to—"

"Halt, woman, or I'll be on fire again," the disappointed alien teased to silence her talk about his dead half brother who could never have made love to her like this, to whom she could never have responded like this.

Jana grinned as her fingertips played over his lips. "If so, my desirable husband, I will extinguish your flames in a delightful manner."

He chuckled and guided them to sitting positions. "Right now, my love, the flame I'm experiencing is in my belly. I am hungry, and this time for real food! Will you release me from your spell for a while, my golden temptress, but stay on a slow burn for me, only me?"

"As you once told me, I do, all the time."

Jana reclined in bed with a book in her hands as they neared Rigel. She sipped on fruit juice and pretended to read while her husband worked at a desk nearby. She couldn't stop thinking about what she might confront tomorrow if Varian dared to show up at the meeting. How could she face him, knowing what he had meant—still meant—and had done to her? She tried to push thoughts of him out of her mind. After the passionate bout last night with Ryker, it should be easy. If only she knew why he had betrayed and discarded her, she could deal with the tormenting matter. She had been certain Varian Saar loved her and wanted her. It was apparent he had lied about his feelings. Or he had felt that his sacrifice was critical. If they had been given more time together, perhaps he wouldn't have made—

Stop it, J. G. Don't do this to yourself again. You belong to Ryker.

Jana yawned. Her lids were heavy. She felt limp and relaxed, warm and cozy and comfortable. She leaned her head back to rest her tired eyes a minute. They didn't open again, and she was lost in slumber.

Varian peeked over his shoulder and saw she had succumbed to the drug in her juice and that the glass was empty. He stood and went to the bed. He scooted her down to her back, tucked her in, and kissed her forehead. "Sorry, Moonbeam, but I have a secret meeting to attend tonight. Sleep well, Jana; tomorrow will be difficult for you. I wish it didn't have to be this way. I wish I could tell you the truth, but it's too dangerous. Ryker had a spy in my last crew; Taemin or Cass could have one concealed somewhere in Star Fleet. I can't take any chances of fouling things up when we're so close to victory." He thought about their precaution of using a new crew on his ship this time to prevent a close friend from guessing his identity. Until the mission was done and Ryker's death was exposed to the public, Jana had to be kept in the dark. But it was possible one more cunning trip to Maal's would be necessary. *Soon, my love, this deceit will be over. We can be happy again.*

Kadim Tirol Trygue greeted Jana with a warm smile and embrace. "It is good to see you again. You look radiant. How are you?"

The Earthling raked her chilly eyes over the eighty-year-old ruler of the Maffei Alliance, a man who had helped—and perhaps ordered—her betrayal by his grandson. Because of his high rank and her good manners and desire to conceal the anguish and shame inflicted upon her, she was polite to him. "I'm fine, sir. I will be even better after my world is saved and I'm back home with my husband."

"Are you sure you want to go on this long and dangerous journey?"

"Yes. I prefer staying with my husband. Where he goes, I go."

"As you wish, Jana, but please stay safe. You are very special to me."

You lying alien! Though the look in his light-blue eyes said he was sincere and he projected an aura of kindness, Jana was bitter and resentful of his interference in her life. Her warring emotions caused her to act aloof and reserved. "My husband will make certain of that fact, sir," she replied, stressing the words "my husband" each time. She noticed what appeared to be a shadow of sadness and dismay in his eyes. *It's too late for you to be sorry for what you helped do to me. Don't expect my forgiveness and friendship. I liked you and trusted you. I was a fool.*

Tirol looked at his disguised grandson and nodded. "We understand and accept your motives for wanting to take command of this mission, Prince Ryker, but I wish it had been handled differently. You made your request sound more like a demand or a threat instead of a favor. That is not necessary between allies and friends. If it is that important to you and Jana, we are happy to comply with your desire. The deed is what matters, not who does it. No one is more qualified to carry it out than you are."

"If I sounded demanding, *Kadim* Tirol, it was not intentional," Varian replied. "And yes, it is very important to me to do this task for my wife."

As the two men talked, Supreme Council member Draco Procyon joined them. Draco smiled at Jana and said, "It is good to see you again."

She started to snap that those were Tirol's exact words. Instead, she smiled. "Congratulations on your new marriage. It's very romantic to recover a first love and marry her. I hope you two will be as happy as Ryker and I are. Perhaps we'll see each other under different circumstances."

"I hope so, Jana. I've missed you and thought of you often since you left Karnak. You look as ravishing as you did the last night I saw you. I can tell you're happy. I'm glad."

"So am I, sir," she responded, not using his first name as she had done in the past. This handsome, amber-eyed blond with his classic features had helped Varian trick her at her fake auction and during the many weeks she had lived and studied in his home. In addition, as a Council member, he might have assisted her final defeat.

"You remember Supreme Commander Breccia Sard, don't you?"

"Yes, I do. Good day, sir."

Brec nodded as his black eyes scanned her flawless features. There seemed a tightly leashed hostility surrounding her regal exterior. Her emotions were understandable, but he still hated to see her and Varian being hurt. He pushed an ebony lock of hair from his temple. "It is an honor to see you again, Princess Jana. I hope you both realize how vital this mission can be."

"We do, Commander Sard, and thank you for letting my husband take control of it. I assure you that Ryker will do his best to succeed with it."

"I have no doubts he will or I would not have agreed to it. The Council and I are hoping that this show of friendship, cooperation, and faith will strengthen our alliance with Prince Ryker."

Varian nodded and said, "It will, Commander Sard, it will."

They sat down at a conference table. The genial Maffeians were on one side, with Jana and "Ryker" on the other. A false briefing was presented in less than thirty minutes, then lunch was served.

Jana was afraid Varian would appear at any minute. She hoped Tirol had enough compassion and intelligence to have ordered his grandson not to come. Surely Varian would obey his ruler, no matter how singed his pride and how strong his anger. Their hosts did not mention Varian or anything of the past. Perhaps they were being cautious to avoid offending the Prince and Princess. Even when Tirol mentioned the *Wanderlust*, he called it "my grandson's ship." Jana noted that Council member Segall Garthon, Canissia's father, did not attend the meeting. It was possible the missing tri-leader had been excluded on purpose because of his reputation as a loose talker. Little would please Jana more than for the spiteful and arrogant Canissia to be exposed before her wedding could take place.

Jana pushed aside her personal thoughts and worries to listen while the four men completed their discussion of Project Starguard, any possible problems, and how to handle a failure with . . . Stardusting.

She was relieved when the briefing and meal ended. At the side of the blond alien and her hands on his arm, she said courteous farewells. Then, she and her mate left for their shuttle which would take them aboard the *Wanderlust*. Her possessions were already loaded on the shuttle, and she hoped they were proper for the trek ahead.

During the short flight to the starship, Jana scoffed, "They pretended to be so nice and caring about me. What a farce!"

"How could they help but be nice to you, Jana? It was obvious to me that they truly like you and are concerned about you." He didn't want her breeding ill feelings toward Tirol, Draco, and Brec, so he said what he thought was necessary: the truth. "In fairness, they aren't responsible for what Varian did to you. They were not on his ship when the trouble began with his defiance. They simply found a safe and logical way to clean up the mess he had made by taking a *charl* in training for himself."

"That doesn't explain or justify their letting him give . . ."

He had forced himself into a rash corner and was compelled to get out by saying, "Present you to me as a birthday and truce token? He owned you, Jana, so he could do as he pleased with you."

She almost refuted, *No, he couldn't; I was free!* But she realized that was part of her delusion. She had been freed later, by Ryker's demand. "From talks I overheard, they were in on his sport. On the tape Canissia played during our trip to Darkar, Varian said: 'If all goes as *Grandfather* and I plan, I intend to make Ryker an offer he can't refuse.' "

Varian recalled the false statements he had made to Cass to dupe the redhead. His "offer" had accompanied a shake of his fist and his meaning had been: peace or defeat. Soon, he would explain her misinterpretation. He dropped the plaguing subject, as they were in the docking bay of his ship.

Jana grasped Ryker's hand as they exited the craft in case Varian was there. Her carefully guarded gaze touched on one past friend: Martella Karsh. The rest of the group gathered in the docking entry were strangers.

Jana smiled and greeted the female First Lieutenant whom she admired and respected, though she wasn't certain whether or not the officer could be trusted.

Martella smiled. "It's been too long, Jana. You look wonderful."

Jana's gaze roamed the alien female's leaf-colored eyes and red hair that had a few hints of gray in the short and bouncy curls. "So do you, Martella." She noticed Martella was wearing a red uniform with gamboge chevrons, instead of the perse with silver stria of her last known rank.

The *charl* ex-trainer saw Jana's line of vision. She explained, "I'm head of security on this voyage. I'm the only one you know aboard. The rest of the crew and your old friends are either on leave or have been assigned to other ships for this task." Then, the Elite Squad member who knew the truth lied out of necessity and orders: "The Council wanted the lead ship to have the best trained and qualified staff available. I hope we can have a catch-up chat during our long voyage."

Though Jana was relieved to learn only Martella from the past voyage was present, it made her suspicious. "I'm sure that can be arranged," she answered sweetly.

"Let me introduce you and Prince Ryker to the rest of the officers." As she was told the officers' names, ranks, and positions, Jana saw each man or woman nod a greeting which Ryker returned in like kind along with a clasped wrist gesture which she had learned was the equivalent of a handshake on Earth. During this session, she did nothing more than nod.

Only one of the two Elite Squad members present—Martella Karsh—was aware of Varian's secret identity and the motive behind it. Zade, who had taken Nigel's place, was ordered to prevent any dissension among crew members about "Ryker Triloni" taking command of this ship and mission. Martella was present to handle any problems that might arise and to carry out any secret communications necessary. She also provided a friendly face for his beloved Jana.

"My wife and I will get settled in this afternoon then join you for dinner and a briefing tonight at seven," the disguised Varian said. "I'm sure we'll get along fine during our long voyage. Officer Zade, I hope you'll have reports from any affected areas with you tonight."

"Yes, Prince Ryker," the dark-haired officer replied. "We'll use the conference room near your quarters. I'll direct you there myself if you're ready, sir. Crewmen will bring your things to you within a few minutes."

"Yes, we are ready. Come, Jana." He clasped her hand.

Jana glanced at Martella, smiled, and departed with her husband. She had dreaded facing the crew again and enduring their gossip. It was with trepidation that she entered Varian's quarters once more. This was her ex-lover's room. She was back where it all began: her abduction, training, ill-fated love affair, and betrayal.

Shortly after entering the haunting location, Jana made a shocking discovery. She opened the closet in the dressing room by pressing a button release and found that all of her old clothes, possessions, and gifts were there! She didn't know why Varian had removed them from Tirol's—the last place she had lived before going to Darkar—and placed them here, but she wondered if it was his way of reminding her of the bittersweet past they had shared. Was it a selfish attempt to evoke memories and emotions best left buried? She couldn't grasp why he had even kept them. Canissia would be furious and jealous if she made this curious discovery.

Jana looked at the miniature painting of a *Talias* in full bloom; it was a souvenir from a trip to a local museum shortly before her phony auction. Varian had purchased it because it had reminded them of the flowers they had seen near a waterfall during her voyage here. He had plucked one near the streambank and given it to her, proving he could and would break the law when it suited him! Just as he had disobeyed orders by making her his mistress! She picked up the necklace he had given her along their treacherous path; it was a cluster of flowers on a gold chain with stems that formed the Maffeian letters for *V* and *S*. As if a foreboding, the piece of jewelry had been made by a craftsman on Caguas, the planet Darkar orbited. When she had teased him about "advertising his prior ownership," he had chuckled and said, "I wouldn't want you to forget me." As if she ever could! She lifted the flowers to expose five tiny pictures of the two of them at special moments. She gazed at the sapphire-eyed, sable-haired alien who could still cause her heart to flutter and her body to enflame. She remembered each occasion and wanted to sob in anguish. She snapped the gold flowers shut and flung the item into a drawer. Perhaps Varian had wanted her to know he hadn't forgotten her. Perhaps he hadn't wanted to get rid of her. Perhaps he still wanted her. It was certain he had never expected his half brother to marry her and . . . Take her out of his reach forever? Her dilemma always returned to the starship commander's motive for betraying her.

Jana recalled that her birthday present—a gold bracelet—had been discarded in the trash after the heart-rending garden scene on Auriga. His last gift, the farewell ring, was in a drawer on Darkar. *Damn you, damn you, damn you! Why did you put these things here?*

She looked at her old garments, reflecting on the times she had worn some of them. She lifted the one she had worn to her auction.

"How are things going?" Varian inquired as he entered the dressing room and halted to lean against the closet entrance. When his gaze touched on the object she was holding and then on the open jewelry drawer, he cursed himself for not thinking to have them removed. He had put her belongings here during his long and agonizing search for her after she had vanished. During that tormenting time, he had touched, smelled, and looked at them often to call forth even the tiniest memory when he feared he had lost her forever. When this mission was born, it had sprung to full growth instantly. He had worked and studied in Ryker's complex and had forgotten about what awaited her on this return.

"Varian is cold, cruel, and vindictive, my husband. He put these things here to taunt us. I'll pack them and have them stored out of sight."

"I'm sorry, Jana," Varian said sadly. "I should have checked out this room. I never want you hurt again."

She went to him and entered his arms, resting her head on his broad chest. "You've become a very kind, gentle, and caring person since our first meeting when you terrified me to the bone. Or perhaps you were always this way and didn't have a chance to reveal your wonderful traits. It wasn't your fault, my love. And it wasn't an oversight by him; it was an intentional taunt that he assumed would distress me and vex you. Perhaps he's saving them to use on his next helpless victim. I'm sure Canissia wouldn't want anything that had been touched by me, and I can imagine her reaction if she found these things."

Perdition, Varian, you're making her fall in love with that evil bastard! "I'll get rid of them for you so you won't have to touch them or look at them. Why don't you go into the other room and pour us some wine while I handle this unpleasant task. We'll have to get ready for dinner and the meeting soon."

She lifted her head and sent him an imploring gaze. "Must I go, Ryker? I'd rather eat here and rest. I don't want this new crew to make wild speculations about me, about us."

"I thought you'd enjoy seeing Lieutenant Karsh again."

"I do, and I'm glad she's aboard. But I don't want to see her again so soon. In a few days after I've gotten accustomed to being here."

Was this part of the ruse, he worried, too much to ask of his love? "Will it bother you to stay in these rooms for a few weeks? If so, we can use the guest quarters down the hall. I was told they're smaller but still very nice."

"No, that won't be necessary." Besides, the Gold Room held just as many bittersweet memories for her, as that suite had been hers in the beginning.

* * *

Following a briefing last night between Ryker and the officers, the *Wanderlust* left orbit around Rigel at dawn and headed for rendezvous with the other starships between Saturn and Jupiter. From the *transascreen* in their borrowed quarters, Jana eyed the vast span of space before her. Wherever she looked, all she saw was sky that looked like one endless rippling of white waves. They were under way, traveling to her galaxy at starlight speed, their fastest pace. By Earth timing, the voyage would require three weeks; and by Earth's calendar, they would assault the rogue less than two weeks before Christmas.

Thanksgiving . . . Christmas . . . New Year's . . . Friends, turkey with all the trimmings, shopping, decorations, parties, funny hats and noise makers. . . . Holidays: how she would miss them.

Jana thought about Andrea being on the colony at Anais. If Project Starguard failed, her best friend would lose all of that and her family. She would also be forced to make a new life here in Maffei. But if the mission was successful, Andrea might be sent home. *I have to see you at least once before that happens. I need to see you. I need to talk with you. You always teased me about being in full control of my emotions and life. You always said I knew what I wanted. That's no longer true. I have control over nothing—not even the air I breathe or food I eat. How wonderful it would be to make my own decisions again. Please, God, let this mission succeed. Give Earth another miracle for Christmas.*

For three days, Jana didn't leave Varian's quarters. She ate, read, and exercised there to avoid the new crew. She didn't want to make friends with any of them, as she had with the old one. Besides, she would never see these men and women after this trip, so why make any overtures that might be laughed at or ignored?

If she desired to leave the suite, Ryker had told her she had free run of the ship. She turned and let her gaze roam the sitting area. It was roomy, masculine, and comfortable. She could close her eyes and almost picture Varian sitting and working at his desk as he'd done in the past. Several times when Ryker had used it, she had experienced gnawings of irritation at the unnatural sight. As if he'd become a ghost, Varian seemed to haunt this room. His lingering spirit seemed to lurk in here, in the adjoining bedroom, and even in the bathroom. Worst of all, sometimes it was as if she were suddenly and helplessly yanked into the past when she was the captive but willing mistress of that ebony-haired blue-eyed space pirate. She expected to glance up to see Varian strolling through the door, but it was always her blond-haired, green-eyed husband. Nearly every area of this ship held special memories of those blissfully ignorant days when she had fallen in love with him, and perhaps that was the real reason why she didn't want to view them again. Yet, she couldn't remain locked in here for six or more weeks.

And that was emphasized the following day when Varian said, "You can't stay cooped up in here for the entire voyage, Jana. I'm sure everyone is wondering why you haven't made a single appearance since our arrival. Do you want them to think you're afraid or embarrassed to face them or that you're being held captive in here by me? You said you didn't want them gossiping about you or us, but this is a sure way to inspire that. This is a big ship with plenty to do on it. Get out and enjoy yourself. Do something with Martella to stop her from being my shadow." He chuckled before using one of Tristan's favorite sayings. "She sticks to me like *gracon* to a beaker to make sure I don't see or do anything I shouldn't. Come on, woman, get dressed. Let's eat and dance in the Stardust Room. I've seen it, and it's very romantic."

So had she! She had spent many "romantic" evenings there with Varian. "You're right, my intelligent and caring husband. I suppose it's past time for Princess Jana Triloni to grace everyone with her presence. I'll be ready in thirty minutes."

* * *

Chief Medical Officer Mirren said to Martella and Zade, "Tris told me wonderful things about Jana and her skills. Nothing would have pleased him more than to have gotten her as his assistant. From what I heard, everyone aboard thought she and Varian would get together, that they were perfect for each other. I wonder what happened to prevent it."

"From the way it looks," Zade replied as his gaze pointed at the dancing and smiling couple, "Ryker Triloni happened."

"Whatever it was that split them apart, it's too late now. She looks happy and so does Prince Ryker. I guess if Varian had been in love with her, he wouldn't be marrying that Garthon woman. What a waste of a good man."

"And waste of a good woman from where I sit," Jarre added. "How could any woman leave Varian Saar for a man like that?"

Martella silenced the annoying conversation. "Some things are meant to be and others aren't. If a mistake is made, one can never tell when fate will step in and correct human error. But I don't think we should be gossiping about them. We wouldn't want to be overheard and cause problems. This task is too important."

Jana felt as if Varian was standing in the dark corner and watching them with a mocking grin on his handsome face as they made love in his bed. She soon realized she had no choice except to fake pleasure and a climax. She hoped and prayed pretending wouldn't become a necessary habit for her. What she needed was an antidote to Varian Saar, something to cure and heal her and make her immune to his continual torment. She had to face the reality that Ryker was not a panacea or substitute for that daring space rogue.

Varian comprehended her predicament, but he was given hope at surmising she was still haunted by him and bound in heart to him. He pretended not to notice her deceit.

* * *

Two days later, Jana sneaked into the Gold Room to see if anything had changed there since her departure. She found only the monitor for spying on her and for giving her orders had been removed, and she quickly left.

She entered the officers' gym to exercise on the walkometer. For the time being, no one was present, and she was glad. She stepped on the treadmill, set the time, pace, and incline she wanted, and pressed the start button. She moved slowly at first during her warm-up period.

"Hello, Jana. So we finally have time and privacy for a talk."

Jana was surprised to see Martella coming toward her, as Ryker had alleged the woman stuck to him like glue. Perhaps he had told the new security chief that she would be coming here, as she had told him her plans earlier. "Did you finally manage time away from Ryker's demands to get in some fun and exercise?" she jested as the machine's pace increased.

Martella began her warm-up. "I must admit he's doing a superb job."

"Did you expect otherwise?" Jana asked. "Ryker does *everything* superbly. He's a perfectionist, or didn't the Alliance know that?"

"You've also done well for yourself, Jana. You look wonderful and radiant. I'm glad to see you so happy, and I'm delighted you're free."

Happy and free? Jana caught her breath before replying, "You and your training team taught me well, as did my ensuing experiences."

"But not to become Ryker's wife. I had hoped . . ." Martella halted and looked embarrassed by what she wanted to appear a slip.

The treadmill's speed increased again and Jana's legs moved faster. "So had I, Martella, but it didn't work out like that. I'm really fortunate he gave me to Ryker instead of someone else who might not have felt about me the way that my husband does. Our life together is perfect because we have similar interests and skills. I'm lucky, and happy.''

''I'm glad, Jana, because I want what's best for you.''

Jana believed that was a true and sincere sentiment. She had always been able to speak openly and candidly with this woman. ''I'm unsure anyone knows what that is, including me . . . How's Tristan? I've missed him. I'm sorry we never had the chance to really work together.''

Martella beamed with love. ''He's doing fine. He's on one of the other ships. Upon our return, we will be getting married.''

''That doesn't surprise me. You two were made for each other. I caught hints of that when I was here. Congratulations. Give him my best wishes.''

''Why don't you do that yourself by attending our wedding?''

''I don't think that would be wise. I'm sure your friend Varian will be there. Frankly, I don't care to ever see him again.'' Jana changed the topic from that of her lost love. ''We've never minced words, so I want to ask you a question and I hope you'll answer with the truth. Would you mind telling me why there's a new crew on the ship? It strikes me as odd.''

Martella began working out with weights. ''It was Varian's orders. They were assigned to other ships for this mission because Varian thought it would be better for you and for them not to be placed in an uncomfortable position of being thrown together for weeks under such . . . different circumstances. He didn't want anyone, especially you, Jana, to be uneasy and embarrassed.''

''How nice of him. Why are you here?''

Martella noted the coldness in the tawny-haired Earthling's voice during her first response. She wished she could say something to ease it. She experienced pain for her two friends. ''Varian and the Council wanted someone aboard they could trust implicitly as head of security.''

The treadmill speeded up again, causing Jana to go into a run. ''You mean, someone of your special rank to watch Ryker with an eagle eye?''

Martella looked surprised. "You say that like you know—"

"I do, but I wouldn't tell anyone else."

"Anyone?" It didn't matter if it were "Ryker," but a slip to Maal . . .

"Ryker knows, too, but I didn't tell him. In fact . . ." Whatever, Jana asked herself, was she doing? Was she getting light-headed and witless from lack of oxygen to the brain? She couldn't tell this Maffeian that Ryker knew the names of all Elite Squad members! Yet she wished she could because it placed their lives and assignments in jeopardy, from Maal.

Martella changed weights. "In fact *what*, Jana?"

"Nothing. I heard you're working hard to have *charl* laws abolished. Is that true? Will you succeed?"

"I think so. I hope so. The practice is outdated. I have plenty of influential and powerful people assisting my cause: Draco, Tirol, Varian, Tristan, and many of the *avatars* and *zartiffs* and elite citizens. Naturally some of the *charl* owners will back my issue. Needless to say, many of them are discontented since you won your freedom and married your ex-owner."

"I thought that might happen. And I'm glad. We abolished slavery on Earth long ago. I'm surprised a society as advanced or 'superior' as yours would have continued it this long. If your males can't romance and woo a female into marriage, they don't deserve a mate or a wife."

"That's a logical and accurate assumption."

"It wasn't mine; it was *Kadim* Maal's, my new father-in-law. We've just returned from a visit with him in Androas. It seems I've become quite the intergalactic traveler since I was stolen from Earth. How long do you think it will take to push through your change in the law?"

"Why are you so interested? It won't affect you, not anymore."

Jana had to catch her breath again before answering. "I'd like to see Kathy Anderson and Ferris Laus married before their first child arrives. I'd also like to see Heather Langdon become the wife of Spala Rilke. And all the others from our voyage and the ones before and since it." The treadmill began to slow its pace with gradual decreases every few minutes. "Speaking of Rilke, how is my old *laius* partner doing? I had hoped Tesla or Nigel would be aboard so we could continue our quest for a championship."

Martella wondered why Jana asked about Tesla. If Varian had her convinced her rescue and his death were delusions . . . "Tesla is fine. He's on Commander Jaekle's ship, the *Maffeian Wind*. Nigel was given the command of the *Kiunterri*. Of course, Varian stayed where he was."

"I'm glad. I'm sure he has lots of plans to make since his wedding to Canissia is so close."

The bitterness in the Earthling was blatantly obvious. Martella wished she could say something to ease Jana's anguish and to give her hope, but she couldn't. The officer didn't like this feeling of helplessness and seeing two close friends in such torment. She disagreed with Varian and Tirol about keeping Jana excluded from the ruse, but she had no authority to disobey orders. What she was witnessing and hearing worried her because it appeared as if Varian was pushing Jana away from him and toward Ryker. Even when the Earthling learned the truth, it might be too late to make a difference since their relationship might already be damaged. Obviously Varian was also aware of that risk and that was why she sensed such panic in him to have the affair finished.

Martella turned the topic away from Varian and back to the *charl* matter as a distraction. "I don't want to deceive you, Jana; the facts are, we have plenty of opposition in high and low places to freeing the *charls*. Change will require lots of time and work. Some owners are afraid their *charls* will not want to marry them and will even want to return to their homes; they're afraid abolishment of the practice will break up their families and disrupt their lives. Some might not want to wed their mates because marriage is a serious and permanent relationship, more than they bargained for when purchasing mates for reproduction and companionship. As you know, divorce is hard to obtain and is frowned upon in our culture. Currently, owners can, with a good reason, trade or sell their *charls* to another, something they can't do with a wife. Captive mates have been like their possessions and would suddenly—with marriage, citizenship, and freedom—be their equals. Many are intimidated by that untested reality. What I'm trying to say, Jana, is that the matter will require a lot of changes in law, customs, and emotions; and most men don't like drastic changes."

Jana knew from experience with Varian Saar that Martella's last statement was true. "Please, keep working on abolishment," she implored her. "No one deserves to be a prisoner to another and certainly not for life. These women did nothing to provoke or justify their captures and entrapments."

The officer wondered if she was referring to herself. "Jana . . ."

She looked at the Maffeian redhead who put down the weights. "Yes?"

"Nothing. It's just that I didn't think things would turn out this way."

Jana couldn't bring herself to ask her any questions about Varian, particularly why he had done this to her. She didn't want to be hurt and shamed further, and the truth might do both. "Nor did I, Martella, but perhaps it's for the best. A liar and deceiver could never be trusted again."

"But . . ." *Don't say another word, you stupid female.*

Jana was intrigued. "What is it you're trying to get out, Martella?"

"Something best left inside and unsaid. At least for now. I'm sorry."

"For what?"

"I came here to talk of happy things and times, not the past. How much do you know about self-defense and weapons?"

Jana wondered at the sad look in the woman's eyes. "Excuse me?"

Martella repeated her question. A confused Jana asked, "Are we expecting problems?" Was there trouble in the wind after they finished?

"In your new role of princess, trouble can ensnare you at

the most unexpected moment. I want you able to defend yourself. Can you do that?''

Jana mused, *Role?* ''I took a course once in self-defense for women.''

''Could you battle an attacker and escape from him?''

Jana recalled the night in Andrea's garden when she had confronted the thugs, then the aliens. ''Evidently not or I wouldn't be in Maffei.''

''Would you mind if I teach you self-defense and use of our weapons? We could meet here every afternoon for lessons and practice. It will give us both something to do during our travel time. How about it?''

As the treadmill halted, Jana shrugged. ''Why not? I'm game. Teach me all you know. I might need such skills and knowledge one day. I'll tell you what: I'll agree to be your student if you tell me about Andrea McKay, my best friend on Earth. Varian promised me she would be rescued before this final mission got under way. Was she? Is she on Anais?''

''She was, and she's fine; that's all I can tell you about a secret project.''

''Is there any chance I can see her or get a message to her?''

Martella took a deep breath and considered the request. She decided that Jana shouldn't have to suffer over Andrea as it would be known to her soon. ''As a favor to you, Jana, I'll check on it after our return home.''

Two and a half weeks passed while Jana became skilled in self-defense and with the use of weapons. She, as well as the crew, spent time reading books from the ship library, playing sports and games, exercising, and all the daily tasks. Though she had intended to avoid the new crew, she had communicated with most of them many times because they had turned out to be nice and kind people. Except, she amended, for Mirren. The doctor always remained reserved and watchful as if he had a private grievance against her for marrying Ryker or for committing some unknown offense.

Jana had observed a few of the meetings on strategy as the men searched for the rogue's weak points and how to best attack them. Conferernces were held in the geology and astrophysics labs, while facts and theories were analyzed in the data-processing area.

Only once had Jana visited sick bay and the med lab, and it was a brief visit. Mirren, whose family was the third richest in Maffei, was polite, but he wasn't anything like the genial Tristan Zarcoff, her friend.

Jana found it odd that during all the time she had spent with Martella, the officer had not asked her how she had gotten away from Varian, met Ryker, and married the Prince. She had come to assume Martella knew the truth of the offensive matter. She was sorely tempted to question the Maffeian about how and why Varian could do something so cruel and wicked, but she didn't want to put her friend on the spot. Besides, knowing the truth couldn't alter her situation.

Three times she had made passionate love with Ryker, but not in Varian's haunting quarters. Once had been in the locked botanical garden with the scent of exotic flowers swirling around their heads. Another had been in the conservatory bubble, also locked, beneath the stars and a colorful blend of nebulous clouds. The last time had been in the private shower in the officers' gym. Each time, Ryker had intoxicated and tantalized her beyond her will or wits to resist. Away from Varian's intrusive and inhibiting spirit, she had surrendered and had taken great pleasure from her husband. She couldn't possibly have denied either of them of his bewitching skills when he had wanted her with such urgency, tenderness, and love, as if he could not resist her.

"My stars, Ryker, it's so big!" Jana shrieked in astonishment and dismay as they approached the rogue worldlet. "It must be the size of Darkar or larger. How will you ever smash it to pieces?"

"Don't worry, love, we'll overpower it and win. If nothing

more, we hope to change its trajectory and send it into a different orbit from Earth's. It must have taken thousands, or even millions, of years to orbit your solar body after it was formed or arrived from deep space. Perhaps another one struck Earth long ago and sheared off enough mass to form your moon; that happens often anywhere. It's not alone; there are many similar bodies orbiting your sun. Collisions with planets can pulverize attacker and target."

Jana was alert and tense as he told her more about the potato-shaped object. She prayed they had accurately guessed locations of its weak points. If not, it would plummet to Earth with unimaginable force, as only five to ten percent of its size would be eaten away by friction upon atmospheric entry. If impact was imminent, Stardusting would be used. Yet, she worried, how could these aliens ascertain if that "merciful" action was necessary? How could they be sure *all life* would be in jeopardy of eventual and total annihilation by aftereffects?

Jana listened as her husband contacted the bridge and told the navigations officer to match the intimidating body's course and speed. He asked if the other ships had arrived either before or after them. They had, and all were in safely spaced orbits around the enormous rogue.

"Tell the crew and the other ships we'll get a good night's rest and begin our assault in the morning. I'll be on the bridge at first light."

She couldn't take her eyes off the dark threat to her civilization. "Will the lasers truly work, Ryker?" she asked. "Can you stop it from destroying Earth?"

"I'll do my best, Jana love. Stop looking at it and let's get to bed. Tomorrow will begin a busy and exhausting period. This task could take days . . . weeks. We've never tried it before."

"This is the first time you've tried something like this, ever?"

Varian saw her panic and wished he hadn't made that slip. "Yes, with these new weapons and this size body. Have faith in me and them, my love. Let's get to bed; morning will arrive before we know it."

Jana did as he said, to lay in his possessive and comforting embrace. For once, she felt free of Varian's ghost, or was it an illusion because so much depended upon the green-eyed blond at her side, her husband. They kissed and cuddled for a while, a momentous event looming ahead.

Chapter Eleven

One starship took its assigned location between the rogue worldlet and its ignorant target to send out deflective pulses to shield the mission against discovery by people and instruments on Earth. Its task was to mock a Black Hole that even a ray of light, such as a laser beam, couldn't escape.

While they waited for the energy shield to be readied, Science/First Officer Zade said, "It is fortunate Earthlings do not have any deep space probes nearby. Their Voyager missions ended years ago. That data unit malfunctioned before Neptune after passing and photographing Jupiter, Saturn, and Uranus, as the Earthlings named those bodies. Of course we know the pictures did not reveal the life on Uranus, or Earth would have begun another unmanned voyage immediately to make contact. Their probe's instruments could not penetrate the cloud barrier. They do not realize it is not freezing as they assume it must be. They do not suspect a source of internal heat that warms the planet and makes it livable for humans. Nor have they surmised accurately that something enormous, possibly the size of their world or the rogue out there, struck Uranus and tilted it on its axis. Soon, they will be studying the phenomena of an assumed Black Hole that suddenly appears and then mysteriously vanishes."

"What about the Uranians?" Jana asked. "They'll know we're here."

"It is fortunate Saturn is blocking us and our work from them," Zade told her. "When we passed within their detection range, we deflected their signals. They were and remain unaware of our presence."

"Are you sure Stardusting is necessary if you fail?" she asked the genial scientist. "Wouldn't at least the other side of the planet be all right?"

Zade wished she hadn't asked that question about her endangered world, but he replied with honesty. "The rogue's speed is swift now and will increase when it enters your atmosphere and gravitational pull. It will strike with cataclysmic force and evoke terrible aftereffects. The cloud of dust kicked up on impact and then explosion will cover the globe and shut out the sun's life-sustaining rays. After plants, animals, and fish die, man will use up his stored food supplies and he will perish, too, a horrible death if we do not prevent it. Too, there will be chain reactions around the planet: nuclear explosions, floods, quakes, slides, tidal waves, and more that will spread disease and contamination and certain death. Wars will break out among the survivors to take possession of what little is left. It will become a savage and barbaric place. I am sure you would not want to doom your world to such a fate when you can prevent it."

"I don't want to think about Stardust unless the situation becomes hopeless. If you can't smash it into harmless chunks, you can try to alter the rogue's course, can't you?"

"We analyzed that possibility but cannot be assured of not creating a worse disaster if it struck a smaller planet and disturbed the balance of your solar system. If the alignment of the planets was different, we could try to divert it past Earth and let the rogue carry itself into the sun and to its destruction.

Their positions will not change in our favor before it is too late. We could not keep altering its course past each planet in its path until it is beyond the last one; that would place our ships too close to your solar body and would ensure certain destruction of them.''

Officer Para, who was in charge of processing all data, reminded Jana, ''Star Fleet has relocated as many Earthlings as possible during the time we had. It would be cruel to inform those left behind of their impending peril. It would be wrong to instill terror when they are helpless to prevent it.''

''If you doubt the success of the rogue's destruction, why aren't you using this valuable time to save more of my people?'' Jana asked Zade.

''We believe the mission will succeed. If we do not use this time to try to accomplish it, far more people will perish horribly. Maffeians are familiar with the threat and fear of extinction, so we have made certain your race will survive, as we were forced to make certain ours did. We are doing our best to help you and your world.''

Jana did not remind him that she was a captive because of their desire to survive at any cost. Wouldn't she do almost anything to save Earth? She smiled at him and said, ''I know you are, Zade; thank you.''

Chem halted the talk by relating that the force shield was in position.

''Are the ten ships ready for testing their lasers?'' Varian asked.

Jana was surprised by the great number of starships being allowed away from Maffei at one time. Obviously they assumed there was no threat from Androas with her and Ryker in attendance. It warmed her heart to realize how important Maffei considered this mission.

''Yes, Prince Ryker. Five are in stack formation on both sides as you ordered. Each has matched course and speed with the target and other ships.'' Chem added that they could be in jeopardy at such a close range.

''To cut through the largest section, this range is necessary,''

Varian explained. "Order covers removed from the beam reflectors and raise them into position. I want all lasers aimed at the same stress point on the first shot to check the effect of the combined force on the rogue's composition. If it doesn't require all beams on the same spot to weaken the interior rift we believe is there, we can spread out our beams and bombard the entire section at the same time. Once it splits, five ships will attack each end. We'll shear off chunks until we have pieces small enough to be chased and disintegrated by particle-beam accelerator and photon blasts."

Varian's dyed-green gaze traveled from one officer to the next as he played his role of Ryker with skill. "Officer Jarre, make certain our course and speed do not vary even in the slightest." The navigational officer acknowledged the command. "Chief Jasani, keep a sharp eye on your indicators and handle any engineering troubles immediately."

"Yes, sir. The *Wanderlust* is cooing like a happy baby today."

"Excellent, just make sure it doesn't pitch a temper tantrum at the wrong time." Jasani grinned and nodded. "Officer Chem, keep us in contact with the other ships at all times; no break in communications, and pass along my last three orders." After Chem acknowledged the command and sent out the messages, the blond alien issued orders to the other men to check their sensors and scanners during the test to detect any problem. "Well, gentlemen and ladies, are we ready to begin our attack?" Varian asked.

Everyone nodded; they were all impressed by "Ryker." Varian hated making his evil half brother look good in their eyes.

Jana observed everything on the semicircular bridge. On her first visit long ago, the sights and sounds she witnessed had staggered her senses. She had viewed this setting at Varian's side, this complex conglomeration of computers, panels, and instruments. Officers and crew members were busy but attentive. She glanced at the wide window span which curled around on both sides. The heavens were an intense blue-black with hints of indigo, as they were partially shielded from the sun's illumination by Jupiter, the largest planet in her solar system. Off in the distance, vivid and harmonious hues of blue, red, and green cloudlike formations dappled the slowly brightening sky. They seemed adrift in a dark sea filled with millions of glittering fish and strange aquatic creatures.

"Officer Chem, alert the others we're ready to position the mirrors."

Jana observed with bated breath. Her husband certainly seemed to know what he was doing, and the crew was totally obedient and responsive to him. She was relieved, as much was at stake for her people and world. She also was impressed at how well her husband interacted with others. It seemed as if Ryker Triloni never ceased to amaze her and please her.

Jana glanced at the monitor as the reflector for the laser beam was raised from its parallel position during travel. As the giant device lifted the mirror upward, an apparatus clutched the protective cover and removed it. Ryker had told her that even a small scratch by space debris could pit and ruin the aiming unit. The lasers were mounted atop the front center portions of the starships while the mirrors were attached at the two rear ends of the U-shaped crafts. The reflectors were positioned at a height to avoid striking the vessels when the beams were fired backward to glance off the mirrors' surfaces and hit their mutual target. The laser worked by chemical reaction of gases formed from *Xenarogen*, *Tremolite*, and *Osorillium*: weapons and products by Trilabs and their creator, Ryker Triloni. Stardust was also one of her husband's formulas.

"Sir," Chem called out, "the *Star Fire* reports their reflector won't raise into position. It's stuck halfway. They'll send someone out to free it."

Varian knew it would look and sound best if he—as Ryker—handled the situation. "No, I'll go over in the shuttle with Tje and Kurtz. They've been programmed to specifically handle problems like this. Androids won't require life-support units to work outside. They'll save us time, and using them won't endanger any crewmen. I'll go with them to be on hand to check out any unexpected trouble. Alert Commander Gys we're enroute to do the repairs, and tell the other ships to stand by for further orders."

Jana grimaced at what she hoped and prayed wasn't a bad omen. She returned the encouraging smile her husband sent to her. She hated for him to leave the ship and put himself in possible peril. If anything happened to him . . . A terrible and wicked thought crossed her panicked mind. Surely the Supreme Council would not dare arrange "an accident" for him . . .

Everyone watched the monitor as the mission leader and two androids approached the *Star Fire* and halted the shuttle near the stubborn reflector. They observed with interest as the two mechanical beings left the craft and began repairs that required two hours.

Jana awaited her husband's return with rising suspicion and dread. She prayed it wasn't a cunning trap that would provoke trouble for everyone, including herself. She didn't know what she would do if something happened to Ryker, or what Maal would do in retaliation.

At last, Ryker, Tje, and Kurtz began their return to the *Wanderlust*. Jana sighed in relief, and chided herself for such foolish worries. She told herself they wouldn't dare harm a man who was so valuable to them.

Afterward, the disguised Varian said, "Officer Chem, tell the other ships we're ready to proceed with the test shot, to fire on my command. Officer Coran, raise the eye-protection screen."

Jana was almost breathless with suspense and trepidation. She stared at the moving rogue. *Die, you evil beast!* She heard the mission leader give the order to initiate Project Starguard. She saw five beams fuse into one large one at the point of attack, like flashlights combining power to focus one great light on the same spot. If not for the protective barrier over the *transascreen*, they wouldn't be able to watch the brilliant action without risking eye damage. The weapon emitted a loud buzzing sound that soon melted into a roar like that of hurricane winds or a jet at top speed passing within inches of her ears.

As far as she could tell, the combined force had no effect on the target, but they had calibrated the units with perfection.

"Cease firing," Varian commanded over the open communication system. "Any problems anywhere?"

"This is Lieutenant Commander Nigel Sanger on the *Kiunterri*. Our laser did not function. What do you suggest, Prince Ryker?"

"We need all the firepower we can get, Commander Sanger. Do your scanners indicate where the problem lies?"

There was a brief pause, but no one interrupted the conference in progress. The area and channel remained silent as a response was awaited.

Jana knew that voice and man, a dear friend. No, she fretted in lingering sadness that pinched her heart like cruel fingers, a deceitful *past* friend. A man who had carried out Varian's treacherous orders to drug her and ship her off to Ryker like unwanted baggage, with an apology from him as he did the dirty work for his best friend and commanding officer.

"Our sensors show no liquids reaching the reaction cylinder to form *Barine*," Nigel replied. "Do you want us to check the triaxial connectors and shut-off valves, or would you prefer to handle the malfunction yourself? None of us know much about your new weapon or the chemicals."

"I'll come over with Tje and Kurtz to handle it. Everyone stand by."

Once more, Jana eyed the monitor as her husband and the two androids left in the shuttle. She watched the small craft hover over the giant starship while the androids exited and approached the device to see if it could be repaired before too much time was lost. Suspicions gnawed at her gut again and her imagination began to run wild with crazy and fearful thoughts: a set-up? Trap? Sabotage? Had she been allowed to tag along as a witness for Maal that Ryker had died in an accident? Was her husband as irreplaceable as he and others had told her? Would they attempt to get rid of what they perceived as an enormous threat to their safety? If anything happened to Ryker, she would be a widow in an alien world, yet a free woman and citizen of Maffei . . . available for Varian to try to enchant again. Had her being a gift to Ryker been a clever ruse from the beginning? Had she been sent to the Prince to get under his skin so they could get rid of Ryker, let her inherit Trilabs, then hope Varian could get the powerful complex through the widow who had once loved the Star Fleet commander? Was that why Varian wasn't along on one of the other ships, to prevent his being a suspect in Maal's eyes? Was a deadly trap the reason why the Supreme Council and Varian had allowed Ryker to take charge of this mission? Was Varian so conceited that he believed he could win her back after betraying her?

Soon it was learned a pipe was bent and the chemicals couldn't flow past the damaged location. The nonhuman team, wearing magnetic boots and attached by cables to the top of the *Kiunterri* to prevent drifting off into space, went to work to correct the problem. A spurt of fluid shot out, was ignited, and almost eradicated Tje. At the ready, Kurtz extinguished the blaze with a special formula then shut off the escape of flammable liquid.

"Don't anybody panic; we have everything under control," Varian said over the speaker; he knew the small fire was in view. He hauled the damaged android inside while the remaining one continued the work alone.

Jana's tension mounted. If that had been Ryker instead of Tje, he could have been killed after Nigel lured him over there. She knew she wouldn't relax until he was back aboard and safe. She wished he had sent someone else or only the androids to do the repairs. She was certain Ryker did not plan the malfunctions in his weapons just to prove how much he was needed here. Besides, Star Fleet had installed them and should have noticed any defective parts. Surely the apparatuses had been tested after mounting. She hoped the mission wasn't doomed to fail.

Time passed slowly for Jana. She began to pace, a worried expression on her face that told everyone how anxious she was over her husband's safety.

"You should not worry so much, Princess Jana," Zade

comforted her. "Who better than the creator of the weapons and chemicals to repair and direct their use? He will be fine. He is staying in the shuttle away from danger."

She wanted to scream, *What if the shuttle explodes? Please, God, don't let me be a witness to such a tragedy. Don't allow these people to harm my husband as they've harmed me. He's risking his life and using his weapons to save my world, your creation. Protect him, please.*

More time passed, and Jana wanted to send another shuttle to check on Ryker. It had been quiet—too quiet—for a long time. She went to Chem and told the communications officer she wanted to speak with her husband.

The man sent her a strange look. "Now, Princess Jana? He's busy."

She used a firm but calm tone to respond, "Yes, now."

"Perhaps he shouldn't be disturbed. We're running behind schedule."

"I know, Chem. But contact him anyway, please."

The officer did so on a closed channel.

"How much longer will it take?" she asked. "I'm worried about you."

"Soon, Jana," her alien husband replied. "We're almost finished. And I'm fine."

"Be careful and hurry back."

Varian detected fear and tension in her voice. "I will."

Martella noticed the expression on Jana's face, the mingling of undeniable affection and fear in her gaze, and the sound of them in her voice. The alien female tried to distract the worried Earthling with light conversation.

Jana guided Martella away from the others. "Would you tell me if there is something very wrong going on?" she asked.

"What do you mean, Jana? He has the repairs under control."

Jana voiced her suspicions aloud to the woman in a tone only Martella Karsh could hear. She watched shock register on the Maffeian's face.

"How could you think such a terrible thing about us?"

"In light of how and why I came to your world and what's happened to me since I arrived, I have just cause to be suspicious of anything involving Varian Saar and the culture that imprisoned me. I've been told what all Maffeians think about my husband. If this is a trap, you had better warn them to stop it right now. I will not be used as a pawn to get rid of Ryker and get Trilabs for your side."

"You're mistaken, Jana. I promise, he's in no danger."

"If you're wrong and anything happens to him, everyone involved will be sorry. I won't tell *Kadim* Maal it was an accident, if that's why I was permitted to come along. I warn you now, if I'm made a widow, it will not profit Varian or the Alliance in the smallest way. If Varian thinks he can get control of Trilabs by sucking up to me later, he's dead wrong. He can't even compare to my husband, so Ryker had better come back safe."

Martella wanted to shout the truth at Jana to open her eyes: *That isn't your husband! It's the only man you love!* Yet, she felt guilty and ashamed to realize that part of the ruse had to do with what Jana suspected: obtaining and controlling Trilabs for the protection and survival of Maffei. Since Jana had been captured and enslaved for that same reason of safeguarding Maffei, learning it had occurred again was not going to sit well with the Earthling. Martella glued her gaze to Jana's and vowed, "The man out there will come back safe and sound, and he'll remain safe and sound. I swear."

Jana thought her response was odd, but she nodded and accepted it. "Thank you, Martella. I just don't want any more trouble. I've endured enough, and all because of Varian and his selfishness."

"I understand. You'll be back where you belong soon."

Again, Jana thought her reply and tone were strange. She didn't have time to question them as Chem shouted, "They're heading back."

Jana rushed to the *transascreen* and watched the shuttle approach from the *Kiunterri*. She couldn't wait to see her husband, so she rushed to the docking bay. She flung herself into his arms and hugged him in relief. "You scared the wits out of me. Don't leave this ship again! Please, Ryker, no more risks. I would die if anything happened to you."

Varian, with a tormented mind and heavy heart, gave her a quick hug and kiss. "Let's join the others; we have work to do. Time's running out."

All day, Jana heard a series of long laser blasts with brief cessations every so often while the apparatus cooled and formed more *Barine* gas. She felt as if she were standing trackside at Daytona Speedway while race cars whizzed past at top paces. Every six hours, the task was halted for a longer period while more chemicals were added to the devices. It looked as if the rogue refused to split in half. Maybe, she fretted, it was too thick and solid to be sawed in half by anything, including Ryker's powerful weapons.

It was late the next day when an elated shout went up as the rogue cracked. The ships and beams continued to attack the weakening rift with new zeal. A small piece of rock that was sheared off struck the reflector of one ship between automatic blasts, too fast to push a stop button to prevent the next shot. The pitted area caused the laser beam to fire upward instead of forward and to strike the ship above it in the stack formation. The powerful beam knifed into the vessel's underbelly in the engineering section before the device could be shut down. An explosion rent the air. The ship was crippled and in danger of being destroyed any moment.

Assault on the worldlet stopped while an emergency rescue went into effect. The uninjured, wounded, and the few dead were taken aboard other starships. By remote, the burning craft was piloted to a location in which it couldn't endanger the other ships. Within twenty minutes of reaching its final destination, it exploded and sent debris in all directions.

Jana looked up at her frowning husband as they observed

the alarming episode. "I never expected any of them to get killed. I hope they don't treat us differently because they lost lives and a ship. What else can go wrong? Will they call off the mission?"

"No, Jana, we'll keep working with the remaining nine ships. We'll just be more careful. Being this close presents peril, but it's necessary. We'll start up again soon. Go on to bed; you need rest."

"So do you, my love. You didn't come to bed last night."

"I took occasional naps. I'm fine. I've gone without sleep plenty of times. There's nothing you can do here . . . Except distract me," he added with a tender smile to conceal his irritation at being unable to handle this emergency while playing Ryker instead of being commander of his ship.

"Will you call me if anything happens?"

"I promise. Don't worry so much. We expected it to take this long to sever the stress point. It might take until morning or longer. Go to bed."

Far away from the battle in progress with the rogue worldlet, Canissia Garthon was speaking with Prince Taemin Tabriz on the planet Cenza in the Pyropean Galaxy. Her body quivered with eagerness to share her astonishing secret, but she waited in order to enjoy the intoxicating suspense a while longer. "Tell me, my salacious treat, does that little Tarterrian you wed a few months ago please you as much as I do?" she questioned Taemin.

"There is no comparison between you two. You know I married her because Father insisted; he wanted a strong bond with the Maffei II Galaxy where her father is the ruler. Jurad thinks it is necessary in case we lose Androas as our ally. At least the bride he selected and foisted onto me isn't totally plain. In the dark or with my eyes closed, I can pretend she is anyone I desire. Sometimes that is *you*, Cass. I suppose I am fortunate she was trained to obey her superiors without question; so far she has never refused any order I have given.

Recently when I demanded certain acts, I saw hesitation in her gaze, but I made her too terrified to expose my treatment and epicurean preferences to anyone. If she finds the courage to defy me in the future, I have ways of forcing her to do as I wish."

Canissia peeled a colorful robe from his body to find him naked underneath. Her gaze sparkled as she stroked the virile chest of a man who was magnificent in bed and a strong ally out of it. They made a good team, she concluded, as the young Pyropean ruler had dark and greedy appetites to match her own. Besides, Taemin was the perfect tool to help her extract revenge on Varian and Jana while he was trying to increase the size of his empire. "Have you considered an accident to be rid of your puny bride?"

"Of course, my sweet Cass, but it is too soon to carry out that plan."

She fondled his body with boldness and familiarity. "Your father will object to her loss unless she first provides you with an heir."

"Let that offensive creature mother my children? I am neither crazy nor desperate. I take precautions to make certain that can never happen. If Father gets in the way of my plans, he'll follow the same path into the ground where she will go soon. But I cannot act in reckless haste; I must be certain I have no need of her or ties to her father's empire. Tarterria is too small and poor to tempt me to slay him, so I can rule and rape it through my wife as its heir. Few things sound more distasteful than sitting on the Tarterrian throne with that stupid weakling at my side. I do not even want to fuse that offensive territory to Pyropea. I only agreed to the temporary union to make Father so content that he is blinded to my real desires and plans. When I take Father's place, Pyropea will know a greatness and power such as she has never possessed until my glorious reign."

The redhead smiled in sadistic pleasure. If Jurad and Taemin's bride were slain, Taemin would become the Supreme Ruler. If she married him, as Ruleress, she would be safe from all enemy threats and would have an elite position in which to do as she pleased. As she sank to her knees, Canissia drifted her hands and lips down his body to his most sensitive area and brought it to instant life. Because of that Earthling witch, her mind scoffed, she had lost both Varian and Ryker! But Jana would pay soon, she vowed. For now, the only thing she could do was become closer with Taemin and kill Varian, who was no doubt setting a trap for her and would spring it the moment she showed herself. She wouldn't give the ebony-haired god the chance to ensnare her; it was he who would become *her* captive. Yes, she mused, the lascivious prince was the answer to her problems, but not as his mistress.

Amidst her stirring siege, she murmured, "If you become ruler here, my lusty prince, you can conquer the Tri-Galaxy with my help. In addition to the secrets I've stolen from Father for your benefit, I can help you get control of Trilabs. With its powers and weapons, its takeover will be easy. Of course, there is a tiny price for being your ally."

Taemin writhed and relished as she licked, nursed, and made playful nibbles at his manhood. He groaned in bliss as her skilled tongue swirled around his throbbing manhood. "What will it cost me, you talented enchantress?"

Canissia halted only a moment to glance at him and reveal, "I want to become Ruleress of the Tri-Galaxy we shall own."

The lascivious man deliberated the seriousness of her words. He knew how greedy and insatiable the woman was: for sex, for wealth, for expensive possessions, for power, for status. Until recently, that list had included Varian Saar and Ryker Triloni, though she had tried to keep those facts from him. "That can be arranged, and will be most satisfying for us in many ways, including this one, my flaming-haired temptress."

She drove him wild by running her tongue around the pleading tip of his fiery shaft, then paused to grin and say in a merry tone, "I thought you might agree." She worked on him again for a few minutes before halting her tantalizing task to talk, but her moisture-slick hand continued to stroke the ravenous prince. "I had Father check on the marriage registration between Ryker and Jana; it's legal and binding. I'm certain it shocked Varian to discover his lost puss was bound to his worst enemy. Since he had freed her, there was nothing poor Varian could do about the matter, not even about my part in it. Jana believed that little tale Ryker and I told her about being given to him. She hasn't and will never deny the claim that she escaped with my help. Allegedly I took her to Ryker's because she felt that was the only place she would be safe from Varian's clutches. As a scientist, she supposedly went there to work for and with him in Trilabs. But they fell in love and got married. How sweet and romantic and deceitful,'' she scoffed, then returned to her task.

Taemin licked his lips as he envisioned the exquisite Earthling *charl* his father had attempted to purchase to become his wife. It would be sheer heaven to be training Jana to serve him instead of the repugnant creature his father had chosen for him after Varian and the Supreme Council had denied their matrimonial request: a decision ''controlled by Maffei law.''

As he had done many times since meeting Jana, the debauched prince closed his eyes and pretended the woman giving him pleasure was that golden-haired goddess. He groaned in achingly sweet torment. He writhed and squirmed as his urgency for release mounted. His hands gripped Canissia's head and held it tightly as his hips made forceful thrusts. Within minutes he pumped his climactic nectar into the redhead's mouth. He praised Canissia's talents as he helped her from her knees, then the merry couple collapsed to the bed to relax and talk.

''Do you think Ryker takes her to bed?'' he asked. ''You know he never seemed to care much for most women. But then, Jana Greyson Triloni is not most women. She is unique and highly desirable. I would love to ravish her from head to foot.''

Miffed by Jana's appeal to her new target, Canissia retorted, ''Possibly he raped her or used his sex drugs on her before he died.''

Taemin propped up to stare at her. ''What do you mean,

before he died?'' he asked. ''I have not heard that shocking news. How? When?''

Canissia related her discovery. ''From the date on the marriage registration,'' she added, ''Varian isn't the one who wed her in the cunning disguise he's using these days, but that doesn't matter to us. What matters is that she's Ryker's widow, or will be as soon as news of his death is revealed. That means our little alien puss owns Trilabs. I have the feeling she doesn't know Varian is impersonating Ryker, which fits perfectly into our scheme. As soon as he finishes playing his half brother, I'm sure he intends to woo the rich and powerful widow and win her back to get Trilabs for the Alliance. I have no doubt Jana will fall into his arms the first moment he curls his finger at her. But he won't get the opportunity, my tasty treat. Once we get our hands on her, Trilabs is ours.''

''You think she is going to hand it over to us even as our prisoner? She is not dumb. Nor did she strike me as being a coward or a weakling.''

''With the little treasures in my possession, she won't be able to say no to us about anything. I'll even let you have her to use for a while, as many times as you please, in any way you please; and I know what pleases you most. I can see her in chains, your lash striking her body all over, you red and slick with her blood from mounting her from every direction. Imagine the fun you can have with her at your mercy, especially with her drugged into compliance.'' Canissia painted erotic sadistic word pictures to tempt Taemin into aiding the brazen and dangerous trap she would suggest soon. Before she had finished creating the clever perverted images, she witnessed his eagerness to join her side.

''Pain is a potent stimulant, Cass. I look forward to many hours of titillation and satisfaction with her as my obedient and helpless slave. I am sure you will enjoy watching me with her as much as you will enjoy taking sweet revenge on your ex-lover. Even without your drugs, I am sure either of them will do anything we say to keep the other alive and safe; that lie will serve us well with them.''

The deviant Canissia trembled with excitement. "I can hardly wait to get them in our clutches. What can anyone do to stop us? Nothing. Tirol and the others involved in this ruse can't expose the fact Varian is impersonating Ryker. They can't find an excuse to justify a rescue or attack here if they even suspect we set a trap for those two. After we have our fun and extract the complex code from them, we'll arrange an accident to cover our sweet success. We'll blow up the ship supposedly taking your guests home. You won't mind sacrificing one ship, captain, and crew for our protection?"

"Of course not. As long as the last Saar dies and we get what we want from Jana, I will do whatever is necessary to make our plan work. We must not let anything or anyone stand in our way."

"Right now, my greedy prince, our desires need sating in another way. It's my turn to experience rapture beneath your talented hands and lips. Reward me generously for what I shall soon give to you: the Tri-Galaxy to rule and myself at your side as your new wife."

In his secret haven, Taemin appeased her rampant urges many times and in many ways. He knew how far to go in his pain-and-pleasure games to give her supreme and enthralling satisfaction yet make her beg for more. He savored how easy it was to drive her wild with his skills and with his knowledge of her deepest and darkest desires. He would let the conceited bitch serve him in and out of bed and let her believe they were partners. After he had taken all he needed or wanted from her, he would rid himself of the valueless and untrustworthy Cass and his sickening wife, then lay claim to Ryker's matchless and captive widow and take possession of his father's federation.

At ten the next morning in the Milky Way Galaxy, the stress point of the potato-shaped rogue gave way and it parted into two uneven ends. Four ships bombarded one piece to reduce it into smaller chunks to be chased and disintegrated, while five ships worked on the other section. Whenever a large fragment was carved away by laser knife, a ship left the group to pursue and destroy it, then returned for another piece.

Jana eyed a fragment before it began to drift off in the vast space that surrounded them. It was dark brown with an olive-like exterior similar to the meteorites she had seen on display and on videotape at Meteor Crater in Arizona: a huge hole created long ago when an enormous body impacted with Earth at forty-three thousand miles per hour. The inner surface exposed mostly a black interior with green, tan, white, and silver bits. In a few places she saw silvery white with blue to greenish blue speckling. Ryker told her the body was made up of stone, iron, a little nickel and cobalt, a few amino acids, and scattered space debris.

For a while, she observed the difficult work at her husband's side.

At night, in bed alone, Jana was awakened by blasts of the lasers as they were fired down the area between the sides of the U-shaped vessel and bounced off the reflector mounted nearby. Varian's quarters were located at the top rear of one side, while the Stardust Room and botanical garden were positioned in the same place in the other side. With three decks, the *Wanderlust* was gigantic and magnificent. It had everything required to sustain life, to carry out their assignments, and to provide needed amusements. This time, their assignment was critical to Jana.

Each time the noises disturbed her slumber, she would remind herself of what they were trying to do and would pray again for success. During lulls of the noise when chemicals were being added and the lasers were cooling, she would nap in spurts and dream of Ryker.

Four days of nerve-wracking and body-wearying work were required until the last largest fragment was shattered into harmless chunks. For many, including Varian, it was days and nights of short naps, swift or no shaves, quick meals, no love-making, and rapid changes of clothes.

When the shouts of victory sounded in the *Wanderlust* and over the communications system from other ships, he was exhausted. Yet, he was ecstatic to know that Jana's world was safe from catastrophe. Surely when she discovered he and not Ryker was the one who had led this Earth-saving mission, she would be grateful to him, and perhaps lenient toward him for his critical ruse. At present, she hugged him and praised him.

Varian leaned over to the communications panel and said to all the men: "Together we accomplished a great deed. On behalf of me and my wife, thank you for your hard work and cooperation. To the families, friends, and loved ones of the four men and one woman who died on this glorious mission, we extend our sympathies. I think everyone should relax tomorrow before heading to Rigel with victory flags flying high. A celebration would be in order and, I'm sure, appreciated by your crews. Thank you and good night. Ryker Triloni out."

Varian turned and looked at the officers and crewmembers on the bridge of his ship. He wished his friends, especially Nigel and Tris, were here to celebrate with him and Jana. He smiled and asked, "Well, is everyone too tired to party tonight?"

Kurtz was put in control of navigation of the ship while almost everyone headed to the appropriate areas for celebration. The officers and two guests entered the Stardust Room, while crewmembers partied in the crew mess hall and rec room. Varian wished everyone could have fun together tonight, but rank was never cast aside for any reason. And in his disguise, he had no authority to change the situation.

Jana liked the elegant setting and allowed her gaze to take in its beauty. The decor was intended to give one the feeling of dining on an open terrace beneath the stars and moonlight. There were scenic outdoor murals on two of the side walls, while the remaining two were of a transparent glasslike material. The ceiling was a retractable panel that could be moved aside to reveal the heavens. Small pin-size bulbs were mounted in such a fashion as to blend unnoticeably with twinkling stars overhead. The remaining fixtures, furniture, and decorations were a careful harmonizing of amber, sky blue, and forest green. Soft music seemed to come from every direction at the same time. Muted laughter and quiet chatter filtered between the dreamy strains. The room was filled with gaiety, excitement, and tranquility—all of which Jana was feeling at that moment in her husband's arms as they swayed to romantic music.

"It's over, it's really over," Jana murmured. "Earth is safe. And it's because of you, my husband. How can I ever reward you properly?"

Varian, his wits dulled by fatigue and her nearness, grinned and said, "I'm sure I can think of a way you can thank me properly, Moonbeam."

Jana wished he wouldn't call her by Varian's pet name for her, but she didn't chide him, not tonight of all nights. Later, she would ask him to check on what would happen to her people on Anais. "It's like an early Christmas present for everyone on Earth, a miracle, the miracle of life. Do you know how wonderful you are and how lucky I am?"

"I can say the same thing about you, woman."

After a few dances and delicious meal, he said, "If you've partied enough, can we leave? I'm too tired to hold my eyes open another minute."

Over three weeks later, Jana and the blond alien were standing in the planetarium bubble atop the ship and gazing into space. After several days of rest and recuperation, Varian had been so relaxed and jubilant that this ruse would be over soon that he had been much too romantically attentive to Jana. Yet, he had promised himself he would not take her again as his half brother and, hard as it had been, he had kept his word.

Despite that physical denial, Jana had been drawn closer and closer to "Ryker" and had finally begun to feel as if she had conquered her past with Varian. She leaned against the clear *transascreen* and gave a dreamy sigh. "I believe we've come to trust each other enough to say anything within our hearts and minds. Am I right, my husband?"

"Of course you are, love."

"The past is finally over, Ryker, for both of us. I'm free of Varian, and you said you've taken your last revenge on him. All that stands ahead of us is a happy future. I love you and want you, only you. I believe you feel the same way about me. From this day forth, it's just the two of us."

Varian's heart almost stopped beating as he heard those alarming words. A sensation akin to sheer terror washed over him when he realized he had carried his Ryker ruse too far. He had planned one last visit to Maal's before arranging Ryker's "death," confessing all to Jana, and starting over with her. He realized he could either let her join in on the remaining task or he could go see Maal alone. Either way, he had to tell her the truth before it was too late, if it wasn't already.

"Jana, there's something important I must tell you."

She turned to face him fully and smiled. "What is it, my love?"

He decided to blurt it out then explain. "I'm—"

"Prince Ryker, there's an urgent call for you, sir."

"Urgent?" Varian murmured, then stepped to the panel and said, "This is Ryker. An urgent message about what and from whom?"

"From Prince Taemin Tabriz," Chem replied. "He says it's important."

Varian glanced at Jana in confusion as he asked, "He asked for me?"

"Yes, sir."

"How did he know I was aboard?"

"I don't know, sir. Shall I put him through?"

"I'll take it in Commander Saar's quarters. Tell him to stand by until I get there," Varian told him, as the line on his desk was protected in case Chem thought he should listen in on the odd communication.

"I'll tell him, sir."

Varian looked at Jana. "Wait for me here; I won't be long."

"How would Taemin know you're here?" Jana asked in confusion.

"Grandfather must have told him to prevent an attack on us or to boast about me taking Varian's place and his ship. I'll see what he wants from me."

The blond was gone before she could ask why he couldn't take the message in front of her or why he wanted to be alone when he heard it.

When Varian finished talking with Taemin, he summoned Martella to his quarters and explained the astonishing situation.

"You can't do this, Varian! It's too dangerous. Ryker didn't make any plans like these with Taemin; you came up with the idea of taking your place on this mission. How did he get such information?"

"Maal has to be behind it."

"Are you certain you have Ryker's grandfather fooled?"

"Positive. And Cass's ship is under surveillance at Zenufia. It has been since shortly after she gave our shadows the slip."

"Canissia is cunning and daring. Don't underestimate her evil."

"With *Moonwind*'s type of system, any message from Cass to Taemin would have been detected by our sensors. At first, I suspected Taemin was removing us from danger before attacking the group, but I doubt that's his motive with those chemical lasers mounted on our ships. Taemin said he had something vital concerning both of us to discuss with me. He refused to give any clues over the air. It could be a revelation of an imminent or future attack on Maffei. He did say he had a foolproof way to get rid of my 'worst rival and his only kin.' How can I protect Grandfather and myself if I don't learn where those threats will rear their ugly heads? Imagine what I can accomplish, Martella. I have to go and discover what he's up to. I'll get him in a talkative mood that will supply information about his past or future plots. It'll give us leverage against him and the Pyropeans when treaty time comes. We need that truce badly or Taemin will keep things stirred up. If he isn't stopped or weakened, he'll find a way to use Ryker's death to his advantage. I would be stupid to pass up this chance to get evidence on them and to coax them toward a truce. You report to Grandfather and Brec, and tell them not to worry about us."

"Us? You really are taking Jana with you?" As he nodded, she reasoned, "That isn't wise or safe. For many reasons, Varian. Including the fact that this will stall your confession to her. You were going to tell her everything after a final visit to Maal to show him you returned safely and to impress our strength on him. You know that must be done; Maal is sure to have the same suspicions Jana had. Another delay has me worried. This ruse is taking too long."

"I'm worried, too. Talk about sorry timing, I was about to begin my confession when this cursed call came in, but I only got one word out of my mouth. As soon as we leave the Tabrizes, I'll tell her everything. If she doesn't understand and won't aid my final ruse with Maal, I'll go there alone while Nigel keeps Jana on Darkar. I can't confess the truth tonight, not with her heading into Taemin's perceptive presence. She believes I'm Ryker and she's half in love with him. Her behavior will help dupe Taemin. Between our new marriage and her beauty, that devious prince should be distracted enough not to guess it's me. If I told Jana the truth, her reaction would surely expose us because she wouldn't have time to adjust to my confession. And I certainly can't tell her then leave her captive on this ship. *Kahala* help us for the unmerciful demands this is making on me and Jana for intergalactic peace!"

"Are you sure you know what you're doing, Varian? Please refuse. She could make a slip and endanger both of you."

"Damn the stars, I have her completely fooled, and that scares me, Martella. Right now, I have her closer to him and more in love with him than with me. But how could I logically explain coming to Cenza alone and not bringing her when she's aboard? Ryker promised Jurad a visit weeks ago. If I don't accept, I might not get another chance with them as Ryker. I must halt Taemin's threat and power. If his ship wasn't nearby, I would have said we'd visit later. As much as I hate to take her there, it would seem too strange to leave her on the *Wanderlust* with a Maffei crew and heading for Star Base where Varian is supposed to be. If that lookalike cyborg was used a few times at a safe distance as we decided, everyone should believe I never left Rigel and Altair. As soon as we're gone, inform Nigel about this predicament and tell him to place the other ships on alert status. Tell him to keep an eye and ear open enroute and at Taemin's, in case anything goes wrong and we need help."

"How could you get a message to him if problems or dangers arise?"

"I'll find a way; I always manage to get myself out of trouble."

"This time, you'll have Jana as an additional complication. If she's in peril, it could cost you your lives. I'll make sure Nigel doesn't lose contact with you two. I just have a terrible feeling about this situation."

"You can distract yourself from worry by handling that other matter. You and Tris take care of the return home of the Earthlings on Anais. While I'm gone, send everybody back except Andrea McKay. Take her to Darkar with you. Before Jana and I arrive there, she'll be told the truth, all of it. Maybe knowing her best friend is safe and awaiting her will soften her heart toward me. Use those mind implants and none of the Earthlings will remember their misadventure. And don't forget to embed those medical cures in Dr. Martin's mind. We can share that much with them."

"What did Prince Taemin want?" Jana asked. "Your talk took so long."

"To extend an invitation for us to make an official visit to Cenza. Our ship was picked up on their tracking system and he knew we were aboard. It seems Grandfather boasted of my action to him and warned off any attack on the fleet by letting

Taemin know we're aboard. He has a ship waiting nearby for us. After our visit, he'll have an escort take us home; the *Wanderlust* and others will continue on to Star Base."

"You accepted? We're leaving with his men?"

He forced a smile and caressed her cheek. "That's right, my love. Taemin says he has important matters to discuss with me, business and personal. I couldn't refuse. Do you mind? He insisted on seeing you again."

"I really don't care to see Taemin or Jurad again," Jana admitted. "I didn't like them. But I suppose since it's an official visit, you can't reject his invitation."

"No, I can't, and I'm intrigued by what he wants. Grandfather must have told him I'm against an alliance with them for any future attack on Maffei. He probably wants to convince me otherwise."

"The Tabrizes plan to attack Maffei and want Androas's help?"

Varian tried to sound casual and unconcerned to calm her fears. "The Tabrizes are always talking about a vengeful conquest of Maffei; they have done so since Jurad lost Mother to Galen. If they were serious, they wouldn't have waited this long. Don't worry, it's big talk, nothing more, especially without the help of Grandfather and me. And I'll make sure that doesn't happen."

"If you're blocking his path, will it be safe for us to go there?"

Varian chuckled as if amused. "Taemin is bold and arrogant, but he isn't a fool. He can't afford to provoke Grandfather against him by harming us. And he certainly doesn't want to anger me." He watched her fret over the unforeseen and unpleasant situation, as he was doing inside. Yet, he couldn't pass up this golden opportunity to dupe Taemin and Jurad as Ryker. Nor could he deny himself the chance to obtain details from Taemin about the clues he'd been given today. "It will be over soon, my love, and we'll be home together. I promise. Pack light because we're not staying long. I have important work to do."

Jana realized the matter was out of her control, so she acquiesced by dropping the subject. "What did you start to tell me before Taemin called you? Something important, you said."

Varian pulled her into his arms and kissed her. Then he grinned and said, "I was going to tell you how much I love you."

Jana couldn't venture a guess as to why her husband wasn't being honest. Perhaps something that had taken place with Taemin prevented him from saying what had been on his mind. "I love you, too. Let's get moving; you said our escort is waiting."

Varian took a precaution to prevent problems with the new crew. In the docking bay where a shuttle would deliver them to Taemin's ship, he spoke with the First Officer who was taking command of the *Wanderlust*. "Taemin and I are allies of a sort, Lieutenant Zade, but initiating an alert would be wise. Since he knew we were aboard, he knows too much about this affair. Taemin is unpredictable at times, so be on guard for trouble. If you don't mind, have the rest of our things put on the next Trilabs ship that makes deliveries at Star Base."

The moment the Pyropean ship crossed the galaxy boundary, Varian found himself and Jana taken captive by Taemin's men. He cursed himself for allowing his love to fall into this cunning trap with him. He admitted that Martella was right about her fears of duplicity. He berated himself for being too overconfident in his Ryker ruse and too desperate for peace. He tried to bluff his way out. "This is an outrage!" he exploded. "Release us this instant! My grandfather, *Effecta* Maal, will have your heads for this. Does Pyropea challenge Androas to war? Are you fools?"

"Check them for weapons and communicators," the leader ordered as he ignored Varian's threats and questions.

"We don't have any and didn't think we needed any," a furious Varian scoffed. "We never expected trouble or threats from friends and allies."

As they were hand-searched by two men, the leader said, "There won't be any trouble if you two behave."

"There will be as soon as Grandfather, *Effecta* Maal," he stressed the ruler's name and rank to strike fear into them, "hears of this."

"That's a problem for Prince Taemin, not me. My orders are to bring you to him, uninjured if possible, in chains if necessary."

Jana gasped in fear and gaped at the three towering blonds with ice-blue eyes who reminded her of ancient Viking Norsemen. How could they dare do this? "In chains? Why? Has he forgotten who we are?"

"Orders are orders, Princess Jana. You won't be harmed by us, unless you do something stupid. You can say anything you want to the prince when we dock. It won't do any good with me. To disobey him is certain death."

Jana observed in panic as the men refused to answer any questions.

"Take the woman to my quarters and lock her in. Take him to the cell we made and confine him there. Remember, no tricks and you're safe."

"You'll regret this offense and will pay with your lives," the blond alien said. "If you harm a single hair on my wife's head, I'll slay you with my bare hands. Perhaps you should warn Prince Taemin that I contacted *Effecta* Maal before we left the Maffei ship. I told him to be on alert for trouble. If he does not hear from me each day by sundown, he will move against Pyropea. Is that clear?"

"Clear, but we have our orders. Don't expect company where we're headed, Prince Ryker. A decoy drone was launched at the same time our detection deflectors went up. If anybody is in pursuit of us, they'll follow the drone's signal; we're shielded from their scanners and sensors. Don't cause trouble because I also have orders to escort you two home as soon as Prince Taemin finishes his meeting with you."

Varian didn't believe the man's claims. They were not only in jeopardy but were also out of contact with Nigel and the *Kiunterri*. If he didn't have Jana along, he would wait until he reached Taemin and risk bluffing his way out of this predicament. A gut instinct warned him not to let them get near the devious prince. If he couldn't come up with a successful escape plan, this unforeseen incident and his recklessness might unmask him and destroy all of the work he had paid so dearly to accomplish. Worse, it could get them killed.

A terrified Jana was taken to the captain's quarters and locked inside. She didn't trust the Tabrizes and sensed that something awful was afoot, something Ryker had never expected. She had seen her struggling and angry husband hauled off in the other direction while shouting over his shoulder to her to do as they said and to stay calm.

Stay calm? Like you're staying calm? You know we're in terrible danger. No doubt Prince Taemin thinks you've joined the Maffeians and betrayed him. And he probably thinks it's my fault for changing and influencing you. What evil is awaiting us ahead?

Chapter Twelve

Garus, leader of the captors, shoved "Ryker" toward a compartment opening after letting the prisoner out to go to the lavatory before he turned in for the night, as there were no facilities in the rigged cell. Though he appeared distracted, Varian was alert for an opportunity to overpower the Pyropean, who was armed and seemed to be taking no risks. As far as Varian knew, there were only three enemies to best, and he had defeated greater odds in the past, and with less at stake than the lives of him and Jana.

"Prince Taemin ordered me to keep you two separated after we reached a safe distance from the others and you were taken captive," Garus said. "He said you weren't to be harmed unless you were disobedient. If you do, I'm to use any force necessary to deliver you to him. I doubt you would be stupid with your wife in my care."

"Don't worry about me. I'll do my talking with Taemin."

"Prince Taemin also said to tell you, and only you, that he and Cass are eager to see you and Jana. He said to tell you they've learned your secret game and the four of you will be playing it. You're heading to his private dwelling and not the palace, so you won't be disturbed. We're the only ones who know about your secret visit, and it will remain that way. Now get inside."

Varian pretended to obey but whirled at the last minute and sent a chopping blow across Garus's wrist. The weapon went skidding across the floor. Varian attacked the Pyropean with all his energy. A fist into the Adam's apple then one to the groin sent Garus to his knees, struggling to breathe and defend himself. Varian seized a metal object and clobbered Garus on the head, rendering him unconscious. He shoved his foe into the compartment and switched on the electrical beams that guarded the door in case the villain awoke before they escaped.

Varian realized his opportunity hadn't come a moment too soon. He could imagine what plans Taemin and Cass had in mind for them! He would kill Jana before allowing her to fall into their wicked hands. He sneaked from the area, slipped up on the man at the control panel, and clubbed him on the head. With stealth, he went from room to room to disable any crewman he found, but there were only the three aboard. He checked the emergency escape pod for supplies, weapons, and a communicator whose signal he hopefully could alter to summon Nigel. He studied the self-destruct mechanism to make certain he knew how to give the correct code in a hurry. He went to the captain's quarters to fetch Jana. He had left her until last to save time and arguments after she discovered his plans. Until he had her safe, he wouldn't start any delaying trouble by telling her who he really was.

Jana was in a light doze when she heard the door open and saw a tall shadow framed there for a moment before it swished closed. She readied herself to use the self-defense skills Martella had taught her. Her heart pounded and she wondered if her impending attacker heard the change in her breathing.

"It's me, Jana. Let's get out of here."

"Ryker? My God, how did you get away?"

"I overpowered my guard and another man, but I don't

know how many others might be elsewhere on the ship, so there is no time to talk now. We have to sneak to the emergency escape pod and get off this ship.''

''Escape pod?''

He grasped her arm and pulled her toward the door, then released it. ''There is no time to explain. I'll show you. Be quiet and stay behind me.''

Jana obeyed, but a hand kept contact with his body for courage and reassurance. At the bridge, she nudged him and motioned to the man who appeared to be resting his head or sleeping at the control panel.

''It's all right,'' he whispered. ''I got him earlier. The ship's on auto-pilot.'' He led her to a hatch that he opened. ''Get in the pod. Put on that helmet and strap yourself in tight. It's going to be a wild and bumpy ride. I'll be back in a minute.''

She panicked and grabbed his hand. ''Where are you going?''

''To lower the force shield so the ship will appear on their radar. I also have to set the self-destruct code. I want Taemin or his men to see the explosion so they'll—''

''Explosion? You're going to blow up the ship?'' He nodded. ''What about the men aboard? They'll be killed.''

He cupped her face in his hands. ''It's them or us, Jana. If I don't blow up the ship, they'll come after us as soon as they regain consciousness. We can't get far in an escape pod and we're in Pyropean territory. We need time to get clear and hide. We have no choice.''

''Can't you bind them to give us time to get away?''

''It wouldn't be long before they're found, freed, and came after us. The ones I knocked out will wake up soon and know we can't be far away. A pod's range and power are limited. They'll begin a search. Or Taemin might come to meet us and discover his captive crew and our escape.''

''Why don't we take over the ship, hold them prisoner, and use it for ourselves?''

''We'd never get across the Pyropean boundary without being discovered and then recaptured. We can't use them as hostages; to get us back, Taemin would sacrifice those men's lives. I must blow up the ship and get rid of this threat. It has to be scheduled to perfection. We take off almost at detonation time; that way, the pod might be mistaken for debris being shot off by it. There's a large planetoid nearby; we can make it there."

"Then what? We'll still be stranded in their territory."

"Only until we can be rescued by our forces. I sent a message to them from the *Wanderlust* telling them to watch out for us. If this ship is sighted when I lower its cloaking shield, they'll know where we are, for a while. The pod has a rescue beacon, but we can't use it. I've taken one of their communicators to see if I can rig it to signal our side. Right now, our only hope of survival is to get away in the pod and cover our escape with the explosion. With luck, Taemin will think either the ship blew by accident or I destroyed it rather than allow us to be captured."

"Why did he do this to us?"

"I'll explain later. We have to hurry, woman."

Jana climbed into the only available pod, donned the protective helmet, and strapped herself into one of two seats. She told herself they had no choice but to blow up the ship and let their captors perish. If her husband did not fear for their lives, he wouldn't be making this daring attempt to get away.

Varian returned in a near-run. He leapt into the seat, yanked on his helmet, and buckled his harness. He readied the controls and continued the verbal counting which Jana knew not to interrupt. When he reached the chosen number, he pressed a button to jettison the pod. Almost the minute they were outside, the ship began exploding from the engine room upward and outward. When debris was flung in all directions, he turned on the thrusters and off they went at a speed that bobbled the tiny craft.

Jana remained silent, rigid, and alert. Varian concentrated on his flying task to make them appear a shooting fragment of the ship. He hoped Nigel wasn't too far away chasing the decoy drone to notice the brief blip on the radar screen and to surmise its meaning. No matter, he couldn't risk sending a signal to his friend. With luck, Taemin and Cass would think them dead, or quickly give up the search for them.

It was a bumpy, scary, swift ride as they zoomed through the atmosphere of the planetoid Luz at the edge of Pyropea. Varian used the optical scanner and sensors to crash-land the craft. Just before impact, he gave her a warning of what was to come and told her to brace herself.

Jana obeyed, but it didn't do much good. The rocky terrain and rapid pace made for a rough and tumbling touchdown that seemed to jar her every bone. Her head spun as they twisted and turned and collided with objects. Her body pressed against the tight restraints. Her head was yanked about on a neck that would be sore later. Shrieks of panic were torn from her lips. She feared they were going to be killed, either in the crash or from obstructions.

When all movement ceased and the engine was shut off, Varian looked at her and asked if she was all right.

Shaken to the core, she glanced around to see if they were really stopped and still alive, then nodded.

He relaxed a moment. "I couldn't slow it down or anybody on radar would suspect something. No fragment or debris has brakes. Let's get out of here. We need to unload the gear and skuttle this pod. I brought along a charge to handle that for me. We have twenty minutes before the auto-beacon turns on. We need to find a safe place to hide from Taemin's scouts, possible bad weather, and any other perils on this hunk of rock."

"What if they come after us?"

"I brought along weapons, and we have enough supplies for a week. Let's move, woman; we don't have much time."

Varian released her straps and his. They doffed their helmets and tossed them into the seats they vacated. The supplies and weapons were hauled to a safe distance. Jana remained with them while "Ryker" set the charge to destroy the escape vehicle. He raced to her and flopped down on his belly beside her.

"Duck your head and cover your eyes from flying debris,"

he got out before the loud blast. When it was quiet and all scatterings had settled, he lifted his head and took a deep breath. "That takes care of that threat. I want you to stay here while I check for a good place to hide. Keep one of those weapons handy; Martella said she told you how to use them."

"Why don't we stay here until morning when we can see?"

"Too risky. If they come over the area tonight in shuttles with light beams, we'd be spotted on their monitors."

"Shuttles with searchlights?"

"Yes. Stay put. Yell if you hear or see anything."

Jana accepted the weapon he placed in her grasp. She sat on the rock seat and waited for him to return. Not once did she allow her attention to stray. She strained to follow him in the full moon with her eyes and ears; then he vanished from sight and hearing. She focused on watching the sky for approaching ships, enemy ships. She waited, and waited, and waited; and became nervous and frightened. "Ryker!"

"I'm coming, love." When he joined her, he said, "I found a rock shelf that will shield us from detection. Let's get us and our stuff under it."

She followed his lead, then was left under the overhang while he covered their tracks. Her gaze grew accustomed to the darkness in the sheltered spot. Beyond it, there seemed to be plenty of moonlight for his task and for sighting dangers. She was relieved when he returned.

"That was not an enjoyable journey!" he joked to relax them. "You sure you're all right, love?"

"A few bumps and bruises, but fine. You?"

He leaned against the stone and stretched out his legs. "Fine. Relax, love. We're safe for now. Snuggle up to me and get some sleep."

Jana propped her back against his torso and rested her head on his shoulder. It felt good when his right arm crossed her chest and his fingers curled around her left arm to hold it there. She raised her hand and pressed it over his. "You timed our escape perfectly. You're a good pilot. Your skills and wits never cease to astonish me. What now?"

"We try to get some sleep; we'll need it. Tomorrow, we move farther away from the crash site and cover our trail as we go. If the pod is located, there will be nothing that would indicate it was occupied. Hopefully they'll think it was thrown clear during the destruction, crashed, and finished exploding. We could be here a long time, Jana, so we'll need to be careful with our rations and look for others. Mostly water. We can do without food for a while but not liquid."

"Whatever you say, I'll do."

He hoped and prayed that was true. As soon as he put a safe distance between them and this spot, he'd confess all. "Thanks, love, it could save our lives. Sleep now. I want to move out at first light."

"Shouldn't we take turns standing guard or something?"

He chuckled. "No need, I'm a light sleeper."

The moment dawn appeared, Varian had them up and traveling away from the crash site and the scouts Taemin was sure to send eventually. He urged them onward all day with nothing more than short breaks for rest and nourishment. Jana did not complain or hold them back, despite the fact that she was in a dress and heels. At one point, she tried to lighten the grim situation by joking about her inappropriate hiking wear and shoes. She jested about packing better the next time. The blond alien had grinned and agreed. He seemed to enjoy her sense of humor in such a precarious predicament. He praised her stamina, courage, and good mood. Yet, he journeyed in dread of what faced him at dusk: his confession.

They trekked over rough and difficult terrain that was filled with craggy peaks, arduous hills, large boulders in giant piles, and rocky ravines. They skirted bluffs and jutting mountains, walked around craters, avoided prickly plants and sticker trees, and challenged dry scrubland. Most of the large formations on the landscape were in browns and blacks that sent out gloomy messages.

In one spot, the rocks and grit around them were a mingling of light and dark blue, but the blond alien told Jana they held nothing of value. In places where sand was abundant, it was in large grains and was the color of carrots. So far, they hadn't come across water, and that worried Jana.

"Is the entire planetoid this rugged?" she asked during a short break. "Have you ever been here before?"

"Yes and yes." He wasn't ready to tell her that all Star Fleet officers made it a point to know the terrain and demands of most places in enemy worlds and in their own in case that information was vital to them one day. He hadn't been here before, but he knew where he was leading them: to a destination he hoped was safe. "I travel all over in search of things I need to know and gather." That was misleading but true.

"Do you remember your way around? Is there any water available?"

"In a few places. We're heading for one. We'll make camp there."

"Won't Taemin or his searchers look for us at water holes?"

"He doesn't know I'm familiar with Luz; that's where we are."

Jana took a deep breath and slowly released it. "That's a relief and good fortune. Mercy, I hope we have plenty more."

"So do I, Jana love. After we camp and sleep, I'll begin work on the communicator signal in the morning. Blink your eyes and hope we have good luck with it. If so, we could be rescued soon."

Jana didn't ask, *But what happens if our luck runs out?*

Sunset neared and the horizon became blood-red with streaks of bright orange. The clouds overhead were indigo with lavender bases. In the distance in both directions, the largest and tallest formations looked like black silhouettes against the lighter or vivid backgrounds.

They finally reached their destination. They were hot, sweaty, tired, dusty, and apprehensive. Their muscles ached from their exertions. He ordered her to hide while he proceeded onward to make certain the location was deserted. When he was convinced, he waved her into what would become their camp.

"The seep's around that big rock. We don't want to camp beside it. Whatever kind of animal life Luz has in this area will come to drink there. We have enough trouble without tangling with strange or ill-tempered creatures. Let's eat and settle down. A lot might happen tomorrow. We need to be rested to face whatever comes." Varian wondered if he should make his confession tonight while she was weary in mind and body or wait until morning when she was fresh and alert.

"Are you sure that shuttle we hid from this morning was one of Taemin's? What if it was help for us? We might have given up our only chance of rescue."

"I promise you it wasn't one we wanted; it was Pyropean."

Jana assumed the size, or shape, or sound, of the shuttle had given him his answer. "Why did Taemin do this to us?"

Varian took a seat on a large rock and sipped water. "He thinks I've sided with Maffei and I'm working against him. He's right, Jana."

"What if he's the one to pick up your signal tomorrow?"

"I won't use the communicator unless I'm sure it will work."

Jana sat on the ground before him and between his parted thighs. She drank from her own portable container, then replaced the top and set it aside. She rested her cheek against his left leg, facing away from his body. Contact with his strength gave her courage. Yet, she was afraid and tense, and knew it was obvious. "If it doesn't, and we know we can't surrender to Taemin, we'll die here, won't we?"

Varian stroked her tawny hair and wiped a smudge from her

cheek. He had to relieve some of her fears. He summoned his courage and replied, "I've been in worse binds. With Nigel's help, I'll get us out of this trouble; I promise." He felt her stiffen. "But right now, I have to tell you something important. It won't be easy for me to say or for you to hear. Listen and feel with your heart, Moonbeam, not with your head."

Jana turned her body to sit facing him on the ground. With wide eyes and parted lips, she stared at the sunny-haired alien. She realized in disbelief that she was hearing . . . Varian Saar's voice! Even before he continued, she had no doubts who and what he was . . . perhaps she never had.

Varian fused his solemn gaze to her shocked one. In a tender and contrite tone, he said, "I'm sorry I had to trick you along with everybody else, Jana, but it was necessary. It was the only way to save both of our worlds and our lives. After I explain the truth, I hope you understand and forgive me. I realize I shouldn't have come here and I certainly shouldn't have endangered you by bringing you along." Frustration entered his voice. "It just seemed like the perfect chance to get evidence on Taemin to force the Tabrizes away from war and into a permanent treaty. As Ryker, I've already accomplished that feat with Maal. Or I will after one more visit to let him see I made it back from the mission alive and to tell him Maffei is too strong to be attacked. Since Ryker is dead, he can't provoke his grandfather and ally against us anymore. Your world is safe now, Jana, and mine will be, too, in a few weeks. As soon as I arrange a new death for Ryker, we can put this all behind us. I'll handle it after I get us out of this mess. With luck, Nigel didn't fall for that decoy drone or he saw Garus's ship appear briefly on the monitor. He might be on his way here to rescue us. Before we left my ship, I gave him orders to shadow us in the *Kiunterri* and to be ready to respond to trouble, so don't lose hope."

Varian's gaze and tone softened as he vowed in earnest, "I love you, Jana; I have since the moment I saw you. Forgive me for duping you. Please understand I had no choice but to seek peace and safety for all of us."

Varian waited for a response and reaction, and it wasn't the one he had expected. Jana just sat there and stared at him as if in a trance. "Say something, my love," he coaxed. She didn't move or speak, only continued to stare at him with a near blank expression. He had to reach her.

"Your rescue wasn't a delusion and you were never ill. I kept you drugged for a week while Tris, Nigel, and I made the changes in me and on Darkar. Shara was alive, and she did try to kill you. Cass did kidnap you from me and take you to Ryker. I was the one who freed you so we could marry. Everything I told you on my ship that night was true, *is* true, Moonbeam. I used a lookalike cyborg on Auriga because I knew you doubted my identity. I couldn't take you to Maal's until you were convinced I was Ryker, and that seemed the only way. I couldn't risk you being questioned by him or other enemies with *Thorin*, and I couldn't arouse any possible captor's suspicions by making you immune to it with *Rendelar*. I know I've hurt and deceived you many times, but never again, I swear. No matter what happens or what's involved, from now on, I'll tell you the truth."

Varian didn't know what to think when she did not scream at him, curse him, pound him, cry, or vent her anger and hurt in any visible manner. He wondered if she was in shock; he had brought along a medical kit; maybe he should see if it held *vitricine*.

Finally Jana spoke in a deceptively calm and soft voice, "Whose idea was this charade? Were you under orders again to dupe me?"

"It was my idea, Jana; but Grandfather, Draco, and Brec agreed to let me attempt it. While you were asleep and recovering from your ordeal with Shara, I read that evil woman's journals and I viewed videotapes she and Ryker had made with Maal, Taemin, Cass, and others. They showed me how much danger we were in. I felt I had to do something to send all that evil to the grave with Shara and Ryker. I realized the only way to beat them was to do it as Ryker, make Ryker correct his mistakes before I laid him to rest. Only he could get to Maal and Taemin to prevent war. I realized too late I was cruel and rash in my plan and actions, but so much was at stake, Jana, so very much."

She noticed how he stressed certain points by expressing the same thing in a different way to make sure she grasped his point, his bloody excuse. "You believed *only you* could save everything and everybody? It was *your sole* responsibility so you appointed yourself savior of it all?"

He ignored her sarcastic tone. "I was the only one in a position to do the job because I knew I could pass for Ryker: in looks with a little help from Tris, in character and personality because I knew my half brother well, and in traits and secrets because I had the journals, tapes, and the complex entry code. Shara even recorded the codes for the androids and computers and safes. She never imagined anyone could get into the complex to take advantage of them. Thank *Kahala* she was wrong. During my final showdown with Ryker, he taunted me with the entry code. He told me you were locked inside, that you two were married, and he was planning to kill both of us. He said if I won our battle, you and Trilabs were the prizes. I didn't want to kill my own brother, Jana, but he forced me to do so in self-defense. I think he's better off dead; he was irretrievably evil and mad. Don't you see? I had all I needed in my possession to impersonate Ryker."

"Along with my unsuspecting assistance."

He perceived her sadness and disappointment. But where, he mused, was the fury he had anticipated? How could she stay so calm and controlled? "Yes, Jana," he admitted. "And I'm sorry. I love you, woman, and I need you. Can you forgive me? Do you understand why I did what I did? I promise I won't ever do anything like this again."

There was pleading in those fake emerald eyes and deep tone, but, she told herself, they could be another pretense. She chilled her own tone and gaze and put emphasis on each of her next words. "You used cruel and intentional lies to deceive and delude me. You made me doubt my sanity. You convinced me you didn't love me or want me. You convinced me Ryker did. You put everyone and everything above me and above our relationship, our happiness, even our survival and safety. No, Varian, I can't forgive or forget, or come back to you. I would always be second choice after duty."

He slid off the rock seat to his knees before her. He grasped her shoulders. "No, Jana, it won't be like that. I swear, never again."

She pushed away his hands. "You can't make a promise you can't and won't keep. You would do something like this again and again, if I permitted it. If it were the first time, perhaps I could be lenient. But it isn't; you've tricked me, used me, and betrayed me before."

"I've explained all those times, Jana. Don't you realize my burdens and responsibilities? I'm a Star Fleet officer, a ship commander, a member of the Elite Squad, the *kadim*'s grandson. I can't behave like other men. Don't you realize most of the hostilities in the Tri-Galaxy are because of what happened in my family, with my father, with my half brother? I, more than anyone, should help destroy them."

"That's supposed to make whatever you do all right? When duty calls, you're expected and determined to make any sacrifice and take any risk to answer it? You can simply cast aside conscience, honor, compassion, right and wrong, and anyone in your way just to carry out your orders?"

"You make duty and loyalty and love for my world sound terrible. You make *me* sound terrible. I've been reared by an officer and a ruler, and I've been trained as an officer, trained to obey. I had no choice."

"Yes, Varian, you did. You've always had other choices. And so do I for the first time since we met. You said this ruse was your clever idea, so you have only yourself to blame for the consequences."

"I didn't do it for glory, Jana! I can't ever reveal it."

"I don't care why you did it. I want you out of my life, Varian, totally and forever. I don't want to see you again, if we ever get off of this enemy ball."

Varian's heart thudded with trepidation and his skin crawled with fear. He told himself she couldn't be serious, only angry and hurt. "I can't do that, Jana, I love you. I need you."

"*Need* me? For what this time? For what next time?"

The bitterness in her voice and coldness in her multicolored eyes caused him to wince in torment. "For myself, Moonbeam, only for myself."

"For how long? Until your next secret assignment? Next burden?"

"Until the Universe ceases to exist. I can't lose you, Jana. I can't."

"You already have, Varian, the moment you let me wake up on Darkar with Ryker as my husband instead of in your arms on the *Wanderlust*."

"You have to understand and forgive me, Jana," he insisted.

She shook her head and glared at him. "No, I don't and I won't, not today, not tomorrow, not ever. It's over between us, Varian. Over!"

"I'll find a way to change your mind. I have to."

"So you can get your hands on Trilabs through me? Ryker, and even Shara, warned me you might try something like that. To try to get me back will be a waste of your time."

"You're worth all of it and more."

"But you aren't worth mine. You don't deserve my love and trust."

"Perdition, woman, I'm not after Trilabs! If that was my goal, I could take it by force. Give me another chance to prove you're wrong."

"You've had plenty of them, too many. Now that you've obtained the goals most important to you, I'm the only thing left you crave, at the bottom of the stack, where you've always put me and will always keep me. I would be a fool to let you hurt me again, and I'm not a fool, you bloody traitor."

"I swear on my life and honor I won't ever hurt you again."

"I know you won't, because I'm not going to let that happen. Go marry Canissia like you planned. I don't want you anymore."

"I never intended to marry that wicked bitch. It was only a

ruse to draw her out of hiding after she kidnapped you. I never imagined Ryker would use it to coerce you into marrying him. I suspected she was in on your disappearance, but I had to get my hands on her to question her. She had to believe I didn't suspect her and think she had something valuable to return for: me. She disappeared because Ryker arranged her death, but she foiled his attempt. That day she came to see us, I knew the truth from those tapes and I managed to convince her she was wrong, or at least I thought I had her fooled. Something I said or did that wasn't recorded by Ryker and Shara caused her to suspect the truth. She eluded the tail I had put on her: Command 10. When her ship was located and put under surveillance, it was at Zenufia. The trouble is, she wasn't on it; she's with Taemin. She must have told him her suspicions and they planned this trap for us. As a taunt or terror tactic, they had Garus drop clues to me that he didn't understand. I had to get us off that ship. The only reason I didn't arrest her on Darkar was to prevent exposing my ruse. I will have her in custody and prison soon. She'll pay for her crimes."

Varian tried to hold her hand, but she jerked it away and glared at him. "What we have is special, Jana. We can't just throw it away over a misunderstanding, over something vital I was compelled to do. I'm sorry for the past. Let me make it up to you."

"No, not now, not ever."

"Never is a long time, Moonbeam. I won't let you end it for us."

"Can't you get it through your thick and conceited head that you already *have* ended it for us. Give it up, Varian; I did weeks ago."

"When, Jana? Was it the day I used that cyborg on Auriga? Until that trick, you didn't believe I was Ryker, no matter how well I played him. Even afterward, you still had doubts."

"But you played him so well that you made me fall in love with him and want him, not you."

"You couldn't possibly love a man like Ryker Triloni! Remember all Shara told you about him, about them. Remember how Ryker treated you. He would have killed you if things had gone differently when we met. You can't be in love with Ryker; you never got to know the real man. You lived with me, you loved me, you wanted me. I was the one with you all this time, not him."

"But you were impersonating him, you were being him, not Varian. If you hadn't played him with perfection, you wouldn't have fooled everybody. The fact you have should prove I was, in all ways but one, with Ryker."

She saw a look of panic cross his face that surprised her. "You let everyone think I practically eloped with him, a near stranger. You made certain our marriage was revealed and is legal. When his death is exposed, do you think the grieving widow would run straight into your arms? Return with eagerness to the man who had treated me so badly? The man, by your own plot, I escaped. You fooled me, but I'm not a fool. If I came traipsing back to you after pretending to be happily wed and in love with Ryker, I would certainly look like one. I would appear a money-grubbing bitch, a liar, a cheat, a schemer."

"It won't be like that, Jana."

"Almost as soon as you free me, I race off, meet Ryker by sheer chance, enchant him, and marry him. Then, he's no sooner allegedly killed and buried when I leap back into the arms of my ex-captor, my ex-lover, my betrayer! I become your mistress. I do all of that and I won't appear anything but sweet and innocent Jana Greyson? Fat chance!"

"Not as my mistress, Moonbeam, as my wife."

"That would be as bad and repulsive. And about Cass . . . you spread the news you two are eagerly awaiting to be married. But as soon as your ex-lover is widowed, you dump her to get me back? How will that make you look in the eyes and hearts of your people? You can't ever reveal you impersonated Ryker, or this was all for naught. Without exposing the truth, you've entrapped us."

Varian read Jana's anger and bitterness. He was almost glad the emotions had surfaced so he could deal with them and hopefully dispel them.

"Who's going to believe such garbage, Commander Saar? No one."

"All we have to say is that you ran away from me because you didn't know I loved you. I was going to wed Cass to get over your loss. Lovers torn apart by cruel fate and reunited by generous gods . . . Who could resist believing such a romantic tale?"

"Hog wash! Bullshit! This is real life, you bastard, involving real people, intelligent people, not some fantasy. Besides, Maal would kill both of us if I dishonored Ryker's memory by getting involved with you again. Be realistic, you space pirate, no one will fall for such a story."

"I admit we'll have to be persuasive and careful for a while, but—"

"But nothing, Saar. No deal, no more chances. You've had your last one with me and you blew it. You enjoyed your little pretense and were proud of yourself for being so good at it."

"I enjoyed being with you, Moonbeam, but not fooling you."

"You liar! Is that why you slept with me as him?"

"I couldn't help myself. I loved you and needed you. I missed you."

"What you needed and missed was sex, and that's all you got from me."

"You made love to me, woman; it wasn't just physical sex."

"I did not make love to you; I was responding to Ryker."

"To me, Jana Greyson, to me! In your heart, you never doubted it was me. You always wanted it to be me. You pretended it was me."

That was true, but she taunted, "Are you positive?"

"Don't do this to us, Jana. We've both suffered too much for my missions and mistakes. Let's make peace and be happy."

"Just like that," she scoffed as she snapped her fingers. "Forgive and forget? Just pretend this so-called misunderstanding and betrayal never happened? It isn't that easy or simple."

"It can be, my love, if you let it. I love you. I need you. I'm sorry. I want to marry you. Doesn't any of that matter to you?"

"No, and you have a strange way of showing your feelings. On Earth, we say: 'Practice what you preach.' You certainly don't."

He lifted his unballed hands and, with palms upward, shook them, an alien sign of being open and honest. But it was as a gesture of frustration tonight because he knew he wasn't getting through to her. "I've made mistakes; I've admitted that. Are my words not translating into your language correctly to get my meaning across to you? Perdition, woman, I said I was sorry, but I had no choice."

Jana saw how upset he was, but she didn't let it affect her. "I have no choice, either, Varian; I can never trust you again. Without trust, it's over. When we get out of this mess, if we do, we go our separate ways."

He narrowed his gaze in denial. "No, Jana, I won't let you get away from me. I can't lose you."

"You already have. Are you listening to me and understanding my feelings? Is your aural translator malfunctioning? It's over."

"I don't believe it; I won't believe it. True love doesn't end."

"*True* love, that's the key word, Varian; you've never been true to me and I doubt you have the capability to do so with me or any woman. Whether or not you choose to believe it's over, that's up to you. But if you doubt it, you'll be fooling yourself this time."

"I'm not fooling myself, and I'm not lying to you. You lit a fire in me that can't be extinguished."

"Without the right fuel, all fires die. Or didn't you learn that scientific fact when you trained to impersonate Ryker?"

He frowned. "Is it so hard to understand what I had to do?"

"Understanding the situation isn't the problem. How you

handled it and why you handled it that way is; that's what stands between us and will always stand between us and keep us apart."

"You know why I did it, Jana, to save lives and two worlds, to prevent intergalactic war. Aren't those things important, too, as important as we are? What else could I have done?"

"You could have trusted me and loved me enough to let me help."

"Without endangering everything I was trying to accomplish? I told you I couldn't risk using *Rendelar* to protect our secrets."

"You found ways to do everything else the mission required. You and your team of experts are so good at things like this that you could have found a way if you had tried hard enough. You didn't because you wanted to take the quick and easy way out, which included using and betraying me."

Provoked by panic, he shouted, "*Easy* way? You think it has been easy to dupe you? Stars above, woman, it's the hardest and most painful thing I've ever done! I hated every minute I had to keep you in the Shadows. You don't know how many times I panicked over losing you and started to reveal the truth, even if it wound up costing me everything I had worked for."

"But you didn't ever reach that point, Varian. You saw the damage and suffering you were causing me . . . *us*. Yet, it didn't matter enough to call a halt. I didn't matter enough for you to risk all to keep me. The damn mission was your priority."

He gritted out between clenched teeth, "The damn mission saved millions of lives and many worlds, Jana, including yours."

"For that part of your deception, I'm grateful."

Varian stared at her as he tried to calm himself and regain self-control. "You don't want to understand or forgive."

"Dr. Jana Greyson *Triloni* doesn't have to be either one."

His heart ached as he witnessed the full extent of what his ruse had caused. "I can't believe you could think and feel this way about something so important. You want to hurt me and punish me. You want revenge. You want me knocked to my knees. You want me humiliated. You want to do to me all the things you think I've done to you. You're wrong, Jana, and it isn't necessary. I am ashamed. I have been punished. You had revenge every time you called me Ryker and it seemed as if you were being drawn to him. It pierced my heart and soul to think I could lose you. I am on my knees, Moonbeam, and I am begging you to forgive me."

Jana broke the bond of their gazes. Hers darted about aimlessly as she thought about his words. She looked at him again. "I can't help what I feel and think, and you're responsible for those emotions and doubts. I don't want revenge, Varian. I don't want to humiliate you. I don't even want to hurt you or see you grovel. What I do want is for you to leave me alone and let me find peace and happiness. If I have to force you to honor my wishes, I will. This time, I have the freedom and rank to prevent you from using me again; I'll use them if you make it necessary. I suggest we concentrate our energy and wits on getting out of Pyropea alive and unharmed, then we'll go our separate ways."

Varian watched the effect of his confession on her. He realized the shock of his revelation and her anguish were too fresh and deep to make a difference on her tonight. He concluded it was going to take time, work, patience, and love to win her back. Somehow he must find a way out of this trap, with Jana at his side. "Let's eat and talk again in the morning. We're both exhausted."

"I'll eat, but my appetite is gone." As she forced down the food in the tins and clear bags that he had passed to her, she stared at the ground. All along she had been with Varian and she had never given herself to Ryker. Everything she had said and done while believing he was Ryker flooded her mind like one tremendous gush of drowning liquid. She reflected on how she had behaved with "Ryker" when they visited the *avatars*, Maal, Tirol, Draco, Brec, and on the *Wanderlust* with the new crew. She thought of her ridiculous confrontation with Martella when she feared for "Ryker's" life.

Varian had made a fool of her. He had trampled her feelings and pride, when he could have prevented or halted the torment and fears and shame she was experiencing. Love him and desire him or not, could she ever forgive him? Could she ever trust him again? Her dazed mind said *no*; her bruised heart said *no*; her tormented soul said *no*. Was there anything that handsome space rogue could say or do to change her mind and feelings? *No, no, no!* they all shouted again.

Varian observed her mood and suffered, too. Perhaps once the shock wore off and she had time to think clearly, she would soften her stubborn and destructive stance. He couldn't give up on her and their love.

Chapter Thirteen

As Varian worked on the stolen communicator the next morning after eating their scant rations, he and Jana talked with control at some points and quarreled with a loss of it at others.

"Will that thing work and get us out of here?" she asked.

"I think so."

"What about that decoy drone Garus mentioned? Won't that have drawn Nigel out of hearing range by now?"

"I hope not. I told him to stay on alert for trouble."

"Does he obey orders as well as you do?"

"How long are you going to stay angry and hostile?"

"Until the feelings wear off, just like you did. Just as I get over you and fall in love with somebody else, you storm back into my life and I'm told he doesn't exist, never existed as I knew him. You duped me to get your hands on Trilabs, didn't you? Why not admit it?"

Varian stopped working to look at her. "I won't deny how important Trilabs is to us. But more than we want and need to own or control it and its secrets, we want to prevent it from falling into the hands of our enemies. You must grasp that reality, Jana. Whoever rules Trilabs has the power to rule the Tri-Galaxy. Maffei does not want that role, but Taemin and Maal do, and Ryker did. Only Trilabs stands between us and them, only Trilabs can prevent their attack for conquest."

"If it were true that Ryker wanted to conquer and rule the Tri-Galaxy, he would have made an attempt by now, before he died; he had the power and means to take control."

"He was biding his time until he was ready. He enjoyed holding that threat over our heads and watching us squirm, especially me. The only reason I didn't confront him sooner was because I knew I would endanger my world and loved ones. He provoked me at every turn, Jana. He wanted either me or him dead. I had no way of getting to him and halting his threat until he gave me the entry code to his complex. He was so insane by then that he didn't even think to give me a fake one that would result in killing me and creating a sector catastrophe with the destruction of Darkar. He must have thought if I won our final battle, Shara would be waiting inside to take revenge on me. He never imagined I would impersonate him and dupe her."

Varian captured her gaze and held it. "When I entered that lab disguised as Ryker and saw you strapped to that table and without any signs of life, I almost went as mad as they were. Shara tried to pretend it was an accident, that she had tried to save you after your attempted suicide. She thought I was dead. She boasted of victory over the Saars. I wrapped my fingers around her evil throat and almost squeezed the life from her before I realized what I was doing. When she exposed their plan for her to take your face and place and she revealed their incestuous affair, I was repulsed. I told her it was over. She took her final plunge into madness and tried to kill the man she saw as a traitorous Ryker, perhaps as our father, too."

He lowered his troubled gaze to the task in his hands as that dark memory surfaced vividly. "During our struggle for the knife, she fell on it and was killed. Then, I discovered you weren't dead, just being prepared for cryogenic suspension.

All *Gehenna* broke loose. Everything that could go wrong to prevent awakening and saving you, did. Solar flare-ups knocked out communications. The life-support unit had been destroyed. The shuttles and bay were demolished. One *Spacer* wouldn't work and one exploded with Tesla aboard.'' He fused his gaze with hers once more.

''Hours passed in sheer terror, Moonbeam. Tris barely saved your life and it took agonizing time to do so. I was exhausted from the weeks of thinking you lost forever and my having to kill my half brother, scared by your near death and frantic rescue, and my discovery of the extent of their evil. I was trying to figure out a way to explain Ryker's death to Maal to prevent retaliation on Maffei. When this ruse came to mind. I saw it as the only answer. Maybe I still wasn't thinking clearly when I put everything into motion. But once it was under way, there was no turning back and no safe way to get rid of him. His death had to appear an accident, in one of his guarded locations, with witnesses Maal would believe—like Ryker's own men and androids, I could not be around to blame. To set that up, I had to play him and had to place my men at the chosen location: the mine on Caguas. I honestly believed you would understand and accept it. Even when you scared me with doubts, I kept telling myself it would be over soon and everything would be all right.''

''So much clever work and planning and yet you couldn't find a simple way to include me, only *use* me. It all comes back to the fact you would do anything to get your hands on Trilabs.''

''Keep it out of their hands, Jana; there's a big difference. Can you blame me for trying? Do you have a real concept of what intergalactic war would be like, especially with the advanced and powerful weapons we possess? You witnessed what ten ships and lasers did to that rogue threatening your world. Imagine what ten similarly equipped enemy ships could do to a populated planet in our galaxy. I couldn't let that happen. Why do you refuse to grasp and admit the truth?''

''What you refuse to grasp and admit, Varian, is there was

never any need for this cruel ruse. After you killed Ryker and Shara and rescued me, we had Trilabs in our control. I was Ryker's wife and would become his widow and heir. No one knew how or where he died. We could have arranged an accident on Darkar that would have fooled Maal. A lethal spill in one of the labs or something. You had the entry code. You had the journals. You had the videotapes. You had Ryker's secrets. All of that gave you the power to save and protect both worlds. It provided the evidence you needed to force Maal and Jurad into treaties. If they refused, it supplied the power to defend Maffei or to even attack them. You held victory in your hands; instead of using it, you began another conflict and put me in the middle.

"By confiscating Trilabs in that manner, through you to me, it would only have provoked more trouble and certain war with Maal and the Tabrizes. You were already my ex-lover. If Ryker allegedly died with only you present then you and I married, it would cast suspicions on both of us. Maal and Taemin would have come after you. This way, Ryker is the one who talked them out of attacking. What I did will accomplish peace in a peaceful way. After all the evil he's done in his life, what harm did it do to let him supposedly do some good before he dies publicly?"

"If no harm was done, Varian, then what are we doing stranded here in danger? The very two people who saved everybody else might die for their good deed. You had the right to endanger your life, but not mine, not without my permission."

"Isn't your life worth risking to save your world? Isn't my life worth risking for mine?"

"Yes, but that isn't the point."

"What *is*, Jana?"

"You're only seeing and hearing your side."

"Why can't we be on the same side, Moonbeam?"

"Because of who and what you are."

"What is that, Jana?"

"A man who puts his duty above everything."

"Why is that so wrong in a critical situation?"

"If you don't understand the difference and my meaning, I could never explain in a way you would grasp and accept."

When his frustration caused him to get angry and snappy because she wouldn't accept his apology and forgive him, Jana became even angrier because he seemed to expect to say those words and everything would magically be all right when he didn't appear to realize how wrong the matter was from her point of view. She knew she still loved and desired him, but she could not trust him, or was afraid to do so again. He had inflicted—yes, in the line of duty—great suffering and shame on her. She truly believed at that time that he might do it again in the line of duty. She couldn't open the door to an already abused heart and risk further damage to it. If there was a chance for them to get past this dilemma and make a fresh beginning, he had to prove his fealty and love to her. She had to give him time to worry, experience her loss, and correct his flaws and weaknesses, his misguided conceptions.

"Martella knew everything all along, didn't she?"

"Yes. But she resisted and argued against my plan. She warned me many times of the risks involved with duping you. She even had bad feelings about this trip; I should have listened to her."

"Who knows you're Varian?"

"Nigel, Tris, Martella, Grandfather, Draco, Brec, Kagan, and the two Elite Squad members I assigned on Caguas."

"What about your crew who saw me rescued, saw Tesla die, saw you go to Darkar disguised as Ryker?"

"They were given mind implants to make them forget that happened, chemically induced partial amnesia that affects recent memory. My crew remembers our search for you but not your rescue. They were sent on leave while Tris, Nigel, Martella, and I prepared for this ruse."

"Why didn't you give me amnesia, too? It would have been kinder and safer for all of us. At least taken me back to before Shara's murder attempt."

"Because I didn't want you to forget what we said after your rescue. I didn't want you believing the lies Cass and Ryker told you."

"You didn't want me to forget it, but you would go to great lengths to convince me we were never reunited and you didn't confess your love and arrange for my kidnapping; it was only an hallucination? That's contradictory and cruel."

"That was one case where I was being selfish, Moonbeam. If I had blocked all of that out and played Ryker as I have, you would hate me by now. I had to fool you, but I had to leave you with doubts and hopes, with good and honest memories of me even if you believed they were dreams."

"How dare you tamper with my mind and emotions?" Jana screamed at him. "How dare you come to my bed as another man?"

"I never intended to make love to you as Ryker. But that night before our trip to Maal's, you were so close and tempting that I couldn't resist you. Once we'd started an intimate relationship, I thought it would look suspicious to halt it. And, Ryker was romancing you before he died. I did try to control myself, Jana; remember how I attempted to slow things down between you and him?"

"So, sex became just part of the mission, part of your role."

"No, I wanted you and needed you. I admit I excused my weakness and desires by telling myself it was necessary, but I knew inside it wasn't."

"You're a damn good actor, Commander Saar. You fooled me and Maal and everybody else. I hope you're reveling in your many successes."

"How can I enjoy my successes when they might cost me the only woman I have ever loved?"

"On Earth, we call that flaw 'wanting your cake and eating it, too.' In real life, it doesn't work that way. I'll admit, you were a most enjoyable lover. You're good, very good. I should have known no two men kiss and make love exactly alike. But how could I know I was right since you're the only man I've bedded?"

"I never forced you to sleep with me as Ryker; I wouldn't have."

"Mental and emotional coercion don't count. I suppose?" She saw him flinch from that stinging barb. "Why did you leave my old things on the ship? Were they supposed to taunt and hurt me?"

"That wasn't intentional. I honestly forgot about them being there. I took everything with me when I left Grandfather's on Eire when I went to search for you . . . Now can I ask you one question and you answer it with honesty?"

Jana grasped a change in his tone and direction. "Perhaps."

"Do you still love me? Do you still want me?"

She stalled to think by asking, "With honesty?"

"Yes."

"Honestly, I don't know. Honestly, even if I do love and want you, I don't think it matters any more. It changes nothing in this predicament."

"It changes everything, Jana. And it does matter. It matters to me, to us, to our future."

"We have no future, Varian; you destroyed all hopes of one."

"I'll repair my damage, or I'll create a new one for us."

Jana tore a strip from the bottom of her dress to use as a cloth for bathing off at the seep. She was relieved her period had come two weeks ago during her stay on the *Wanderlust*, as it would have been a problem for her here. Also, there was another predicament she didn't have to worry about: getting pregnant. The men in this alien world were in charge of birth control measures and when reproduction took place with their *charls*, they held that power in their hands with the use of three-month injections of *Liex*, a "no-accident precaution and formula." Varian had told her about *Liex* before her affair with him, and she was certain he wouldn't allow her to become pregnant with "Ryker's" baby during his charade. He wouldn't do that even to have a hold on her afterward, as people would view his firstborn as the child of his half brother.

* * *

"You're certain only Nigel can decode your message?"

"Yes, and I sent it fast and turned it off so Taemin couldn't target my pulses. All we can do is wait and be careful until he comes."

"*If* he heard you."

"We have to believe he did, Jana. We'll be rescued, so don't worry."

Twenty minutes passed as Varian put away their gear and swept the area of tracks visible to optical scanners. His head jerked northward and skyward. "Get into that crevice fast!" he shouted to Jana. "A shuttle is coming this way!" Before she could react and obey, he shoved her into the concealing location he had prepared for such an emergency, the spot where their supplies were already out of sight. He wriggled in beside her and pulled the sticker bush in place, ignoring the painful pricks on his fingers that brought forth blood.

"Maybe it's Nigel with help."

"Not this quick."

"Taemin must have picked up your signal," she said in rising alarm.

"No, it's just a fly-by check of the area. Stay still and quiet so we can elude their sensors."

In mounting dread, Jana obeyed. She leaned her head against a rock and closed her eyes, her heart pounding. She didn't want to think about their grim fates if they fell into that evil alien's hands. She heard the shuttle as it made a slow circle of the location. She panicked when it hovered a moment above them to study it.

The crevice was a tight fit which held their bodies close together. Jana opened her eyes to look at her ex-lover. Sweat beaded on his forehead and above his upper lip; moisture caused his nose, chin, and cheeks to shine. They weren't manifestations of fear, as Varian Saar feared nothing and no one, but from his exertions and the heat. As several drops rolled toward his dark brows and sensual lips, he made no move to wipe them away. He remained rigid, alert, and silent. He exuded self-assurance and immense power even amidst this peril. He was a complex and contradictory man of surprising gentleness and strength. He possessed highly developed reflexes, keen instincts, and honed skills.

Jana's gaze roamed his handsome features. She missed the tiny smile creases near his eyes and mouth, as Ryker didn't have them. She missed the cleft in his chin, that deep and short slash she had fingered many times in days past. She missed the rich sapphire shade of his eyes. She missed the sable color of his hair. She had missed the sound of his deep and husky voice while he was playing Ryker. His strong jawline was stubbled from days without shaving and smudged where he had mopped at his face with dirty hands, as he hadn't had time to wash up after his tasks. The dark hair and dirt made him look earthy and appealing. She found herself aroused by contact with him. She realized they could be dead soon . . .

Varian was aroused, too. He knew the shuttle was gone and the area had passed inspection. He remained in the tight confines because he perceived his good affect on her. Maybe it was using another trick, but again he had no choice, as he must use every charm he possessed to win her. He turned his head to fuse their gazes. He allowed his eyes to roam her exquisite face, enflamed by her beauty and perfection. He noticed how her tawny hair was mussed. He saw how fear darkened her multicolored eyes of blue, green, and violet encased in a deep green band. He saw glistening perspiration from the heat and the tension of the situation on her creamy flesh. He yearned to kiss that lovely nose and small chin. He craved to feast on her lips. Uncontrollably his left hand reached out and captured the right side of her face between his strong fingers. His thumb drifted back and forth over her parted lips, and drew her head toward his. He kissed her, long and deep and tender. His pulse raced. His heart thudded. His breathing became ragged. His loins blazed with need. "I love you, Jana Greyson," he murmured.

"Don't you think you should be quiet and still? Sensors, remember? Are you trying to get us captured with such lustful foolishness?"

"They're gone, and it was one of Taemin's shuttles."

Jana frowned in annoyance. "Is it safe to get out of this crack now?"

"Yes, but it's nice being—"

"Then get out and stop squashing and fondling me."

He pushed aside the thorny barrier, crawled out, then extended his hand to assist her. "You didn't enjoy that as much as I did?"

Jana dared not lock gazes with him and give away her excited state. She pretended to brush off her clothes as she replied, "It was nice, but I didn't resist because I was obeying orders to stay quiet."

Varian exhaled in matching annoyance. "As you wish, Jana."

"Good. Thank you. From now on, no stunts like that again."

"How will you know it's over if you don't test your feelings?"

"I don't need to test them or want to test them. Understand?"

"So be it."

As you wish. So be it. Lordy, how many times I've heard those two responses in the past. She needed a distraction from him. "We seem to be stranded alone together for a while and you have my full attention, so tell me how you pulled off this charade so convincingly? How did you know all that scientific and medical information? How did you get your eyes green without contact lens? How did you know Androasian? And use your right hand? How did you always stay one step ahead of me?"

Varian lifted the water container and a rag from her dress. "First, let me get that blood off your beautiful face."

Jana felt her sticky cheek then looked at her hand. "From where?" she asked, then saw his injuries. "What happened?" she asked in alarm. "You're bleeding."

"The bush snagged my fingers in a few places."

"Get the medical kit and let me tend them. Some thorns have poisons or irritants on their tips. I can't let anything happen to my protector because I certainly don't want to be stuck here alone or with you ill."

Jana cleaned his hands with water from the canteen and a strip torn from the bottom of her dress. She applied antiseptic to kill any germs, then an antibiotic cream to prevent infection and to heal the small holes.

As she worked, he jested, "If you keep ripping up that dress, Moonbeam, pretty soon you won't have any cover left. That would be pleasant for me, but it will be much too stimulating for our rescue team."

"I'll try to heed your caution, sir, before I reach the indecent stage. It was pretty and expensive, too, I'm sure, but it can't be helped. I had no choice but to use it."

"That sounds like a familiar quandary and resolution to a problem."

Jana let go of his tended hand and glared at him. "Demolishing a dress doesn't compare to devastating my life. Which reminds me, you were about to answer some questions for me when that craft interrupted."

Varian took a deep breath and explained.

"I'm amazed and impressed. I would be even more so if they hadn't been used against me, you bloody traitor. When and if we get out of this trouble, you won't have an opportunity to do so again."

"The ruse can't be halted until it's finished, Jana. Since you know the truth now, you'll have to assist me and cooperate."

She looked stunned.

"Or you'll do what? Imprison me? How? On what charge?"

"Of course not! But I'll need your help."

"You need my help to finish your bloody mission? If that's true, you should have kept me in the dark until it was over. No way, Varian, no way."

"I couldn't keep you in the Shadows any longer because you've suffered too much as is," he explained. "I was also worried about you getting even closer to Ryker and about us dying with this lie separating us. I was about to confess the truth when I received that deceitful message from Taemin." He told her what the prince had said to compel him to remain silent a while longer. He related how and why the ruse must continue. He surmised to himself that if he wasn't wearing Ryker's face and image, his own would influence her. He concluded he had to finish this business fast and get back his own appearance.

"You want to involve me in your dangerous deceptions? Risk my life again? Are you crazy? I want to get away from you as soon as possible. I'm not going to lie and dupe like you did. How could you do this to me, to yourself, to us? How could you tell such horrible lies about yourself and the past? You tried your best to convince me you never loved me, and I came to believe it was true. You tried to make me fall in love with Ryker when he's dead. You let him replace you in my heart and body."

He decided to provoke her into seeing and admitting the truth. "It didn't take much persuading. You did a good job of that on your own. If you had truly loved me and wanted me, Jana Greyson, you wouldn't have turned to my brother so fast. Real love can't die that quick and easy. Real love is understanding, kind—"

"You don't know what real love is! Besides, how could I turn to Ryker when I was always with you?"

"But you thought you were with him, didn't you?"

"Not until you pulled that cyborg trick! No matter how many times you removed clues or dropped phony ones, I knew it was you and I knew my rescue wasn't a delusion."

"If you believed it was me and you truly came to hate me as you now claim, why did you keep responding to me as him?"

"To evoke a confession or to discover why you were lying. I thought that if you loved me and it was a trick, I could make you feel guilty or scare you into halting your game. But I failed to coax out the truth."

"You know the truth now, so you'll be my partner until it's over."

"Like hell I will! This time, you space rogue, I have a choice in my life. Thanks to your charade, legally and publicly I'm Ryker's widow and heir. I own Trilabs and all of his holdings; me, not you or the Maffei Alliance. As a citizen and free woman, you can't coerce me into doing anything. I don't belong to you or to any alien anymore. You had plenty of chances to win me, but you chose to discard them and me. Now, I have something more important than you."

"What?"

"My freedom. And my self-respect. Things you stole from me."

Varian didn't want to argue those touchy points with her. "You'll have to work with me, Jana. You don't have a choice."

"Yes, I do. If you try to force me to stay with you, I'll expose you."

"And get us killed? Provoke intergalactic war? I can't let you do that."

"Would you kill me to silence me? Is your ruse that vital?"

"You're talking crazy, woman. Of course I wouldn't kill you. And I won't let anybody else harm you. I've saved your pretty skin too many times to lose it now or ever. I have one other option. If you refuse to cooperate, I'll hold you captive until I'm finished. And if you recall, my love, I can be a very demanding captor."

Jana realized it was futile to argue with him here. She would handle getting away from Varian when they were around others and he couldn't stop her. She changed the subject. "What about Andrea? Is she all right?"

Varian grinned, delighted to be on a pleasant topic. "Do I have a surprise for you!" he teased to snare her interest and alter her mood, which he obviously did judging from her look of eagerness and anticipation.

"She was taken to Anais as I promised, and is safe. She was told everything about you, except the recent events, of course.

Actually, I have two surprises concerning your best friend." He sipped water.

"What? What? Don't keep me in suspense."

"She'll be joining you on Darkar soon." He saw Jana's eyes widen in astonishment and confusion. "If you'll agree to become my partner in the remaining ruse, she can live there with you until we marry, then live wherever she and Nigel settle down."

"She and Nigel? What are you talking about?"

"It seems my best friend and your best are in love."

"Andrea and Nigel? How did they meet? When? Where?"

"Incredible and wonderful, isn't it? If Nigel has his way, she'll marry him soon. From what he's told me about her, she's willing and ready. Nigel was on Anais recently, along with Tris and Martella. They told Andrea about you, about us, about Earth's threat, and about our imminent attempt to save it. If you agree to be my partner, I'll have the Earthlings returned to your world and have medical cures implanted in one of the doctor's minds."

"You can block out memory and yet embed information?"

"Yes, in certain matters. We'll implant the clues to take Dr. Martin in the right direction. How about cures for cancer and AIDS? Along with saving your world and bringing Andrea to you and helping to get the *charl* laws changed, will you agree to help me with the rest of the ruse?"

"Are you serious?"

He smiled and nodded.

"Do you have the power to carry out those promises?"

He smiled and nodded again.

Jana thought about his tempting and unexpected offer. "Is that all I have to do?"

"I would like to add 'marry me' to the list but that might provoke a negative answer. But I warn you now, Moonbeam, I'll do everything I can to get a yes to that question, just like you promised on my ship long ago."

"Don't push it, Varian."

"I'll even order some how-to-save-your-environment-facts embedded in one of the scientist's minds. It will take only a few weeks. Is it a bargain?"

She could risk becoming his captive to protect his mission or she could accomplish many positive things by assisting it. And it wouldn't be for long. Did she have a choice? That question caused nibblings of guilt, because she realized she would do just about anything for those goals, as he had done for his. "Supply the medical cures and science facts, reunite me and Andrea, and free the *charls* and you have a deal."

He waited for her to include, and leave me alone afterward. He was relieved when she didn't. "You'll trust me to keep my word on such an important matter but you won't trust me with your love and marry me?"

"If there's one thing I know about you, Commander Varian Saar, it's that you'll keep your word of honor. You never promised me anything, so you didn't break your word to me. True, you implied promises, but that isn't the same thing, I suppose."

"I've promised never to do it again, so what's the difference?"

"Earn my trust and prove yourself, then . . . Who knows? But don't get any false hopes because I truly believe it's over between us."

He was all smiles as he murmured, "We'll see."

Jana frowned and said, "Yes, we will."

Far away on Rigel, Jana didn't know one of his promises, the one concerning the *charls*, was being carried out that very moment. Nor did she suspect that the other three were already in progress . . .

It was afternoon of the next day when trouble struck the couple. Varian had sent out his coded signal again last night and this morning. So far, no shuttle—foe or friend—had appeared at or near their hiding place. They were discussing his plans for the remainder of the ruse when Varian pulled her to his chest and kissed her with unsettling thoroughness.

Jana heard a sound she recognized and shuddered. She yanked away.

"Give us a chan—" Varian urged.

"Hush! Listen!" As Jana glanced about, he obeyed, but it was suddenly quiet. "I heard a *keelar*, one of those sand snake creatures."

Varian had been so enchanted by her that his guard had been down for a moment. He looked around and listened. He decided it was a trick to halt his romantic siege. "I don't see or hear—"

The "pssst" sound came again from several directions. She was right. He had become dull-headed and that was foolish and dangerous. *Keelars* were deadly, especially without an available antidote to their venom.

"They sometimes live and travel in packs. Climb out of their reach. Now!" he shouted and nudged her when she seemed frozen to the spot.

Jana scrambled up the boulders and Varian followed. They watched the ground seem to come alive with movement as the creatures earthed their way into sight. Varian shot one, two, three, but more and more surfaced. The air was filled with their angry hissings.

He checked the weapon in his hand. He had only seven blasts left. The other two weapons were in the crevice with their supplies, out of reach with those lethal snakes everywhere. "I have to save my fire. We'll wait them out up here."

"We can't! We're in plain sight of any shuttle that comes along."

"We can't climb down. One strike and it's over, Moonbeam. I've never seen so many in one group. They're plenty mad, too. When one dies or is wounded, he gives off an odor that attracts others."

"Then why did you shoot those three?"

"I was going to kill all ten so I could get to the other

weapons, but then more surfaced. They're around the crevice; I can't reach them. Maybe they can't smell us up here. Maybe they'll take their dead and leave."

"Smell us?"

"That's how they track prey. The scent of fear makes it stronger."

"If that's a caution or suggestion to calm down, I'm not sure I can. Do you think they'll give up now that they've found a tasty meal?"

"Sit and relax," he responded evasively. "We'll be here a while."

She did, not because of his words but because her legs were about to give way. Her panicked gaze scanned their surroundings. It looked as if more *keelars* were arriving every minute. Jana shuddered and stared. They were trapped, without food and water, with weapons out of reach, and in view of a passing enemy. For the first time, she truly believed they might die on this barren wasteland. Until now, she had been confident Varian would find a way to save them. If only his signal would reach Nigel in time.

"At least they can't crawl up here," Jana remarked. "Can they?"

"Not with the rolled or sheer edges of the rocks."

Both fell into troubled silence as they sat within two feet of each other. Hours passed as the heat and their thirst increased. Their gazes shifted between looking at the skies for enemy crafts and looking at the ground for a retreat of the *keelars*. Many thick-bodied creatures had secured sharp teeth into their dead then dragged them away, possibly for food. Only the heads and about eight inches of sinewy necks of most were visible from their freshly tunneled holes. The snakes twisted their heads and shifted their bodies as if continuously keeping vigil in all directions.

Varian didn't want to make their precarious predicament worse by discussing a lack of options with Jana, but the snakes appeared firmly lodged in and around their campsite. He tried to come up with a plan to get their supplies and weapons, but there seemed no way without endangering himself. If he died, Jana would be in worse danger. He wanted to kill Taemin and Cass for luring them into this peril. He was apprehensive about enemy shuttles discovering them, after they had been so clever in eluding them. If the *keelers* didn't leave and even if they weren't caught by Taemin, they couldn't stay on the rocks and starve or die of thirst. He had to come up with a plan.

Jana was analyzing the grim situation, too, and her thoughts matched Varian's almost perfectly. She stood and walked to the area above their supplies. The alien joined her.

"We don't have a rope or hook. The limb across the crevice is too thick for retrieving the water and weapons by their handles. The thorn bushes are too short and limber to reach them."

Jana eyed the limbs he had placed at haphazard angles, atop which he spread the prickly brush for concealing them with what should pass for a wild thicket. "If we shove the thorn bushes away and move that sturdiest limb to there," she said, pointing, "where the ledges try to meet, I can hang by my knees and reach our water and weapons."

"You could fall and those *keelers* would be all over you before you could escape the crevice and climb the rocks. No, Jana, it's too risky."

"I took years of gymnastics and aerobics. I've climbed plenty of trees, fences, and rocks. I'm agile and steady. That limb should bear my weight for a short time. You can even hold on to my ankles in case it gives way. We have no choice."

"I thought you said we always have choices."

"We do: we can try my idea or we can sit on our butts and die."

"I'll do it, Jana. I don't want you getting hurt. That wood is abrasive."

"You're too heavy. If you try, that limb is certain to break and drop you right into a nest of those vipers. I need to keep you alive to get me out of this mess. Have faith in me for a change. I might prove to you I have more to offer than just a body for sex and reproduction."

"If that was your only value, Moonbeam, I wouldn't be

desperate to win you back. I know your immense worth, Jana; that's why I want you to become my wife."

"This isn't the time or place to be harassing me with marriage proposals or subjecting me to your cunning charms. Keep your mind on the business at hand or we won't survive to face that dilemma."

"All right, Jana, do it your way, but just be careful."

Varian used his booted toe to kick the branches to the ground. With him on one side and Jana on the other, they shifted the limb to a lower spot. He arranged verbal signals for avoiding danger.

When she asked him to help her out of her dress, she noticed his startled reaction. "Get that lusty look off your handsome face, Rogue Saar. I just don't want it hampering my vision and movement when I turn upside down." After the garment was removed, Jana warned, "And don't let it fall off this rock. I'm not fond of the idea of Taemin or his devils capturing me half naked." She took off her slip and shoes and tossed them near the ruined dress, leaving her clad in a lace bra and matching panties in sky blue.

Varian was surprised and pleased when her anxious gaze locked with his worried one for a moment and she smiled at him.

Jana took a deep breath and murmured, "Here goes our one chance."

"If you fall, woman, I'll thrash you good."

"You won't have to; I'll be dead in two hours from the bites of those critters."

Varian seized her by the shoulders and shook her. "Don't even joke about such a horrible thing."

"Why not? It's a lesson I learned from you: show contempt for danger and death so their powers are weakened."

"Bluffing foes and having a healthy respect for threats isn't the same thing, woman. *Keelers* can't be deluded and double-crossed like men can."

"I'm sorry, I was only trying to lessen our tension. I'll be careful."

His gaze roved her shapely body, then he ordered himself to alert. He flattened himself on his stomach on the rock above the ledge and dangled his arms over it to be ready to offer any help he could provide.

Jana eased her way to the center of the limb by straddling the branch and using her hands to wriggle herself forward. "Ouch. Ouch. Oh-ee. That smarts. This bark bites as badly as those snakes must. Ouch. I don't hear it groaning and complaining, so I guess it's strong enough to hold me. I'm ready. Wish me luck, and watch those ugly critters."

For a moment, their gazes fused and spoke unbidden messages. Varian smiled and coaxed, "Don't worry, love, I've got you. I'm sure you can do it. Get busy before they wise up and head for you."

Jana didn't want him to know how scared she was. Much depended upon her success, so the risk must be taken. *If you fail, J.G., and those* keelars *refuse to hit the trail, you and Varian are finished.*

Jana shifted to her buttocks and clutched the limb between her calves and thighs. With caution and with her hands gripping the wood support, she began to ease backward. She felt the muscles of her abdomen tighten from her strenuous effort. Her legs quivered from tension. When her long tresses fell downward, she thought about a *keelar* leaping at her and getting entangled in them. She wished she had torn another strip from the unfortunate dress and secured her hair in a ponytail at her nape. She felt blood rush to her head. Before she was in position to do her task or to sight the slithering predators, she heard their hissing increase. At the same time, she felt Varian seize her ankles as he shouted a warning to her.

"Get back! They're heading for the crevice! Up, woman. Fast!"

Jana was glad she hadn't lowered her arms yet because she knew the reptiles were almost within striking range. Varian applied pressure to her ankles to give her added strength and security. Her hands reached for the limb and she struggled to lift herself. Varian released one of his grips and held out his hand. Jana strained to grasp it. At last, their fingers interlocked and he pulled her to a sitting position on the branch. She raised her feet as she didn't know how far the elongated creatures could spring. Shaky, she let Varian lift her from the makeshift beam and place her beside him. She looked down to see the crevice writhing with numerous *keelars*, covering life-sustaining supplies and life-saving weapons. She locked her gaze with his. "It didn't work."

"It was a good idea, but I should have thought to use my last seven shots to create a diversion on the other side with dead bodies." After seeing her at work, he was convinced she could succeed and he told her so. "We'll give them time to settle down and get back into their holes before we try again. That is, if you want to try again; I think it's our best hope."

"Yes." She forced out the intimidating word. She pulled the slip and dress over her panties and bra in case they had unwanted visitors first, then they sat down to rest while the *keelars* calmed.

"I hope you'll come to forgive me for tricking you, Moonbeam," Varian said. "I want us to have a chance at real happiness when this is over."

"*We're* what's over, Varian. How could I come back to you without everyone thinking I'm crazy?"

"It doesn't matter what others think, Jana."

"It does to me, and it should to you, too. People look up to you. Young men and boys want to be like the illustrious Commander Saar. Your recent example tells them they can do as they please without fear of repercussions, especially where women are concerned. At least it would if I returned to you after how you've treated me."

"The public doesn't know and won't know of my deceits."

"They know you had romance with me. They were led to believe I was forced to escape your cruel clutches. Some of them know—and will probably gossip to others—about how I behaved with 'Ryker' during that first trip we took and how we acted on the *Wanderlust* during the Earth mission. They saw those lovey-dovey pictures that sneaky reporter took of us on Auriga: kissing in that romantic park, wasn't it? I suppose you also arranged that. From everyone's point of view, I've been Ryker's wife for months. Now, as soon as he dies, you want me to race back to you. People will think me fickle, phony, opportunistic, and shallow. You may not care what they think of me and say about me or yourself, but I do, very much. I already have the stigmas of being an alien and a *charl* to overcome. I certainly don't want more stains on my reputation."

"Everybody will think Ryker ordered you to display affection and happiness in public. They'll—"

"Are you forgetting you've made him seem a nice guy lately? And you plan to further brighten his dark image before your charade ends. You've made it appear he was so in love with his cherished wife that he changed for the better. But how do I repay him? By betraying his memory with you."

"People will think that you were being grateful to Ryker for freeing you and marrying you, or that you were trying to conceal or remove any lingering feelings for me, or that you were trying to be a good wife and friend."

"You're dreaming, Varian. What about Maal and the Androasians? Remember how we behaved at their party for us? For heaven's sake, Varian, our wedding portraits are hanging there!"

"The Androasians and Maal will think you're assuaging your grief with Ryker's half brother."

"You mean, my husband's archrival and foe."

"Not for long. Ryker and I are reconciling soon."

"If we get out of here alive. Anyway, Ryker's been disguised since birth, correct?"

"Yes, but everyone knows he and I look like Galen Saar."

"How can they if he's always . . . Ah, yes, the genetic law of your world: fathers reproduced in their sons. How nice that daughters are spared that replicating process." She gave an exasperated huff. "That resemblance makes it worse for us."

"How so, Moonbeam?"

"I leave you to marry your reflection, then he dies. I bury

Ryker, then elope with his mirror image. People will wonder which one of you I love."

"When they see us together, Moonbeam, they'll know it's me."

"Like everyone knew it was him when they saw us together?"

"You were never with my brother in public."

"Thanks to your ruse, I was, many times, and always appearing to be in love with him. You don't seem to grasp what an impossible predicament you've put us in. What you should have done was expose my kidnapping and declare my marriage illegal; then, perhaps I could have returned to you without problems. Ryker was dead, his threat and power gone. You could have stripped Trilabs and arranged a phony death for him. You could have found other ways to obtain your two treaties. But, no, you had to use this elaborate ruse that's ensnared us like a spider's web. We can't break free; you wove too many captivating strands. Now just drop it," she ordered. "We have work to do and I don't want to discuss it anymore today."

While they waited in moody silence, dark purple clouds moved into the area. Wind gusted with an odd whooshing and whining sound. Red lightning with countless dazzling branches illuminated the horizon within a few miles of them. Air waxed muggy and oppressive, while sand creatures became noisy and agitated. The vanishing sunlight cast them in ever-darkening shadows.

Jana observed the air currents and unusual shades of rip-roaring nature in this alien setting. "Just what we need, a violent storm with us exposed to its fury up here," she said. "Surely we'll be zapped by lightning and won't have to worry about *keelar* bites, or Taemin's claws."

"You should be delighted, Moonbeam; it's good luck. *Keelars* hate rain. They can't move through wet ground. It hurts them. They'll burrow deep. It'll give us a chance to get our things. Maybe even drive them away."

"You mean we're having good luck for a change?" she muttered as she watched the sky.

The ominous threat of nature's violence moved closer. Jana squealed as scarlet lightning bolts snaked to the ground like flaming vipers seeking cover less than a half-mile from them. Its brilliant fingers sounded like whips snapping as they clawed through the humid air or attacked objects with their fiery tips. Thunder boomed and echoed overhead, often with almost ear-splitting peals that lowered in volume as they drifted away from the two stranded captives. A deluge of water began to fall suddenly, and the only hissing heard now was from the cool rain and hot objects making contact.

Jana and Varian were drenched in minutes. Hair almost the same tawny color was plastered to their respective heads. Clothes were soaked and glued to their bodies. Rain rushed into emerald and multihued eyes, over noses, across mouths, and flowed over both exposed and clothed flesh.

Varian's fake green gaze tried to penetrate the downpour. He didn't see a single *keelar*, but they could be lurking just below the surface until the ground was saturated and became uncomfortable for them. For certain he couldn't hurry his love beneath any overhang that offered dried earth beneath, a definite lure for the creatures. He explained why they couldn't seek cover, shouting it over a blend of wind and rain and thunder.

The heat decreased with the sun's disappearance and weather's abrupt change. Breezes became stronger, whipping at their hair and garments. Thunder rumbled like a stampeding heard on Jana's Texas ranch. The couple felt vibrations from the potent storm. They watched red lightning dance wildly in jagged lines across the indigo sky. It seemed as if the heavens had been ripped open by the lightning's sharp nails and every drop of moisture stored there was being released in their confining location.

Jana realized it would be beautiful and exciting had it not been so dangerous. "Why don't we grab our stuff and run to another spot while those vile beasties are trapped underground?" Jane asked.

"The signals, woman," Varian explained. "They gave these

coordinates. I may not get another one out to correct it. I'll get our things, but we need to stay here."

"Be careful; those vipers might be hiding in there."

"No, it's too wet by now. Get ready to catch the things I throw up to you."

Varian tossed everything atop their refuge and they soon sat down and ate from tins protected against rain by body shelter. The rations tasted delicious to them after being without food for hours. The wind and lightning lessened but rain continued to pelt them in large and rapid drops.

Goosebumps raced over Jana's drenched head and body. Her teeth chattered and she shuddered. She draped the ragged material of the thin silk skirt over her folded legs and bare feet. Her hands felt like ice and she was cold from head to foot. She crossed her wrists and massaged her arms with opposite hands to warm them; the temperature had taken a drastic and swift drop like the Texas northers she remembered that always chilled her to the bone.

"Why don't you sit closer and share my body heat?" Varian suggested. "If you get too cold, you can take a chill and we don't have proper medicine." He noted that Jana didn't wait for a second invitation, as if she'd forgotten about her quarrel with him. She snuggled into his arms as he said, "I should have thought to grab some covers or jackets."

"You can't think of everything. At least we have supplies and weapons."

Varian rubbed his hands over her back, shoulders, and bare arms to spread warmth. He decided not to tell her just yet that the sand creatures had torn open some of the pouches and yanked others into their holes. One weapon was missing from the crevice, and he hoped he could find it when daylight returned. Diminished food and weapon power wasn't news to share at this depressing moment.

"If there was a *sparker* in the emergency kit, we'd be warm. It's the size of a small stone and gives off lots of heat and some light, even in rain."

"We could use one about now. The dress has no protection and my shoes are full of water. I'm freezing!"

His hands stroked and caressed rain-slick flesh. His lips teased over her face and ears as he murmured, "I know how to heat you up if you're willing." His hot breath, fiery lips, and blazing hands soon ignited more than warmth within both of them; they kindled white-hot desires in bodies denied passion's pleasures for weeks. He meshed their lips with feverish ardor, cradled her in his embrace so his mouth could ravish hers with a wildness to match the storm's while his body shielded her face from rain.

Jana wondered if this might be the last time they could join their bodies before they died on this barren planetoid so far from home. It was possibly the only span of time when shuttles wouldn't appear. In spite of all the unfair things Varian Saar had done to her, she loved and desired this irresistible alien. Even if they escaped this peril, she knew she would agree to a secret love affair with him as they continued the charade he had begun so many weeks ago. For once, her ex-captor and traitorous lover would be in her power and at her mercy because he needed her for the success of his ruse. In exchange for all he had offered and promised for her assistance, she also would be his lover. Why deny herself? As their lips parted, Jana asked, "Did you order up this bad weather and *keelar* attack so you could take advantage of me?"

He chuckled and smiled as he comprehended her responsive mood. "Of course. But I plan to take even more advantage of you, woman. I plan to remove these wet garments." As he talked, he pulled the dress and slip over her head, then released her breasts from the soaked bra. "I plan to heat you up in grand style."

His greedy lips covered hers while his deft fingers captured and stimulated her nipples, brought erect by a combination of the cold and sexual excitement. His hands labored there until his hot tongue took control of the loving chore. She made no attempt to slow or halt this heady madness, not even when he removed her panties and tantalized her with daring caresses.

She admitted that he knew how to evoke achingly sweet sensations, how to make her flesh quiver, how to fan her coals into smoldering embers and then into a roaring wildfire. Jana ignored the near stinging rain and chill. She ignored the wet and hard rock. She ignored the rain dripping from his hair and face onto hers. Her desire was too great to be restrained, and it was the same with him.

A savage intensity of primal need coursed through their veins. Primitive longings gnawed at them. The dangerous setting and elements evoked an erotic and potent wildness. They needed a frenzied union, a swift and urgent fusion of uninhibited bodies and unleashed emotions. Her hands sought the Velcro-type closing of his jumpsuit, yanked it apart, and peeled the stubborn garment from his torso with his assistance. Together they shoved the snug sapphire garment past his firm buttocks to release his manhood. "Take me," she urged him and guided him inside her.

"I need you so much, Jana," Varian whispered. "It's been so long since I've loved you as me."

Soft and throaty moans came from her throat, from the core of her being where anticipation was mounting at a rapid rate. The cold and rain were ignored and forgotten. All that mattered was being with her daring space pirate one more time. Each time he entered and withdrew, she savored heaven and endured hell. Her hands journeyed over his broad back, along his narrow sides, across his strong shoulders. She felt his sinewy muscles as they moved beneath her exploring fingers, moved because his hands and body were tantalizing and delighting hers. He was like a heady drug that numbed her wits and took command of her body. Every time his manhood plunged into her receptive body, his kisses would deepen and his tongue would dance with hers. He challenged her to give him the same splendor without speaking a word, and she accepted.

Varian blocked out the reality of the torrential rain as it pelted almost painfully on his unprotected back and buttocks. He took and gave with zest. He enjoyed the way she kissed and sucked and licked raindrops from his chin, his ears, his brows, and shoulders. He savored the way she cast aside reservations and handed control over to him. This was one area in which she always trusted him. He continued and increased his movements and resolve. She arched and writhed and clung, and almost drove him mindless with pleasure and stimulation. Her body as well as his cried out for appeasement. The intensity built to a point where they could no longer wait to be sated.

She murmured over and over, "Don't stop. I'm ready. Take me now. Take me. Take me. Now. Now." Her entire body experienced a rush of heat and tingling. She held tightly to him with arms and legs as the blissful climax rocked her to the core. Wave after beautiful wave of sheer ecstasy washed over her and swept her away. His mouth seemed to demand kiss after kiss as she heard him groan and recognized movements that said he was now in the throes of sweet release from which she was still reeling.

Varian continued to thrust and thrust within her. He was exuberant, sated, contented. He was also misled about her fiery response. "I love you, Jana. I knew everything would be fine."

Reality had returned for Jana, and she was chilly in more than flesh again. "Everything is not fine, Varian Saar, you treacherous snake. This changes nothing. It was nothing more than physical release."

"Why don't you admit you love me and this proves it?"

"We're accustomed to having sex and it's been weeks since we've been together like this. We were horny, that's all. For certain, we're well matched in bed, even one this hard and wet and uncomfortable. I made a deal with you to work as allies. We have an old song on Earth that says: 'I'll be your friend and I'll be your lover,' but nothing more, Varian, nothing more."

"All right, you stubborn female: ally, friend, lover, and partner—I'll settle for that much of you for now. But I'm not giving up on getting more. I'll chase you at every turn until you weary and surrender."

"That would be smart because we need to continue the romantic ruse between your brother and his wife."

"I won't be pretending or faking anything with you, woman."

At sunrise, Jana was awakened to a hairy and naked threat that was squatting beside her and poking her with fingers that were dirty and fuzzy. She came to instant alert. She scrambled to a sitting position with a shriek of surprise that caused the ugly cavelike man to become agitated. He jumped up, stared at her from a crouched stance, and sent out a menacing air. His huge balled fists plummeted his hairy chest as if telling her he was the leader. It was a gesture similar to ones she had seen on nature shows about gorillas, of which the male reminded her in body shape and appearance, though his enormous head did not. Scraggly, smelly hair grazed his shoulders. His nose was like a pig's snout, his black eyes round and beady like a weasel's except for their large size. His protruding facial bones revealed big lumps and long, sharp ridges. Dark, wiry whiskers struck out from all over his face. His flesh was pale yellow and his thick lips were brown. When he opened his mouth to form unintelligible words, it looked as if there was enough old food around his teeth to make a meal for a small animal. As he puckered his lips and made blowing sounds like signals, his breath stank like rotting vegetables combined with spoiled meat.

Jana wanted to retch and run. Her frantic gaze located Varian near the flat boulder's edge almost behind her. Two naked creatures cut him off from her and their weapons. He nodded but didn't speak, as if talking would be a threat to the Neanderthal-like creatures. She knew she must not make any sudden moves against the intruders. She assumed that if communication were possible, Varian would be doing it. Her gaze swept over the surrounding area to sight a group of mutants. The band looked ready to scale the rocks and attack them the moment a signal was given by the three atop it.

Jana realized that even if she and Varian could get to the weapons lying near her, they had only seventeen shots left, nowhere near enough to defeat this large band of savage primitives. Her frightened gaze searched the horizon in vain for a shuttle. She wished the *keelars* hadn't left the saturated area or would return to scare off these beasts. She knew Varian, even with his great strength and skills, couldn't attack the two strong males entrapping him. To do so would risk being thrown into the growling crowd below and perhaps be torn to pieces and devoured.

As the wild brute near Jana stopped studying her and inched forward, she trembled in terror and revulsion. The way he fondled his exposed manhood while eyeing her revealed that the filthy animal had mating in mind. The panicked Earthling prepared herself for the alien beast's assault and her defensive battle with him. Yet she feared there was no way she or Varian could prevent impending ravishment by the stalking beast.

Chapter Fourteen

Jana knew she must make an attempt to save their lives. With caution and a slow pace, she wriggled backward by moving her palms and buttocks against the flat-surfaced stone. As she did so, she forced a relaxed gaze on the foul-smelling, furry creature who watched her with curiosity but without advancing again. She was relieved that she had redressed last night after her lovemaking with Varian, as a naked woman might drive this beast crazy with lust.

Her groping fingers made contact with the two weapons. She grasped one to use and the other to toss to Varian when the opportunity came, if it ever did. She surmised that the moment she presented a threat to the wild men, she and her lover would be pounced upon and further imperiled. With only seventeen bursts of power left in the two weapons, she couldn't risk wounding these beasts. She glanced at the creature a few feet to her right, his enormous and erect maleness pointing directly at her. It was telling her that if she didn't remove his grim threat she would be brutally raped by this primitive gang. She must kill him first or he might leap forward and disable her. Jana reasoned that her sudden defeat of the pack leader should take the two beasts standing near Varian by surprise and freeze them long enough for her to shoot them next. Then, Varian could assist her in confronting the many others on the ground who were sure to rush them.

Stop stalling and do it. J. G. You have no choice. This is a life-or-death struggle. Do it before it's too late.

Jana's armed hand rounded her body and she fired the alien weapon. It gave off a loud "bzzzt" and an iridescent beam as the charge blasted into the mutant's heart with full power. He howled and thrashed then collapsed to the rock as the others gaped in astonishment. She wasted no time before whirling and firing at the other two, striking both motionless creatures in the center of their chests. Close to the edge, both lifeless bodies tumbled to the ground amidst startled and rigid primitives who continued to gape. Their slow recovery of courage and simple wits gave Varian time to rush to Jana's side and take the weapon she held out to him.

"Back-to-back position," he ordered, and she obeyed without question or hesitation. "They'll rush us as soon as they realize their clansmen are dead. Make every shot count, Moonbeam, because we don't have many." As his keen gaze kept a lookout for trouble, he asked over his shoulder, "Where did you learn to shoot like that? Three direct hits, and under pressure! Martella said you were trained before she gave you lessons."

Jana pressed close to his muscular back as she responded. "My father taught me. We used to target shoot, hunt quail, and such. Thank goodness Martella showed me how to use these weapons. There was no denying what was on my cave man's mind: heavy mating."

"You're right. That big leader had me worried. I was afraid he'd grab you and snap your neck before I could defeat the two separating us. I'm glad you kept a clear head and snatched us the advantage."

"Advantage? You call what we have an advantage? Fat chance, Saar."

Jana watched the confused mutants gather around the bodies to sniff and nudge their companions as if they wondered how the three had been defeated without a physical battle. After the truth settled in, they began to jump up and down and wail like injured animals. They growled, snorted, stomped, and made clawing motions at the couple.

"I think I made them a little bit angry. Where's the other gun?"

"The *keelars* rooted it into the sand and I couldn't find it in the dark. I planned to look for it this morning but never got the chance. I was relieving myself over the edge when those two sneaked up on me."

"They sneaked up on you? I can't believe that's possible."

He chuckled. "Caught me with my pants down as you Earthlings say. I heard a shuffling noise behind me but thought it was you sneaking over to tempt me again. If the wind had been in my favor, I would have smelled them. We'd been having a silent showdown for thirty minutes while the others gathered around. Since they don't talk, they take speech as a show of threat. I was glad you caught my hint to stay silent."

Jana watched naked men gather into small units and make signs with their hands, no doubt plotting their offense against the stranded couple. She chatted to lessen her tension. "I dared not take my eyes off him, so I hoped you were watching me and catching my line of thought."

"Actually, I was about to try to toss my two over the edge and dive for the weapons when I realized what you were doing. You didn't panic and you reasoned out the course of attack with perfection. You're as brave, smart, and daring as you are beautiful and delicious."

"Thanks for the compliments. Just save the last shot in case we don't scare them off, which appears unlikely. I don't intend to become a slave to a band of horny and savage primitives."

"Don't worry, Moonbeam; I won't let them get their dirty

paws on you. I'll make cert— On guard, here they come. No wounding, Jana, or he could require another shot to disable him and we have none to spare.''

From a defensive back-pressing position, they stopped nine mutants from scaling the formation to reach them. While she watched the enraged men cluster for another rush, Varian rolled the apparent leader to the ground in case he was their objective. They had five blasts left, two in her weapon and three in his. A few of the creatures began another assault, taking the couple down to three charges of energy before they retreated.

''You would think this loud noise and bright light would panic them. They must be too dense to realize we're using powerful weapons. We'll be in big trouble as soon as they comprehend we have no more shots of magic.''

''At least some are being scared off, Jana love. They might be stupid, but they've caught on to our superior strength and position and their danger. The dead are being carried away now.''

Jana glanced over her shoulder, eyed the situation, and refuted, ''Not far, Varian. Look; they're piling the bodies and returning for one last big attempt. They'll probably come at us at once. We'll—''

He felt her go rigid and silent. ''What's wrong?''

''A shuttle just materialized from nowhere. We're doomed now. It's too late to run or not be seen. Damn!''

Varian whirled and eyed the approaching craft as it dipped its right wing twice, then its left one three times. He recognized the signal, relaxed, and lowered the weapon in his hand.

She stared as the vehicle opened fire on the mutants and scattered them. Soon the barbarians were running for survival and leaving the dead behind in their frantic haste. ''It appears Taemin wants us for himself,'' she murmured in dread as the craft came to hover about ten feet above them. She knew an escape was impossible and any attempt was hazardous. With sunlight cut off, it was almost dark beneath the large vessel. She heard the steady hum of a healthy engine as the shuttle seemed to park in midair. She was surprised there wasn't any strong rush of wind; it was almost deathly calm. Varian put his arm around her waist and drew her close.

She sent him a resigned smile. "Well, Rogue Saar, we gave it our best shot, but it's over for us. I'll never forgive you if you let me fall into the evil hands of Taemin and Canissia. Do what you must and kill me fast."

He cuffed her chin and smiled. "We'll be fine, Moonbeam. That's—"

She cut him off with, "No, we won't. They'll torture us and kill us. Our good luck has been used up. We'll never get another chance to escape their clutches or to survive their trap. Please, use your last shot on me."

"Tell me you love me. There isn't much time to be honest before they open the hatch and reach us."

She fused her gaze with his, and noticed he didn't appear worried. "All right, I do love you and want you. Now, shoot me. Quick." She watched an expression of mingled joy and victory spread over his face.

"And let you miss a reunion with Nigel? That's his shuttle. See."

Jana whirled and stared at two men in Star Fleet uniforms who lowered a rope ladder for them to climb. She was about to scold Varian for tricking her when a rescuer shouted for Prince Ryker and Princess Jana to hurry aboard before their presence was detected with the cloaking shield down. Jana grasped the sturdy but swaying rope and mounted it, with the disguised Varian close behind and coaxing her to rush. The distance was short, so she didn't have time to experience much, if any, fear.

After they were inside and the hatch was locked, the detection deflector went back into effect to conceal the craft from enemy radar. The cloaked shuttle was piloted toward a rendezvous with the *Kiunterri* that, with cunning wisdom, remained in sight of Pyropean sensors.

In front of the regular crew on the *Kiunterri*'s bridge, Jana and "Ryker" Triloni were told that Nigel Sanger had received "Ryker's" emergency transmission and coordinates, after being ordered into this border area by Varian Saar to check on them because Taemin's invitation and timing were suspicious. The temporary commander of this starship had set his course to allow a slow pass over Luz on its way to pretend to "make an official call on the Tabrizes" to inquire about the couple's whereabouts and motive.

Jana looked at the hazel-eyed man with thick and curly brown hair who had been a close friend of hers. Once more, she reminded herself he hadn't betrayed her long ago, that someone had faked Nigel's voice while drugging her. He was one inch shorter than Varian's six-four frame, and was the same age of her lover: thirty-one. "Thank you, old friend, for rescuing us in the nick of time. Can we get out of this enemy sector fast?"

"As soon as I meet with the Tabrizes to ward off suspicion. I'm sure the shuttle wasn't detected because we shielded her while she was visible for rescue." Nigel explained "Varian's" clever ploy to them, one that would be used to explain their rescue in public soon. "You'll hide while I dupe the Tabrizes. We can't afford to make them suspicious or to enlighten them before we can get you two out of any danger lurking here. I'm sure you're both eager for a good meal and hot bath. We'll handle that now." The creases deepened around his hazel eyes and full mouth as he grinned; so did the dimples in his cheeks.

"That sounds wonderful, Nigel, as if you read my mind. Needless to say, I feel a wreck in this torn and dirty dress." She assumed it was hard for Nigel and Varian to conceal their twelve-year friendship and genial rapport during this pretense. She was glad she didn't have to try.

The shielding device was remounted in the starship to avoid suspicion and all clues to the rescue were destroyed. Nigel explained to the couple in the presence of others how, after being ordered by Commander Varian Saar to keep a close eye on them, he had used debris and sensitive instruments to track them to this sector. With the aid of the signal "Ryker" had sent, he had located them. Following "Varian's" suggestions, he rescued them in secret. "Not a moment too soon from the way it looked on monitor."

"It was getting a little hairy down there," Jana quipped.

"As soon as we finish here, you two can thank the man responsible. Varian's waiting to greet you two on Rigel at Star Base. Do you have any objections, Prince Ryker, Princess Jana?"

"None. In fact, a genial meeting with my brother is long overdue."

"I concur with my husband's decision."

Varian and Nigel talked while Jana lazed in a tub of bubbly water for an hour. The best friends decided to let Jana believe for a while that the ruse demands were being met because of her promise to aid Varian.

"I can hardly wait to see and hear Taemin's and Cass's reactions when they learn it was Ryker they tried to kill," Varian gloated. "Those two played right into our hands with their treachery."

When she had dried off and dressed, Jana joined the two men in Nigel's quarters to chat and sip wine. "Thanks again, Nigel. And thank whoever loaned me this outfit and shoes. Mine was ruined."

The hazel-eyed man embraced her with affection. "You're more than welcome, Jana, and it's wonderful being with you once more."

"For a while, I thought we were dust in the wind. Varian has a knack for getting us into deep trouble. I'm thankful he has the skills to get us out again. By the way, Rogue Saar, how did you know it was Nigel's shuttle?"

Varian chuckled before he informed her of the signals used to alert a stranded party to the arrival of friendly help. "Nigel stalled opening the hatch to give me time to caution you against exposing my identity to others."

"You and Nigel are very clever and make a good team," she said.

"So do we, woman, I told him how skilled you were back there. If not for your quick thinking and courage, he would have arrived too late."

"I'm glad to see you two on the same channel again," Nigel said. "I've missed you, Dr. Jana Greyson, almost as much as I'm missing Andrea."

Jana made herself comfortable as she coaxed, "Why don't you tell me everything about this romance with my best friend?"

Her question began a long and stirring tale from Nigel Sanger as they headed toward Cenza to carry out their ruse with the Tabrizes.

Later in the quarters assigned to her and "Ryker," Varian offered to tend her leg where it had been scratched on the rough bark on the limb she had straddled. "I've already doctored them, thank you. If you don't mind, I'm exhausted."

"You're just going to bed after what you confessed before our rescue?"

"That was a bloody trick you pulled on me back there and it didn't work," she scolded in a soft tone. "I only said it to let you die happy."

"What was that Earth slang you used: Fat chance? I'll leave you be for a few days' rest and recovery. Then . . ." He chuckled and licked his lips.

Canissia Garthon hid from the group of Maffei officers who shuttled down to speak with the ruler and his son, and she was relieved that Jurad did not know of her presence. She felt thwarted and enraged by the explosion that had snatched Varian, Jana, and Ryker's holdings from her grasp. She was furious that Taemin's search had revealed no survivors. She had surmised the "accident" would evoke questions and an investigation and perhaps another search, but she hadn't expected them to come from the Alliance or this quickly. It was almost as if they had expected a trap.

Taemin informed them that the Trilonis never arrived. "An explosion registered on our screens," he explained. "We searched the entire area, but found nothing. We never received a warning and do not know what happened. We suspect treachery from an enemy, but have found no proof of it. Within two days, I would have been on that ship escorting them to Darkar after their visit, so perhaps the explosion, if it was sabotage, was aimed at me, not the Trilonis."

Nigel used a deceptively pleasant smile and tone. "It is to everyone's interest if you don't report they're missing to the public until we're sure you can't locate them alive or recover their bodies. I'm sure this will not sit well with our mutual ally, *Kadim* Maal. We will appreciate it if you continue the search until there is no hope. We feel that Prince Ryker and Princess Jana were our responsibilities, and we're certain *Kadim* Maal will view it that way, too. If you have further news, you can report it to us at Star Base. As soon as we're certain they're lost, we'll inform Maal and issue a news release from Rigel."

While enroute to Rigel, the curly-haired man told Jana, "As we speak, the Earthlings are being prepared by Tris and his staff for their return home, minus any memory of their sojourn here. The medical cures and scientific facts are embedded in the correct heads. In accordance with your last demand, the *charl* laws have been abolished, and a team headed by Martella has been chosen to help the women get settled according to their wishes. Martella said to tell you that Kathy and Ferris, and Heather and Spala, and many of the others on your voyage are already wed to their past owners. She said to tell you that few men and women have chosen to go their separate ways."

"As soon as Tris and Martella finish with the Earthlings and *charls*," Varian added, "they'll meet us on Darkar to go to work there. In case anything goes wrong in Androas, we'll have all we need from Trilabs.''

''Confiscating my inheritance without my permission?'' Jana quipped.

''You wouldn't withhold such secrets from us, would you?''

''Perhaps. You and Maffei captured and enslaved me, stripped me of my freedom and pride. On the other hand, Ryker wed me and gave them back. I was accepted in Androas and have family there—my father-in-law. My golden-gowned wedding portrait even hangs in the hallowed halls of their palace; so does yours as Prince Ryker. How can anyone compare a bleak and lowly *charl*'s life with the glorious one of a princess?''

Nigel saw Varian grimace and remain silent, so he changed the subject, ''I'll go after Andrea myself while you two visit Maal a last time. We'll be waiting on Darkar for your victorious return.''

Jana glanced at Varian to ask, ''Isn't it dangerous to go to Androas? What if Taemin and Canissia warned Maal about the truth?''

''It wouldn't matter, not with the little charade we have in mind.'' He grinned and chuckled as he gave her the cunning details.

''Are you sure all of these tricks will work?''

''They must, Moonbeam, and they *will* if we don't make any mistakes.''

''I don't have to worry about you fooling Maal; you already have. I just hope he doesn't hear from those two villains and start asking you questions to which only Ryker knows the answers. Even if you have those journals and tapes, they don't cover everything that happened in the past or with Maal. If he decides to test your identity, we'll be in deep trouble.''

''Be optimistic, love; I am.''

''I'm afraid that's a quality you stole from me, you space pirate.''

''Then recover it; you won't be sorry; I promise.''

How many times have you heard him make those last two

statements? Too many times you believed them and trusted him but got hurt. This time, be alert for lies and tricks. ''We'll see, Varian. We'll see.''

Taemin, Canissia, Maal, and others viewed the live news broadcast of Ryker Triloni and—thanks to the lookalike cyborg, Varian Saar shaking hands after a daring rescue of the Androasian prince and his wife. It was alleged that after Star Fleet officers went to consult the Tabrizes about the Trilonis's disappearance and a joint search, it was learned their shuttle exploded and no survivors could be located. As the *Kiunterri* departed and was passing over Luz, they received an urgent signal from Ryker who had managed to repair a communicator in time to summon them while in range of its beacon. The false tale related that the couple—after being attacked by space pirates—had escaped in an emergency pod from the escort ship and had crashed on Luz in the edge of Pyropea. Lieutenant Commander Nigel Sanger and his team rescued the couple and took them to Star Base to thank the man responsible for ordering a protective shadow and immediate search, none other than Ryker Triloni's half brother, Varian Saar.

The reporter's lead and final lines were: ''Brothers reunited after daring rescue on barren planetoid.'' Many watching it were stunned.

Varian sat down at the communication panel and—as Ryker—called Maal to let his ''grandfather'' know he and Jana were all right and were headed to visit him to explain everything. From Maal's words and actions, Varian and Jana assumed he wasn't aware of Canissia's suspicions.

Next, Varian—still as Ryker—contacted Supreme Ruler Jurad and his son. ''I don't know if you were involved with Taemin and Cass's plot against me, but I warn you now, Jurad,'' he threatened, ''it will not be forgotten or forgiven by me or Grandfather. My wife and I almost died on Luz at the hands of mutants and the other perils there. From the message Taemin gave to Garus to pass to me, I assume you are not involved and I hope that is true.'' He repeated for the astounded Jurad what the ship captain had said to him. ''I can also assume the 'secret' he mentioned has to do with Cass getting it into her stupid head that I tried to kill her, which is absurd. When she visited me recently, I told her she was wrong. Obviously she did not believe me and she raced there to involve Taemin and perhaps yourself in her revenge. I find it incredible and offensive that my friends and allies would believe such foolish lies and would conspire against me. Taemin cannot possibly love or desire that bitch more than what he can obtain from me. Consider yourselves and Pyropea cut off from Trilabs until I receive a convincing explanation for your traitorous acts and a full apology.''

With the viewer screen left on, Jurad looked at his son and asked, ''Taemin, what do you know of these accusations and Garus's treachery?''

''They are not true, Father; I swear it on my life and honor. I do not know why Garus lied. Perhaps the Maffeians bribed him to create an intergalactic rift between us. You are wrong, Ryker; we are not responsible for the trouble. You said yourself it was an attack by space pirates.''

''That was a lie to keep the black truth from the public. Do you think I want the Tri-Galaxy to learn the Tabrizes and Canissia Garthon tried to kill me and Jana? No, I will handle my retribution in my own way.''

Taemin was duped by the news-communication ruse and by other sightings of ''Varian'' on Rigel during Ryker's presence on the *Wanderlust* far away. He was furious with Canissia over her costly and stupid mistake. He was also vexed with himself for believing her wild talk and for getting involved in her crazy and desperate scheme for revenge. At the time, her claims had sounded logical and potentially very profitable for him. If he had gotten his spy's report on Varian's location sooner, he would not have alienated Ryker and Jana. Somehow he had to repair the damage to those crucial relationships.

"We have been friends and allies a long time, Ryker," the guarded prince said. "Even if that were not true, I would be a fool to destroy our vital link to Trilabs. I did not try to capture and slay you. I have not seen Canissia Garthon since she attended my nuptials months ago. If the traitorous Garus had not been killed, we could have forced the truth from him. I will make every attempt possible to unravel this mystery and to capture those responsible. How could you doubt my loyalty and friendship? How can you accuse me of such wickedness?"

Varian used every word and expression he could think of to evoke doubts in Jurad about his son's guilt. "Because I am sure Garus did not lie and was not working on his own or for someone else. Your longtime captain would carry out any order you gave him. There is no amount of money or coercion from anywhere to compel him to betray you. He also said things only you could have known and told him. You and Cass hoped to torture my wife until you forced the entry code to my complex from my lips to halt your cruelties. Until I married Jana, there was no weapon or tool to use against me. But any man or woman who dares to harm her will pay dearly. Do you forget I know how much you crave to conquer and rule the Tri-Galaxy?"

"At one time, that was your dream and goal, too. Before Jana."

"So, that is why you hate her and wish to destroy her. I promise you, Taemin, you will never get near her again. Neither you nor Cass. If any harm ever comes to her, I will destroy you. And if any harm ever comes to us or to me, Grandfather will use Trilabs' powers to destroy you and Pyropea."

"Your threats and anger are wasted on lies, Ryker. I am innocent."

"Why did you not signal us for help?" Jurad asked. "Why were we not informed of your rescue and have to learn of it by news communication?"

"Now that you've heard the ugly truth, Jurad, surely you don't think I could have allowed the Maffeians to inform you we had been located and rescued so Taemin could attack us again. His deceit forced me to rely on a previous enemy for survival, for rescue from a so-called friend and ally.''

Varian glared at Taemin. ''How dare you two plot against me and my wife! I suggest you and Cass watch yourselves carefully, and don't either of you expect to make any future purchases from me. If the *Moonwind* or any Pyropean ship comes near Darkar, it will be attacked and destroyed by my automatic defense system. And tell Cass that if I ever see her devious face again, I'll remove whatever remains of her beauty with acid. If either of you try another trick, I'll play a few videotapes from my private collection across the Tri-Galaxy. I doubt you or Cass want certain, if any, people to hear and view you while revealing your dirty and dangerous secrets.''

''Explain your meaning, Prince Ryker,'' Jurad demanded.

''I'll leave that up to your *loyal* son, for now. Remember my warning and hear me well, Taemin, harm Jana or me and you're dead. To you, Jurad, watch your son with keen eyes. Prince Ryker Triloni signing off.''

Jurad locked his gaze on his son's face. ''What did he mean, Taemin?''

''I do not know, Father. Perhaps he has become as mad as his mother was at the end. Since he met that Earthling temptress, he has changed. He fears some man will steal her from him, so he sees evil spirits and threats where none exist. Because of a wild delusion, he has made peace with his half brother and Maffei. I do not know how Varian and the Alliance accomplished such cunning deceit to turn Ryker against us, but it has worked, for the present. The day will come when Ryker learns it is we who are his true friends and allies. Be patient, Father, and trust me.''

''What of the Garthon woman? Perhaps the treachery was her doing.''

Taemin had speculated on that idea himself and did so again for a moment. He knew now he should never have allowed Canissia to convince him of such a crazy tale. Even if Ryker and Varian were near-twins and Ryker's treasured wife was Varian's cherished ex-lover, it was reckless for the Maffeian starship commander to kill the Androasian prince. After seeing them together while shaking hands and talking on the viewer live and before many witnesses, he concluded that an impersonation ruse was impossible. Taemin finally answered Jurad's question. "If it was her doing, Father, I will find out soon. And if it was intentional deceit, I will slay her."

Enroute to Tartarus in Androas, Jana remarked, "At least your cyborg trick duped Taemin like it duped me on Auriga. Whatever you said or did to cause Canissia to doubt you, he has to be convinced she was mistaken."

"With luck, those two are at each other's throats and will stay out of our way. That will give us time to finish our tasks with Maal and on Darkar."

"If you take all the secrets from Trilabs, what value will it be to me?" Jana asked. "With it, I have the wealth, power, products, and knowledge to help my people on Earth."

"That isn't possible, Jana. The products are from plants, minerals, and animals located here, not on your world. Those formulas would be useless to your people."

"Not if I make them here and transport them there. I can afford it."

"And create an imbalance of power on your planet? For your country to have such things would entice attacks from others, those called terrorists, to steal or take them from America. Advancement and progress on any world must come at its own rate, by its own hands, from its own caring. Can't you imagine the fears you would evoke by revealing our existence? Your bargain with me was for a limited supply of knowledge, not for the continual feeding of it to your people. That would create chaos."

"Are you sure you trust me to carry out my end of the bargain? Have you forgotten I have just cause to betray you and seek revenge?"

"If you toss me away, Moonbeam, you will miss me and my love. Where would you ever find another love as perfect as ours? Find a man who loves you and needs you as I do? You're too intelligent and tenderhearted to throw away what we have. You could never love or respond to another man as you do with me. Think of what we have, Moonbeam, and how we make each other feel. Think of the good times we've shared. Don't they count for something? We've learned a lot and both matured. I've made mistakes, but I've learned from them and from almost losing you."

"You *have* lost me, so face that reality. You did the tossing away, not me. You are the one who didn't allow what we had—*had*, Varian—to count for anything. If our love was so perfect, you wouldn't have slain it in such a cold and calculating manner. What I am is too experienced to trust you again with my heart."

"Haven't there been times where you've unintentionally hurt someone because you did what you knew you had to do for the good of everyone involved? What kind of man would I be if I went against my conscience or didn't do what I knew could save so many lives and obtain peace? If you'd tell me why what I did was so wrong, perhaps I can understand your feelings and thoughts better and make up for wrongs you believe I committed against you." Her expression warned him that his last sentence was another mistake, so he hurried past it. "I know you don't like being tricked. But knowing what you do now, tell me what I could have done differently to accomplish my goals without losing you, my greatest personal treasure."

"This isn't the time and place to be thinking about us, about Varian Saar. It's vital to your charade for me to keep seeing you as Ryker. I can't if you constantly remind me of your true self. If you don't back off, you'll have me calling you Varian by mistake and that could ruin everything and cost us our lives. This ruse has cost us plenty, so don't make it fail by thinking about me when it's too late to matter."

"Jana, please lis—"

"No, Va— Ryker, I've heard enough today. I can hardly wait to see Andrea," she began as she changed the topic to a safer one. With wisdom, he allowed her to do so.

* * *

Maal gaped at the green-eyed blond as he related his facts and suspicions about Taemin and Canissia. "We must not trust the Tabrizes again, Grandfather. No doubt they hoped to slay us and blame the Maffeians to provoke you against them. They know we're leaning heavily toward a new treaty and refusing to join them to war against the Alliance. They know I am the one trying to persuade you toward peace. But don't worry, Grandfather, I will take care of them when the right time comes. First, they will endure my painful pinch by being cut off from Trilabs."

That revelation stunned the older man, but another did so even more. "How could you make peace with the son of the man who betrayed and destroyed your mother, my daughter?"

"That was many years ago, Grandfather, and we've both changed. To hate for so long and so deeply eats into a man until it is he who is destroyed, not the enemy. We have lived and fed on thoughts and plans for revenge until that meal has grown sour and expensive. On Rigel, I had a talk with Varian. Just as I am not to blame for Mother's deeds against the Saars and Trygues, Varian is not responsible for the deeds of his father against us. I have grown weary of our private war; it is past time to end it. We are half brothers: we carry the same blood and genes. There is a bond between us which we have both denied and resisted. To do so is self-destructive. He reminded me of something long forgotten: Galen never denied I was his son, and he did plead with Mother to let him raise me. Surely you recall it was you and Mother who refused, and he had no choice except to honor your wishes. Our parents are dead and buried, as the past should be. Before the Tri-Galaxy, Varian claimed me as his brother. Am I less of a man than he is? Could I have refused to accept his offer of peace?"

"What if he lies, cherished flame of my soul?"

"There is but a slim chance he fooled me. In our deepest of hearts, Grandfather, we do not know what happened between my mother and father years ago. Only they knew the truth and it is buried with them. Varian did not accuse Mother of being to blame because he does not know the truth, either. It is only natural for him and Tirol to accept Galen's words, just as we accepted Mother's. Perhaps it was a cruel twist of fate and neither Mother nor Father were at fault. Perhaps even they didn't know the truth. Perhaps a chemical in the food or water worked a tragic spell on them. We know such things happen, Grandfather. Whatever took place between them, it is over for me and Varian."

Maal had always suspected his beloved, but selfish and defiant, child was to blame for ensnaring Galen, but he could not admit it aloud even now. "So you have made up your mind to push for a treaty with the Alliance?"

"Yes, Grandfather, for many reasons. They risked a confrontation with Pyropea to rescue us; they saved our lives. During the voyage, I discovered that Maffei is much stronger than we realized, too strong and well trained to challenge recklessly. It will also prevent a rebellion among our people. I am convinced Varian and the Maffeians are sorry for the past and that their offer of peace is sincere. I will not tell you what to do or say, Grandfather, but I urge you to sign a treaty with them for everyone's sake."

Varian paused a moment for those suggestions to sink in before he added, "Taemin will seek revenge on me for exposing his black deed. If anything happens to me, look to him, Grandfather, not to Varian or Maffei. But do not worry too much as I will guard my back and my wife well."

Maal reflected before answering. "I will wait, watch, and listen, cherished flame of my heart. I must have time to think on this matter and on your change of position. I have never known you to be wrong in the past, so there must be value in what you advise."

"That is good, Grandfather, because we all need fresh beginnings."

As Maal and Jana chatted, Varian thought about his impending talk with Agular to expose the breach with Pyropea and strengthen the ties to Maffei.

* * *

Enroute home, Jana asked, ''Do you think we convinced him to go for the new treaty?''

''I hope so, Moonbeam. We did our best. You were perfect.''

''Thanks. So were you. If your ruses with Maal and Jurad don't succeed, you have the journals and tapes to use for blackmail.''

''If I can obtain treaties without using them, I will.''

''Why? Don't you want them to know your father was innocent?''

''As you've told me over and over, many people have been hurt by the past, and I think they've been helped by my ruses. If I don't have to use that ugly evidence, it will prevent more pain. Besides, instead of settling them down completely, discovering such a horrible truth could provoke them again—especially Maal when he learns about Shara and Ryker.''

Jana was surprised by his intentions, and she was warmed by his kindness. ''You like Maal, don't you?''

''Let's just say he isn't totally to blame for his feelings and actions. He had Shara and Ryker provoking and duping him at every turn. The same is true with Jurad; he had Shara and Ryker and Taemin doing the same to him. He suffered a great humiliation before the Tri-Galaxy by what she did. He loved her and wanted her, so naturally he hated my father for stealing her even if it wasn't his fault. I know I have the power and means to clear my father's name, but the price could be destruction of all I've worked and sacrificed for to achieve. Father would understand and agree.'' He didn't think it was wise to remind her there was another reason to keep his evidence concealed: many of Maffei's secrets were revealed and discussed on those tapes and pages. Many of them were entwined with portions he would need to use to persuade Maal and Jurad of the truth. He also noticed how Jana responded favorably to the motive he had mentioned for withholding them. It was selfish and even deceitful, but he didn't want to destroy any progress he was making with her.

"Is my part over? Is that all you needed from me?"

"Not until Ryker is killed in that mining accident on Caguas. You'll have to play the grieving widow when we take his body home to Maal. That will be your last assignment, Jana, then you're out of this situation."

"What if Maal still points a finger at you instead of at an accident or at Taemin?"

"I have an alibi arranged: Varian Saar will be a long way from Caguas."

"The cyborg again?"

"Until I can switch places with it and visit Jurad."

"You're going to see Jurad and Taemin? As yourself? Why?"

He explained the importance and motive for his "official" visit.

"You two being seen in different places at the same time should cover you when the news breaks. What about me? I'll be a widow, Ryker's heir. You know the leeches will come out of the walls to try to suck me dry."

Varian caressed her cheek. "I promise you, Moonbeam, nothing and no one will harm you again, not even me."

"Good. Now, make love to me."

"What?"

"We did agree to be allies and lovers and friends, didn't we?"

"Yes, but you've been pushing me away."

"I told you why, so I wouldn't forget you were Ryker before we saw Maal. After we reach Darkar, you'll become Varian again so I don't have to worry about that problem anymore. Besides, I have to test your pull on me before I reach home and everything gets crazy."

"You want me? Now?"

Her hand reached up to caress his taut jawline and to trace the fake scar there. "You know I've never stopped wanting you in that way."

That physical contact and her mood called out to him to accept her offer to share herself. The ship was like a warm cocoon that encased them in a romantic haven that drew them together. It also separated them from the outside world that threatened to yank them apart and destroy their beautiful bond. Their pull on each other was too great to resist, and neither wanted to do so. Fate had drawn them together, parted them, and reunited them. Their hearts and lives had been changed by meeting each other: souls bound as one spirit, hearts beating until eternity with love, and bodies burning until infinity with desire.

Varian captured the hands that were stroking his cheeks and pressed them to his lips. As his gaze remained locked with hers and he absorbed her mood, his lips and tongue played sensuous music in her palms. He stepped closer to her to remove all space between them. His arms banded her receptive body and his mouth seared over her ear. It murmured sweet and passionate endearments before drifting down the silky column of her throat. He felt her tremble and sway against him, as aroused as he was. His hands removed her nightgown and robe with speed and agility, then discarded his boots and pants. Pressing their supple frames together, he savored the touch of her tawny flesh against his tanned body.

Jana's arms encircled his waist as she used her torso to caress his. As if on cue, her fingers buried in his blond hair as his slipped into her tawny tresses. Their mouths meshed to share a kiss which stole their breath and ignited their smoldering desires into a raging blaze of urgency.

One kiss blended into another until there was no beginning or ending to any of them. His hands roved her bare shoulders and sleek back, admiring the silky feel of her unmarred skin. His fingers were ravenous in their search for more treats; they wandered to her soft curves to caress her firm buttocks and upward to rove her tempting breasts.

Jana shifted sideways to allow him easy freedom to explore her aching body. He cradled her in the curve of his right arm as his mouth feasted at hers and his left one closed over a firm mound. When her peaks responded without haste and became taut with need, his mouth drifted over her chin and down her throat to ensnare one with his teeth in a gentle and stirring grasp. His lips had left a trail of kisses behind that still tingled. The rosy-brown buds bloomed beneath his questing mouth and tongue. She was always astonished by how his actions affected her from head to foot. Even her tummy quivered in suspense and delight. And the core of her womanhood, it ached with pleading. Her entire body was alive and burning, as was his.

Varian returned his mouth to hers for a short while and kissed her with almost feverish intensity. He wanted her now, fast and fully. Yet he knew this moment must not be rushed, even if his self-control was hard to maintain. She had come to him of her own free will. She was showing him she wanted him, loved him, needed him. He must do all within his power and skills to give her exquisite pleasure and supreme satisfaction.

Jana felt afloat on dreamy clouds as his hand moved past her abdomen and stroked enticingly along its predetermined path. She quivered when his deft fingers stroked the sensitive flesh between her parted thighs. They labored with a skill, eagerness, and gentleness that left her breathless. She felt as if her legs would give way at any moment as a languid weakness washed over her. He caressed her until she was trembling and limp, until she murmured, "Take me, Varian; please take me."

He was thrilled to hear his name escape her lips. In gratitude and joy, his mouth seared over hers, parted her lips, entered her beckoning recess, and allowed their tongues to mate first. His grasp on her was snug and possessive. "Stars above, Jana, I cannot resist you. I knew that the first moment I saw you. *Kahala*, how I do love you." Varian guided her to the bed and they collapsed to it because neither would release the other to brace their fall. They laughed in amusement and began their play anew.

Jana inhaled his manly scent which mingled with an arousing cologne that was perfect for him. His mouth tasted like spearmint; it was delicious and provocative. Her tongue danced with his in an erotic and stimulating manner to a seductive beat they heard only inside their heads and hearts.

Once more Varian's mouth trailed down her neck, kissing

and sampling every inch of it along the way. His tongue played with both succulent breasts with an intent to conquer and delight them. Her nipples hardened even more under his loving siege. Again, his fingers journeyed to the dark triangle between her thighs. They stroked the downy soft hair surrounding her portal to love. The heat of her arousal warmed his hand, the mist of it dampened his fingers.

Ecstasy, sweet and tormenting, enthralled Jana. It began deep within the core of her being, mounted and teased, searched and found, then sent charges like tiny lightning bolts over her flesh in all directions. She writhed and moaned. She clung to him. Every part of her was sensitive and susceptible. She yearned for more of him. She locked her softened gaze with his fake green one and smiled. Yet, not once did she think of him or see him as Ryker Triloni. Her rosy-eyed vision saw her sapphire-eyed, ebony-haired lover who had won her heart long ago.

Both knew they had plenty of time to love as long as they desired tonight, but passions soared and urged to be sated. It was as if they were exploring emotions as well as passions, allowing spirits to mingle as well as bodies, allowing hearts to reach out and speak without intrusive words.

Varian was thrilled and encouranged by her fiery need. He obtained extra pleasure from the rapture he was giving her. He eased atop her, parted her thighs, and obeyed her mute summons to possess her to the limits of love. The contact between their private regions almost staggered his senses and stole his mastery. He wanted and craved to drive within her over and over.

Jana's legs curled around his thighs as she matched his rhythm. Her mouth clung to his and her flesh melded with his. She rode the stormy waves beneath him as the marvelous forces mounted in power. She felt like a glowing star shooting across the heavens.

Both realized this wasn't just raw sex taking place. Both knew they were speaking from their hearts and souls, with their whole beings. It was more than a fusion of starving bodies; it was a union of spirits, a forging of their cores, a flight toward their entwined destinies. Their desires, pace, and patterns matched. Their ardor inspired them to hold nothing back. Passion's flames engulfed them in a blaze that only fulfillment could extinguish.

Jana arched to meet each thrust, then relaxed a moment before returning for the next one. She wanted the tantalization to continue, but she also wanted release from the achingly sweet torment. The bud and core of her womanhood began to spasm wildly. "I love you," she murmured in the throes of ecstasy without realizing she had spoken those revealing words.

Varian heard and his heart drummed with happiness and relief. He knew she wasn't conscious of uttering them, but they had come from her heart, the very place she was guarding against being hurt again. He kissed the tip of her nose, her cheeks, her eyes, her ears. He cast aside his control and chased after her to join her in a serene paradise. His release spilled forth within her in rapid, joyous, and uncontrollable splashes.

Afterward, they nestled together in the golden afterglow of their loving. They cuddled and caressed, stroked and kissed, until, at last, they slept.

Following days of a fragile truce, the moment Varian dreaded arrived. "We're orbiting Darkar, my love, so there's one last promise you have to make before we shuttle to the surface for your reunion with Andrea."

Jana was filled with excitement. In the past few days they had made love many times and in many ways. She realized he was weakening her resistance and was winning her heart and trust again: perhaps, she decided, that wasn't bad. "What promise do I need to make?"

"When you see Andrea, you can't tell her the truth. She'll meet me as Ryker, your husband. She won't meet Varian until this mission is over and my brother officially dead. You can't ever tell Andrea about my ruse." As he related his order,

Varian witnessed an array of emotions in her reaction: she was stunned, hurt, disappointed, and suspicious.

Every time he nodded after each of her ensuing questions, her heart sank more and more. "You mean downright lie to my dearest friend? Let her believe Varian Saar coldly and cruelly betrayed me? Believe I'm Ryker Triloni's wife of my own free will and I've been living with him all this time? Dupe her like the others? Forever?"

"It has to be that way, Jana. I'm sorry, but too much is at stake. If anyone ever extracted the truth from her, it would tear down all the good we've built. This risk is too great. She must never know the truth. Never."

She had looked forward to a soul-cleansing and comforting talk with Andrea. She couldn't ever imagine deceiving her. "I can't lie to her. I *won't* lie to her. Damn you! Always your duty!"

"Think, Jana: she could drop a clue and ruin everything."

"How? She'll be secluded with me on Darkar."

"Not permanently if Nigel marries her and she leaves with him. In the near future, she could make a slip to a visitor, a client, a friend. Even if you swore her to secrecy, accidents happen. If she doesn't know anything, she can't expose anything. It has to be this way."

"I trust Andrea completely. She wouldn't betray me as you have. I will not lie to her or deceive her. She won't endanger our secrets; I swear."

"Your blind faith isn't good enough in this crucial matter."

"If you asked me to keep something from her for a while, I would. But you're demanding I lie to her for the rest of our lives. Besides, she knows me; she would know I'm being dishonest. That would hurt her deeply. How could she ever trust me again? Our relationship would be damaged. What if I were demanding you lie to Nigel or Tirol?"

"That's different. They know everything and are trustworthy."

"So is Andrea! And me, too!"

"I chose my word badly, Jana. Calm down. I meant, they're trained and experienced in guarding secrets. Because of those traits and *Rendelar*, they can't be tricked or forced into exposing vital secrets. That isn't true of Andrea. She's susceptible to potentially perilous slips and coercion."

"You're asking me to risk destroying the closest friendship I have. Once trust and loyalty are gone, Varian, it's never the same. I can't tell her such horrible lies about my entire life here. I can't imagine you wanting her—my best friend and Nigel's fiancée—to think you so terrible. She'll be prejudiced against you before you even supposedly meet. How can she ever change her mind if she's fed those malicious tales?"

"You refuse to protect all we've worked for by misleading her?"

"I refuse to lie to my best friend forever; it isn't necessary."

Varian took a deep breath and released it. "You leave me no choice; you won't be allowed off the ship until the mission is over. Afterward, you'll get a mind block so you can't remember the truth. If you won't give me your word of honor and keep it, I'll have to make sure you believe the ruse, too."

Jana gaped at him. "You wouldn't dare, not if you love me and want me."

"I do love you and want you, Jana. Please don't force me to challenge you. Think about what's at stake, love. What will it be?"

"You're serious, aren't you?"

"Yes, Jana, I am," he said, but knew it was a desperate and offensive bluff to safeguard their priceless secret. He knew he could trust Jana to hold silent to others, but Andrea McKay might not have his love's wits and courage; Andrea could destroy everything they had accomplished.

"Damn you, Varian Saar. You've had me for the last time, so I hope you enjoyed yourself. I was just about convinced you had changed, but you haven't and you never will. Do your blasted duty and let it keep you warm at night. Let it give you love and pleasure because *I* never will again." She saw him wince and grimace but remain unyielding in the stance he had taken.

"I need your answer, Jana. Do we shuttle down or not?"

"Yes, you sorry snake, you have my word. I want to see Andrea."

"If you break it, Moonbeam, Andrea will also pay for your guile."

"I'm not even going to ask what that threat means. I promise," she gritted out as she plotted how to return this fresh pain to him.

Part III
Moondust And Magic

As the playful Gods gather to watch mortals below,
The helpless Fates warns sadly, for only they know:
Beware foolish men with bold dreams and false pride;
Dangers abound for loves lost from your side.
On wings of magic, passion and victory wish to ride;
But how can they conquer a Universe so wide . . .

Chapter Fifteen

Varian grasped Jana's forearms in a firm grip. "Listen to me! I'm not being mean, selfish, or unreasonable; and protecting the use isn't my sole concern. If you tell Andrea—or *anyone*—the truth, it will endanger all of our lives, including hers. Have you forgotten Taemin and Cass are out there somewhere plotting against us? We think we have them fooled, but we could be wrong. If they thought they could extract information from Andrea and use it against us, they would. But if she knows nothing, my tender-hearted love, she's no threat to us or to herself and no help to them. Then there's Maal. After Ryker's death, he'll be crazy with grief for a while. If Cass goes to him with her suspicions about me while he's in that state, there's no telling what he'll do to seek the truth. If Andrea is captured and questioned under *Thorin*, she'll have to tell the truth, what she *believes* is the truth. If Andrea and your friendship with her are the only important things to you in this grim situation, then do it just to protect her life and safety."

"It isn't fair for you to put me in this difficult position."

"You and fate did that, Moonbeam. You asked me to sav Andrea from Earth's doom. If I hadn't loved you and done tha favor for you, she wouldn't be here to tempt you to endange our mission. I can't let that happen."

"Are you forgetting about Nigel and Andrea's romance? I I tell her you're awful and all you've done to me, what is sh going to think about him being the best friend of the man wh nearly destroyed me? She might think Nigel has her fooled an is just like you, that he'd do similar things to her. It could rui their relationship. Is the ruse worth everything it's costing Varian?"

"How do we place values on saving lives and creating inter-galactic peace? What are they worth, Jana? Or do they mea nothing to you because it isn't your world or people in jeop-ardy? I wonder if you'd feel the same if your world were involved in the decision instead of mine."

Ouch, J. G. "What about me? I know the truth. Enemies o doubters would come after me before capturing and questioning my best friend."

"You won't be at risk much longer because I'm putting you through the *Rendelar* process. It won't seem strange for Ryker to do that for you, not in your position as his wife and heir and his assistant in Trilabs with all of its secrets to guard. After Tris finishes the process, no one will be able to extract anything from you. I can't do the same for Andrea because that would be too suspicious."

Jana stared at the alien. Dangers abounded for anyone near him. She had ridden the wings of magic in his arms, but there was a universe of differences between them, perhaps a span too wide for her to cross to reach him. He was right, she admitted with reluctance, about his precaution and their possi-ble jeopardy. But did protecting the charade and their lives justify so many deceptions? His loved ones knew the truth. It wasn't fair for hers to be kept in the dark forever, to be fed horrible tales. She and Andrea had always told each other everything. Her best friend would know she was lying. Too, the restriction kept her from having anyone with whom to share her fears and doubts. Jana couldn't help but wonder why he could use those reasons to explain her being *Rendelared* now when she couldn't be earlier.

"I know what you're thinking, woman; it's written in your eyes. Ryker wouldn't have done this until he was certain of you. Since you two had just met and married, he would have waited a while."

"Are you a mind reader now? If so, you know how much I hate this trap. All right, my lips are sealed. But I'm doing this for everybody's survival and for peace, not just for mine and Andrea's. I only hope this demand doesn't cost me her friendship."

"If she's anything like you, Moonbeam, it won't. Thanks, Jana. I was confident that once your anger subsided, you'd understand and agree."

"Just get this nasty, sacrificial business over with so I can get on with my life." She had made the promise with good intentions, but she didn't know if or for how long she could keep it.

He seemed to read her mind again when he added, "All right, Jana, I'll compromise. As soon as this mess is cleared up, which shouldn't take much longer, I'll also have Andrea treated with *Rendelar* so that you can tell her everything. Will that appease you, woman?"

"Are you serious? You swear? You promise?" After each question, he nodded and his sexy grin broadened. She knew he could carry out his earlier threat, so she was pleased he had relented. A compromise was fair.

"Well, are we still a team? Total silence until the mission ends?"

She smiled and hugged him. "Yes, and thank you, kind sir. As you're always telling me, you won't be sorry; I promise."

"For all our sakes, I hope not."

Jana hurried down the shuttle steps to be reunited with her auburn-haired friend after eight long months of separation. She almost squealed like an exuberant child at Christmas, "Andrea! Andrea! Mercy, you're a soothing sight for sore eyes."

The young woman raced forward to greet her in a heavy Texas twang. "Jana! Jana! You're finally here!"

They hugged, kissed, and shed tears of joy. Then, each studied the other as words tumbled forth in excitement.

"Heavens, Jana, it's good to see you. When you vanished, we went crazy with fear. I'm so glad you're alive and safe. But this . . ."

"I know, incredible, isn't it? I'm sorry I got you into this fix. When they told me Earth might be destroyed, I begged them to rescue you. If you want, you can go home now. I'm sure your parents are out of their minds."

"They shouldn't be. When I was captured, I was told about you and informed I would be joining you soon. They let me write a letter to Mom and Dad telling them I was going away on a trip for about a year. They're probably miffed and concerned, but they believe I'm all right, and there on Earth."

Jana was amazed to see the twenty-four-year-old bundle of energy was smiling and at ease in what most females would view as an intimidating situation. "You must tell me everything, Andrea, everything that's happened since we were taken captive. I still can't believe you're here with me."

They hugged again and shed more tears of relief and happiness. Jana unintentionally ignored Tristan, Martella, and Nigel during her excitement for a short time.

The disguised Varian joined them. "Why don't you go inside? You have plenty to tell each other. Ine can serve you refreshments. Andrea McKay, I'm Ryker Triloni, Jana's husband. It's an honor and a great pleasure to meet the woman my wife has talked about so frequently."

Andrea studied the handsome man's features before meeting his emerald eyes. "Do I bow or what?" she asked with a glance at Jana. Without awaiting a reply, she smiled and said, "It's nice to meet you, Prince Ryker. I hear you've made my best friend very happy. Thank you."

A pleased Varian smiled. "The pleasure and satisfaction are

all mine, Andrea. You're welcome to remain on Darkar with Jana as long as you wish.''

Andrea looked at Nigel as he joined them. The love and desire that glowed both in her eyes and in his were unmistakable.

Nigel slipped his arm around Andrea's waist with familiar ease and deep affection. ''It's good to see you again, Jana. I'm glad you suffered no ill effects from your recent predicament. I told Andrea about the crash and rescue that you and Prince Ryker endured. She's been eagerly awaiting your return. She has many things to tell you.'' He eyed the lovely female at his side with posessiveness.

Jana looked at the glowing and smiling redhead who snuggled closer to Varian's best friend and second in command of his beloved ship. For a moment she envied Andrea for not being as controlled by cruel fate as she herself was with Varian. Perhaps Nigel had to deceive Andrea for a while, but he wouldn't be called upon to vilely use his love as Varian had his. As soon as this mission ended, Andrea would be astonished by the truth! Yet, Jana was very happy for the couple, as Nigel was a good and strong man. She decided they were perfectly matched. ''I appreciate you fetching Andrea for me and keeping her safe,'' she told him.

Nigel's dimples were prominent when he grinned and replied, ''As Prince Ryker said, 'The pleasure and satisfaction are all mine,' Jana.''

Martella Karsh and Dr. Tristan Zarcoff came forward. Jana and Tris hugged and chatted a moment as she told him how much she had missed him and congratulated him on his impending marriage. Tristan and Nigel had been good and steady influences on Varian, or so he had told her. She liked the tall and lanky doctor with his sunny disposition and easygoing manner. He had an affable smile and gentle sky-blue eyes. She had liked him from the first moment they met and hadn't changed her mind.

The doctor sent her a boyish grin and said, ''I've missed the best assistant who ever stepped into my lab and picked up an instrument. You look wonderful, Jana. I'm pleased to be here with you."

"It will be fun to work together again, particularly on Ryker's new project. It's nice of Star Fleet to loan us three of its best officers, especially its top medical man." She smiled at the twinkling-eyed Tristan. "And its top two scientists," she added as her gaze went from the doctor to Science Officer Nigel Sanger. "I'm also glad Martella was assigned as liaison. I hope our research takes a long time so we can catch up on everybody's news."

"So do I, Jana," Tristan concurred.

Varian was thrilled by the ease with which Jana handled Tristan before her friend. "Nigel, I'm sure you told Andrea our research project is a big secret and that no one must know you three are here."

"Yes, sir, I explained the need for secrecy. If anyone visits Darkar, she knows not to reveal our presence. She realizes how important our work is. We're delighted you let us become a part of this new project. It will benefit a lot of people. We certainly don't want news of it falling into the hands of spies or competitors."

Jana turned to Martella, smiled, embraced her, and smiled again. "Thank you for handling the *charl* situation so quickly and compassionately. And thank you for teaching me self-defense and how to use the weapons; those skills came in handy sooner than we both imagined they would. You're a wonderful and special lady, Martella Karsh, and I'm glad to have you for a friend. I know you and Tris will be happy. You're lucky to have each other."

Tris edged his arm around Martella's shoulder, almost blushing at his bold display of feelings. "She gave me a long and slow chase, Jana, but I finally captured her. I had to wait until she reached the top of her field before she would give me a chance with her."

"Tris, you teaser, you know I've been after you for years. We just couldn't seem to travel in the same sector long enough to get things going. We're lucky we were both assigned to the

Wanderlust for a lengthy mission. Imprisoned on the same ship for so long, it was bound to happen."

Jana enjoyed seeing the older couple so in love. In a way, her assignment had brought them together, just as it had thrown her and Varian together and the meeting between Andrea and Nigel. So much love and happiness had come from such a demanding task.

Before the two reunited Earthlings headed for the house, Varian halted Jana to tell her, "Why not take Andrea to our bedroom where you two can have privacy? She's using the guest one adjoining ours. Tris and Martella are staying in the complex suite."

Jana's back was to the others so she was able to conceal her astonishment at that news. She realized the intelligent and cunning Varian must have had her things moved into his bedroom to protect their charade. "Thanks, we will do that." She turned to the others. "We'll see you all later."

Jana and Andrea sat on Ryker's bed in cross-legged positions to chat for hours as they had in their Texas homes and in the apartment they had shared during most of their college days. "You should be in Paris making a big name for yourself in the fashion industry, and I should be at Johns Hopkins in research. We're a long way from all that, my friend. Mercy, how our lives have changed in less than a year."

"The fabrics and styles I've seen in this world," murmured the hopeful designer, anticipation glittering in her eyes. "I can't wait to work my magic on them. Many ideas have come to mind. I drew some of them while Nigel was busy. In no time, I'll create a name for myself here."

"Confident and cocky as ever, I see," Jana teased. Turning serious, she asked, "You've decided to stay? Because of Nigel?"

With romantic sighs, Andrea fell sideways to the bed as if swooning. "Oh, Jana, he simply takes my breath away. He's handsome and virile and brave and smart and good and kind and funny and simply wonderful. I've never met any man so perfect, so . . . so everything,'' she said, bubbling over with enthusiasm. She sat up and clasped Jana's hands in hers. ''I love him so much, and he loves me. We're going to get married soon. I know this sounds too fast, but we can't help ourselves. Love at first sight . . . We're so lucky.'' She laughed and hugged herself as deep emotions warmed her all over. ''Did we ever imagine we would meet and marry aliens and live in another world?''

''Not in our wildest dreams, Andrea McKay.''

''And you, Jana, what about you? You're married to a prince. You're a future queen. Heavens, of an entire galaxy! Tell me every juicy detail. Nigel was too sketchy with his version. He said it was best coming from you. The wait has been torture. How? When?''

''First . . .'' Jana stalled because she hated the impending lies, ''what happened after I disappeared? My story is long so I'll cover that last.''

Andrea leaned close and almost whispered as if revealing a secret. ''A servant taking out trash found your open car and scattered things halfway through the party. I was in a panic. The police came. They questioned everyone and searched the grounds. They found two abandoned motorcycles but never located their owners. All three of you just seemed to vanish into thin air. After two months without ransom demands or clues, the case was closed and you were ruled dead by foul play. Mr. Purvis executed your will as you had made it out with all your money and holdings going to research for terminally ill children. I'm sorry about your things, Jana, but we thought you were dead. We even held a service for you and placed a stone near that of your parents. Heavens, how many times I've cried. And Alex, he still isn't over you.''

''I'm sorry you all had to suffer, but I had no power to contact you back then. You were lucky they allowed you to prevent your parents' worries with a message to them. I'm sure Nigel has told you the threat to Earth was destroyed, so your family and our friends are safe.'' Andrea nodded as Jana continued. "As for Alex, we had broken up and had no future. The snake actually wanted me to give up my work and live with him until he decided it was time for us to marry. I never loved him, Andrea. He just became comfortable like an old boot. I should have called things off sooner, but I was too busy and distracted with work and studies. I'm sure he's moved on to someone else by now. From what I learned just before we broke up, as my grandmother used to say, he kept honey in jars in several places because he couldn't trick any out of mine. Lordy, Andrea, I really never knew how bad he was."

"Well, Jana, you certainly made a better choice than that handsome and conceited devil. Ryker is quite a catch. I bet you were terrified when those aliens kidnapped you."

"I was. Three men in strange shiny jumpsuits with impenetrable helmets surrounded me in the garden before I could reach the house. The music from the party was so loud I couldn't be heard over it. They didn't say a word, probably because they knew I couldn't understand their language; they just drugged me in silence and hauled me away like pirates collecting booty. I woke up in a beautiful gold-and-ivory room with all kinds of ultramodern equipment. After I was intimidated into obedience, I was told I was on a spaceship heading for another galaxy to become some stranger's mate for reproduction. I was sure I was having a nightmare. The ship's commander made certain I was convinced it was real and I was helpless."

Andrea squeezed her friend's cold hand sensing the bad memories that must have washed over her. "Nigel explained the *charl* practice to me and how you girls were selected and trained for your new lives. If that had happened to me, I would have lost my mind. I was lucky I was rescued and told part of the truth from the beginning, at least as soon as they got something implanted in my ear so I could understand them. When Nigel came to Anais and we met, he explained the rest to me. He's so fond of you, Jana; so are Tris and Martella. I like all of them. I'm sure they made it easier for you."

"Yes, in a way. But I resisted tooth and nail for a while. Then I realized how useless and dangerous defiance was, so I decided it was to my advantage to fit in the best I could." Jana decided at that moment not to tell Andrea all the horrid details of her enthrallment. Andrea had accepted her new life here and was in love, so why spoil things for her and Nigel by creating doubts and dismay? "The man who captured me was on a cover mission. Did Nigel tell you that?"

"Yes, to study the threat to Earth. They had to keep it a secret because of trouble here with other galaxies. Heavens, Jana, on Earth we only worried about attacks from other countries; here, they speak of intergalactic wars with awesome spaceships battling among the stars."

Jana chose her next words with care and cunning. "Commander Varian Saar had, or rather *has*, many enemies and rivals. He . . . was fond of me and pleased with me, but he said he couldn't keep me because my life would be in danger from those forces. That was true. He pretended to auction me like the others to a close friend of his, a rich and powerful man, one of three members of the Supreme Council. Do you know what that is?"

"Nigel told me about their political set-ups. He said the man who captured you and wanted you is his best friend and commanding officer. He said Varian Saar is the grandson of their highest ruler, the *kadim*."

"That's true. After Varian completed another mission, he came to get me back; he hadn't sold me; he had purchased me on the sly. Needless to say, I was furious and hurt and confused when he allegedly sold me and then walked back into my life as casual as you please. While we were at his grandfather's on another planet, one of his many enemies attacked. I got in the middle of the battle and earned my freedom. I came here to work with Ryker. We hit it off fast like you and Nigel, so we married."

Nigel had cautioned Andrea not to delve deeply into the relationship between Varian and Jana too soon because it was not resolved and both were still suffering from their unhappy and "unplanned" parting. Andrea knew that when the time was right, Jana would tell her the whole story. "You've had many misadventures in such a short time, but you're in research here, so you have your two loves close by.''

Jana smiled to dupe Andrea, and felt surges of guilt as she did so. The only thing that kept her from confessing everything was Varian's promise to make the truth possible soon. ''Yes, I do,'' she replied with an honesty that was exposed in her gaze and tone. *For all the good they do me, my unenlightened friend.* ''Ryker is . . . How shall I put it? Complex, kind, a genius, and good to me. It doesn't hurt that he's handsome, virile, rich, and powerful. The man I'm with is a rare treasure, Andrea. Despite a few bumps in our lives here and there, we love each other.''

Uh oh, the redhead thought, *you are in love with him. Oh, my, and Nigel thinks you're in love with his best friend and pining over his loss*. From the way Nigel had looked and sounded when he gave her a brief explanation, Varian was still hooked on Jana. It appeared as if those two men were in for a disappointing surprise. Even with what little she knew about the recent past, she couldn't blame Jana for feeling betrayed and ill used by her mysterious and quicksilver captor, and she couldn't blame Jana for falling in love with a man like Ryker. Besides, Jana and Ryker were married, so it had to be over between Jana and Varian, at least from Jana's side. ''So what is life like on Darkar? Your own private world. How utterly fascinating and extravagant. What do you do here with him?''

Jana talked about research and Darkar for a while. Afterward, she set the next part of the ruse into motion. ''Ryker has some important business that will take him away tomorrow for about a week. When he returns, you can get to know him better. I'm sure you'll like him, Andrea. Everybody does. He has irresistible charm; I know from firsthand experience! Have you and Nigel set a wedding date? And where will you live afterward? He's a starship officer, so he'll travel a lot, I guess. You're welcome to live here with me, and I hope you will. In fact, I'll build you a lovely studio where you can work on your marvelous creations. Is that tempting enough?''

''It sounds wonderful, Jana, but . . .''

"But what?"

"Nigel said we would live on Rigel, their capital planet, near Star Base. We plan to marry within the next few months, as soon as he finishes his current assignment. Until then, I can stay with you if Ryker doesn't object."

"Of course he won't object; bringing you here was his idea. Until we heard about your romance with Nigel, we thought you'd live on Darkar if you didn't return home."

"That's very kind and generous of him and you, a real down-home welcome. I'm sure I'm going to like him. By the way, I found my graduation presents in the driveway. Thanks. I wish I had those delicious nighties with me. You must realize Nigel and I are . . . sleeping together. He's been staying in the other room with me. He'll be moving to the shuttle complex now that you two are home. Does that surprise you about me?"

Jana tugged on a long auburn curl and smiled. "Yes and no. Love can't be controlled, Andrea, and sharing sex is a big part of a relationship. You and Nigel getting together was the big surprise, and a pleasant one."

"You know I slept with Tom. I thought I loved him and was going to marry him. I admit I enjoyed it, but I wish now I had waited. After meeting Nigel, I know what real love is. It didn't seem to bother him he wasn't the first. He's so wonderful, so perfect."

"Don't worry about it. I'm sure it doesn't change his feelings. Nigel is a wonderful person. We became good friends on my way here."

"We should join the others," Andrea suddenly said. "We've been talking for hours. With Ryker leaving in the morning, I'm sure you want to spend time with him tonight."

"You don't fool me, Andrea McKay; you're just eager to get back to Nigel. I know he's leaving tomorrow, too. It's all right. We'll have lots of time to talk after our men are gone. Let's go see what everyone's doing. Oh," Jana added, "Nigel can stay with you tonight. Ryker and I won't mind."

"Are you sure? I mean, I wouldn't want your husband to

think badly of me. But Nigel doesn't know how long he'll be away. Heavens, I'll miss him."

"Without a shadow of a doubt, I can promise you he won't object if you spend the night in the next room with Nigel. Honest."

As Jana brushed her hair and prepared for bed, Varian said, "I like Andrea. She's made Nigel a happy man. She's a lot like you, Moonbeam. I can see why you two are best friends and why you missed her so much. Did you have a good visit this afternoon?"

Jana knew that when the doors were closed, all rooms were soundproof, so she didn't have to worry about Andrea and Nigel overhearing them. No doubt they were making love before Nigel's departure with Varian. Probably Tris and Martella were doing the same in the complex suite. Both couples were happy and carefree, and she envied their uncomplicated loves.

"Well? Did things go all right between you two this afternoon?"

"If you mean, did I break my promise and make slips, no."

"That isn't what I meant, Jana. I trust you."

Jana's nerves were frayed and she was strangely fatigued; even a little queasy. She assumed it was the result of all tension she was under recently. She looked straight at the cause. "I wish I could say the same about you."

"One day, you will. Right now, you might want to kiss your husband goodbye. This will be the last time you see Ryker. When I return, I'll be my old self again. You'll be a widow soon, and maybe you'll marry me then."

"Frankly, I prefer the fake Ryker you played over you or the real one."

"My, you're in a testy mood tonight. I thought you'd be happy. You have Andrea, the ruse is almost over, and you have me."

"So what more could a sane person possibly want, right?"

Varian approached her and studied her slightly pale face. "What is it, Jana? This isn't like you. Something's troubling you."

"I guess so much has happened recently that I'm out of sorts. It must be the strain of lying to everyone, especially to Andrea. I'm sorry. You have been good and this will be over soon."

He leaned against the wall. "Yes, I leave for Caguas first thing in the morning, then head for Jurad as soon as I'm finished there."

Jana put the brush aside and looked at him. "Finished? But you're not supposed to be around when Ryker dies tomorrow evening."

"I won't be, so don't worry. I'll enter the mine as Ryker, with his body in a crate. It's been kept sealed and treated until now. The two agents I planted there on our last visit will help me sneak out another way in a disguise. A ship will be waiting to transport me to Star Base to fetch the *Wanderlust*. My cyborg has made a few distant showings on Rigel today and will do it again tomorrow until I take his place and destroy him and make myself highly visible far away from the accident scene. At superstar speed, I'll be there shortly before the explosion that kills Ryker."

"An explosion? But you said that mine would burn forever. What about the *tremolite* you'll lose? I'll lose, because I'll inherit his holdings."

"We're doing it in the control room and have things set up to contain any fire that might result. We're timing it so that *Avatar* Faeroe and others will be approaching the site for a visit; our witnesses. I've already talked to Maal this evening for a final time as Ryker. I told him I'm heading his way after stopping at the mine; he's still fooled and leaning toward a treaty. In fact, Taemin contacted me and will be in orbit at the precise moment of the accident. That should cast some suspicion on him as a possible culprit."

"You're framing Taemin Tabriz for Ryker's death?"

“Not exactly, just drawing eyes away from me and Star leet. If he does get entangled, that will get a dangerous and vil man out of our way. In case you have forgotten, Moon-eam, he tried to kill us recently. Once Ryker is dead and his owerful secrets are in our hands, neither Jurad nor Maal hould refuse to sign treaties with the Alliance. As for me, urad himself will be my alibi while his son is sitting atop the rouble. I'll be on the viewer screen with him from Star Base, nforming him of my official visit to present a treaty.” He ollowed her into the bedroom as he went on. “That is one hange I made today: we'll get the news while we're talking, o I'll tell him I have to go to Caguas and Darkar to handle the ituation and will visit him afterward. I'll call Maal from Star Base and give him the bad news, then tell him I'm headed to nvestigate my brother's death. I'll tell him I'm going to pick ou up so we can deliver the body home. At superstar speed, can be back the next day. That way, we can head for Maal's efore he's tempted to come here. I realized today that the riginal plan to head for Jurad's would put me too far away rom the action and any repercussions.”

Jana sat on the edge of the bed, relieved her nausea had assed. “It's a very clever plan. I'm sure it will work because ou seem to have thought of every angle. I'm impressed.”

Varian sat down sideways near her. “Thank you, my love. While we're gone, Tris and Martella will complete their tasks ere. It's best if all secrets in the complex are taken away, and hose that can't be will be rendered useless when you offer it o Maal before marrying me.” He hurried on before she could rotest. “If Maal becomes unstable like Shara did, we can't urmise his behavior. I'm sure Jurad and Maal will realize Trilabs is worthless to them, so peace with us will look very good. If they refuse, I'll use parts of the tapes to expose the extent of Taemin's evil to Jurad and force him into compliance. I'll even expose the ugly truth about Shara to both rulers if hey make it necessary, but I can't do that until Ryker is fficially dead and I've had time to ‘find’ that evidence. I doubt either ruler wants a scandal like that, so they'll agree. I don't

want to do it that way, Jana, but I will if forced into a corner
I want those treaties fast so I can get us out of this mess an
we can put our lives back together.''

The mission seemed to become more and more complicate
and perilous every day, with every step taken toward a saf
termination. Yet, despite Varian's vows of love and display
of fiery passion, Jana couldn't seem to take the last step towar
him for a reunion. Things kept coming between them as i
some dark force were determined to keep them apart and wa
intent on destroying not only their love but their lives. If onl
Trilabs, the Alliance, and the treaties weren't so important t
Varian. Not that they weren't crucial, but she wondered wh
they should always come before their love and their future.

''Tris is giving you the *Rendelar* process tomorrow after I'n
gone. I hope this is over as soon as Jurad realizes he's los
Ryker as an ally and lost Maal, too. In light of Taemin's recen
and imminent treacheries, he shouldn't have a choice. I'll be
talking with him when Ryker's death is revealed, so I'll pres
him for his answer. When we take Ryker's body home, I'l
press Maal for his. If we succeed, Moonbeam, it's over. A few
more weeks at the most. I'll have Nigel with me in case of
trouble.''

''If Jurad doesn't believe Taemin is guilty of trying to kil
us and of killing Ryker, you still have that evil prince to dea
with. Canissia, too. What are you planning to do about her?
Your marriage announcements are still circulating, I presume.''

''I've already had them withdrawn and cancelled. By now,
everyone knows I've jettisoned her like the dirty debris she is.
My lookalike partner has already taken a couple of ladies to
dinner to show that my disinterest in her is real.'' He saw
Jana's surprise at that news. ''Just so you won't worry or get
jealous, he hasn't made any advances toward them. He's been
well trained and programmed. As soon as Cass is sighted, and
she can't stay in hiding forever, she'll be arrested and sent to
a penal colony for life. We won't ever have to worry about her
again. The colony is escape-proof.''

''How can she be arrested, charged, and convicted without

ing evidence you can't reveal? To expose the fact she kid-
pped me will make my marriage to Ryker illegal and will
rip me of all the benefits of being his widow—of being heir
Trilabs and all of his assets. And you can't use the proof in
ose journals and tapes, if you choose not to expose them."

"You forget, Jana, this is Maffei. The Supreme Council will
dge, sentence, and exile her without explaining what the
idence is to anyone."

Jana twisted to sit cross-legged on the bed to face him. "Her
ther is on the Council. Do you think he's going to vote against
s only child?"

"He won't be there much longer. Segall Garthon is going
be forced to resign to avoid a nasty scandal after he's told
out his daughter's treason and treacheries. He can't refuse
ter he learns how his loose lips aided them. Brec will take
s Council seat, and I'm to take Brec's place."

"You're going to become the Supreme Commander of Star
leet, the Alliance Force, and Elite Squad? You're replacing
reccia Sard?"

"If I say yes. My answer depends on what happens between
s."

Jana didn't comment on his last statement. "It's certainly a
owerful and prestigious position. The only people with more
nk are the other two councilmen and the *kadim*. Congratula-
ons. I'm sure you've more than earned it, especially in light
f your current assignment."

It was Varian's turn to ignore *her* last statement and sarcastic
ne. He smiled as if he didn't notice. "Thanks. The android,
riep, will be shuttle pilot for me to the mine. I'm leaving
agan here in charge of security and whatever comes up when
e news is released. I wish I could be here with you, love. Will
ou be all right? Can you handle what's ahead tomorrow?"

"I've had plenty of practice with lies and deceptions lately.
fter the *Rendelar*, I'll be as good at them as you are. No one
ill be able to drag the truth from me then, not even you. That
as one of your old threats, I believe. Let me see . . . Ah,
es, when you took me from Draco's home."

"Please don't do this to us, Moonbeam. It's almost ove When I return to you, it will be as myself. I promise, no mor secrets or lies. I love you, Jana Greyson. I want you to be m wife. Can't we put the past behind us and begin our life anew?

"I don't know, Varian. I need time alone to think."

He sent her a broad smile. "At least that isn't a definite no.

"And it's far from a yes. I have to be convinced I can tru you."

He moved close to her. "If I have my *Rendelar* reverse and let you question me under *Thorin*, will you believe m then?"

Jana leaned back as he was much too near and tempting, to witstealing. "You can do that? You *would* do that?"

He captured a hand and kissed it. "Yes, for you, for *us*."

As she fluffed his blond hair, she asked, "Aren't you afrai to reveal what might really lurk in your unconscious mind?"

"Not where you're concerned. Well, is it a bargain? If pass your tests, will you come back to me and marry me?"

"Is this another way to trick me? You'll pretend you'r vulnerable?"

"I'll let you read the medical journal and do the treatmen yourself. You'll know there's no way I could be lying to you Well, is it a deal?"

"I'll give you my answer when you return."

He bounded forward and trapped her beneath him, a positio from which she didn't try to escape or protest. As he showere her with kisses, he teased, "Ever the cautious and cunnin female, aren't you?"

"It's kept me alive and safe so far. From every peril excep you."

"All right, Moonbeam, when I return."

"Aren't we being cooperative tonight?" she quipped with laugh.

"We always try to be where you're concerned." His mout covered hers and gave her a deep and yearning kiss.

Soon, clothes were discarded. Their hands stroked, stimu lated, and pleasured each other. Their mouths explored tempted, and enticed. Their bodies joined, labored, sought appeasement, and found exquisite rapture. They nestled together in contentment without replacing their garments and slept peacefully in each other's arms.

Jana and Andrea stood outside and watched "Ryker" and Nigel leave in the shuttle. Jana knew that when it reached Caguas within two hours, Nigel would slip aboard the other ship. The disguised Varian would enter the mine with Ryker's hidden body, set the phony accident into motion, sneak out, and leave for Rigel with his best friend. The long and damaging ruse was coming to its explosive culmination. Soon she could tell Andrea everything, then seek some good advice from the person who knew and loved her best. She dreaded what lay ahead this evening when she became a widow and dreaded her next trek to Maal's. Just a few more weeks, she reminded herself, then . . . then what? she wondered.

At ten, Jana headed to the complex for her *Rendelar* procedure. As she walked along, she wondered how Ryker's "death" would change her life. She asked herself if she could even trust Varian again. If not, she mustn't return to him and risk another broken heart. He was trying hard to win her back, but could he build a bridge over their troubled waters so he could reach her? Dare she, should she, impede his progress or demolish every attempt he made in order to protect herself? How long would he continue against thwarted efforts and stinging defeats before he lost heart and hope? If he gave up on obtaining his alien goal, in what condition would that leave her stranded on the other side of their breach? Was permanent separation what she truly wanted? Somewhere deep inside, buried beneath anguish and doubts, dwelled the truth and she must locate it before his return.

She entered the complex and went to join Dr. Tristan Zarcoff.

In the medical laboratory, Tris asked, "Are you ready to begin, Jana?"

"Nervous and ignorant, my friend, but more than ready. How long will this procedure require? How does it work?"

"It takes about two hours. And *Thorin*, our most potent truth serum, comes from the venom of creatures similar to *keelars*; it attacks the nervous system in the brain; it's activated by involuntary physiological changes in the body when a person lies. To stop excruciating agony, one has only to tell the truth. *Rendelar*, which comes from a derivative of the creature's brain cells, prevents that from happening. Those cells are few and hard to come by. The extraction process demands the most minute and skilled microsurgery. If mishandled, they're damaged beyond use, but you can do it. Ryker Triloni was indeed a rare genius with gifted hands. During the time I've been in his labs and gone over his notes, I've been astounded by his creations. I'm glad you're back to help me finish my task."

"It sounds exciting, Tris. I'm eager to get back to work. I must admit I'm impressed by his research and products. I'm almost sad I never got the opportunity to work with him. He could have taught me a lot."

"He could have taught all of us a great deal. I found the formulas for *Rendelar*, *Thorin*, and one of his most secret prizes. You probably know he had an unknown additive that made his formulas self-destruct if anyone attempted to analyze their contents. It comes from that leech project Varian demonstrated for you. Of course, we didn't know it at that time."

"It makes sense, Tris, coming from an unnatural test tube. Inside their bodies, they can produce a chemical unknown and unreproducable elsewhere. We'll get busy as soon as I'm made trustworthy," she teased.

"I'm ready. First, we need to do a complete physical to make sure you don't have any problems that could interfere with its success."

"I'm fine. No ill effects from the crash and rescue."

"Still, we have to be sure you're in top condition. This

procedure requires a lot from the body. It places immunities in every cell. If any of them have problems, it can be most uncomfortable and damaging."

Tristan did a thorough examination that included all tests. He repeated one before returning to the lab where she was awaiting him.

"Let's get started," she said with a cheery smile. When Tristan looked at her as if at a loss for appropriate words, Jana asked what the problem was.

Tristan sat down and met her curious gaze. "I don't know how to tell you this, Jana, but we can't do the *Rendelar* procedure."

"Why? Did something show up on my tests? What? Speak up, old friend, you're making me nervous. Do I have a disease? Is it that bad?"

"It's not bad, but bad timing. You're . . . you're pregnant. Four weeks."

Jana gaped at him. Surely her aural translator was malfunctioning. "Pregnant?" Tris nodded. "Me?" He nodded again. "Are you sure?" He nodded again. "How? I mean, it's impossible. The *Liex* . . ."

"There's only one way I can surmise. Schedules are kept on wrist computers. Varian's has been locked in his ship's safe since he became Ryker. It's apparent he missed his last one when he wasn't reminded it was due. It happened four weeks ago while you two were stranded on Luz."

Jana's face flushed a deep red and her cheeks burned. The color splashed down her neck and onto her chest. The heat rush itched and her hand lifted to rub her collarbone area. It was embarrassing for anyone, even this close friend, to know such intimacy had taken place on that barren planetoid. "I can't believe this. The test must be wrong."

"I ran it twice, Jana, to be sure."

Suspicions flooded her. "Why would you even run a pregnancy test?"

"The medical analyzer picks up on anything unusual and tests it."

"Is this a trick to tie me to Varian? Did he do this to me on purpose?"

"No, it was an accident, an oversight."

"Accident? Oversight? How do you know? That bastard is capable of anything! Dammit, he doesn't need me to get his greedy hands on Trilabs! He's already stolen the complex blind, or will have soon. Didn't he realize how this would complicate everything? Has he forgotten I'm married to Ryker? Has he forgotten I've supposedly been living and sleeping with Ryker? Babies won't wait for missions to be completed. As soon as everyone learns I'm pregnant, they'll think the baby is—oh, my God—Ryker's, because Varian won't ever reveal his ruse. My child's paternity will always have a shadow over it. Damn him, Tris; this is unforgivable! He'll use anything and anybody to get his way, even his own child."

"Settle down, Jana. Getting upset isn't good for you or the baby."

"Nothing is good for me, Tris, and hasn't been since I met that devil."

"Maybe you're looking at this situation all wrong; maybe it was meant to be. Maybe he did have his *Liex* and for some fated reason it didn't work."

"This is all his fault! He should have been more careful. He's the one responsible for birth control, not me, not any woman in your world. He probably got me pregnant on purpose to force me to marry him. If I had known this could happen, I would have taken other precautions. No, I wouldn't have allowed the treacherous snake to touch me again!"

Jana paced back and forth as she cursed Varian and the predicament. She halted and looked at Tristan. "I can't have *Rendelar* because of the baby?" After the doctor nodded, her eyes narrowed and chilled. "That's why he finally offered to let me have the procedure. He knew I couldn't because he had gotten me pregnant. The sneaky, low-down, conniving, selfish son-of-a-bitch!"

"Jana, Jana, you know Varian better than that. He wouldn't—"

"Yes, dammit, he would and he has! He's making me Ryker's widow, then stealing any inheritance I would get so I'll be penniless and dependent on him. Now, this! No, I don't know him, Tris. I never have and I never will. He isn't the man I thought he was. It's about time I admit that to myself and stop making excuses for him."

"Wait until he explains."

"Lies, you mean, like always to get his way. He won't do this to me."

"You don't want this baby?"

"I don't want *his* baby. I'll have to figure out what to do about it."

"There's nothing you *can* do; abortion is illegal here unless the mother's life is in jeopardy. That law was passed when our survival was imperiled."

"I didn't mean get rid of it. My stars, Tris, it's my baby, too. I mean, do something about getting Varian out of my life forever."

"Why, Jana? He loves you. You love him."

"Sometimes love can't matter, Tris; sometimes it isn't enough. Please, just leave me alone and let me think. I have to get control of myself before all hell breaks loose this evening after Ryker's death."

"Why don't you go to your room and lie down for a while?"

"And let Andrea and Martella see me like this? I don't want them to know the truth. Damn, damn, damn, what am I going to do? We're supposed to visit Maal as soon as Varian returns. When Maal learns about the baby, he'll fight every demon from here to eternity to get his hands on who he thinks is Ryker's only child, his great-grandchild."

"You're only four weeks pregnant, so it won't show for a long time. You and Varian can be married and on Altair by then. Maal doesn't have to know."

"What am I supposed to do? Hide out there for seven or eight months until the baby is born, then wait two months to fake a birth date like he's faking a date for Ryker's death? What other complications can come along?"

"I'll contact Varian and give him the news. Maybe he'll know what—"

"No! Don't tell him anything until he gets back. If you destroy his concentration, this damn charade will never end."

Tristan wondered if that was her true concern, or if it was to avoid distraction to guard Varian's safety. "If that's what you want."

"Promise me you won't sneak behind my back and tell him."

"I promise you will be the one to tell him about the baby."

"If you break your word, Tris, our friendship is over; I swear it."

Jana left the room with a bold idea in mind.

Chapter Sixteen

As promised, Tristan did not communicate the unexpected news to Varian, but he did confide it to Martella, who was stunned and dismayed.

"What sorry timing, Tris. A baby should be a happy occasion," the sixty-year-old sterile woman murmured. "Poor Jana. She's had to deal with so much. There's something you have to do for her."

Tristan guessed from his love's expression and tone that she had something particular in mind. "What is that?"

"Varian is planning to use the *Rendelar* procedure on Andrea very soon so she and Jana can share the truth. I think you should do it now. Jana needs Andrea's understanding ear and comforting shoulder. I'll take full responsibility for ordering it done. Please, do this for me and for them."

"I will, my sweet, because I believe you're right. Send Andrea to me."

* * *

Jana sat on the sofa in Ryker's bedroom to enlighten her best friend to the stunning truth. She was grateful to Martella and Tristan for making this much-needed purging and comforting possible. When the long and gut-wrenching story was finished, Jana said, "When Varian told me I couldn't tell you the truth, I was angry. I agreed with reluctance after he explained his motives and promised to give us both *Rendelar* soon so we could talk. I suppose it's normal for a powerful man to have dangerous enemies and he has to do seemingly cruel things to defeat them and protect others, as with his reason for that fake auction which ripped out my heart for weeks. Canissia's kidnapping, Ryker's plots, Shara's attempt to kill me, and Taemin's capture prove Varian has a right to worry and to take drastic precautions. I even understand that he abducted me so his race could survive and our world could be saved. They've abolished the *charl* law and practice, but not because of my bargain with Varian."

She looked at Andrea. "I'm sure those medical cures and scientific facts would have been implanted even if I had refused," she said. "You would have been brought here anyway because you wanted to stay in Maffei with Nigel. And they planned all along to send our people home if Earth was spared. I only let Varian think my demands and our bargain were the reasons why I agreed to help complete the charade. I agreed to be near him so I could test my feelings and decide if we could have a future together. I understand why he wanted Trilabs and peace so badly. I know I was kidnapped from him by that jealous and malicious bitch, and he did search heaven and hell to find me. He even saved my life after Taemin's trap and again after the crash. I realize the risks he took during the Earth mission and I know all he's done to protect me from Maal, Taemin, Canissia, and others. I'm truly grateful for all those things."

Andrea was surprised that Jana was being so fair toward Varian.

"The problems start after those things I understand, accept, and forgive. He knew I was coerced into marrying Ryker and he realized what he and Maffei could gain with me as his widow, so he let the marriage stand without challenging it. He let Canissia go her merry way because it would interfere with his mission if he arrested her. He tricked me into believing his rescue was a delusion. He convinced me he didn't love me. He enticed me to fall in love with a phony Ryker. Now I find myself pregnant at a time in his mission when marriage between us is impossible. He's tricked me so many times, Andrea, that I don't know if the baby is just another trick to bind me to him. I don't know if Varian truly loves and wants me, or if it's who he sees as his creation, his property by right of conquest. He can't want me for Trilabs because they're taking everything from the complex they desire. Perhaps he wants to prove he can win back the woman who allegedly dumped him for Ryker, prove to the public he's so irresistible that I had to have him back."

When Jana paused, a dismayed Andrea did not interrupt.

"I admit there were plenty of happy and tranquil times: outings we took, dancing on his ship, days and nights in his arms, those glorious hours on Eire before Canissia's kidnapping, that night on his ship after my rescue from Shara's evil, and many other moments. When Varian is relaxed and his real world recedes, he's like a different person—a kind, wonderful, caring, gentle, and loving man. Maybe we met at the wrong time in his life, when he was confronted by too many problems and perils, duties too demanding for him. I don't know if that's it or if it's Varian himself." Jana met Andrea's sad gaze. "I hate to dump this misery on you, but I needed to talk to someone who knows me and loves me, someone I can trust, someone who can help me decide the right thing to do. I hate to spoil our reunion this way, but I need you. We've always been so close and I'm so glad you're here. Please don't blame Nigel for any of this trouble; he was caught in the middle, too."

Andrea had listened to Jana's astonishing tale with eyes wide and mouth agape. When the long story was finished, she didn't know what to say to her friend who was in such torment. She could hardly believe all that had happened to Jana. She realized how much Nigel had omitted from the tragic and incredulous tale, and understood why now: it was Jana's right to reveal or not to reveal certain parts of it. "I'm so sorry, Jana," she finally managed.

The Earthling scientist wiped away the annoying tears evoked by her emotional state. It was the first time she had been able to pour out her feelings to anyone since she had been taken from Earth. "So am I, Andrea, sorry I ever met him."

The redhead wasn't convinced that was true. "Yesterday I was going on and on about silly stuff when you were in such pain. I was carrying on about Nigel and our romance like a girl with her first crush when you were in a terrible bind with your man. I was thinking how terrible it was that you and Varian had lost each other when all along you were still together. When I thought you were talking about Ryker, it was really about Varian. That's why you knew he wouldn't mind if Nigel stayed with me last night, because they're best friends. You've told me what he's done, but what is he like, really like? He's my love's best friend and commanding officer, and everyone I've met speaks so highly of him. It's as if you're talking about a different person. I've been looking forward to meeting him, but now, I don't know if I really do or how I'll behave toward . . . ." Andrea halted, then shrieked, "Heavens, Jana, I've already met him. Am I ditsy or what? Nobody dropped a clue to me. Heavens, Jana, how do you keep them straight? What's Varian Saar like as himself?"

As his image filled her mind, Jana murmured, "Imagine the most expensive and loveliest shade of a sapphire sparkling under a soft light, and you have his eyes. Think of Russian sable or a raven's wing in sunlight, and you have his hair. Picture Kirk Douglas's cleft chin. Teeth so snowy and perfect that his smile could be nothing less than breath-stealing. He's tanned and tall: six feet four inches to be exact. He's thirty-one years old, with a physique every male star in Hollywood would envy and every woman on Earth would kill to caress. I could say he's handsome and virile but those words are so far below what Varian Saar is. He's Apollo, Adonis, Mel Gibson, Kevin Costner, Harrison Ford, Ron Moss, and Kurt Russell all rolled into one magnificent package. Take away Ryker's blond hair and green eyes and give him a dent in his chin, and you have his near-twin half brother."

"You mean that they look that much alike, but you suspected nothing?"

"Remember when Cindy dyed her black hair blond and switched her brown eyes to blue with contacts and had that complete makeup and wardrobe change? Not even her best friends recognized her. She even behaved differently and altered her voice with lessons. That's how it was when I met Ryker, the real Ryker. Something nibbled at me, but I couldn't put my finger on it. Why would I have thought those two were brothers? One's an Androasian prince and the other's a Maffei starship commander. One is the Androasian *kadim*'s grandson and Varian is *Kadim* Tirol's. But the minute I was told the truth, it all made sense. I realized that was why I wasn't totally terrified of Ryker, because some part of me saw my Varian."

Andrea caught the last two words and stored them away. She couldn't believe that Varian Saar was as wicked and cruel as Jana's story implied. If he were, Nigel would not be his longtime and best friend. There seemed to be extenuating circumstances for the incidents Jana had endured, some which her friend grasped and some which she didn't. Maybe Jana was too hurt and confused to comprehend the truth, and needed awakening. "You've covered his appearance. But what about his personality? His character? Be open with me."

Jana thought for a few minutes, then complied. "Every superior and wonderful adjective that comes to mind fits him to perfection. Every word you used to describe Nigel is the same, if not more, where Varian is concerned. He's self-assured, cool-headed, with nerves of steel, sharp wits, and rigid self-control. His skills, reflexes, wits, and instincts are at the highest level. He's complex, contradictory, mercurial, unpredictable. He possesses and commands enormous strength and power. He attracts the attention and influences the emotions of both men and women. He controls the fates of countless people: friends, foes, and strangers. He's fun and exciting. He can be gentle as a lamb or as fierce as a lion. He's magical and mysterious. Seductive. Raw and tamed sensuality. A highly skilled and generous lover. He knows how to touch a woman's heart, body, and soul."

Jana leaned her weary head against the sofa back. "He's accomplished great things and is, without a doubt, destined to do even more. He embodies power and passion. He's widely respected and admired. He's fiercely loyal to his rank, family, friends, and Maffei. He will slay his enemies if he can't defeat them with his wits and brute strength. He isn't afraid to die in the line of duty, and even sometimes seems contemptuous of its threat." Jana frowned in worry, then her features softened again.

Her voice became almost dreamy as she continued. "He has a way of making one feel safe and brave. It's as if he radiates part of his courage and confidence to you, and you can't help but absorb them. He's coveted and envied, loved and hated. He makes women melt with charms and looks that inspire jealousy in the gods. The sheer force of his will, or just his voice, could make the heavens tremble and obey. He knows he's invincible and irresistible and overwhelming, and he savors and uses that power over others. He's as satisfying as a dream come true. Now do you see why I was utterly bewitched and dazzled by him, why I didn't have the strength or wits to resist him?"

Andrea saw her friend blush when she realized how she was talking about the topic of their conversation. "Do you still love him and desire him?"

Jana's now somber gaze met Andrea's empathetic one. "This wouldn't be so hard if I didn't. God help me, I do with all my heart and soul. The problem is that I think I hate him as much as I love him. Or maybe I don't love him at all. Maybe that's the real delusion. Maybe I just formed some kind of crazy bond with him when my life was in his hands; psychiatrists say that can happen between captive and captor under certain conditions. Of all days for this ton of bricks to be dropped on me! In a few hours, I have to deal with Ryker's 'death' and whatever new troubles that announcement brings. Then, I have to go with Varian to Maal's to take his body home. I promised; it was part of our deal. Unlike Varian Saar, I keep my word."

"Can you forgive him and make a fresh beginning?"

"I don't think so. Too much has happened between us. I don't think I could ever trust him again. I should have known from the start we were star-crossed lovers. It isn't as if he didn't warn me enough times that was true. I didn't listen. I loved him and I wanted him and everything else be damned. Now, all I want is to be rid of him."

Andrea knew she should keep Jana talking out her real feelings. "Do you really, deep down inside?"

"I don't know. Dammit, I don't know anything anymore. My heart says one thing and my head says another. I've followed my heart's advice so far and look where it's gotten me. It's about time, past time, I listen to my head. I've never been this confused in my life. Look at all the trouble and danger I've gotten into and am still in because of him and his lies. With more complications arising every day, I see no end to them."

"There's nothing I can do to help, Jana, but Nigel will know what to do when he returns."

"It isn't your problem—or Nigel's; it's mine. Besides, Nigel is biased in Varian's favor, and that's only natural so I don't blame him. But you have helped; you've helped just by being here with me when I need you most. I'll have to thank Tris and Martella again for making it possible for us to talk. I didn't want to deceive you, Andrea, but I was trapped."

"I understand, Jana, and I agree with what you and Varian had to do."

"You think he's right?"

Andrea looked uncomfortable as she replied, "I think he did what he believed was right. A lot is at stake, Jana. You said so yourself."

"So you think I'm being silly and selfish to feel as I do?"

"No, of course not. After what you've been through, if I were in your place, I would probably feel the same way. I haven't suffered the things you have and I don't know Varian Saar, so I'm giving an unbiased opinion. I can see both of your sides, or at least what you and Nigel have explained as *his* side. I don't like what he's done to you, but I can understand why he did it. It sounds as if he was trapped, too, Jana. It sounds as if he really loves you, so I'm sure it hurt him to trick you."

Jana jumped up from the sofa to pace off her nervous tension. "It's the kind of trick he used, Andrea. He convinced me Varian didn't love me or want me. He forced me to believe I had suffered from hallucinations and amnesia about one of the most beautiful and special moments of my life. He persuaded me to fall in love with Ryker. He even let me sleep with him as Ryker. What kind of man would do that to the woman he claims he loves?"

"Did you fall in love with Ryker? Was he the one you made love to?"

"No, but it wasn't because Varian didn't give it his best shot. For a while, I almost convinced myself it was true. He broke my heart and betrayed me, Andrea, several times. How can I get past that?"

The redhead continued to ask questions instead of giving answers or advice with the hopes Jana would discover the truth on her own. "Do you want to lose him forever?"

"Should I be like a battered wife who keeps a man she loves because he's good sometimes, and ignore or forgive the times he isn't? Where does one draw the line between accepting good and fighting evil at any cost, between duty to his country and loyalty to loved ones? What about compassion, honor, conscience, simple human kindness? Does one toss them aside when duty calls? When do sacrifices become too great to pay?"

"I don't know how to answer those questions. I've never had to. I'm sure there'll be times when Nigel will have to keep secrets or perhaps even fib to me. He has already, in a way. I love him and forgive him and understand. But my situation doesn't compare with yours. Only you can decide how you feel and what you must do. Whatever it is, I'll stand beside you. I'll stay with you as long as you need me."

"Thanks, Andrea. Your arrival was perfect timing. If only things weren't so complicated and painful and so damn confusing. My life with him has been like some Shakespearean tragedy. Only cruel and mischievous fate cast the leading roles and wrote the grim and destructive script."

"It's in your control alone to write the ending you want, Jana. If he's genuinely sorry and he truly loves you, a rejection because of your injured pride and hurt feelings can do as much harm to him and your relationship as he's done to you and your love. You have the baby to think about, Jana, *his* baby. Do you want to raise a child alone in an alien world? Do you want to raise one without its father? Raise it as Ryker's child?"

"No, but do I just tuck my tail between my legs and run back to him as if nothing terrible happened between us, and act grateful he still wants me? Does he only have to say 'I'm sorry' and that's supposed to make everything all right? Being contrite and apologetic isn't enough to repay me for all he's done. It's like a judge slapping a criminal's wrist and telling him his debt to his victims and society are paid in full because he's sorry and he's promised never to do it again. Prisons are overflowing with repeat offenders."

"Don't you see, Jana, you're too confused and you're hurting too much to make decisions right now? You're also pregnant, so all kinds of changes are taking place in your body. You know: hormones and chemicals running amuck. Give it time and you'll make the right choice."

"You've always believed in me and thought I knew everything. You used to tease me about being so confident and decisive. You said I knew exactly what I wanted and how to get it and let nothing stop me. If that were true long ago, it isn't now. I just want to love him and trust him. I just want to marry him and be happy. I just want things to go back to where they were that day on his ship after my rescue from Shara. It isn't possible."

"Part of it is, Jana; the rest you can build anew. Aren't you the girl who used to tell me when things got tough in school: 'Andrea McKay, nothing is impossible if you want it badly enough and work hard to get it?' "

"I said such nonsense because I was blind and stupid and naive. I know better now. And Varian's the one who opened my eyes and educated me."

"As you always told me. Look on the bright side. You've made good friends here: Nigel, Tristan, Martella, and others. I saw the rapport all of you share. You have admiration, respect, and affection. You're in the research that you love so much. You've helped carry out a great mission, Jana, one that saved our world and will bring about peace in three galaxies. You're helping to defeat several terrible enemies and making allies of others. That should make you very proud of yourself; I am. You have wealth, prestige, a royal title, a beautiful home, and your own small planet. You hobnob with this society's elite. You're expecting a baby by the man you love, by a man more than half of the women here crave."

Andrea finished with her best arguments, "You were freed before the other *charls* were, freed by Varian—not Ryker—so you could marry him, not marry his brother so Varian could get Trilabs. You were freed, Jana Greyson, *before* this charade began, before it was even a thought in his mind. If that bitch hadn't kidnapped you from Varian, you two would have been happily married a long time by now. Even with your kidnapping involved, if those journals and tapes and threats hadn't existed, Varian wouldn't have been provoked to begin the charade."

Andrea grasped Jana's hands and pulled her down to the sofa. "But they did exist, Jana. He did read and view them while you were asleep in recovery. He grasped the awesome extent of their peril. He reacted immediately in the only way that came to mind. It might have been impulsive and rash and even cruel, but do you honestly believe he set out to intentionally hurt you? Don't you think he would have taken another road if one had been open?''

Andrea hoped she wasn't pressing too far, and God help her if she was wrong about Nigel's friend. ''All I can go by is what you've told me, and it sounds as if the ball got rolling too fast and too soon and couldn't be stopped. I know I might be making this sound simple, but feelings and situations are never simple. I only want you to make certain you know what yours are and you know what you're doing.''

''I *don't* know at this moment, but I will within the next few days. I need time to settle down and think clearly.''

''Just remember that all these recent events wouldn't have happened if you hadn't been stolen from him, which wasn't his fault, Jana. From what you said, he did everything in his power to protect you. He always seems to be there or to get there when you need him. Despite the fact he was playing Ryker, he's even been with you this whole time, making sure nothing happened to you while he performed his crucial mission.''

''You don't even know him and you're already impressed with and charmed by him. See what tremendous power and influence he has!''

''I'm basing my opinion on what you and Nigel and others have told me. The fact you love him and want him is as clear as a Texas morning in summer. You explained everything with honesty and frankness so I could give you an unbiased opinion; I know that's what you wanted from me. You don't want me to berate him and belabor the bad episodes just because I might think it will make a breakup easier for you. You know I will stand by you, right or wrong, but I do have to be honest with you. It's always been that way between us.''

''You're right, and I wouldn't want it to be any other way, ever. You're also right about me dwelling too much on the dark sides of our troubles and intentionally ignoring the bright ones. I just don't want to be hurt and used again, Andrea. I don't want the good times to influence me too much in his favor. But it isn't fair to either of us or the baby to let the bad ones cause me to make a terrible mistake. Thank you for listening and caring and for helping me see things clearer."

Hours passed and Jana became worried. She should have heard something by now. Her imagination began to run wild. What if Varian hadn't escaped the mine explosion? What if the death ruse had been discovered and exposed? What if it had been postponed? What if there was trouble with Jurad or Maal? What if Taemin or Canissia had ensnared Varian again?

She couldn't stand this waiting. She headed for the shuttle complex to speak with the Elite Squad member, Kagan, to ask him to obtain news for her. She met the man coming to see her.

"Varian contacted me. He said to tell you that it's done and he's on his way here after a brief stop at Caguas. He should arrive tomorrow afternoon. He talked with Jurad and Maal and he'll tell you about it when he returns."

"Is that all?" she asked the officer.

"Prince Taemin was in orbit around Caguas and has fallen under suspicion, which is good. Varian told me to make certain he doesn't visit here. Varian said Maal agreed to let him come here and give you the news in person, so Maal won't be contacting you before your visit to him."

Jana was glad she could speak openly with this officer who was knowledgeable on the matter. "That's a relief. I wouldn't want to make a mistake dealing with him. Varian's too close to victory for me to mess things up for him. Thank you, Kagan, for the news. I was getting worried by this silence."

The agent smiled and said, "You've done an excellent job for the Alliance, Jana. Few people would be so totally unselfish with their time and energies or would take on such a dangerous mission. I'm impressed by your courage and intelligence. It has been an honor and pleasure to work with you. It's a shame so few people will know what a great thing you've done for us. Fate, Jana, is what brought you to us, and I'm grateful to it. Without a doubt, if not for you and Varian, we would be at war this very moment. He's a lucky man to have found a woman like you. I hope I will be as fortunate one day."

Jana was surprised by his unexpected and flattering statements. From his seawater gaze, she knew he was being honest and sincere, and it moved her deeply. "Thank you, Kagan. It's good to know this mission was worth its price to us. I'm glad you're here to handle security. Whatever comes up, be assured I will obey your orders and follow your suggestions. Helping your world obtain peace is my way of thanking yours for saving mine."

Kagan was indeed impressed by the remarkable woman. He had spoken the truth and was glad he did. Maybe it would help bridge the span the task had created between his friend and the woman Varian loved and had been forced to hurt. "One last message from Varian: He loves you and misses you, and he said not to worry, that everything will be fine soon. And it will, Jana, I'm sure of it."

She was astonished that Varian would pass along such a personal message. Perhaps she would get to know Captain Kagan better now that the formality between them was broken. She smiled and thanked him again, and they parted.

Kagan came to see Jana again within the hour. "*Avatar* Faeroe is on approach. He's requested a visit with you. I believe he's come in person to deliver the bad news. Pretend this is the first you've heard of Ryker's death. I'll have Tris, Martella, and your friend hide in the complex until after his departure. I'll come inside with him if you prefer."

Jana experienced a moment of panic at her first involvement with this aspect of the ruse. Very soon Ryker's death would be a known fact around the Tri-Galaxy and surely its effect would be heard and felt from one end to the other. "Why don't you be in here going over papers with me so it won't look suspicious for you to remain in the room? Let him join us and

I won't ask you to leave and hope he doesn't. I may need your support.''

''That's an excellent idea. I'll handle it immediately. We have about twenty minutes to get prepared for his landing.''

Ine answered the call at the door and showed the planetary ruler of Caguas inside. Jana rose from the table where she and Kagan were sitting and pretending to go over shipping orders. She smiled and greeted the member of the Alliance Assembly. ''*Avatar* Faeroe, what a pleasant surprise. Welcome to Darkar. I'm afraid Ryker isn't home; he's at the mine. Perhaps he'll return before you depart, though he isn't scheduled to do so. What refreshment can I have Ine serve you?''

''None, thank you.''

Jana dismissed the yellow-eyed android. ''Please be seated, sir.''

Faeroe didn't move from near the entrance where she had met him. ''I came to discuss an urgent matter with you.''

She sent him a look of curiosity and asked, ''With me?''

''I come with bad news, Princess Jana. I . . .''

When Faeroe halted and glanced at the man at the table, Jana said, ''This is Captain Kagan, head of Darkar security. Ryker and I trust him implicitly, so please feel free to talk in front of him; we do. What bad news? Should I contact my husband and let you speak with him?''

Faeroe clasped Jana's hands in his and said, ''I'm afraid that won't be possible. There was an accident at the mine earlier today involving him.''

Jana forced a look of worry. ''Is my husband all right? Was he injured? Has he been hospitalized? Did he send you to get me?''

''I'm afraid Prince Ryker was killed. There was an explo—'' He ceased speaking when she paled, swayed, and gaped at him. He grasped her by the forearms as if fearing she would faint. He felt her tremble. ''I'm sorry if that came out too luntly. You must sit down,'' he advised. He guided the shaky voman to a sofa. ''I know this comes as a terrible shock and erhaps I'm not doing this well.''

Jana looked at him as he took a seat beside her and placed comforting hand on her arm. ''He's dead? What happened? Iow? When? I saw him just this morning when he departed. This can't be true.''

''I'm afraid it *is* true. There was an explosion in the control oom. Prince Ryker was present. He did not suffer. He was aken away instantly. I was enroute there with some friends to neet with him. We arrived just as it happened. When it was afe for a rescue team to enter the area, they recovered his ody. I had it placed in a casket and brought it home myself. didn't want to tell you such shocking news over the communi-ator, so I came straight here as soon as I could get away. I eft his security team in control. Star Base has been notified. They're sending Commander Varian Saar to investigate and ake his body to *Kadim* Maal. Varian said he would come here o speak with you and to escort you there. Is that permissible?''

Jana's eyes darted about on the floor and she took deep reaths as if to steady herself and clear her head. ''I don't know vhat to say. This is so unexpected. We've been married for uch a short time. Dead . . .''

Kagan came forward and placed a hand on her shoulder as f offering support. ''Don't worry, Princess Jana, I'll handle verything for you.''

''Thank you, Kagan,'' she murmured. She looked at Faeroe and asked, ''You said Commander Saar is coming to investi-gate. Why? It was an accident, wasn't it? Or were you implying omething else?''

''From appearances, it was a tragic accident. However, with a man of Prince Ryker's status and importance, an investigation s normal procedure. We can't be too cautious. I'm sure you can imagine the ramifications if it turned out to be a deliberate attack on him here in our star system. As you may be aware, the Supreme Council and Alliance Assembly are in delicate

negotiations on a new peace treaty with his grandfather. Sabo
tage could be detrimental to those talks. But, as I said, we hav
found no signs of foul play."

"And I hope you don't, sir. I'm certain Ryker would no
want his tragic death to be responsible for a needless an
reckless war. On our last visit with Maal, my husband spok
favorably of peace, and recently he was reunited with his ha
brother after many years of conflict. I'm sure Maal will acccep
the truth. I will do all in my power to convince him to do so."

"You are a wise and good woman, Jana Triloni," he sai
as he patted her hand in a fatherly gesture. "Prince Ryker wa
a friend and a valuable asset; his genius shall be missed terribly
If there is anything I can do to help you through this sa
situation, please call on me."

"You are most kind, sir, and I deeply appreciate your offe
Ryker was a unique man. He took his work and responsibilitie
very seriously. It will seem strange with him gone. I'll nee
time to think and adjust before making any decision." Sh
looked at him again. "You said an explosion in the contro
room . . . Was there a fire in the mine? Was anyone els
injured or slain?"

"Two androids were destroyed, but the fire was containe
before it could spread. Prince Ryker took excellent precaution
for safety."

"That's good. When we visited there, he told me *Tremolit*
could burn forever if it caught fire. I wouldn't want your plane
to face that peril or the pollution it would cause. You and th
Alliance won't have to worry about problems with shipments
Like my husband, I'm a friend, citizen, and ally of Maffei
There will not be any changes in his policies or contracts. H
taught me a great deal about his work and products and abou
the importance of safeguarding them. I have access to hi
formulas, labs, and holdings. You might recall, I'm a chemis
and research scientist myself and I've worked closely wit
Ryker since coming here to live and marrying him."

"I well recall Dr. Zarcoff's high praise of your intelligenc
and skills. We're fortunate Prince Ryker married you and pre

pared you to face this challenge. That means you plan to remain on Darkar and run Trilabs?"

"Yes, Ryker would want that. Besides, it's my home. I . . . I'm sorry, sir, but my thinking isn't totally clear at this time, so I suppose I'm rambling from subject to subject. I can hardly believe this has happened; I saw him only this morning," she repeated for effect on the elite witness, as she knew this Assembly member wasn't aware of the secret mission as he had been with the one involving her capture and the threat to Earth.

"You should be alone and rest now. Captain Kagan can handle the remainder of my business. I'll check on you again this week."

"You're leaving so soon?"

"Yes, I must get back and keep matters under control on Caguas. So far, this news has been told to only a select few. When it breaks, it will create a great commotion. Ripples will be felt across the Tri-Galaxy. Many people and forces were dependent upon Ryker for certain supplies. I'm happy you count us among your friends and close associates, Princess Jana."

'You needn't worry, sir, that will not change. I hold no grudge against Maffei for the way I was brought here. I understand the importance of race survival, but I am pleased the *charl* law has been struck down. I want the friends I made on Commander Saar's ship and the women brought here before us to be as free and happy as I am. As happy as I *was* for a short time." Jana was surprised when tears formed in her eyes and eased down her cheeks. She thanked Kagan for the handkerchief he passed to her, and she removed the moisture on her cheeks. She accepted the glass of green water he fetched for her and sipped it. "I'm sorry, gentlemen; it's just such a difficult and painful moment for me. I don't think the full reality of his loss has hit me yet. I keep thinking this must be a terrible dream."

"I should leave now," Faeroe said, rising. "I leave you with my prayers and condolences, Princess Jana. If you need anything, *anything*, please do not hesitate to call on me. Captain Kagan can show me out, so don't get up."

She clasped wrists with him. "Goodbye, sir, and thank you for coming in person. I shall never forget your kindness and compassion."

Jana watched the two men leave the house. She sank against the sofa back and closed her eyes, lashes still dampened by tears provoked by the stress of the situation and the hormonal changes taking place in her body. Yet, in a strange way, she was saddened over Ryker's tragic life and death. He was Varian's half brother. Ryker, even if only it was a ruse, had been good to her at the end. With Varian playing him so accurately she had gotten to know the misguided man a little. She could not help but wonder what Ryker and his life would have been like if the insane Shara hadn't been in control of it, if Galen had reared him, had reared his two boys together.

At least the impersonation part of the mission was over and she would complete the rest with Varian—as himself—at her side. She wondered if that would be easier or harder on her. As soon as the grim news was exposed, people would consider her Ryker Triloni's widow. In less than a year in this alien world, she had gone from captive *charl* who had no control over her life to a wealthy, powerful, free woman who owned the most feared and envied weapons and chemical labs in three galaxies. What did it matter that the public didn't know Varian and his team had confiscated those powerful and dangerous formulas when they believed they were in her control?

When the door opened and closed, Jana expected Andrea to come to see if she was all right. It was Kagan. She straightened and looked at him.

"Faeroe is gone. I put Ryker's casket in the shuttle complex until Varian arrives to take possession of it. You were magnificent, Jana. You continue to amaze and impress me. Too bad you can't join the Elite Squad; you'd be one of our best agents. Are you all right?"

His concern touched her. "Yes and no. I'm relieved his visit is over and went so well, but I'm drained. Are you sure I did everything right?''

Kagan leaned against the back of the sofa which set near the center of the room in a grouping of furniture. ''Perfect, to be exact. Why don't I get you a glass of wine to soothe your nerves.''

''No thanks,'' the pregnant Jana replied. ''I think Zandian tea and a hot bath will be more relaxing. Did you tell the others it's safe to come out?''

''Not yet. I thought you needed a little time alone first. I know part of it was superb acting, but you're a tender-hearted woman who feels deeply. I know that wasn't a simple task. Strength and gentleness in the right proportions are good qualities. I'll give you ten minutes to calm down before I send the others here. If you need anything, call me immediately.''

''I will, and thank you again, Kagan.''

She watched her new friend leave, then rested until the others were told they could return to the house to be enlightened.

Twenty minutes later, Jana learned that Kagan had related the visit with Faeroe to Martella, Tristan, and Andrea to save her the energy. Still, the three asked her several questions which led to her repeating the entire meeting. ''I want each of you to promise me you won't tell Varian or Nigel about the baby when the men arrive tomorrow,'' she added. ''I don't want to discuss my pregnancy with him until after we return from Androas.''

When Tristan started to protest the secrecy, Jana said, ''Wait, Tris, and listen to me before you argue with my decision. If Varian learns of this, he will worry about me and the baby during our trip to see Maal. And you know I have to make that trip with him to participate in duping Ryker's grandfather. If Varian knows I'm carrying his child, he'll be so concerned about our safety that he'll either prevent me from going or he won't be able to concentrate and could make a fatal slip. He must have his full attention on the situation or he could mention something Maal said to him while he was impersonating Ryker, or vice versa. We can't take that risk. We've come too far and gotten too close to mess things up. I'll depend on you, Tris, to give me something to take to prevent any symptoms—like morning sickness—from exposing my condition. If we're going to stay safe and get this charade over with fast, it's best if he doesn't know the truth. I promise to tell him the minute we reach Darkar again."

It was ten o'clock that night when Kagan came to see Jana. She and Andrea were sitting on the sofa sipping herbal tea. Following their baths, they had donned nightgowns and robes. Jana assumed it was Tristan or Martella when the signal sounded.

"Kagan, what is it? Has something happened?" she asked in surprise as she opened the door.

"I'm sorry to disturb you, Jana, but Princce Taemin is on the com channel in the security control room and he insists on talking to you. He refuses to leave orbit until he does. I told him it was late, that you were upset over your husband's death, and weren't taking any more calls tonight. I even threatened to fire defense lasers at him if he didn't leave our air space. He said I could shoot him out of the sky if I dared, but he wasn't leaving until he told you what he'd come to say. He sounds serious. He said it's private and urgent news, something you should know."

"Give me a minute to change clothes and I'll go with you to see what our enemy has in mind. It could be of vital importance to us."

Chapter Seventeen

Seated before the communications panel in security control, Jana told Kagan, to excuse her French in advance.

''What does that mean? It doesn't translate to make sense to me.''

Jana laughed and explained, ''Earth slang meaning Excuse me if I talk naughty because I plan to be provoking with Taemin to extract information from him.''

Kagan chuckled. ''That's very clever, and an amusing saying.''

''You sit on the counter out of sight from the viewing screen; maybe that devil will be more loose-lipped if he thinks I'm alone.''

Kagan hopped upon the desk top, wriggled his body past the front of the *telecom* monitor, and took an Indian-style sitting position. ''Ready. He's on stand-by. Just push that button.'' He sent her a smile of encouragement and confidence, which she returned.

Jana took several deep breaths and summoned her wits to

full alert. *O.K., J. G., let's do it*, she told herself, and pressed the red square Kagan had pointed out to her. Taemin's visage, which always reminded her of that of a viking warrior, materialized at once. She saw the prince react with pleasure and relief, and come to full attention. Before she could begin, words rushed from his sensual lips.

"Jana, thank you for deciding to speak with me," a thickly accented voice said. "I know it is late and perhaps I was a little demanding, but I wanted to offer my condolences in person before I depart for home. Ryker was a good and longtime friend and ally. I shall miss him."

With a chilled and narrowed gaze and in an icy voice, she replied, "If you make it a common practice to capture and slay your friends and allies, I shan't imagine you have any left." She saw vexation tinge his dark-gray eyes, though he quickly tried to conceal it. As she spoke her next sentence, her eyes raked over his flowing blond hair and noble features as if she were appraising an animal that was under consideration for purchase and found the creature to be annoyingly flawed and worthless. "You might have considered my husband a friend and ally, but it was wishful thinking on your part."

Taemin leaned forward in his seat and rested his arms on the desk. "It is not my fault Ryker is dead. If you had allowed me to rescue you two from Luz or you had arrived on Cenza for your visit, we could have straightened out our misunderstanding and Ryker might still be alive."

Jana widened her gaze to reveal astonishment and disbelief. "Rescue? Visit? Misunderstanding?" she echoed in a sarcastic tone. "Are you insane, or do you take me for a fool? You lured us into a trap. You ordered your captain to bring us to you in chains if necessary. In *chains*, you bastard! You had Ryker locked in a cell like a common criminal. You were going to kill us, perhaps after torturing us for Trilabs secrets. You would have succeeded if Commander Sanger had not arrived to save us and thwart your treachery. You forced us to detonate your ship to ensure our escape. We barely survived the crash on Luz and the confrontations with *keelars* and savage mutants.

Now you dare to come here and call Ryker your friend and ally! You dare to show your deceitful and wicked face to me! I should kill you myself!"

Jana watched him place his fingers on his screen as if to calm her by a touch as he responded in a controlled tone meant to soften and soothe.

"I do not blame you for being angry, Jana, but let me explain. I would not have harmed either of you once Cass's absurd idea was proven false. I cannot believe I allowed her to convince me it was."

"You're not making sense, Taemin, and I'm in no mood for a guessing game. What 'absurd idea' could provoke a trap of 'friends'?"

"That Ryker was dead and Varian was impersonating him."

Jana stared at him in befuddlement but was careful not to expose fear or guilt. "Did I hear you correctly? Or is my aural device malfunctioning? Did you say you thought . . . Varian was playing Ryker?"

"You heard me correctly, Jana. But—"

Jana placed her palms on the counter and leaned forward to demand, "Is this a sick joke? Why did you really come here? My husband has been dead less than a day, a man you tried to murder not long ago. If you think to cozy up to me to win my forgiveness and friendship, you are a fool. And if you're trying to pull some kind of crazy stunt with such a preposterous allegation, I can't imagine why or how you hope to pull it off."

"It was Cass's mistake, Jana. She said she had evidence Varian was playing Ryker. She was going to prove it to me after you two arrived."

"That's the secret Garus mentioned to Ryker?" Jana scoffed. Taemin nodded, but she didn't give him time to interrupt. "He thought you were referring to him persuading Maal to sign a new treaty with Maffei. He thought that was why you were angry and were abducting us. He believed you were going to use me to force him to give you supplies from Darkar, maybe even try to coerce the entry codes from him so you could take what you desired from Trilabs before the treaty cut you off." After her cunning speculations, she sneered, "I can't believe you two would be so stupid and rash. I take that back; I can imagine *her* being that deluded and daring, but not you, Taemin. When we met on Lynrac, I formed a good impression of you and your father. But they have changed—for the worse."

"Please give me an opportunity to prove you were right then and wrong now. If Cass had not come to me with—"

Jana cut him off again. "She can't have proof such a ludicrous thing was true because it isn't and it wasn't. Do you honestly think Varian Saar could dupe Ryker's wife and grandfather and friends into believing *he* was Prince Ryker Triloni? That's the silliest excuse for treachery I've ever heard. And it doesn't explain or justify your vile treatment of us before reaching Cenza for your little test. Whyever would you, a prince and future ruler, act so recklessly upon a few stupid rantings from a scorned and vindictive woman?"

"I realize how foolishly I behaved, Jana. I know now it is not true; I saw Varian and Ryker together on the news broadcast after the rescue. I also know they were seen in different places at the same time. I should not have listened to Canissia, but she has never lied to me or been wrong in the past."

"Don't you think it would have been smarter to check out such a ridiculous tale before you dared to betray Ryker based on her word? I thought you too intelligent to be fooled by her or anyone."

"You are right; she had no evidence to prove her claims to me and I should not have acted upon them before she presented it to me. It will never happen again, Jana. I have severed all ties with her. I ask your forgiveness for any offense and harm you suffered because of my foolishness."

"You sorry bastard! You dare to come here while I am dazed with grief to weasel your way back into business with Trilabs? Not in a thousand years, Taemin Tabriz! Ryker cut you and Pyropea off and I shall honor his decision. Trilabs is mine now and you will never see another product from here. If you don't take your ship out of my air space, I will have it destroyed.

You have thirty minutes to comply before I order Kagan to open fire on it."

"You cannot do this to me and my federation. Ryker asked me to meet him on Caguas to make peace. He understood and accepted my mistake."

"You liar. He would never have made peace with you after what you did to us. He told me what he said to you and your father."

"I entreat you to let me come down and talk to you in person."

"Fat chance of you getting close enough to harm me again! If you make any attempt to do so, your shuttle will be disintegrated by my force shield. I swear to you I will not lower it. I will sit here and watch your craft explode with you aboard; maybe that will return you to the hell from which you came, you devil. Get yourself and your bitch out of here."

"If that is why you are reluctant, Cass is not with me. She is in hiding on Zenufia. It seems the Alliance is eager to speak with her on a few delicate matters." Taemin continued in a cocky tone. "If you reinstate Pyropea as one of your best clients, I will not reveal to anyone that your marriage to Ryker was illegal and you have no claim on Trilabs."

"What?" After the arrogant man repeated his words, Jana refuted, "My marriage is very legal. If you doubt it, check the Androas and Maffei records. Whatever new trick you're trying to pull, it won't work."

"I know the truth, Jana, so do not force me to use it against you. If we make a deal, I will keep silent and allow you to inherit Ryker's holdings. Your marriage resulted from a crime, so it is illegal. Cass kidnapped you from Varian and gave you to Ryker as a slave, a captive, a beautiful toy."

"Have you gone totally mad like your fiery-haired accomplice? I was free to come and go as I pleased, and it pleased me to come to Darkar to participate in research with the greatest scientific genius of all time. Surely Canissia told you I was liberated for saving *Kadim* Tirol's life during an enemy attack at his home on Eire. That incident is also a matter of public record and easily verifiable for a man like you with spies everywhere. It pleased Canissia to help get me away from the man she desired: Varian Saar. It also pleased me to marry Ryker when he proposed. Didn't you learn anything from Canissia's recent lies and tricks? She fooled you again, Taemin, because she did not kidnap me. If she had, I would press charges against her because I'm free to do so. And if she had, Varian would have hunted her down for punishment and he would have demanded my return from Ryker. Since you have so many sneaky ways of obtaining facts, why haven't you discovered those truths? Why don't you get Canissia to come forward to challenge and discredit my word and holdings?''

''You know she would never admit to a crime. She is in enough trouble as is. All I have to do is spread the news to cast doubts on your status as Ryker's wife and heir. What will Varian do when he learns how he lost you?''

''No one is more acquainted with those reasons than the man responsible for them. Even if what you think is true, which it is not, who would believe you and Canissia? It's on record at Star Base and with Maal that you two tried to lure us into a trap to kill us. Ryker told both sides the truth about how we got on Luz, but he told them he would handle revenge in his own time and way. That's the only reason he didn't expose you two in public. If you doubt me, ask them. Besides, he told you and your father the same thing. You said you knew Ryker well. If that's true, would he take a captive wife almost everywhere with him? Would Maal believe such a crazy lie after spending so much time with us since our marriage? He knows how happy we are. *Were*, that is, until today when we were parted forever.''

She glared at Taemin. ''I suggest you leave before I contact *Avatar* Faeroe and the Alliance Force stationed on Caguas nearby. I'm sure they will be interested in coming here to talk with a man who made a recent attempt on Ryker's life. Did you make another one and succeed? Is that why you were on Caguas when he was killed?''

''Of course not! I did not harm Ryker today or any day.''

"You might have to prove your innocence very soon," Jana warned. "When *Avatar* Faeroe brought my husband's body home this evening, he told me Commander Saar is on his way to the area to investigate this possibly suspicious accident. If you are involved, your father and people cannot protect you from the combined wraths of Maffei and Androas."

"I had nothing to do with the mine explosion. Nothing."

Jana pretended to catch a slip he had made. "How did you know he was killed and that it was in an explosion?"

"I have ways of learning such things."

"From your hirelings who did the dirty work for you?"

"From friends on Caguas."

Jana made herself seem suspicious of him. "How, when the news has not been released yet except to family and the authorities?"

"I cannot name my sources unless necessary. They are friends."

"You have some left that you haven't betrayed and killed?"

"I have never slain a friend, Jana, and I would not."

She realized she was increasing his anger and frustration. "You tried to murder Ryker five weeks ago and you called *him* a friend."

"I explained that error."

"Well, if you claim you never kill friends, then I should worry about future threats from you because we'll never be friends or allies."

"I will not allow you to destroy or humiliate me and the Pyropean Federation, my daring and exquisite Earthling."

"Threats already? Getting scared and desperate, Taemin? Is your father threatening to disown his bad boy for losing the Trilabs connection?"

"Do not taunt or mock me, Jana Greyson; it is foolish and dangerous."

"I am beyond your power and skill to reach and harm. I have no fear of you, Taemin. Ryker taught me strength and courage and wisdom."

"After Varian Saar took them away after he captured you as a slave."

Jana sent him a look that said he had gone too far. "I will not discuss either Commander Saar or my past. But if you recall, Ryker reconciled with his half brother after our rescue from your treachery. In fact, my foolish prince, it was your reckless stunt that precipitated their reunion. It proved to Ryker that it was wiser and safer for him to trust and ally himself with Maffei than with Pyropea. He and Commander Saar settled their problems and became friends. I assure you I'll honor that pact. Commander Saar is welcome on Darkar any time it is necessary for him to visit."

"Ryker Triloni would never make peace with Galen Saar's son—*never*—and you are foolish to do so. It was a trick."

"You saw the meeting yourself; you told me so. Do you doubt your own eyes? Was anyone's arm twisted into compliance? Are either of them susceptible to coercion by drugs? It wasn't a trick, Taemin. They made genuine peace. Ask Maal if you doubt my word."

"I saw Ryker pretend to reconcile with Varian. He must have had a clever motive for doing so. He hated Varian and wanted to destroy him. If he had lived, he would have. Ryker has always hated the Saars and Maffei and plotted their total destruction."

"That's a lie. He moved to Maffei and became a citizen here. He was their ally and friend. He sold his powerful products and weapons to them. That isn't something a sane man does with his alleged enemies. Surely you aren't implying Ryker was crazy?"

"Of course not. But the reconciliation was a trick, Jana; you are being duped. I know how much he hated Varian and wanted him dead."

"Perhaps years ago, but not recently. Their bond as brothers became too strong to resist. Both men were ready and eager to finally make peace and to halt their foolish rivalry. Ryker was no longer controlled by the past and he wanted both galaxies to feel the same. That's why he talked Maal into signing a truce with Maffei. If you had talked to Ryker since we met months ago, you would know how much he changed before his death. It's clear to me that you're as deluded as Canissia is. How dare you speak about my husband like this, especially on the day of his tragic death? Be gone, twisted-tongued devil, before I lose my temper and patience and annihilate you for your wickedness against us and smear on his memory."

As she glared at him, she slammed her hand on the control button to sever the communication link. She fell back against the chair and let out a loud exhalation of air to release her tension. She looked at a grinning Kagan who had admiration, amazement, and affection sparkling in his seawater eyes. "Well, how was that performance, my friend?" she asked.

"Excellent. No one could have done better. You must be exhausted after all you've had to do today. Come, I'll walk you to the house."

As they left the control room, Jana glanced skyward. "Do you think he'll hang around or make an attempt to land? Pretending to be fearless and actually behaving that way aren't the same. I admit that I'm scared of him. Men like Taemin can be unpredictable and dangerous. Especially when they have someone like Canissia egging them on to bolder plots."

Kagan grasped her hand and squeezed it. "Don't worry, my friend. Taemin won't try anything with the force shield activated and the automatic destruct system in operation, not to mention your warnings. His sensors know he can't get through our protection barriers. Nobody was smarter about defense than Ryker Triloni and no place has a better system than Darkar. It's totally impenetrable to all attacks. You're safe, Jana. I wouldn't let anyone or anything harm you. Varian is going to be very proud of how you handled yourself with Faeroe and Taemin. I am. So will *Kadim* Tirol, Supreme Commander Breccia Sard, and Councilman Draco Procyon when I report it to them tomorrow morning."

"I'm glad I have you here to help me and protect me, Kagan."

"I'm glad I was the one chosen for this special and secret assignment."

"So am I. Good night and thanks," she said at the door.

Kagan looked at it a moment after it was closed. Yes, he concluded again, Varian Saar was one lucky man—if he didn't mess things up with her.

It was hours after dinner the following day when Varian and Nigel arrived on Darkar in a *Wanderlust* shuttle. To allow the two couples privacy, Tristan and Martella had retired to the complex suite. Andrea awaited Nigel in the living area, while Jana had chosen the secluded bedroom for her first meeting with Varian as himself after over four months as Ryker.

She reminded Andrea to withhold the truth from the men, then hurried to the bedroom. She was glad her love hadn't been present when she received the news of her pregnancy. That had given her time to adjust and plan after her talk with Andrea had clarified many things. She thought of the tiny life growing within her and of becoming a mother. She imagined holding their baby and wondered which parent it would favor.

Perhaps the baby was fate's way of removing a difficult decision from her hands. Love, marriage, a child, a golden future—were they possible after all that had happened? First, she had to be sure this wasn't another trick to obtain control of her again. She also had to be convinced of her own feelings, that she was doing the best thing for everyone involved. *Prepare yourself, Rogue Saar, for the most important test of your life. If you fail, we all lose.*

In the living area, Nigel greeted an overjoyed Andrea. When their lips and arms parted, the curly-haired man introduced his two loved ones. "Andrea, I want you to meet my best friend and commanding officer; Varian, this is the woman I'm going to marry very soon."

The ebony-haired man clasped wrists with her and smiled. "It's a great pleasure to finally meet you, Andrea McKay. Nigel has told me all about you. Congratulations on snaring my best friend. You couldn't have chosen a better man to share your new life with in our world. Rest assured I shall make certain he has plenty of time to enjoy it. I must add, it looks as if he couldn't have made a better choice for a wife."

Andrea eyed the handsome alien and was charmed by him. "It's nice to see you, Commander Saar. Nigel has told me many things about you, too; so has Jana. I've looked forward to our meeting."

"I wish it could have been under different circumstances. I hope Jana is doing all right in this grim situation. And please call me Varian."

You are a superb actor—and a hunk! "She's holding up fine, Varian. She's waiting for you in her suite so you two can speak in private."

"Thank you, Andrea. I'll go see her now. I look forward to us getting better acquainted after things settle down."

"So do I, sir."

"Good night. We leave early tomorrow so enjoy yourselves." Varian smiled then headed for the bedroom where Jana awaited him.

From her position at a window, Jana heard the door open then close. She couldn't imagine how she was going to feel when they looked at each other with so much torment between them. She saw his reflection in the glasslike material. His image grew larger and clearer as he approached. Her heart fluttered while her stomach played host to countless active butterflies. She trembled but didn't turn. Her gaze took in his sable hair and handsome face. Somehow, she hadn't expected to react in this instantly weakened way. In light of the predicament he had put her in, she had assumed anger would be her predominant emotion. It wasn't.

"Hello, Moonbeam, I'm back. I spoke with Grandfather earlier. He, Brec, and Draco can't stop singing praises for your work with Faeroe and Taemin. Neither can Kagan. It seems you've made a conquest there. He told me I would be a fool if I didn't do whatever it took to keep you."

A romantic and stirring attack on my warring senses right off the bat. Don't let him disarm and enchant you before he's proven himself. "How did things go on Caguas?" she asked.

She kept her back to him as she tried to master her wayward feelings and cool the desire that flamed within her.

"No problem. Taemin stayed around to answer a few questions, so we wouldn't track him down. Of course he loudly proclaimed his innocence. I told him he was free to leave but that Star Fleet might want to speak with him again considering that recent trouble on his ship and Luz. The fire at the mine was minor and repairs are under way. It went off without suspicion pointing at us. We're one step closer to completing our task."

Afterward? she wanted to ask but didn't. "What about those threats Taemin made against you and Tirol to Ryker? Did you question him about that part and about his plot against Maffei? Since you and Ryker made peace, it wouldn't appear odd for him to have warned you of treachery."

"I didn't mention any of that to Taemin. Telling me about a threat to me and Grandfather was only a trick to make sure I was lured into his trap. He wouldn't have added that enticement if he hadn't believed I was Varian."

"Are you sure it was a trick and he won't attack you two?"

Varian warmed as he assumed she was worried about them. "Yes, and he couldn't succeed if he tried. Maal told me as Ryker that he hadn't been the one to tell Taemin we were on the *Wanderlust*. That proved to me and him it was Cass's traitorous doing. The way it stands, neither Maal nor Taemin will trust her or help her again. With Ryker gone, too, that leaves Cass without allies and sanctuary. She'll be caught soon."

"She could have allies elsewhere. She's clever and surely desperate by now. All she has to do is move to another galaxy and hide out until it's safe to sneak back for more malicious mischief. Or she can do as you did: alter her appearance and stroll around as free as she pleases."

Varian placed his hands on her arms to stroke them but felt her stiffen. He dropped them to his sides and said, "I won't let her get away with all her vicious crimes."

Jana wished she could fall into his arms and forget the dark ast, but it wasn't that simple. She felt a desperation of her wn to stop him from assailing her senses before they settled atters between them. To do so, she said, "You may have o choice. You do recall that frequently used statement and ondition, don't you?" When he didn't defend himself or repond, she asked, "Do we leave in the morning for Maal's as lanned?"

Varian had expected her reserve and coolness. He was disapointed to learn he had been right. "Yes, if that suits you."

"The sooner we get this over with, the better."

A short and heavy silence ensued. Varian worried over her rigid mood. Before leaving to dispose of Ryker's body, he ad believed he was making progress with her. Their last night ogether had been glorious, and their farewell had been genial. t was apparent he either had been wrong, misled, or something ad changed her mind during his absence. What? Or was it *vhom*? Had the lies Jana was forced to tell Andrea become too eal? Had Andrea told Jana that Varian couldn't possibly love er and do the things he had done? Had Jana broken her vow f silence and turned Andrea against him as Ryker and Varian? The redhead had been charming, but she had looked at him ddly when they spoke, he recalled. Had it been a grave misake to allow their reunion at this delicate time?

"What about Shara's body?" she inquired to break the tenion.

"It's been buried here. If we have need of it later, we can xhume it. If not, Darkar will be her final and secret resting lace for all eternity. I have agents checking on what Taemin aid about Cass being on Zenufia. If she is, we'll try for extradiion. I'm sure they will hand her over to us. I did give Taemin strong warning about his threats to you; he's been ordered to tay out of this area and away from Darkar. For now, he'll bey."

"How did you manage your change back to yourself without Tris? What about the crew on the ship that picked you and Nigel up? Did they see you as Ryker? Do they now know the truth?"

"Brec came for me with an android crew. No one else is the wiser and it will remain that way, Moonbeam. I was disguised when I left the mine and when I entered Star Base. A specialist in the med complex there reversed Tris's work on me, then had his task blocked from his memory."

"That's a relief. Thank you for taking those precautions. The fewer who know about your ruse with me the better."

Jana turned to look at him, assured she was strong and calm enough to do so by then. Her heart rate speeded up again. She warmed from head to toe. Her body, heart, and mind responded to him. There was a roguish gleam in his molten gaze and broad smile on his sensuous lips. His wide shoulders and stalwart chest were concealed in a wine dress uniform with gold markings. Stripes banded each wrist with a star on either side of them. A gold sunburst was placed over his left chest muscle. He exuded an undeniable and irresistible aura of strength, power, and passion. He was totally magnetic and she was drawn to him.

Jana's wits reeled as she viewed the perfect male who was enslaving her will and leaving her without the power to resist him. The storm raging within her body threatened to wash her away in its flood of potent desire. A warming glow pulsed through her womanhood and she scolded herself for feeling in this wanton way. He was a tower of masculinity, and she had to break his hypnotic hold over her. She told herself it was sexual attraction, but she knew it was more, much more. "He did an excellent job. You're perfect."

He assumed bringing others in on the ruse had been her concern and what had changed her mood, as she appeared to relax a little after his response. "Thank you," he murmured, aware of how they were affecting each other. He yearned to yank her into his arms and cover her with kisses. He wanted her to forgive him, to let him make things right.

As he smiled, she remarked, "You even got the creases back near your eyes and mouth. And that sexy cleft in your chin seems unchanged."

"I'm glad you're pleased. The hardest part was extracting that green dye. For a while, I feared I was going to be stuck for life with blue lenses."

Jana studied his sapphire eyes. "I think not. The shade is perfect. They look the same color they used to be."

"How are you doing after your difficult tasks here?"

"They were scary, but they worked with Kagan's help and advice."

"He gives *you* the credit, Moonbeam."

"That was nice of him. He's a good agent for the Alliance."

"Andrea and Nigel were so glad to see each other," Varian observed. "You'd think they'd been apart for months instead of two days."

"Lovestruck couples behave that way."

He hoped that wasn't a clue to her feelings. "I like her, Jana. She's quite a woman, as you are."

"It's been wonderful having her here. Thank you."

"Any problems with her or the cover story?" he asked, and was pleased at her negative response. He changed his line of questioning abruptly. "I suppose she dislikes me after what you told her. She gave me a strange look when I saw her earlier."

"That's only natural; she was seeing and meeting Varian Saar for the first time. She's only met Ryker until tonight. Remember?"

"In a way, I'd forgotten. Nigel introduced us and we chatted for a short time. Perdition, Varian Saar shouldn't be in here with you!"

"Don't tell me you made a slip for once?"

"Absolutely. That shows how easy mistakes are made."

"Don't worry; I told her I wanted to see you in private."

"In your bedroom?"

"Why not, brother-in-law?" she replied, stressing their relationship.

"But I just smiled, spoke a few words, and strolled past her."

"After she told you I was waiting for you in here, right?"

"Yes, but I didn't even ask for directions."

"In your brother's home, it shouldn't be necessary."

"It'll be suspicious, Moonbeam."

"No, it won't. Besides, I'm sure she's too captivated by Nigel to notice anything unusual—even your good looks and charms, Rogue Saar. Relax, it's natural for my best friend to be curious about my captor and ex-lover. I did tell her I had exaggerated my feelings for Ryker so she'd understand why I'm not consumed by grief over my husband's loss. I'm afraid I couldn't fool her that far. Others, yes; Andrea, no. She's been very understanding."

Another short period of silence took place as if each was waiting for the other to select their next topic.

Finally, Varian said, "I've run out of small talk and reports, woman."

"So have I. If that's all, I'll take a bath. We leave early tomorrow."

Varian perceived that something else was bothering her. Perhaps seeing him as his old self reminded her of the charges of deceit against him. She was clearly as moved by their close proximity as he was, but still she was distant and cautious. He decided it might be best not to pressure her tonight about her feelings for him. "I've already checked things with Kagan to make sure we'll be ready to leave on time. We should get a good night's sleep. We'll travel at starlight speed and be there fast. During the voyage, you can ask any questions you may have and we can practice our next ruse."

"Fine." She headed toward the bathroom.

"I suppose a welcome-home kiss is out of the question, so I'll be a gentleman and let you escape my snare for a while."

She halted and gave a mocking bow. "How gallant of you."

"I see you're still testy and moody."

"With just cause, you space pirate." *I'm pregnant with your child.*

Varian was surprised when she grinned and used a mellow

tone. He did the same. "At least I have some kind of affect on you, Moonbeam."

In an exaggerated southern drawl and with lashes fluttering to ease the tension, she purred a seductive, "See you later."

"I'll see you in the morning, love. Good night."

Jana looked at him as she headed for the door. She read reluctance to leave her in his voice and movements. "Where are you going? It's late. We have an early departure time and busy schedule ahead. We need our rest. I'm sure the others have turned in and aren't expecting a visit and chat with you tonight."

"I can't stay here, Moonbeam."

"It may be your last chance to dazzle me for a long time. And how can you pass my test if you don't take it?"

Varian was tempted to stay but thought it too risky. "I'm not Ryker anymore. I'm Varian now."

"So?"

"What will the others think? You're Ryker's widow."

"Everyone here knows the truth, except Andrea," she fibbed. "By now she's totally consumed with Nigel and will be none the wiser."

"My ship is orbiting Darkar, Moonbeam. What about my crew?"

"Tell them you're staying in the shuttle complex because it's late for a return flight and you'd have to make another trip down early tomorrow. You have Nigel, Tris, Martella, and Kagan present to ward off gossip."

"My crew doesn't know anyone's here except Nigel. Tris and Martella are supposedly on leave somewhere. They don't know Agent Kagan. We did tell them about Andrea and Nigel, so it's fine for him to stay."

She shrugged. "Suit yourself, Rogue Saar; you always do. As for me, my bath is waiting."

Varian couldn't help but say he would make his report and return soon.

Jana grinned and jested, "A wise decision, Commander."

* * *

Jana watched Varian leave the bathroom after a quick shower and shave to join her in the large bed that seemed deceptively small. He radiated heat and enticement as he drew her to him. If the bold idea she was planning to use failed . . . *Don't think about that now, J.G., just test his feelings and yours.*

Jana gravitated toward him until her yearning body made contact with his. A full moon was in a direct angle overhead to cast light through the clear dome roof; it illuminated them in a romantic glow. Their gazes met. She saw him smile, an almost shy and nervous one. Jana let her eyes roam his face. Her hand seemed to lift of its own volition to allow her fingers to trace the cleft in his chin and trail over his lips.

Jana propped her elbow on the mattress and rested her chin on a balled fist. Moonlight played over Varian's features; it glowed in his sapphire eyes; it shone on his ebony hair and on his white teeth. Her body came to life and a fiery flush teased over her from head to foot. His hair was tousled and that stubborn lock was out of place again, one of the clues which had originally caused her to suspect he wasn't Ryker. It made him appear rakish and sexy, as did his expression. The concealing sheet did not come higher than his waist, baring his naked chest to her scrutiny. His tanned flesh was unmarred, soft and sleek over hard muscles and strong bones. She wanted to lay her head there and listen to his heart beat with vitality, life, and hopefully with love for her.

She did not speak as her gaze and hands communicated with him. Varian Saar possessed the most potent magnetism and enchanting power she had ever encountered, and sometimes it alarmed her to see and feel the enormous force of his irresistible magic. She felt tension and suspense laced with anticipation and desire mounting within her, within him, and between them.

Varian was alert and perceptive. Eagerness and pleasant surprise washed over his body and danced within his heart. Her gaze said she wanted him and was reaching out to him. She was like a tractor beam pulling him toward her; he couldn't refuse to obey and didn't want to refuse. He wanted to whisk her away in his ship of love and carry them to a safe port among the stars to live forever as one. As he gazed into her limpid eyes of blue, green, and violet, he did not battle the multicolored currents that were setting him adrift in a sector of wonder. He didn't move or speak, just basked in the radiant glow of her admiring gaze that ignited his passions to a glorious height.

Varian sent his eyes on a voyage over her exquisite terrain. Her tawny hair flowed over the arm bracing her head, spilled over his right arm, and pooled on the bed. No features could be more perfectly sized or shaped to enhance her beauty and appeal. Her rosy lips were parted as if in invitation to him to capture and sample them. Her golden complexion was unblemished and was as soft as Mailiorcan silk. Her dark-blond hair was like gentle waves on Zamarra with sunlight sparkling off of them and brightening certain strands. She was the most beautiful woman he had ever seen. Yet, her beauty was more than physical; it was all parts of Jana Greyson combined.

The alien commander's heart thudded with emotion and need. She caused him to lose sight and reality of all except her. He feared doing or saying the wrong thing at this delicate moment in their relationship. He wanted everything to be perfect for her and for them from this day onward. He wanted to win back her heart and her trust. He craved every part of this unique woman, far more than just her body. This could be her decision-making time, their destiny-sealing episode; and he didn't want to hinder, destroy, or rush it.

Unable to keep from touching her any longer, Varian's quivering fingers slipped into her shiny hair and pleasured themselves in its fullness. He watched her shut her eyes, lean her head into his palm, and nuzzle it. His hand eased behind her head and pulled it downward so his lips could brush kisses over her features, flawless flesh that was fragrant and beckoning. With leisure and delight, he trailed his lips over her forehead,

brows, temples, eyes, nose, cheeks, and chin, then finished hi
exploration at her mouth where he fastened his to hers in
search for splendor.

At first, the kiss was slow and gentle. After she snuggle
closer and clasped his face between her hands, the next one
became fast and deep and exposed intense longings in both c
them. He groaned in urgent need for her and embraced her wit
possessiveness. She moaned in matching need. Their tongue
touched, savored, and teased. Their hands joined their sensuou
and heady quests as they delved into the magic which enthralle
and united two hearts from two distant worlds. It was as if the
were striving to strengthen a predestined bond. It was Varia
and Jana in each other's arms without another man's imag
between them, together at last.

Jana rolled to her back as if on cue. Varian's seeking mout
wandered down the satiny column of her neck. His teeth nib
bled with gentleness at her collarbone. His tongue played i
the hollow of her throat. His mouth suckled at her earlobe. Th
tickling sensation and her pulsing joy caused her to laugh an
wiggle.

He whispered in a husky tone filled with deep emotion, "
love you, Jana. I want you to be mine, all mine, forever.
want your name to become Jana Saar as soon as possible. Ever
day this mission gets harder because it's keeping us apart
Please don't let me lose you because of it. Please trust me an
stand by me, stand with me for all eternity. I swear on the star
I love you with all my heart. Eons can pass and that truth wi
never change."

Varian had difficulty breathing and speaking in his arouse
and worried state. He had trouble thinking, moving, holdin
still. His body felt heavy, yet light. He was uncertain of he
decision, yet sure she loved him and wanted him. He wa
tense, yet relaxed and enlivened. He lifted his head to gaze int
her glowing eyes. He wished she would reply in the affirmativ
about her own feelings. He knew she had just cause to doub
and distrust him. He knew he must be patient and loving t
guide them back to where they had been that night on th

Wanderlust before this ruse threatened to tear them apart. He prayed his skills and experiences were sufficient to accomplish his goal of winning peace and holding on to Jana. He wanted to restrain his cravings long enough to give her rapturous pleasure and immense satisfaction, long enough to show her his desire for her was far more than physical.

Varian's lips captured hers as his hand slipped down her torso and covered one breast. As his tongue invaded her mouth and tasted its sweet response and minty flavor, he caressed the fleshy mound and thumbed the taut peak on it. He felt the bud grow harder and was amazed by the contrast in the rigidity of the point and the softness of its base. He trailed his mouth down her throat and closed it over the nipple, then hovered over one then the other, at first simply brushing them with his lips, then stopping to lavish moist attention there.

Jana felt his hands and mouth working blissful magic on her and dazing her wits. Her spinning senses lost awareness of all except him and their lovemaking. Her hands roamed his bare torso, sliding with leisure and delight over his back, shoulders, and arms. Her fingers dipped into the depression of his spine and tracked each connection until she could reach no further. She stroked his firm buttocks, glided up his hips, over his lean waist, across the ripples of his rib cage, and wandered between them to a furry chest.

Jana loved everything and anything he did to her: each caress, each kiss, each unspoken promise of what was yet to come. Her teeth nipped at his shoulders and neck. She waxed between tension and relaxation. Her breasts responded wildly to his lips and fingers as his tongue circled and flicked the rosy-brown flowers now in full bloom. The core of her womanhood tingled and pulsed with pleasure and with rising need. Her reactions encouraged and urged him to continue his conquest. Fiery blood raced through her, heating her to a feverish level and burning away all inhibitions and reservations for now. Every inch he touched was sensitive, susceptible, alive, pleading.

Varian had titillated her and restrained himself for as long as he could endure the blissful torment which surged through him. At last he slipped between her parted thighs, kissing her as he slid inside her silken heat.

Jana's legs curled over his as she matched his rhythm and speed. Time passed as they labored with love, pleasure, and unsteady control.

"Be mine, Moonbeam, tonight and forever."

As Jana moaned and squirmed, Varian knew she was reaching her climax. He was glad because he could hold back no longer. He continued to thrust and retreat until they were left limp in each other's embrace. As sated and content as he, she nestled into his arms and they shared tender kisses.

Jana closed her eyes and imagined their child's appearance. A boy would look like his father, as she'd been told was the genetic pattern in this alien world. But what about a female? Would a girl also favor Varian? Would her Earthling genes be totally dominated by his potent ones? A baby . . . Their baby . . . How would he react when she told him? She couldn't do so before their trip, and it was mostly for the reasons she had told Tris, Andrea, and Martella. She did have to safeguard their lives, which a lack of concentration and worry could endanger. If he was told and he refused to imperil her and his baby with a trip to Maal's, the charade could require longer to complete, time she—no, the baby—didn't have, not without causing its paternity to be questioned. But the main reason for keeping her secret was to control the timing of her demand; it had to be issued when it could be carried out by him. She also wanted and needed a short span with Varian as himself. Only then could she determine if she could trust him and a future together was possible. Until such time, she could not confess she still loved and wanted him. Her bold demand, it would come as soon as they returned from Maal's.

The following morning while their things were being loaded on the shuttle, Andrea couldn't stop talking about Varian. "Wow, Jana, he's magnificent! No god could have designed him better. He's so nice, too, Jana, utterly charming. I see why you were dazzled by him."

"But is he trustworthy, my friend? So far, I haven't had good luck with men, so maybe I'm a bad judge of character. Look what happened with Alex and Ryker, and now with Varian. Maybe using women and being dishonest with them are flaws men can't help."

"Varian Saar doesn't strike me as having many flaws or weaknesses, but I don't know him as well as you do."

"I'm not sure I know him, either."

"How did it go last night between you two?"

"Fine. But please pretend you don't know he stayed with me. You didn't drop any hints to Nigel, did you?"

The redhead giggled. "Of course not, Bootsy."

"My heavens, Andrea, it's been a long time since I heard that nickname. I thought I had outgrown it when I stopped clopping around in Father's cowboy boots."

"You filled his shoes well before you were brought here to live. In fact, there aren't any shoes too big for you to fill."

"Not even the ones I'm trying on for size in this alien world, Miss Scribbles?"

They shared laughter as they chatted about how Andrea received that nickname in seventh grade for getting caught numerous times "scribbling" and passing notes to Jana until they learned a more effective method.

"Did anything special happen last night? Don't keep me in suspense."

"I didn't break down and tell him about the baby, if that's your meaning." Jana explained her plan.

Andrea, who was convinced they loved each other and could be happy, wanted to help patch things up between the couple. She and Nigel had decided last night to do all they could to keep them from being too stubborn to see the truth and to work out both of their differences. "Isn't an ultimatum like that dangerous, Jana? He loves you; Nigel said so, you said so, he said so, and I believe it's true. I like him, Jana, really like him. Don't say again that sometimes love isn't enough; if it's strong and true, love is enough because it helps you work out any problems.''

''I don't want to get my hopes up again, then suffer when those beautiful dreams fail to materialize. You're being as rosy eyed as I was when I met Varian. Just loving and wanting someone doesn't make it the best thing for me. I have to make certain he loves me enough, loves me in the right way. He must prove his feelings and vows this time. I have to be sure I can trust him; if I delude myself, it will cause worse problems later.''

Andrea couldn't forget or ignore what Nigel had told her about all the grim situations Jana had endured. ''Varian's explained everything to you, and you admit he had no choice. You know what was at stake. Why do you continue to feel as you do, Jana? I don't understand.''

''His goals are good, Andrea, but not how he carried them out.''

''He couldn't tell you or include you at first.'' Andrea attempted to justify Varian's actions.

''He says so, but I'm not convinced there wasn't another way to do it.''

''True love comes around so rarely, Jana. Are you just going to throw it away because he made a mistake?''

Jana surmised that Andrea was being influenced by Nigel who was Varian's naturally biased best friend. Yet, it was obvious Andrea believed what she was saying and only wanted the best for Jana and the baby. ''I've told you my decision; the rest is up to Varian.''

''You want to punish him before you agree to take him back?''

''No, just to be convinced I can trust him and that he loves me as much as his duty and people. Is that so wrong?''

''Don't act impulsively, Jana, please. You might regret it. Varian Saar doesn't strike me as a man who can be threatened or tricked.''

''I'm not doing either one. I won't be rash or reckless, my worrywart friend, just . . .''

"Jana, Jana, this crazy plan worries me."

Jana patted her friend's shoulder and smiled. "Once and for all, I'll learn the truth about his feelings. At that point, it should be simple to prove himself. If he fails, so be it and I'm out of his life for good."

"Where would you go? What would you do?"

"I'd go to my father-in-law's on Tartarus and be a scientist and mother. I'd raise the next heir to the Androasian Empire and live in peace for a change."

"But it isn't Ryker Triloni's child, isn't *Kadim* Maal's grandchild."

"If Varian waits too long to lay claim to me and his child, it will be viewed and accepted as Ryker's by everyone who doesn't know about this charade. Since it can't ever be exposed, the truth will be buried with Ryker. Besides, I've told you that children here resemble their fathers, not mothers. Since Ryker was Varian's near twin and they both look like Galen, my baby will also look like a Saar, like his father and half-uncle. Don't you see why that makes it even more imperative to rush? As far as everyone knows and will ever know, I've been living with *Ryker* as his wife. Who would believe this isn't his child? My hands are tied, Andrea. So many times Varian has said he had no choice in his actions. Well, this time he does, and so do I. But there is a time limit on him making it. I'm not to blame for getting pregnant at the wrong moment; he is. If he doesn't solve this complication, it will be the last one he makes in my life."

As they eased into orbit around Tartarus in the Androasian Empire, Varian confided in Nigel. "I don't know what, but something is up with Jana. She's been strange and distant ever since we left Darkar."

"Relax, Varian," he attempted to comfort him. "It's natural for her to be nervous. Think about what she's gone through, first with your impersonation of Ryker, then her demanding confrontations with Faeroe and Taemin. Also, she's been locked in her quarters to avoid her old friends because she's here as Ryker's widow while traveling with her ex-lover. Give her time to settle down. I'm sure things will be fine. So is Andrea. She likes you and she's working hard on Jana to influence her in your favor."

"I wish I were as confident as you and Andrea are about us, and thanks for the help; it appears I'm in desperate need of all I can get."

The two men stopped talking when Jana arrived in the shuttle bay. Nigel smiled and greeted her, and she did the same.

"The casket is loaded and everything's ready," Varian said. "Let's get this task finished so you can get home. After all you've endured, I'm sure you need to rest. Any questions or worries?"

Jana took a deep breath and released it. "None that words can change at this time. Let's do it, Commander Saar. *Kadim Maal* is waiting for us."

Chapter Eighteen

Jana was relieved when *Effecta* Maal was not hostile or hateful to Varian as, in a gentle tone, the Star Fleet officer explained the circumstances surrounding Ryker's "death." The silver-haired man was somber and near dazed with grief. Jana empathized with his pain, as she had lost her own family and understood what he must be feeling. She did not try to withdraw her hand from his as he gripped it for comfort.

After what "Ryker" had told him about Taemin, Maal was open about his suspicions of the Pyropean prince. "If he is guilty, you must punish him for your brother's death. It is your right and place to do so, as I am too old to seek the truth and subsequent vengeance. Promise me you will do this, Varian, and I shall grant you the treaty the Alliance seeks."

"I swear it upon my life and honor, sir, not because of the treaty but because he was my brother. If any man is to blame for Ryker's death, he will suffer." *And I have, more than you can imagine.*

"My grandson was right when he said both of you had

changed. You are responsible for saving his and Jana's lives when Taemin closed his treacherous trap around them. I shall remember that deed always. We shall never be enemies again. The past is dead, with the cherished flame of my soul, as he desired it and spoke it to me on his last visit and the last time I heard his voice the day of his death. After Taemin and Jurac learn we have made peace, they will offer no threat to the Alliance who befriended my grandson. He will become more than willing to sign a treaty, too. My grandson cut Pyropea off from Trilabs; do not forget that, my sweet Jana."

"I will remember, sir, and honor my husband's wishes." She told him about Taemin's attempted visit and threats, and how she had thwarted him with the aid of Kagan, the head of her security. She told him how kind *Avatar* Faeroe had been, and the others, as well. "Ryker was widely respected and admired, sir, here and in Maffei. Many have sent their condolences. I brought them for you to read and keep."

The older man asked Jana to stay for a visit after Varian departed.

She hoped her excuse sounded plausible. "Ryker would want me to take care of Darkar, sir, at this critical moment. So many people depend on his products and weapons, and he was careful with his great responsibilities. Too, there are several research projects in progress and at crucial stages. He taught me everything about his work and customers. I can and will carry on his important work and make certain no one forgets it or him. He has left a great legacy behind, one I must continue in his name. I'll visit again as soon as things are settled there."

The clear oblong casket was brought inside and placed next to the one which allegedly held Shara's body. The display room where both would lie in state echoed with their footsteps and voices. Jana was relieved, for Maal's sake, that someone had dressed Ryker in his royal robe and placed his gold circlet on his blond head. The medallion around his neck rested on his lifeless chest. He looked handsome and serene, and perhaps his tortured soul was finally at peace.

As the three seemed to honor a short silence, she reflected

on how she had met him and what had transpired between them months ago. The stranger lying there was her husband, and she was a widow. If he hadn't tried to slay his half brother, he might still be alive and her life would be very different. She recalled how Varian had impersonated him, how that robe and circlet and medallion had looked on her love. Yet, it was as if she were gazing at the man she had spent the last few months with, and that feeling was unsettling. If it hadn't been a ruse, the child in her body could have been his . . . She couldn't help but think that if not for Canissia and Ryker's evil, she would be happily married to Varian and be far from this awful episode and its possibly damaging repercussions. Or she could be dead if Shara had succeeded in the attempt on her life. If the princess had slain her and if Varian had died at Ryker's hand, Shara would be living as Jana Greyson Triloni at her son's side this very moment. So much suffering had been endured by many because of those two insane people. Perhaps God, in his infinite mercy and wisdom, had ended their malicious reigns.

Jana cast aside her troubling thoughts. She looked at the aged ruler. Maal was quiet; he seemed crushed, defeated, very old and tired. She watched him stroke the transparent covering as if touching his grandson's body. The agony in his voice and faded green eyes made her want to cry.

"The last cherished flame of my soul has been extinguished. They are both gone and I am alone. Soon, the Triloni bloodline will cease to exist after hundreds of years of ruling the Androasian Empire. I am old and weary. How I wish you two had been married longer, my sweet Jana, and had been given the time to birth an heir to assuage the pain in my heart."

Jana's heart lurched in panic. She envisioned a terrible battle over the child she was carrying, between father and acclaimed great-grandfather. She couldn't let that happen; Varian couldn't let it happen! The conflict between the Trilonis and Tabrizes had almost shattered Varian's life and provoked intergalactic war. Those five people had compelled the charade and might ruin her future. She wanted to hate them and curse them, but what good would that do, especially now? Two of them were dead and powerless, Maal was a broken and enfeebled man, and the Tabrizes would be weakened or defeated within weeks. Yet, that didn't change the damage they had caused to her life; only Varian could do that, and if he didn't do it soon, it would be too late to matter. Her pregnancy would be exposed in a few months, and another complication would stand between them.

Varian pretended not to notice how strange Jana looked and acted. Somehow he knew it wasn't the result of the arduous pretense at hand. Something else, something serious, was gnawing at her. Later, he must urge her to confide in him. For now, he must concentrate on the task before him. "After years of being foolish enemies, *Effecta* Maal, my brother became my friend. I shall mourn his loss and the years we will never share. He was a good man, sir, and will be long remembered. I'm only glad his death was swift and painless. I'm also glad he found happiness and peace during his final days."

Maal looked at the quiet beauty nearby who was gazing at his grandson with sadness in her eyes. "He was happy because of you, my sweet Jana. I am grateful you entered his life to share it, if only for a brief time."

Jana felt she must respond. "I shall miss him, sir. He became a very important part of my life. It will not be the same without him. I will not allow his memory to die with him. I am sure the entire Tri-Galaxy will mourn his passing. I am here today because of what he was and did. I shall never forget him or his effect on my life."

Maal embraced her for a long while, and both were teary-eyed. Jana did not glance at Varian as she pretended to grieve over the loss of his fierce enemy and archrival, the man he had secretly slain months ago. She knew it must be horrible to be forced to kill your own brother and Varian Saar was a man of deep and strong emotions.

Dakin Agular entered the oppressive room, his alert gaze taking in the three people present. He nodded a greeting to Varian and smiled at Jana. He approached the ruler and bowed.

"I came to see if there is anything you need, *Effecta* Maal, and to pay my respects to Prince Ryker. His loss is a great and painful one for all of Androas. You should be proud of him; he died seeking peace and honor for himself and his people."

"Peace, yes, my grandson wanted peace. I am too old and tired and sick at heart to seek it for the Empire. You must do it for us, Agular. Tomorrow, I will proclaim you my successor and you will carry out my grandson's last dream, his last request to me. Go, speak with Ryker's brother on the matter before he departs; I grant you that power and authority. I must be alone for a while with those I loved and have lost."

Agular, Varian, and Jana were astonished by the ruler's unexpected words and hasty plans to abdicate! Jana realized he was giving over the reins of his empire to Agular, a man Varian and Jana knew wanted peace, wanted one of the valuable treaties Varian had sought with his charade.

Jana's heart was plagued by anguish as the old man wept over the two glassed tombs. Her gaze drifted over both deceased people. She wondered what Maal would do if he learned it was not his daughter's body resting there, and if he learned of Ryker and Shara's incestuous affair for seven years while everyone believed her dead. That discovery would hurt him deeply. She couldn't help but hope it wouldn't be necessary to expose such evil to him or to anyone. Varian had told her while shuttling down that this wasn't the time to reveal the treachery to the suffering ruler, if that time ever came. Not only because it might upset Maal and provoke him into doing something rash, but because of Varian's compassion even to an ex-enemy. Maal, Ryker, and Shara had made Varian's life a torment, and Jana was glad he wasn't being vengeful when it was within his power and means to do so. She left the room with her true love and Agular to await Maal's presence in another area while the two men discussed peace.

An hour later, Maal sent a servant to bring Varian to him for a private talk. An anxious Jana remained with the new ruler. They conversed and sipped hot tea while she tried to look as relaxed as possible.

Varian followed the woman to Maal's suite. He found the older man slumped in a large chair, which made him appear small and frail. "You sent for me, sir?" he asked softly. Pale-green eyes lifted to meet vivid blue ones, and the agony in them tugged at Varian's heart. "I wish there was something I could say or do to ease your pain, sir, but I can think of nothing. I'm sorry."

Maal straightened in his chair. "There *is* something important and generous you can do for me and your brother."

"What, sir?" he asked curiously. "Tell me and I will try my best to accomplish it."

Maal read honesty and sincerity in the man who reflected his grandson's true image. His voice was low and strained by emotion as he spoke. "In the days since I was given this tormenting news, I have thought much and I have searched my heart and mind for the right thing to do. I entreat you to protect his wife, our sweet Jana, our ray of sunlight."

Varian took a seat on a firm ottoman so the ruler wouldn't have to crane his neck to meet his gaze. Nor did he want to tower over the man like a lingering threat. "I will, sir; you have my solemn word on it."

"Do more than guard her life and holdings. Until her grief passes, be her friend and defender. Afterward, make her smile and be happy again."

Varian's suspense increased. Could it be that the seeds he had sown many times and in many ways in Maal's mind had flowered? But so fast and in this wintry season? "What do you mean?"

"Ryker told me of your love for her and how she came to be his. He loved her and would desire her happiness, as I do. She was a good wife to my cherished grandson. She filled his last days with joy and peace. She must not suffer endlessly over his tragic death." Maal paused a few moments to let his faded emerald gaze roam Varian's face. "I never noticed how like him you are in so many ways. We were too busy hating and battling to get to know each other. I became accustomed to his disguise, for I rarely saw him without it since he was a child when his mother concealed his Saarian image to ease her pain. Each time I saw you, I saw Galen, the foe who had taken Shara from us."

Varian became nervous at those words until Maal continued.

"You are not your father; you are Ryker's half brother. I know you did not give Jana away; nor did Ryker kidnap her. He was unable to return her or tell her the truth after she captured his heart. You must understand and forgive his painful deed against you."

If you have an advantage, Varian, press it, but gently and carefully. "I did so when we reconciled, sir. I saw how much he truly loved Jana and I realized all they had done for each other. When I lost her, I could not battle him for her return against his powerful threats. But their union became a good one, so I was compelled to leave them in peace. I could not bring myself to destroy her new life. Nor can she be faulted for turning to him when she did not know of my love and need for her. I have only myself to blame for our misunderstanding. But why are you telling me this today?"

"You are the only man with enough power, skills, strength, and love to protect our Jana from being harmed or tricked by the countless men who will pursue her now that she is his widow, a rich and free woman. She was stolen from you in spite while you two were enemies, but you became friends and true brothers. You made a great sacrifice for your world and her by not challenging him for her return. For that you should be rewarded."

Varian's heart pounded in anticipation. *Please end this torment for us*, he prayed in earnest. He waited for an answer to his plea.

"Perhaps it is fate's way of finally uniting a Saar and a Triloni as it should have been long ago. Perhaps your father was forced by an unknown power or threat to give up Shara as you were forced to give up Jana. They are both dead now and the truth is lost forever. Ryker said there had been too much anguish and to let the past die. He said you must be the man to take his place with her. I beg you, never tell her how she came to be my grandson's wife. I beg you, do not tarnish his glowing image in her eyes. Now that he is gone and she is free again, you could destroy his golden memory with the dark truth. She loved you once and may do so again. Give her time to recover from her loss and pain, then woo her with gentleness and patience. Do this for me and Ryker and I promise to speak to her in your favor. In time, she may forget and forgive what she sees as your betrayal, for she has a tender and peaceful heart. Will you do this good and merciful deed for us? Do you still love her and want her?"

It was difficult for Varian not to break into joyful smiles of relief. After a proper mourning period, Jana could return to him with Maal's blessing! He kept his expression and tone controlled. "Yes, sir, I do love her. I will do as you ask and as my brother wished."

"You are a good man, Varian Saar. I am grateful. Now, my grandson can rest in peace. So can I when my time comes to join him and my child."

At last, my love can come home to me in a few months . . .

Jana knew the *Wanderlust* would reach Darkar within hours so she needed to relate her news to Varian. He had revealed what Maal had said to him, results of "Ryker's" clever enticements. But news of the baby would change Maal's mind and heart, and there was no time to provide a mourning period. She had listened in amazement and had been disappointed to have that obstacle removed at a time when it couldn't matter. She had disappointed Varian, too, when she hadn't leapt into his arms and agreed it made everything safe and right for them. Today, now, she would explain.

They sat in his quarters as they had done many times, with him as himself and with him as Ryker. So much had happened in this masculine suite and on this starship. Those contradictory times filled her troubled mind, as did the necessary ruse with his old crew. She had confined herself in the guest quarters down the hall to avoid the men and women she had spent so much time with in the past. She could not bring herself to play Ryker's grieving widow before them, especially in light of a possible marriage to Varian. For now, she must allow the misled crew to think what they did about her and her astonishing marriage to Ryker Triloni when most of them had expected one to their commander and friend. The few times she had seen them, all parties had been pleasant but reserved, as if neither side knew what to say or how to behave under the circumstances. She had given herself time to settle down before she came to visit with Varian today to expose their new predicament.

Varian left his desk to take a seat beside her on the short sofa where she was almost curled into a ball. Her right arm rested across its back and her cheek lay upon it. She had seemed nervous when she arrived, so he had given her a few minutes to calm herself. He had also stalled asking the reason for her unexpected visit, as he dreaded to learn why she had been in a somber mood for a week. He studied her serious expression, but she didn't return his gaze or even glance at him. "You're so quiet and withdrawn these days, Moonbeam. You haven't been yourself since I returned to Darkar."

Without looking at him or lifting her head, she asked, "What is being myself, Varian? I've changed so much since meeting you that I don't even know who or what I am anymore. I was just thinking about how much happened to me and between us on this ship, in this very room."

Her tone didn't sound promising. "It wasn't all bad, was it, Jana?"

"No, we've had many good times, too."

He was relieved she admitted that much, but he was still worried. "What's bothering you, Moonbeam? Tell me, Jana, please. You're scaring me with this chilly distance."

"You don't fear anyone or anything."

He lay his hand atop hers. "I fear losing you and what we had."

She lifted her head from her arm and gave a reply he didn't expect or want in response. "You have one treaty down and one to go. Maal has stepped down, so he won't be any more trouble. You've won that battle. Soon, you'll go to Jurad's and do the same. Peace will rule the Tri-Galaxy and your charade will have succeeded. You should be proud and happy."

His strong fingers curled around hers and he looked deeply into her sad eyes. "I can be if it doesn't cost me the only woman I love."

"Do you truly, I mean truly, love me and want me?"

"Yes, Jana, I do. If you doubt everything else I say, believe that."

Jana freed her hand and stood to move around while she spoke. "That's the big problem between us: trust—being able to believe you after all the lies and deceptions. More than once you have broken my heart and spirit with deceptions and made me journey through what can only be described as the depths of hades. Because of you and with you, I've experienced passion and anguish, good and bad, joy and sadness, love and betrayal, lies and the truth. I can not guess what will come next; that doubt torments me and keeps us apart."

She began to pace again. "Trust, why does it have to be such a fragile thing, so easy to destroy, so difficult to retrieve or rebuild?" she murmured almost to herself. "Perhaps," she answered her own question, "trust is crucial because it makes everything else happen between two people, makes everything else worthwhile and special. Maybe it's hard to yield to you because I'm afraid if I do, you will use me and hurt me again."

She halted once more to lock their gazes so he could grasp her predicament. "You're like a powerful drug, Varian Saar, one I became addicted to, one I craved more than even my freedom and pride, one I needed so badly that I was willing to do anything to have it, to forgive you of any offense so I wouldn't lose the source of it. But when you convinced me that what I believed we had shared was only a cruel delusion, I struggled hard and got over you." She saw him flinch and wince as if she had struck him a painful blow. "Everything was going well until you exposed your ruse and there I was, back in my old pattern again. I finally forced myself to see and admit the truth, that perhaps you aren't good for me."

"Please don't say that, Jana. Give me—"

"No, you give me a chance to finish my explanation. I believe you do love me in your own way. But if that love is destructive and selfish, I can't take it or share it. You told me you didn't understand my feelings and why I saw the charade as an unforgivable betrayal. If I'm making any sense and you're listening, truly listening with your heart, do you now comprehend my dilemma?"

Varian felt as if he'd had the wind kicked out of him. He couldn't argue with the truth. "Yes, Jana, and I'm sorry. But I have learned from my many mistakes."

"Have you, Varian? That's the proof I've been seeking. Only time can answer that vital question for me and we don't have any more of that."

He panicked. Did she mean . . . "Jana—"

She cut him off again in a gentle tone. "Listen to me while I'm brave enough to get this in the open before we reach Darkar. You've done everything within your power to save your world, to prove your love and loyalty to it, even to the extent of making personal sacrifices."

Varian had to jump in before she said what he feared was coming. "You're right, Jana; and I could have done things differently. If I had done so, I would have saved us a lot of anguish. I made a terrible mistake and I'm sorry. The course of action you described to me on Luz could have worked, but at the time, I didn't think of it. I wish I had so I wouldn't have turned you against me. I've really made a mess of our relationship. If it were possible to turn back time, I would. I had to carry out the self-destructive plan I put into motion. Obviously nobody else thought of your idea either or they would have suggested it. But I take sole blame for my actions. I guess men don't think the same way women do; you use your hearts and we use our heads. Maybe if we let our emotions influence us more, we would make better decisions. If you can't forgive me and take me back, I'll understand. *Kahala* knows I've given you ample reasons to distrust and hate me. I wish that wasn't so!"

Jana was moved by his torment and confession. She smiled and jested with him to ease his suffering. "Are you giving up on me, Rogue Saar?"

"*Kahala*, no, not until I'm forced to eat sour defeat. And even then, I would always be there for you, Moonbeam."

"Good," she murmured with another smile. "Now, don't interrupt again or I'll gag you. Where was I?" She found her mental place, repeated the sentence she had used before he had halted her, then continued. "Now, I want you to do the same for me, for us. I want you to use your cunning mind to figure out how you can finish this mission in no more than two weeks so we can get married." Her last few words caught him off guard and he stared at her as if thinking he must not have heard her correctly. "It's then or never, Varian. If you truly love me and want me, you'll find a way to succeed with me, to prove your love and your loyalty to our relationship. We marry in two weeks, or we never marry. Is that being clear enough for you?"

"Marry in two weeks? You're giving me a deadline to prove myself?"

She was glad he hadn't said "ultimatum." "Yes. That's as long as I can wait, as long as I *will* wait. I swear it, Varian, so take this seriously."

"I can see you're serious. Maybe Maal will understand and forgive our impatience. I'm leaving immediately, so as soon as I finish with Jurad and Cass, there's no problem. I need three or four weeks at most. We need those weeks, Moonbeam, to fool everyone into thinking we resumed our relationship while we were working together. With Maal's change of heart, we—"

"We can't wait that long. I can't wait that long. I'll be showing soon."

"Showing? Showing what?"

Just spit it out, J.G., and get his reaction. "A continuously rounding belly that will soon tell the world I'm expecting a baby."

Varian sat up straight, braced his palms on his parted knees, and gaped at her. "A . . . baby? But you . . . and Ryker never. . ."

"The baby will favor Ryker. That is what's been troubling me."

Varian's heart almost stopped beating; it altered to a heavy thudding in his chest. He stared at her as he wondered if a tape had been missing from his brother's . . . He calmed himself and smiled. In a gentle tone, he said, "You must be mistaken, Moonbeam. It's just the tension you're under. You can't be pregnant."

"The test was done twice. I am definitely pregnant."

"You can't be, Jana. You've been with me for almost five months. You would be showing now if you were that far—or more—along. And you had your menses on the return voyage from Earth."

"That's right; I did, my last one. I'm less than two months pregnant. The baby is why I couldn't let Tris do the *Rendelar* procedure on me."

"You didn't have it? You and Tris never told me. I assumed . . ."

"It seems, my fertile space pirate, during all the commotion of your glorious mission, you forgot your last *Liex* treatment."

"Me? Are you saying the baby is . . ." Varian glanced at his wrist. His computer band with his schedule was missing. It was in his desk, had been in his desk for five months, when *Liex* was due every three! Astonishment flooded his body and gaze. "It's mine!" He broke into a smile that kept broadening and softening and glowing more every second. He leapt to his feet, hurried to her, and embraced her. He cupped her face and covered it with kisses. "It's my baby," he said with joy and pride surging through him. "That's wonderful news, Jana. *Kahala*, be thanks. A baby . . ."

"*Is* it wonderful news?"

His happiness and pride increased by the minute, as did his relief. "For me, it is, my love. My first child. *Our* first child . . ."

Jana separated them. "No, Varian, it's Ryker Triloni's child."

His smile faded and he studied her. "What do you mean, Jana? It's mine. Ours. You just admitted it."

"In the eyes of the law and public, as of this moment, it's Ryker's. Are you forgetting your little charade? You've had me living as Ryker's wife for months. If we don't move fast and cover our tracks, the timing of the baby's birth will proclaim him as my husband's. Unless we get married soon, let me hide out on Altair toward the end, then withhold news of the baby's birth for two months, everyone will think your child is Ryker's. In two weeks, I'll be two months pregnant; that's all the leeway we can afford or his size and appearance won't dupe anyone."

"*He*? Is it a boy? A son?"

"I don't know that much yet. I didn't do that test. I just don't want to call my baby 'it.' Do you see why I have to give you a deadline to make a commitment to us? If we want everyone to believe the baby is yours, it's vital, because he will favor Ryker, as well as you and Galen."

"I see your point," he admitted with reluctance.

"If you don't want your child's paternity questioned and gossiped about, finish up your duty fast and marry me. Do it no matter what anyone says, including Maal. If you don't do it in two weeks, I'll know you don't truly love me and that your duty is more important to you than me and our baby. Tris said it happened on Luz, where you gave me the truth as well as your seed."

"Tris knows? Why didn't he tell me? Why didn't you tell me sooner?"

She explained the shocking discovery and her motives for swearing her three friends to secrecy. "That's why Tris gave Andrea *Rendelar*. He and Martella knew how upset I was and knew I needed to talk openly with my best friend after I learned how careless you had been. Tell me, Varian, was it another trick, one you carried out intentionally to tie me to you?''

He tried to pull her back into his arms, but she eluded his reach. ''Don't do that. I can't think when I'm that close to you. I need to keep a clear head to get this matter finally settled.''

''I swear I didn't do this on purpose, Moonbeam. But I admit your news makes me very happy. I promise I will return to you within two weeks and we'll get married.''

''You promised to marry me before and didn't. If you do honor your vow this time, Ryker will have an heir, Maal great-grandchild, and Androas a future ruler. If the baby exposed and accepted as my *husband*'s, he will be born a reared that way. We'll live—''

''You can't do that, Jana. It's my child, *mine*. He'll be Saar.''

''How could you prove that was true without exposing th Ryker's been dead for months and you were not only imperso ating him but the one sleeping with me? I daresay that stunni revelation would spark new feuds with Maal and the Tabriz and would destroy all the good work you've done. You se my cunning and reckless captor, you've entrapped yourself a our child along with me this time. It's up to you to make certa we escape.''

''Are you trying to punish me, Jana?''

''No, just open your eyes to the truth. I will not allow my child to become an intergalactic joke and have people wondering if he's Ryker's child or yours. My heavens, Varian, there isn't even a tiny fraction of a chance he'll favor his mother. By genetically favoring his father, he'll automatically favor Ryker. In any other case or at any other time, that wouldn't matter. In this one, it does very much matter. We can't wait long. I won't wait.''

''Are you angry because I got you pregnant by accident?''

''I believe it was an honest mistake.''

''Thanks, Moonbeam.'' He eyed her abdomen where his child was living and growing. ''Are you all right, Jana? How do you feel? Is there anything you need or want? Shouldn't you sit down and rest? I'll have to study up on this condition."

Jana laughed in amusement. "I'm fine. I'm pregnant, not ill."

"You should have told me sooner, Moonbeam. I wouldn't have let you go to Maal's or deal with Taemin alone. You could have gotten too upset or been injured. All of this tension can't be good for you and our child. I don't want you taking any more risks, woman."

"You've been risking my life for months. But I guess it's different to imperil your child's well-being while I'm carrying him."

"That isn't what I meant. I was always there to protect you. Kagan will guard you while I'm gone."

"So I'm always safe with you? You're invincible?"

He grimaced. "No, the two times Taemin snared me proves that isn't so. I could never connect him with that trap just before Cass kidnapped you, but I can with that last one. You're right; I've endangered us many times. I've been a fool, Jana. I thought I could save everything and everyone by myself, and believed it was my duty to try. That was stupid and vain and wrong. Is the baby why you've finally agreed to marry me?"

"That's a quick change of subject."

"Is he the only reason you're coming back to me?"

"I was angry when Tris told me the big news. I thought you knew and that's why you had agreed to the *Rendelar*, because it couldn't be done with me pregnant. I suspected you'd impregnated me on purpose, and the timing couldn't be worse. Once I got over the initial shock, I felt I had misjudged you. But I don't want my child's paternity to come under a cloud. Can't you imagine what Maal will do when he finds out I'm expecting? He's already going to be angry over the fact that there will be no mourning period for his grandson. I wish we had time to fake a new romance or make up but we don't, so we'll deal with the repercussions as they arrive. If you can't solve our problem in two weeks because of me and the baby, then do it to protect all you've accomplished."

"I'll do it for us, Jana; for you, for our child, not for my mission. If my work comes unraveled because we marry so soon, so be it. I'll deal with trouble later or let someone else do so for a change. The fate of Maffei doesn't rest solely in my hands. I thought that at one time, but no longer. I have you, the baby, and our future to think about; that's my first priority now. But you didn't answer me: Are you marrying me only because of the baby? Have I killed your love for me? Have I lost—"

Nigel interrupted on the communicator. "Varian, we're orbiting Darkar and ready to shuttle down. We only have a few hours before we leave for Pyropea. Do you need to wait a while before heading down?"

"It seems Nigel is eager to see Andrea before departure," Jana said. "Why don't we help the lovers by hurrying?"

Varian went to his desk. "Nigel, we'll be there in a minute." He looked back at Jana. "You're evading an answer, Moonbeam. Or is your refusal supposed to reveal your affirmative responses?"

Jana sent him a seductive smile. "A long time ago, we made a fate-sealing bargain in this room. Let's make another one today. You return and marry me in two weeks and I'll tell you the whole truth. If you don't, my answer won't matter, will it?"

After Varian had a private talk with his grandfather to tell *Kadim* Tirol Trygue about the baby, he and Nigel left Darkar. Varian had told Jana how happy and pleased the ruler was about the exciting event. He had chuckled when he related that Tirol had "ordered" him to make certain he was back with Jana in two weeks and that he was looking forward to having a new granddaughter-in-law very soon. Tirol sent his love, good wishes, and thanks for the excellent job she had done. He also promised to do "anything and everything necessary" to make certain there were no problems to halt their marriage or to shadow their child's identity.

The moment the men were gone, Andrea asked Jana how things had gone. "Nigel is so excited for you two. We'll be his godparents, I hope. I'm so pleased for you two. Nigel even mentioned us having a child as soon as possible. People say babies are contagious, or infectious or something like that, to women. But there's nothing like a little one to also stir a man's thoughts in that direction."

The two good friends shared laughter. "The baby is settled and so is marriage, but what about a confession of love? Did you do it?"

"No."

Before she could explain, Andrea shrieked her displeasure. "Whyever not, Jana?"

"It might do Varian a world of good to worry, as he's made me do plenty of times. He takes for granted I'll always forgive and forget, always take him back no matter what he does. Let him experience how it feels not to know the truth and to fear losing me. Maybe he'll come to understand my feelings and comprehend all he's put me through. If he learns a valuable lesson, he won't be tempted to do it again. Right?"

Andrea smiled and nodded. "This time, I agree."

Jana laughed and gave her a playful punch. "Finally, back on my side, you redheaded traitor."

"I'm on *both* of your sides," Andrea clarified. "I want you two back together where you belong."

"If Varian keeps his promise this time, we will be."

Andrea turned serious. "What if he can't make it back in two weeks?"

"Then, his delay will answer my question of his top priority. Remember that old adage: 'Actions speak louder than words.' This time, they will or my name isn't Jana Greyson."

"It's not," Andrea quipped and giggled.

"Don't point out my error; that slip could be a bad omen."

"Have faith, Jana, your dreams will come true, just as mine have. You do think they'll be safe in that enemy territory, don't you?"

"Taemin is bold and cunning, but he's not a fool. And Jurad certainly isn't one. They wouldn't dare harm Varian on an official Alliance visit, and positively not on the heels of Taemin's last two fiascos concerning Ryker. Varian will warn Jurad of the consequences of refusing to make a new treaty with Maffei. He'll tell him of the new one with Androas, which should spur Jurad into rapid action and compliance. And he'll make sure Taemin is very nervous about being connected to Ryker's death."

"What about those journals and tapes you mentioned to me?"

"Varian has clips from them to use, all disfavoring Taemin. Would you believe on two of them he mentions a possible assassination of his father? That will come as a shock to Jurad. Poor Taemin, he's in for big trouble."

"Is he really as handsome as Martella told me?"

"Oh, yes. He looks like one of those viking heroes on the cover of a romance novel: bronzed skin, deep gray eyes, tall, muscular, strong features, and long blond hair flying in the wind. But his eyes are cold, piercing, and secretive. He has this way of looking at you that makes you feel icy inside. I don't like being near the top of his list of enemies, especially now that I'm pregnant."

"Maybe he'll be put out of commission by his angry father."

"Even so, we're safe. Darkar is unapproachable, and Kagan is here."

"Good. I like him, and he has a tiny crush on you."

"No, he doesn't. Kagan is just impressed by all I've done for this ruse and he's grateful to me. When he came here, I suppose he was expecting just a dumb girl who used to be a *charl*."

"But he discovered you have brains and courage besides beauty. How nice," the redhead purred in a thick southern accent, then giggled again.

"Kagan is very nice, and a perfect gentleman, Andrea McKay Soon-to-be-Sanger. I see we're in a bubbly mood tonight. I don't suppose those two hours in your bedroom with Nigel had anything to do with it?"

Andrea sighed dreamily. "Absolutely. Oh, Jana, he's wonderful. Nigel said he would call on the *telecom* when they left Pyropea."

"They still have to report to Star Base. And there's the matter of Segall to handle. They're going to coerce him into retiring to avoid a nasty scandal and possible criminal charges. I've never liked him, but I hate to see him hurt by his daughter's treacheries. I'm sure that news will be crushing. Supreme Commander Breccia Sard is taking his place, and Varian is to take Brec's. At least he was until the baby came up."

"Nigel said they were also going after that Canissia bitch. If they haven't found her yet, how do they expect to locate her in a week or less?"

"That's my thought exactly and why I issued my deadline. I'm not going to sit here getting plump and waiting to get married while Varian chases that witch around the Tri-Galaxy. Let someone else capture her. I don't think I've ever met a more vicious, sadistic, and vindictive woman."

Andrea recalled Jana's kidnapping. "It's too bad for you she had the means to carry out her spite on you. I wonder why she would keep chasing Varian when he's made it so clear he doesn't want her."

"Because she's too conceited to believe it."

"Well, I hope my path never crosses with hers."

Tris and Martella arrived and halted the private conversation. The four sat at the dinner table a long time chatting, laughing, and enjoying themselves. Plans for three imminent marriages and the baby's birth were discussed.

As Jana went to bed that night, she stroked her lower abdomen. "Soon, my little one," she murmured, "your father will make his final choice. Let's both pray it's the right one. Your mommy will work hard helping Uncle Tris and Aunt Martella in the labs so time will pass faster and easier. Two weeks, little one, and Daddy will be home."

But two busy weeks passed with no Varian Saar. During a break from their tasks, Jana and Andrea talked in the complex lounge.

"Where is he, Andrea?" Jana asked in near panic. "Why doesn't he come back or at least call me? His deadline is up in seven measly hours. I'm worried and scared."

"Don't be, Jana; he'll be here by midnight."

"What if he's calling my bluff? Testing me?"

"He wouldn't do that. Besides, Nigel promised to get him back on time, come hell or high water."

"Unless his all-fired important duty calls."

"Unless it's life-or-death, he won't answer."

"I hope you're right."

"He contacted you after his visit with Ruler Jurad. He had a few things left to do at Star Base before galloping home. He called from there, too."

"Yes, and everything was handled except for the Canissia matter. If he's taken off after her and is delayed, I'll strangle both of them. Time is of the essence for us to get married."

Andrea tried to distract Jana. "Varian had great political and personal successes with Ruler Jurad. Their meeting ended with Prince Taemin's disgrace and exile from Pyropea."

"When Jurad can locate the sneak devil and carry out his royal command. I can't imagine it being against their law for a prince to be executed or at least imprisoned for his crimes. Heavens above, Andrea, he committed treason and would have committed assassination if Varian hadn't exposed him. How could he steal a starship and vanish? Wasn't he being guarded?"

"It seems mighty careless to lose a dangerous prisoner. Varian said he would give us the details after he returned. We're not to worry, Jana; Ruler Jurad has his forces in hot pursuit and we're safe here."

"I'll feel better when he is exiled." She shifted topics to her obesssion. "What could be keeping Varian? The Segall matter has been handled. He's filed his reports. He has his two treaties. We've almost finished our job here. We've had no problems over Ryker's death. Maal is retired and is our ally; he's even given his blessing for our marriage, though he doesn't know it's to be this soon. I doubt that news is going to sit well, but so be it."

"You're working yourself into a tizzy for nothing. You'll see."

"I don't know, Andrea; I'm having bad vibes, very bad vibes. He was using his last two days to track down a clue about that alien witch."

"I bet he's planning a surprise grand entrance at eleven fifty-nine," Andrea surmised. "He might be orbiting Darkar right now, pacing his decks in anticipation of proving himself to you."

"I hope so. Otherwise, I'll have to honor my deadline, won't I? If not, he'll never take me seriously again. Let's get back to work and finish up before he arrives. He'll be here by midnight. He wouldn't dare disappoint me."

Kagan entered the research lab where Jana and the others were working to finalize two valuable experiments Ryker had begun months ago. She glanced up from the high-powered microscope.

"You have a visitor," Kagan informed her. "Maal Triloni is passing on his way to visit with *Kadim* Tirol on Rigel. He says he doesn't have much time and doesn't want to come down to the place where the cherished flame of his soul lived and worked. He's requested for you to come up in his shuttle for a short visit. It's on its way down. I thought you'd want to comply this last time. Am I wrong? Do you want us to come up with an excuse?"

Jana sighed in dismay. "I really don't have a choice. We don't want to spark any suspicion in him at this late date. Have you heard from Varian?"

Ignorant of Jana's deadline threat, Kagan replied, "Not yet, but he might be on his way. From his last message, everything is finished except for that Garthon business. For some reason, he's out of communication. It could be an intentional blackout."

Or something to use as an excuse for missing the deadline. "Maal is no longer a ruler, but he still has access to plenty of power; he shouldn't be offended or angered into calling upon it. He's been kind and good to me, so I must accept. I just wish Varian would contact us if he's going to be late. He promised to return by today."

Kagan saw how upset she was. "It could be a result of those solar flare-ups I see on the sensors," he suggested.

"That has a familiar and intrusive ring to it," she murmured in recall of another time long ago . . .

"If we were any closer or on the other side of Caguas, we might be experiencing difficulties, too. Don't worry, Jana, he'll return soon."

As Tris and Martella questioned Kagan about the unexpected visit, Jana's distressed mind replied: *If only you knew how important it is for that to be today. I told him it wasn't too late for one last chance with me. I thought that was all he needed, but maybe I was wrong again. Can I only have you and depend on you, Commander Saar, until duty calls?*

When the others finished talking, she told the secret agent to contact Maal and tell him she would meet his shuttle and visit. "Just give me a few minutes to freshen up." She said to Andrea, "I'll take you with me to meet him. You can help keep the conversation light. Tris, can you take over here? The specimen and chemical are near merging point and need watching."

Tristan took over for Jana while she hurried to the house to change clothes, brush her hair, and check her cosmetics. Andrea did the same, eager to meet the galactic ruler of the Androasan Empire.

The two women joined two androids in black uniforms with the insignia of Androas on their chest areas. They told Kagan goodbye and entered the craft, then seated themselves inside and strapped the safety buckles. The shuttle took off and made a smooth and safe rendezvous with the large starship. Jana and Andrea were led down a long hallway by one of the mechanical beings. The unsuspecting females didn't know a drone was being released to continue registering a presence on Darkar's sensors while a cloaking device shielded the enemy ship as it departed.

"I'm taking a *Spacer* to Eire to see if I can get through this communications disruption," Varian told Nigel. "Maybe theirs isn't out. Jana must be worried by now. The deadline she set for me is up in three hours and there's no way we can leave the *Galactic Gem* in peril. Why did this emergency have to come along today of all days and with this particular ship! I have a bad feeling, my friend. You know what happened the last time this occurred; Jana almost died while we were trying to rescue her from Darkar, and we did lose Tesla."

As they walked down the hall, Nigel gripped Varian's shoulder in affection and encouragement. "Jana will understand why you were delayed, why we couldn't leave a ship in distress. The crew is being evacuated to the *Wanderlust* as fast as possible. The *Gem* could blow at any time with that unstable cargo of *Barine*. It'll take you at least two hours even in a *Spacer* to make Eire, and communications might be out there, too."

"It's a chance I have to take, Nigel. That woman is important to me; I can't risk losing her, baby or no baby. I hope she'll give me a reprieve when she hears why I couldn't get back on time."

"Especially since you dropped the search for Canissia and gave the assignment to other officers so you could reach her on schedule."

They entered the elevator and Varian gave orders to take them to the swift and agile fighter craft, just like the one that had exploded and killed Tesla Rilke minutes after delivering a dying Jana into Tris's care. That tragic accident still lacked an explanation, and probably always would.

"It seems my grand entrance was timed too close to my deadline. I was a fool to call it this close, Nigel. Some surprise!"

"If we hadn't been passing this area when the distress call was picked up, that ship and crew would be gone before another vessel arrived. Just a little later or earlier departure from Rigel and the *Gem* would be lost. We barely got their weak signal before communications went out, and I doubt anyone else received it. That explosion in her shuttle bay left them with no means of escape without our help. Rescue teams picking them up from the *jerri* hatch is slow work. I hope we can get them all out before we have to take off. We need a minimum of ten minutes to get out of her aftershock and shooting-debris range; that's cutting it close, very close."

"I know, Nigel," he muttered, relieved he had his old crew back with him to work on this dangerous mission. At least almost all: there was a different ships system's officer to take the traitorous Baruch's place, a new navigational/guidance officer to take the slain Tesla's station, and a temporary medical officer in Tristan's lab and sick bay.

The transportation apparatus ceased its sideways movement and headed downward to the take-off area for one of four *Spacers*.

"Their engineering officer is dead so I sent Braq over to see how much time we have left before we have to clear out," Varian told Nigel. "But this incident worries me. I can't explain, but I feel as if something is very wrong with Jana. It's as if I hear Shara and Ryker laughing and taunting me with the loss of Jana or my own death. You know the *Galactic Gem* was Father's old ship, the place where all the trouble began thirty-two years ago. It's as if Shara's wicked spirit is haunting her treacherous territory and she is lying in wait for me today. You know, of course, the *Gem* was decommissioned as a starship and converted into a transport seven years ago after

Father's murder by that insane bitch. Now, she's floating out there loaded with Ryker's *Barine*. It's as if she's itching to carry me into explosive oblivion with her or prevent me from making Jana's deadline. I feel trapped by all those evil ties to that ship. Something is telling me, warning me, to get clear of her and to check on Jana, immediately, old friend. I'll return in four hours at most and catch up with you. There's nothing I can do here but sweat and pace, so you're in charge. You're as qualified as I am to handle a rescue."

Communications Chief Vaiden Chaz signaled his superior, who responded from his moving location. "Commander Saar, Braq reports the *Galactic Gem*'s engineering section was severely damaged and is overheating at a swift rate. He says we have to be ready to get out of here fast. We have one hour maximum until she explodes. Ferris said he'll have the last surviving crewman aboard in fifty minutes or less if progress continues at the current rate, but he may not get the bodies out in time."

Varian acknowledged the messages and rapidly digested them. He ordered the elevator to take them to the bridge. "Things are going to start happening too fast for me to leave. To *Gehenna* with evil ghosts and bad luck! I must have faith in Jana and our love, and pray she's all right."

The door opened and Varian stepped onto the bridge of his ship. As was the procedure during emergencies, no one came to attention; they remained busy at their assigned stations.

"Vaiden, put us on alert status and keep working to restore our communications. As soon as Braq's aboard, tell him I want us ready to hit starlight speed on my command. Jarre, have the course laid in and be prepared to move at a moment's notice. We'll have no time to waste in getting out of here. Nigel, get me a report on injuries from Mirren. Ferris can inform me of casualties when he completes his task."

As Varian thought of Ferris Laus, he remembered the officer and his wife—Kathy, a *charl* from his initial Earth voyage and Jana's friend—were also expecting a baby. He had to make certain Ferris made it back alive from this mission. The same vas true of himself. He could succeed if Shara and Ryker vould stop grabbing at him. *Help me, Father, Mother; don't et that evil bitch and her spawn destroy me and Jana as she lestroyed you two.*

Varian continued with his orders. "We'll take the *Gem*'s crew back to Star Base, then head for Darkar. Maybe communications will be functioning again soon. If not, we can file a eport on this rescue when we reach base. We all had better oray nothing else goes wrong. Coran, run a check on ships systems to make sure we don't have problems anywhere. Keep alert and at the ready, men. We'll be cutting it close."

The daring and valiant rescue continued, as did Varian's eerie sensation that his love and their child were in great peril, while he was stranded a long way from them and in grave peril himself.

Chapter Nineteen

Varian stalked into Supreme Commander Breccia Sard's office with impatience glittering in his sapphire eyes. "You sent word by shuttle you wanted to see me immediately. What's up, Brec? I'm in a rush. As soon as all the *Gem*'s crew are down, I need to head for Darkar. In fact, I need to contact Jana right now. Our communications have been out since late yesterday and she must be worried sick. As we speak, Vaiden and his team are installing that new interference override system so this won't happen again. Surely a report can wait until I'm under way or until after I've spoken with her."

"You did an excellent job with the rescue, Varian, but that isn't why I sent for you," Sard began. "I'm afraid it's bad news about Jana. Kagan reported it to me late last night, but we couldn't reach you to pass it along."

Varian stared at his friend and superior. Surely Jana hadn't given up on him so soon after the deadline expired and left for Androas as she threatened. She wouldn't. She couldn't. "What

re you talking about, Brec? The baby? Has something hap-
ened to her or the baby?"

"Tirol told me that good news," the dark-haired man said, serious expression in his face. "Congratulations, but it has othing to do with your baby."

"Then what?" he asked quickly before Brec could continue.

"Jana and her friend were lured off Darkar and abducted by orces unknown. I have a search on for them and I've—"

"That's impossible!" Varian shouted as icy fingers of alarm ripped his heart. "Kagan's on security and Ryker's defense ystem is impenetrable. Who would dare attack there? How ould any force get through the energy shield and lasers or isable them?"

"There wasn't an attack. They were tricked into lowering heir defenses and leaving via shuttle to rendezvous with a vaiting ship."

"Tricked into leaving? How? With whom?"

"We don't know. The ship they entered simply vanished."

Varian's gaze narrowed. "I don't follow you. How could ey be tricked and not know who did it?"

"Let's get Kagan on the *telecom* and have a conference. He an report the situation better and you can ask questions."

Fear invaded Varian, soul deep, and began a terrifying siege. 'wice before he had almost lost Jana. He shouldn't have left er alone again, but he had believed her safe on Darkar with agan protecting her. If anything happened to her or their hild . . .

Varian called Nigel into the room and shared the grim news bout the women to his best friend. They took seats at the onference table before the large communication monitor.

When the connection was made, Varian leaned forward and emanded to know what had happened. "Where are Jana and ndrea?" he questioned Kagan impatiently. "Who took them? Vhy did you let them leave with strangers, enemies?" He oticed that Kagan's seawater eyes were filled with distress nd frustration. His auburn hair was mussed from running fingers through it, and he looked exhausted, as if he had gotten little or no sleep during the episode.

"I'm sorry, Varian, but we never suspected anything was wrong. I notified Brec and he's begun a search and tightened the boundary patrols. We don't know who took them, where they're heading, or why they were snatched. I shouldn't have told her to go."

Varian shuddered and grimaced as a sensation of déjà vu stormed his body. Gone without a trace or clue, just like before . . . "You aren't making sense, Kagan. Who tricked you into lowering the defenses and who carried them off? And how could they do it without a battle from you?"

Kagan related how the startling event began. "They gave the correct identification code, so I let the shuttle land," he said at the end of his explanation. "The markings on the craft, uniforms, and insignias were Androasian. They even used Maal's pet name for Ryker. They stayed on my sensors, so I didn't realize there was trouble until it was too late to stop them."

"Why would Maal abduct Jana?"

"I don't think he did, Varian. He—"

"But you spoke with Maal; you said he made the request."

"No, his security chief did; that's common practice. I had no reason to doubt it was Maal, and neither did Jana. A short visit, the android said."

Varian was angered by the agent's lack of caution. "So you allowed Jana and Andrea to walk into a trap?" He saw Kagan react as if he had delivered a physical blow to a man already down.

"Yes. They left about five-thirty. When hours passed, I became concerned but couldn't raise them on communications. I thought it was because of those solar flare-ups until a call came through at nine. That made me suspicious. I took a shuttle and went to check on the matter. All I found was a decoy drone sending out the signal that continued to register on my sensors; the ship was gone. I returned and put the scanners on full power. Not a clue or trace of the ship with Jana and Mis

McKay. I contacted Maal on a hunch he wasn't responsible. He was at home and in bed. The security man offered to awaken him if it was an emergency; I thought it best if I didn't disturb him or tell them anything about Jana's disappearance. It still might be Maal's doing; he could be using hirelings to conceal his involvement. But he has an alibi; I don't think he was a part of it."

"Nor do I. He can't be on to us, so he wouldn't abduct Jana."

"I hope it wasn't Taemin," Nigel murmured. "We all know what mood he's in and he's also vanished from sight. We have to find them, Varian."

"We will, my friend, and to *Gehenna* with their captors. No one's contacted you with demands?" he asked the shame-faced Kagan.

"Not a word, sir. I'm sorry. Jana was my responsibility and my friend. I'll do anything you say to help get her back."

"Under the circumstances, I shouldn't blame you, Kagan. Brec, any news on Cass? She could be responsible for this new attack on Jana."

"The plan seems too elaborate and cunning for a woman alone to effectuate."

"So was the last one, remember? But she set it up and carried it out without leaving a clue. We've all underestimated her skills and daring, and her desperation. Have you forgotten she ensnared Baruch and murdered him? She used Moloch and murdered him and his sister. She's plotted with Ryker, Taemin, and others; we have some of that proof on those tapes and in the journals. She tried to entrap and kill me and Jana in Pyropea. And she did abduct Jana once before. That bitch fooled us all for a long time. We know now she's a traitor."

"But her ship is at Zenufia and Taemin told Jana that's where Canissia was headed. Surely she reached there long before yesterday. She knows we're on to her and are searching for her. Surely she wouldn't be reckless enough to cruise through Maffei and dare to commit another crime, one that would certainly provoke all available forces to pursue her."

"The Cass I've come to know lately would do exactly that Brec. She's so vain she doesn't believe she can get caught She's clever and dangerous. She's even more unpredictable now that she's on the run. She probably views Jana as the reason for her downfall and wants to . . ." He couldn't say his worst fears aloud, and it wasn't necessary to do so for them to grasp his point. "When I find that bitch, she will have me to deal with."

"Where could she get a ship of this level, one with a cloaking device, drones and fake markings?" Nigel speculated. "What about the *Ide* code used to fool Kagan? The perfect timing while we were away and Jana was vulnerable? That's a lot for a woman on the run to discover and use."

"She did it last time, Nigel, remember? She even had Jana's captor fake your voice to dupe Jana into believing you were helping me get rid of her. She planned far ahead by making those damned phony tapes with me to use on Jana. She had Taemin's help last time and might have it again. That furious bastard might be with Cass, or it might be him!"

"Or, it could be someone else, but who?" Brec added. "And why?"

"If it's Taemin and he harms one hair on Jana's head, I'll kill him with my bare hands. But I think it's Cass and that she's headed for her own ship in Zenufia. Make sure the patrols along that boundary stay on full alert. I'm heading that way as soon as I can get out of here."

"Before you depart, let me get that new detection device installed on the *Wanderlust*. The boundary patrols already have them. I'll give Ryker credit; he was also an electrical and mechanical genius. We constructed that prototype in those papers you turned in months ago; it worked without a problem. It can penetrate any cloaking shield, but within a certain range. One of its components can pick up and track minute traces of spent fuel."

"If we intercept the course I think she'll take, maybe we can pick up her trail and pierce her shield. Ryker took her from ne; now that bastard's going to help me get her back!'' Varian ooked at his superior. ''Don't keep this news a secret, Brec. t's the perfect explanation for Jana and I to get together again o soon—a daring rescue by her hero. I'll get Braq, Coran, nd Jarre to install the system immediately. For once, my iming couldn't be better. Ryker's genius might help us save our women, Nigel.''

''It must, Varian. I hope Andrea and Jana keep their heads nd don't provoke their captors into harming them.''

''I've seen Jana at work, Nigel; she's intelligent, brave, and quick-thinking. They'll both be fine,'' he murmured, wishing e felt as confident as he tried to sound for Nigel. ''How long vill installation require, Brec?''

''Two hours at most. At starlight speed and with Zenufia nd Rigel's current locations, you should catch up in a day or wo.''

''Let's hope that whoever snatched them is so cocky about eing cloaked that they're traveling at a leisurely pace,'' Nigel emarked. ''If they used starlight speed, too, our women are ong and far gone, Varian. We may not even be heading in the ight direction.''

''We have to begin somewhere, Nigel.'' Varian turned to he other man. ''Brec, see if any of our agents can learn anything about Taemin's location. Check with Jurad. Perhaps, vith our new treaty and his son's treachery, he might be helpful o us. Offer him anything for his assistance, even business with Trilabs again.''

Far away the following afternoon, Jana and Andrea were placed in the same room for the first time since their abduction.

''Andrea, I've been worried sick about you. Are you all ight?''

''Yes, but I'm scared stiff. What's going on? Why did he kidnap us?''

Under the guise of a comforting embrace, Jana whispered in

her ear, "Watch what you say; we're being observed by hidde devices. We can't give away any secrets. Play along no matte what I say or do."

"I'm sure it wasn't Maal," Jana said, aloud. "My fathe in-law wouldn't do this to me. We like and trust each other. was a trick."

"By whom, Jana?" Andrea felt it was safe to ask that ques tion.

"I don't know. Perhaps Taemin or Canissia or another en emy of my husband. Or perhaps someone trying to get thei hands on our products. Ryker warned me to be careful c such traps, but I never suspected this one. He would be ver disappointed in me if he were still alive. I'm sorry, my love," Jana murmured as if speaking to Ryker's spirit.

"Why were we kept separate? Why haven't we seen anyon besides those eerie robots who feed us? Why did they put u together today?"

"It's a terror tactic, Andrea, to show us how helpless an vulnerable we are. We can't allow them to scare us. We hav to remain calm and alert until our captor shows his or her fac and we're told why we're here. I'm sorry I got you into thi predicament. I only wanted you to meet *Kadim* Maal. He' such a wonderful man. As soon as he learns about this, he'l send help. Maal won't rest until I'm safe and back at home o Darkar."

"What about that nice Commander Saar who's investigatin Ryker's death? Maybe he'll come and rescue us. They wer half brothers."

"Don't put much faith in him, Andrea; I haven't found hir to be dependable in the past. He and Ryker reconciled recently but we aren't friends—far from it. I'm sure he won't conside rescuing his ex-mistress as one of his top priorities. Unless h needs to get me back because of Trilabs. That connection ma indeed spur him to search for us. One thing I know for certair Varian Saar never did anything without a motive that woul serve himself. I doubt he's changed much since we parte months ago, which was the only good thing he ever did fo me. Frankly I prefer for Maal to assist us so I won't become beholden to that traitorous rogue. If this was done for ransom or to obtain something from my complex, we should know soon. If that is the case, I'll comply and get us out of this mess; we don't owe these aliens anything—especially loyalty—except for Maal."

Aware of the truth, Andrea comprehended why Jana was badmouthing Varian and she played along with the defensive ruse. "What if it's that wicked prince who captured you and Ryker and tried to kill you two?"

"When he visited me recently, Taemin said he was tricked into that mischief. I know he was angry because Ryker was trying to convince Maal to sign that new treaty with Maffei, but Maal had no choice. If he had gone to war with Maffei, his people would have rebelled, and Ryker told him so."

"Who would have tricked Prince Taemin?"

"Canissia Garthon, that's who he told me. Of course, he could have been lying to cover his guilt and to extricate himself from his troubles."

"Canissia Garthon?"

"You remember, she's the woman I told you about; for some ridiculous reason she hates me and wants me hurt. I don't know why; I haven't been in her way since Varian tossed me aside like garbage. She knows Ryker and I were married and very happy together." Jana feigned a look and sound of bitterness and grief. "It isn't fair, Andrea, for him to be taken from me just when everything was working out so beautifully between us. I still can't believe he's dead. I keep hoping it's a mistake and he'll return home."

Andrea patted her back. "He's gone, Jana; you must accept that. He loved you, so he wouldn't want you to suffer like this."

"But our time together was so short, Andrea. We met as enemies and, wham, we were slapped in the face with unexpected emotions. Those first few days with him are like a bad dream that faded; he changed so fast. We had a powerful rapport. We had so much in common. No man can ever replace him. He was so strong, intelligent, and exciting. Every time he looked at me or touched me, my heart raced and I became as hot as a fire. How will I ever get accustomed to never seeing him again? If he were alive, we wouldn't be in this mess; no one would dare challenge him, except a fool."

"I didn't know him very long, but I liked him," Andrea commented. "He was so kind to find me and bring me to live with you two on Darkar."

"I couldn't have gotten through these past days without you, Andrea."

"How touching and sickening," their captor scoffed from the doorway as it slid open and the two Earthlings turned to face that direction.

"So," Jana said as she eyed the weapon Canissia held in her grasp, "it is you. I suspected as much. What do you want with us, Canissia? What will it take to buy our release?"

"You aren't *that* rich, not even as Ryker Triloni's widow."

"Then let me purchase Andrea's freedom. The conflict is between us and doesn't involve her. It's me you want to destroy, not Andrea."

"How touching to want to protect your little alien friend. No."

"Just like that? No discussion or bargaining?"

"None. After my men and I have our fun with you two, you're dead," Canissia said with a wicked smile.

"You wouldn't dare harm me."

"I have already, and gotten away with it."

Jana and Andrea listened as the evil woman related news of the decoy and cloaking device. She even told them a search was on for them.

"But you'll never be found where we're heading. Never in an eon."

"You can't just murder us in cold blood."

"Oh, I won't do it myself. I'll leave that up to your new neighbors."

When the redhead halted, Jana couldn't help but ask who she was talking about.

"The most barbaric, lustful, and heartless men alive," Canissia explained with glee. "Prisoners on a male penal colony. It's guarded by a force shield, but I happen to know the release code, just like I knew the one for Maal to get through Darkar's defenses. I overheard his grandfather use it. I never forget anything because one never knows when one might need even the tiniest fact. Back to where I was. After you've been sufficiently punished, I'll drop you two off there. I'm sure you'll make new friends very fast." She laughed satanically, then explained it was a prison for the incorrigible male miscreants of Maffei, a place where even the most savage criminal became even more vicious and feral after living like bestial primitives for a short while. "Why, you'll be too busy to miss Ryker. Of course you'll probably be too sore to walk straight, but that won't matter; you'll be spending all of your time on the ground on your back beneath hundreds or perhaps thousands of creatures who haven't had a woman in ages."

Jana experienced sheer terror at what she knew was a realistic threat from the vindictive female who despised her. Where was Varian when she needed him, off doing his duty for Maffei! If he had kept his word and returned on time, this wouldn't be happening to them. Their situation was perilous and looked hopeless. "You'll be caught and punished, Canissia."

"I think not. If anyone suspects me, the search is on toward Zenufia where I left the *Moonwind*. We're far from that location, and no one will ever imagine to search for you where you're going."

Get all the clues you can, J.G. "Where did you get this ship?"

"I stole it from the Pyropean commander who was to escort me to mine. I retrieved my loyal androids, got rid of theirs, and prepared for this little trap. It has all the modern instruments and devices. As soon as I learned Varian was on Rigel and out of my way, I put my plan into motion."

Jana faked a look of confusion. "What does Varian Saar have to do with it?"

"I saw him on the news broadcast on Rigel. He was sighted

entering a private meeting which included my father. They probably summoned poor Father to dismiss him for spilling secrets to me—valuable secrets, I might add."

"I still don't grasp why Varian Saar figured into your plot. I've only seen him twice since you took me to Ryker's: after that thwarted trap on Luz and when he was the one chosen to escort me and Ryker's body to *Kadim* Maal. He wasn't expected for another visit, thank goodness."

Canissia laughed for several minutes. "You're such a blind fool. He would have come soon, again and again, until he won you back."

Jana glared at the woman. "It will be a cold day in hell first!"

"Even if I told you I kidnapped you last time and Varian never discarded you? That the search mentioned was a real and desperate one to locate you? That he only backed off after he realized Ryker had screwed you? He still yearns for you, and he would have been chasing you again soon."

"You're crazy. Varian gave me to Ryker; he admitted it on a taped message to me and in that interview I witnessed on the *telecom*."

"All lies and tricks to trap me. He never stopped craving you."

"Even if that's true, it doesn't matter now. Is that what this is about? You're afraid we'll get back together and he'll be lost to you? Don't worry, Canissia, you can have him. After Ryker, Varian Saar doesn't compare; he can't even stand in his brother's shadow. He might not have tossed me away that time, but he did too many other mean things to me for forgiveness, and he would do similar ones if I gave him the chance, which I won't. You might not care how he treats you and you may come crawling back for more, but I'm not like you. I don't want him or need him. Thanks to Ryker, I'm free and powerful and rich. If you're worried about me exposing what you told me, I won't; you have my word no one will ever know you kidnapped me, if you really did."

"Everything was fine until Varian found you and brought

you here. You ruined everything with him and with Ryker and with Taemin. I was Ryker's ally until you changed him and turned him against me."

"You were his ally, Canissia, until you and Taemin tried to kill us."

"Ryker told you that?"

"I thought he told me everything, but he obviously left out at least one confession, if what you said about me being kidnapped for him is true. I can see why he wouldn't want me to discover that. Even so, it doesn't matter now; he was the best thing that happened to me in your world. You of all women should know Varian Saar only uses, deceives, and discards ex-mistresses. Do you think I could return to a man like that even if he said he loved me? I wouldn't trust Varian Saar for two seconds. He did horrible things to me, and you know about plenty of them. Why you continue to want him after the way he's treated you baffles me. A woman, even one as beautiful and rich and powerful as you are, can't win or obtain revenge against a man like him. To attempt such a goal is rash; that's why I would never challenge him. I'll be satisfied if he just forgets I exist."

"That's the trouble, he *can't* forget you. And he's after me."

"After *you*? For that alleged kidnapping months ago? If that's all, I can handle your problem by calling it a lie."

"You want me to trust you?"

"Why not?" Jana asked the sarcastic woman. "I have a lot to lose if what you say is true. If you and Ryker kidnapped me, our marriage would be illegal; I wouldn't be his widow. If you think I would press charges against you and risk losing Darkar, you're wrong. We can make a deal, Canissia. I want Trilabs and Darkar, not Varian. You want to be free of charges and have certain products of mine. What do you say to an exchange? A truce?"

"It's too late. You see, that isn't the only charge against me."

Jana faked ignorance. "Maybe I can help get the others

dismissed or lightened. I can blackmail them with a cut-off from Trilabs. What are they?"

"Several murders, treason, theft, and so on. I thought Taemin or Maal would grant me sanctuary in exchange for the truth about Varian playing Ryker, but I was wrong there, one of the few times in my life."

"Why on Earth would you think Ryker was Varian? I mean, you've known them both for so long; how could you get them mixed up?"

"Because of what I thought were slips by Ryker on my last visit."

"My husband was tricking you, Canissia. He was trying to provoke you into revealing secrets for a tape he was making to use as blackmail in case you tried to harm me or expose his past secrets. Ryker changed and we were making a fresh start together. He didn't want trouble. He would never have used the tape if you'd left us alone."

"Did he give it to Varian when they reconciled?"

"Of course not. That would incriminate him, too. After he died, I destroyed it because I didn't want it found. I couldn't risk staining his memory. Those were plots he did or planned long ago. He wasn't like that anymore. Despite what you think of him, he was a good and gentle man."

"Did he screw anything like Varian does?"

Jana gaped at the crude female. "Not that it's any of your business, but no; they were nothing alike in that area. Do we have a deal?" She watched Canissia lick and stroke the weapon in an erotic manner as she talked.

"No, never."

"How did you lure us off Darkar with such success and cunning? How did you dupe my security chief, or is Kagan working for you?"

"That trick was so easy to accomplish that I can hardly believe it myself. Have you forgotten your protocol lessons? Rulers never deal directly with the lower class; one of my androids pretended to be Maal's bodyguard and he spoke with your Kagan. He used Maal's nickname for Ryker. You know, that 'cherished flame of my soul' shit. The uniforms, shuttle markings, and insignia were simple for us to make in the work lab aboard."

"What if I convince Maal to give you sanctuary in Androas?"

"Maal isn't in power anymore. I know about the treaty. I also know about the one with Pyropea and about poor Taemin's exile."

"How do you find out such things? You must have powerful contacts."

"My father was my best informer, but that door's closed now. With the help of some of Ryker's best little secrets, all I have to do is whisper a certain sentence into *Avatar* Kael's ear and he tells me anything, everything."

"But leaders and rulers are immuned to questioning, aren't they?"

"Ryker needed information, so he gave me a chemical that caused the *Rendelar* not to work. The planetary ruler of Zandia is my mental slave, among other ways I like to use him with the aid of secret formulas. Your late husband certainly was a genius. I'll miss his products."

"You mean *Avatar* Kael doesn't know he's working for you?"

"That's right. In fact, Kael can't stand me. That's what makes his little enslavement and chores so enjoyable." Canissia licked her lips and told Jana the crude sexual sentence that put Kael in a trance.

"Why can't you use those same chemicals on Varian and enslave him? Then, you and I won't have a problem."

"Ryker only gave me enough to use on Kael; one infusion did it."

"I've been all through his possessions and equipment and I haven't found any mention of such a powerful antidote to *Rendelar*."

"It exists somewhere, because I've used it and it works. That's how I learned about the treaties and Taemin's fate from Kael a few days ago."

"If you're being hunted like an animal, how could you get to him?"

"Simple. In disguise and after uttering my magic words via *telecom*, he gave me clearance. This ship has transport markings outside, Trilabs markings to be exact. Supposedly having valuable, secret, and dangerous products aboard explains my weapons and vessel superiority. Symbols for deadly cargo keep anyone from approaching me too closely, and the androids handle all communications for me. You see, I thought of everything. Even Kael can't recall my visit. Too bad I was too rushed to have my last fun with him. I so enjoy humiliating him. Of course, if I have future need of him, all I have to do is whisper my little message in his ear."

Jana forced her eyes to widen and sparkle with deceptive excitement. "Do you realize what that formula would be worth? No person in an elite position would be safe from questioning. The secrets they possess would be priceless. What did Ryker call it?"

"*Anti-Ren*. But it won't profit you anything, nor me."

"We could be rich and powerful beyond our wildest dreams, Cass." She attempted to ensnare the greedy and conceited creature and used an informal shortening of her name to sound friendly. "With your knowledge and skills combined with mine, we could . . . we could gain control of this damn galaxy. Just think, two female rulers. If we're in control or if we wipe out their memories, you won't be in any danger. We can be a team, Cass. We can even get Varian for you."

"You don't want him back?" Cass asked with open skepticism.

"I was in love with Ryker," Jana stressed. "I'm still in love with Ryker. I do not want Varian Saar. I could never trust him or forgive him."

"Varian loves you more than his own life, even more than his rank and duty or else he would never have taken possession of you during a mission and against orders. He would give anything to get you back. He let Ryker keep you only to save your life, not because Ryker had screwed you. He knew that if he took you back, Ryker would guess he loved you and would kill you. You're blind and naive, my alien temptress. Varian actually loves you."

"How can I convince you that doesn't matter to me? Even if it did, I could never return to him and he would never want me back. I'm carrying Ryker Triloni's child and heir, future ruler of Androas. You know Varian Saar, Cass; he would not accept Ryker's child. He may have pretended to make peace with Ryker, but I don't believe he meant it, and neither do you. He probably thinks he saved Maffei with his deceitful truce."

"What if the baby is Varian's? You screwed him for ages."

"I was with Varian for only two weeks before my auction and then for just a few days after he snatched me away from Draco and you got me. Think about the timing, Cass; that's impossible. I'm only two months. All I want is Darkar, Trilabs, my baby, and our freedom—not Varian."

"The answer is no and will remain no!"

Jana tried another tactic to save their lives. "If what you say about Varian loving me is true, then killing me is a big mistake. He will never know I would never marry him, so he'll hunt you forever, no matter where you go. You know him, Cass, he'll never stop dogging you until he dies; he's very persistent when he wants something. Tell me what it will take to get me and Andrea released and to protect my baby."

"A baby, how sweet. Poor Ryker won't get to see his little seed sprout and grow. How sad. Soon you'll be fat and clumsy and have a whining child clutching at you. Then, my ex-temptress, you won't be appealing to a man like Varian at all. How sad. You're right, Varian would never want you all plump with Ryker's baby, *if* this story of yours is the truth. Come with me to the medical bay for a test of your claim."

"You want me to take a pregnancy test?"

"Do you object? You are telling me the truth, aren't you?"

"Lead on, Cass." She glanced at her friend. "I'll return soon, Andrea."

* * *

Jana was escorted back to the holding room by a silent and heartless android with expressionless yellow eyes. She was frustrated and angered at not having a single chance to overpower Canissia. She hadn't seen a single human crewman during her outing, and she knew androids had no feelings to which she could appeal for help. The mechanical creations were controlled by computer chips that were programmed in Canissia's favor, so no assistance or mercy would ever be forthcoming.

Jana walked to the bed and sat down facing a blank wall. "Andrea, I have something in my eye, perhaps a lash. Can you help me get it out?"

Andrea surmised something was afoot and obeyed. She sat in front of Jana and pretended to do as her friend requested. It was a trick to avoid the hidden camera's eye while Jana used a game they had practiced in class many times in the past: mouthing messages. Jana winked at her friend and gave unwitnessed instructions. "I passed the test," she finally said aloud.

"I got it, Jana. How does that feel?"

They kept their places on the bed. "Fine. Thanks."

"So what happens now, Jana?"

"If Cass is smart, she'll accept my deal and offer of help. Despite the bad blood between us, she and I could make a good team. She's in a lot of trouble, but maybe we can work out something to benefit both of us. If Cass is as smart as I think she is, she didn't leave any evidence behind to incriminate her. All they can have on her are suspicions and maybe light charges. I can't believe she won't call their bluff."

"Do you think she's going to kill us for spite against you?"

"I hope not. If she thinks about it, she really has no motive and it only adds another crime to her list. I told her the truth: I don't want or need Varian Saar. If she wants to save herself, she had better let someone help her, even if it's me. Maybe she'll wise up and realize I'm not her rival or enemy. The best chance to get out of this alive and safe is to be honest with her. To deceive her or attempt to manipulate her would be dangerous. She's far too smart for me to insult her intelligence with lies and tricks."

Jana got off the bed and strolled about as she spoke. "The problem is, Cass believes I'm the root of her problems and unhappiness when the truth is it's her obsession for Varian and his constant rejections. She should realize that was a painful fact long before I came on the scene, so I can't understand why she blames me for it. Ryker and I thought they were getting married; that's what was reported. I'm afraid to ask her what happened to stop the wedding. If Varian called it off, and I presume he did, she must think it's because of me. I haven't gone after him, Andrea, and I *won't* go after him; I'm glad he's out of my life and I want it to remain that way. But if he dumped her to romance me to get his hands on Trilabs for Maffei, he's an arrogant and deluded fool."

Andrea continued to allow Jana to do most of the talking in an attempt to dupe the listening Canissia into releasing them. "Maybe she'll let you give her refuge on Darkar. Nobody would think to look for her there with you. If we help her, she'll release us, won't she?"

Jana gave a loud sigh. "Who are we kidding, Andrea? She'll never believe me or my promises in a thousand years."

"What are we going to do?"

"I don't know. That's up to Cass."

"What if she really dumps us on that horrible prison planet? We'll never survive, Jana. We'll be attacked day and night by awful men. It's bad enough for us to be treated that way, but your baby . . . How can any woman be so cruel as to harm an innocent child?"

"The baby probably doesn't seem real to her because I'm not showing yet, even though she saw the test results. If she loved or wanted children, she would have some by now, with or without a husband. I think we're doomed. I'm sorry, Andrea, for getting you into this bind with me."

"It isn't your fault, Jana. Maybe she'll change her mind."
"No, she won't" came Canissia's response.
Jana and Andrea whirled toward the sound, but no one was there.
"What was that?"
"A hidden communicator, Andrea. She's been watching us and listening to us all along, toying with us. We've been tricked again."
The door opened and Canissia lazed against the side, grinning and armed against a bold attack. "I should warn you, Jana, not to try anything foolish, like taking me for a hostage. My crew are androids: they feel nothing; they only respond to their programming, which is to jettison you into space if I'm harmed. I've ordered them not to bargain with you for any reason, even for my safety or survival. I don't have to remind you being jettisoned is a bloody, slow, and excruciatingly painful death, so none of this threatening to kill me if you aren't released. I assure you, they will call your bluff, then torture you and kill you. If you want that little baby to live a while longer, behave yourself. Understand?"
"I understand perfectly. I misjudged you, Cass; I thought you smarter than this. I can't help it if Varian lusts for me, or Trilabs through me. If he does love me, killing me won't make him desire you or turn to you. Does taking other people's lives mean nothing to you?"
"It actually gives me great pleasure, especially if they suffer a great deal beforehand. You have no idea what delightful cruelties and games Taemin and I had planned for you and Varian; I'm sorry he wasn't playing Ryker and we didn't get our eager hands on you two. Making people bleed and cry and beg and do whatever I command is a delicious and intoxicating sensation. If I had my old crew with me, I'd let them have fun with you two before I discard you. I'd really enjoy watching you take on two and three men at a time, and taping it to send to Varian as his last memory of his lost love. And don't say you wouldn't, that you'd die first; I have chemicals that will make you do anything and everything I desire. I'm only sorry

androids don't have the right equipment to provide that little diversion for me.''

Jana knew it was unwise to say anything provoking at that delicate point in the woman's mental balance. She was relieved Canissia hadn't followed up on her earlier threats of torture. She didn't know why the sadistic creature hadn't kept her word, and she certainly wasn't going to remind her into doing so by hurling curses and insults at her.

''I thought I had gotten rid of you when I gave you to Ryker. I underestimated your powers. You had the same affect on both brothers; even Taemin craved you. Because of you, I lost all three prospects, you alien witch. I was forced to kill Baruch and Moloch and that sister of his because of you. I tried to entrap Ryker because of you. Now, I'm on the run because of you. It's your fault Ryker tried to murder me.''

''You're wrong about that, Cass,'' Jana pointed out. ''Ryker said it was an accident that killed Zan. He told me you were too valuable to him as a spy to kill you. And it wasn't my fault I came here and intruded on your life and plans; I was captured and enslaved. Every place I went, every person I met, and every thing I did was under orders because I had no choice; I was a prisoner in your world. If anyone is to blame for your misery, it's Varian and it's you.''

Canissia glared at Jana. ''Me!'' she screamed. ''How dare you!''

Jana assumed a gentle tone to cover her slip. ''As long as you love him and chase him, he'll abuse you and hurt you. Get over him, Cass, and push him out of your life as I did. He isn't worth it.''

''That public proposal and marriage offer were tricks to lure me out of hiding so he could destroy me and protect you. He never intended to marry me; it was a trap to locate you and get you back. You, you, you, everything for you! But not much longer. I have time and the means to exact my revenge: I didn't rush it. I planned this very carefully. I don't care who gets hurt as long as I destroy you. That's how I will punish Varian. Killing him isn't the way; ruining the only thing he loves and wants will be his living hell. In a few months, I'll tell him where you are. What he finds left of you when he comes, if anything, he'll reject."

"If he loves me that much, he's probably looking for me this minute. Kagan had orders to check on me within two hours if I wasn't back home. You can't have much of a lead on a search party. Give it up before it's too late. Do so and I'll convince them to be lenient with you. If they value their connection to Trilabs, they'll grant my request. I'll give them no choice."

"Let *you* help me?"

Jana watched the fiery redhead burst into soul-chilling laughter. Her aqua eyes glittered with hatred and coldness. Evil and something akin to intimidating madness seemed to shadow her.

"I don't need or want your help or your friendship," Canissia scoffed. "I've never needed anyone's. I can take care of myself; I always have. When you're gone, I'll be happy again and Varian will be punished for all he's done to me. He'll live and die knowing he's responsible for your destruction."

"You're talking and acting like a woman scorned, Cass. Get hold of yourself and think clearly or you'll be in the worst trouble of your life. Maal will come after you, too; I'm carrying his great-grandchild, remember? Between him and Varian and their forces, you won't have a minute's peace to enjoy your revenge. They'll hunt you down like a wild animal and kill you. There's still time to end this recklessness. I beg you, don't do this."

"As soon as I've dealt with you and informed Varian of your fate, I'm leaving Maffei. They'll never locate me to hurt me again."

The woman acted as if she hadn't heard a word Jana had said and wasn't tempted to stop her evil scheme. Jana grasped it was futile to argue and reason further. "I'll fight you on this, Cass; I have to."

"You'll lose, that's a promise. Where you're going, you'll beg and pray for death a thousand times over before it finally eleases you from your suffering. I hate you, Jana Greyson. I hate Varian. We'll be there soon."

Jana watched Canissia leave and the door close.

"She's crazy, Jana; she's going to do it," Andrea shrieked in panic.

"We aren't dead yet, my friend. Don't lose hope and faith. Varian and Nigel will locate us and rescue us; you'll see." *Please, God, let that be true.*

The following afternoon, Canissia came to fetch the Earthlings, and brought two android guards with her. "We're here. Ready to go?"

Jana's heart began to pound hard and fast. Terror ruled her senses. She paled and trembled. *Where are you, my love? We need you.* "Don't do this wicked and cruel thing, Cass. I'm begging you. I'll do anything to save my baby's life. I'll get on my knees. I'll give you Trilabs for protection."

"Shut up, it's too late for bargains."

"It's not too late to change your mind, Cass. I'm begging you."

"No, please!" Andrea shrieked. "We'll do anything you ask."

"Take them to the shuttle," Canissia ordered the androids.

The strength of the mechanical beings couldn't be resisted or overcome. Jana and Andrea were escorted to the shuttle bay and placed aboard a craft. Andrea was crying and shaking. Jana was filled with anger and hatred for their grinning captor.

"You'll be sorry for this, Cass; he will hunt you down and kill you. No matter how far or how fast you run, Varian Saar will find you and kill you."

"No way, no way. Goodbye, Jana, forever this time. Oh, you will have about an hour's rest before the men can reach the place the shuttle will drop you. Make all the defense plans you like, but they won't help you escape their savage lust."

Jana and Andrea huddled together and held hands as the craft

traveled to the surface of the male penal colony. Jana whispere
a message to her.

Andrea nodded and murmured, "Oh, Nigel, my love, wher
are you?"

"I'm sure our men are searching for us. We have to sta
safe and alive until they come. They will, Andrea; I know the
will."

They landed and the two women were taken outside. "Re
move your clothes," one android said in a monotone voice
"Give them to me."

As planned, Jana and Andrea raced for cover as quickly a
possible. The androids were not as swift or agile as the tw
humans. Soon, the women were able to hide. As instructed
Andrea did not move or speak to avoid being detected by thei
trackers' sensors. For twenty minutes, the androids searche
in vain while the two women observed and trembled. The
heard one android report the situation and heard Canissia orde
them back to the ship.

The shuttle zoomed into the sky and Jana and Andrea wer
alone in what resembled a lush jungle. They heard birds wit
strange calls. They smelled an abundance of flowers. They fel
the high humidity and heat.

"What now, Jana? She said those prisoners would reach u
in . . ."

Thirty minutes. "A plan, we need a plan of defense. Damn
damn, damn! I can't think; I'm too scared. We have no weap
ons or food or supplies. And we'll be outnumbered. The bes
we can hope for is male dominance, a leader who might clain
us and keep us from the others."

"Canissia said only the worst criminals were sent here
They'll be battling over us like wild animals over raw meat.'

"Maybe she was lying to scare us. Maybe this place i
uninhabited." *Or inhabited with dangerous creatures and mu
tants like Luz*. The thought of being ripped apart by predator
caused her to shudder in panic. She stroked her lower abdome
and prayed for her child's survival.

"Oh, Jana, they're going to come soon and . . . I'd rathe

die. Kill me, Jana; find some way to kill me. Don't let those beasts rape me. Please.'' Andrea began to sob and Jana tried to comfort her.

After the auburn-haired female regained control, Jana voiced her thoughts aloud. ''I doubt it would do much good to collect makeshift weapons; there will be too many of them to battle and no place to escape to in their world so that would only antagonize them. We should get out of this area as they're sure to come to investigate for new arrivals, but I don't know in which direction to head to elude them. I could walk us straight into their clutches. Just let me think a minute. I—''

Jana went silent. She pushed greenery aside and let her gaze search the sky. When Andrea started to question her actions, Jana ordered her to listen. ''The shuttle,'' she said, ''it's coming back. Maybe Cass changed her mind. Maybe she did this to scare us.'' *Or maybe that evil and deviant bitch wants to hover and watch the action to make certain we're . . . What to do, J.G.?*

Chapter Twenty

"Maybe Canissia . . ." Jana went silent and stared as th craft made curious maneuvers to signal "rescue alert," whic Varian had explained to her on Luz. But was it a friendl shuttle?

Andrea shook her arm. "What, Jana?" she demanded "What is it?"

"Just stay still and quiet. It might be a trick to draw us out o hiding, like the one she pulled at Darkar with those Androasia markings."

Jana peered through the verdant bushes. When the shuttl landed, the door opened and faces appeared. Her heart leap with joy and relief. She grabbed Andrea's hand and shook i in excitement. "It's them! Let's go before those evil prisoner arrive."

Varian jumped down the steps with Nigel and a securit team in tow. His narrowed sapphire gaze shot in the directio of noise and movement in the tangly vegetation. When Jan and Andrea came into sight, he holstered his weapon and ra toward them, as did Nigel. The heavily armed team spread out and took a defensive position.

Varian hugged Jana so tightly that the breath almost was squeezed from her lungs. "*Kahala* be thanked, you're safe and alive. I feared I had lost you, my love. If we didn't have witnesses, Mrs. Triloni, I would cover you with kisses from head to toe!"

When Jana lifted her head to look at him, she saw tears in his sapphire eyes. She knew time was limited for talking and staying. "I knew you would come," she said in a low voice, even though she knew they couldn't be overheard. "I never lost faith. But I was scared witless," she added with laughter to dispell her tension. "We'd better get out of—"

"Just let me look at you for a minute. *Kahala*, I'm ten years older after enduring this terror! I would have returned on schedule," he explained, "but there was an emergency rescue on a ship about to explode. We had to stop and save its crew, and solar flare-ups knocked out our communications. I swear I would have made the deadline or contacted you if—"

She pressed her fingers to his lips to silence him. "I know, and the deadline doesn't matter. All that matters is that we love each other."

Varian gazed at her adoring smile, and his heart melted.

"Yes, Rogue Saar, I love you and I want to marry you. I think the rest of our talk should be in private and out of danger," she hinted, "or the others will wonder why Ryker's wife and brother are being so intimate."

"Are you all right, Moonbeam? Did she hurt you?"

"We're fine," Jana assured him as she touched her stomach. "Cass knows about the baby; she tested me on her ship. She thinks it's Ryker's."

Varian grasped her hand to guide her to the shuttle. "Break it up, Nigel," he teased his friend, "you two can kiss and hug aboard the ship. Let's get Mrs. Triloni and your sweetheart out of here before we have company."

Jana glanced at the well-armed rescue team that was on watchful alert for intruders. She smiled and greeted the security chief. "Ferris Laus, you look wonderful; I'm delighted you made it here in time."

"If we'd been any slower, Varian would have gotten out and pushed. We do seem to have a lot of excitement and adventure with you two."

Jana smiled. "Life is anything but dull around this space pirate. He makes a good friend and brother-in-law," she said for the deluding benefit of the others nearby. "Thanks to all of you."

"You're more than welcome, Jana. You have lots of friends on the *Wanderlust* and elsewhere who will be happy to see you returned safely."

The shuttle took off within minutes of the approach of numerous savage-looking criminals. It docked in the enormous starship that was orbiting the confining location. The force shield was reenergized around the penal colony. Varian, Jana, Nigel, Andrea, and Ferris headed for the bridge.

"Jarre, take us after Miss Garthon," Varian ordered. "Braq, give us starlight speed. Coran, don't lose her on your sensors for a minute. All right, men, we have a big job to do; let's catch us a traitor."

"How can you ever find her? She has cloaking," Jana ventured, as the ship left in pursuit of the fleeing Canissia.

Varian sent her a broad grin. "But *we* have an anticloaking device. There's no place she can hide from our new sensors, if we stay within range. She isn't far ahead. We'll follow her spent fuel trail until we catch up. It's one of your late husband's designs, and it works perfectly. Brec had it installed before we left Star Base after the *Galactic Gem*'s rescue. We also have a new antiinterference system, so we won't lose contact again."

"How did you locate us? Cass said no one would search here."

"She made the mistake of dropping her shield for a few minutes to check the news concerning your disappearance; I guess to see if she was in the clear so far. Brec put out a full alert on you as soon as Kagan realized something was wrong. A patrol ship with the new systems detected her presence but idn't close in to attack and risk endangering you two. They ollowed you and guarded you until we could reach the area nd take charge of your rescue.''

''You mean, you've been closing in on us and we weren't n danger?''

''She had already dropped you when we arrived and scared er off. We have the advantage over her: we can penetrate her hield, but she can't pierce ours. When we approached and letected a shuttle returning from the surface, I guessed what he had in mind for you two. We lowered our shield to scare er into leaving fast so we could rescue you without a delaying attle. She probably thinks we're a prisoner-delivery vessel, o she cloaked and ran. She's gliding along thinking herself afe and alone.''

''And thinking me and Andrea are dead, or worse. And we vould have been very soon if all of you hadn't rescued us. Thank you, everyone, Varian.''

The crew turned, nodded, and smiled, and a few chatted vith her.

''As soon as we capture Cass, I'll take you home to Darkar.'' e promised Jana.

Jana and Varian played along with the last ruse, but it was lifficult, as they wanted to hug and kiss and talk.

''I hope you put her under the jail when you catch her,'' Andrea said.

''I guess that translates to, do our worst to her,'' Nigel huckled. ''We will, my sweet.'' He kept Andrea nestled close o him as the two lovers touched and smiled and savored their eunion. He had already told the crew, his friends, that the voman with Jana was his fiancée.

''She's a terrible person,'' Andrea said. ''Evil personified. f it hadn't been for Jana's wits, she would have tortured us all he way to that horrible place. If she hadn't been crazy, Jana ould have talked her into releasing us. I'm so glad to be away rom that wicked witch.''

''Why did she abduct you, Jana?'' Vaiden, an old friend, sked.

"She held Ryker responsible for betraying her evil deeds to Varian after they reconciled. She was involved in that kidnapping episode with Taemin, among other crimes." Jana glanced at Varian. "I'm sure all of you know she's obsessed with winning your commander. When he broke off their engagement, she thought it was because of me. When I became a widow and was free again, she feared Varian and I would . . ."

The ebony-haired man smiled. "It's all right, Jana," he told her. "I'm sure everybody knows or suspects I never got over you and I'll do about anything to get you back."

Jana was astonished. "Commander Saar, you shouldn't speak like that."

Varian had decided to let the crew, mostly close friends, overhear a few things to initiate gossip about a new romance. "Why not? It's the truth, something I realized after I foolishly let you get away from me. Ask my friends; they raked me over rocky ground about that big mistake, so did Tesla. I hope it isn't too late to correct it."

Jana was amazed by his bold conduct. "Really, sir, you shouldn't talk like this. I'm ma— I guess I'm not married anymore. Still . . ."

"I'm sorry if I'm embarrassing you or making you uncomfortable, Jana; it's just that I've been so worried about you that it's loosened my tongue. The only reason I sold you to Councilman Procyon was to protect you against death threats from my many enemies, and because I was too blind to see I was in love with you. Our good friend Draco realized we were in love; that's why he let me buy you from him. After you earned your freedom, I was going to ask you to marry me. I shouldn't have decided to wait to tell you my feelings and plans until after I finished my mission to Earth. I had you back, so I thought I had plenty of time to confess to you later and I arrogantly believed you had to know how I felt without my telling you. I can't blame you for running off from a captor who had auctioned you and snatched you back without telling you why. I thought you had been kidnapped and Cass was esponsible. She'd dropped out of sight, too. I put out that hony story about our engagement to lure her into the open so could question her about you."

Varian grasped her hand as he continued. "I never suspected ou were working at Trilabs with my brother, that you two vere confined in the complex doing a long experiment and lidn't hear about the investigation, or that my crazy ruse would rovoke you into marrying Ryker. I know you two were good riends and had a lot in common, but you didn't love him, ana; you couldn't have, because you love me. I hurt you by eeping secrets and I'm sorry. When you've had time to adjust o Ryker's death, I'd like us to see if we can get back together. f you'll give me a chance to make up for the past, you won't e sorry. I give you my word of honor."

"Varian, I don't think this is the time or place to discuss—"

"I have to be honest, Jana, before my old ruses do more lamage. When I learned you had married Ryker, I was forced o hide the truth and to let you go. My brother is dead and ou're free again, so it's past time I was totally honest. If I ad been truthful months ago, we would be married today. I ost you to Ryker and almost lost you to Cass's treachery; I lon't want to risk losing you forever. Stars above, Jana Greyson, I love you, woman! How much plainer can I be?"

Jana knew he must have a good motive for what he was loing, so she would play along by feigning surprise. "You *vhat*?"

"I love you. I have since we met."

Varian and Jana pretended to have slipped into a world of heir own, oblivious to the presence of the others around them.

"Why didn't you tell me this a long time ago, before I . . ."

When she paused, he said, "Because I was a blind and tupid fool. Can you forgive me and let me try to make things ight between us?"

The crew remained still and quiet so nothing would intrude n the romantic scene.

"I . . . Ryker has been dead such a short time, Varian. I

shouldn't be thinking about you or your offer this soon, or eve
listening to it. Ryker was good and kind to me. It would b
disloyal to—"

He interrupted in a gentle tone. "My brother, your husband
is dead. We're alive, Jana. Ryker would want you to be saf
and happy."

"But . . . it seems wrong; too soon. Tell him, Nigel."

The First Officer grinned and shook his head of curly brow
hair. The creases around his hazel eyes and near his mout
deepened as his smile increased. "I can't, because I agree wit
him. What's more romantic than best friends marrying bes
friends?"

Jana widened her eyes in astonishment. "Marrying?"

"That's right, woman," Varian clarified with his own broa
grin.

"Ferris," Jana coaxed, "help me get through to him."

"I agree with Nigel; you two were made for each other, jus
like Kathy and I were, just like Nigel and Andrea, just lik
Tris and Martella."

Jana looked at another officer she remembered from her las
time on the ship. "Braq?"

The engineering officer grinned and shook his head in playfu
refusal.

"Vaiden, it's up to you. Talk sense into your friend an
commander."

"It's the most sense he's made since you two parted."

"Am I in the midst of a conspiracy, you guys?" she jested

Varian was delighted when the four men chuckled and nodded. "Don't worry, Jana; I'll try to behave myself, but it'
hard around you. I had to let you know how I felt before othe
men come calling on you."

Jana glanced around the room to find everyone smiling an
nodding agreement with Varian. She looked at him and teased
"You always were persistent and bold, Varian Saar."

"So, you haven't forgotten," he replied and chuckled.

"How could any woman forget anything about you?"

"Or any man forget anything about you." His smoldering aze engulfed her for a moment, then he reminded everyone e had to focus on the task ahead.

"Why don't you two women go to my quarters and relax?" igel suggested.

"They're welcome to use mine, Nigel," Varian said.

That sounds like what we need after our frightening experi-nce," Jana said gratefully. "But if my old quarters aren't eing used, I'd prefer we stay there and not intrude on you wo, if you don't mind."

"Certainly not. You know the way to the Gold Room."

"Yes, I remember it well. Come along, Andrea; you can see Nigel later. The crew has work to do. Thanks again to everyone for saving our lives." Jana halted and turned. "Oh, yes, Varian, Canissia's ship has phony Trilabs markings in case the patrol didn't tell you. It's a Pyropean ship, if that information will help anyone." She related how Canissia had stolen and altered the vessel.

As the elevator whisked the two women from the bridge down the right side of the top deck of the U-shaped vessel, Jana expressed her surprise at Varian's behavior. "I've never known him to use such a lack of caution. He'll have everyone gossiping about us."

"Nigel whispered to me that he was setting his plan into motion to set you up for falling for the hero who rescued you twice. He said that was why Commander Sard issued that full alert for us, to let people know you were kidnapped and that he rescued you. I thought it was very cunning and romantic. The men loved it, and they like you a lot, Jana. The crew that rescued me from Earth was nice, too. I met a few of Varian's men when they came to Anais during our troubles, but Nigel fetched me in another ship to take me to Darkar; I guess to conceal my presence there. You should be happy Varian's crew likes you so much."

"Except for three of the men, I've known everyone aboard for a long time. We were together a lot during my months on the ship. I wish Kara Curri, Tesla Rilke, and Lieutenant Dyk tra were still aboard; you'd like them, too. Tesla was the or killed during my rescue from Darkar after Shara tried to ki me. Kara was our recreational and physical training coach. Sh and I became good friends. She left to get married. Lieutenar Dykstra was in charge of security for the captives; the man called *Mon Spectre* was the one who passed along Varian' orders. He was transferred to another ship after that missio ended and promoted to head of security. I'm sure he'll wor his way up to a commander one day."

Inside the guest quarters she had occupied long ago, Jan looked at Andrea. "This is where it all began, my friend," sh said. "I woke up in here after I was taken from Earth tha night. This was my home for months."

They eyed the furniture that was of an alien material, neithe wood nor metal nor plastic. There was an étagère with expen sive books, statues, figurines, and a model of the *Wanderlust* On one wall was the *servo* and eating bar. On another was a sitting area with a phantasmagorial painting above a sofa, a picture that concealed a *telecom* system. A bed with nightstand and hanging lamp was in another corner. The floor was carpeted in thick material that curled around the feet. Everything was in shades of gold and ivory, except for the painting with its magical hints of blue and black. It was a suite that exuded an aura of wealth, serenity, and excellent taste.

"It was designed to soothe the eye, body, and mind—of a real guest, not a frightened captive. The bath and dressing room with closets are in there," Jana said, pointing to a closed door that worked by floor pressure.

Andrea gazed at the setting. "It's beautiful, Jana."

"Yes, it is. I remember the first time I saw this room. I was scared witless, Andrea. When I checked out that bathroom, everything in there—clothes, cosmetics, and lingerie—was in my sizes and my favorite colors. There were even drawers of expensive jewelry fit for a queen. We had schedules, lessons, and classes. We even had parties to relax us and train us. That's how I got to know the crew so well. I must admit it was a strange sort of imprisonment and slavery. They did try to relax us and teach us to fit in.''

''My best friend was their elite captive, their mission cover; that's so exciting!'' Andrea collapsed onto the bed. ''We're safe, Jana.''

''I told you not to worry,'' Jana said with a smile.

''You were also worried; you won't convince me otherwise.''

''*Terrified* is the right word to describe what I was feeling. But I knew, if it was at all possible, Varian would find us and save us.''

''Will everything be all right between you two now?''

''Thanks to you who helped me see the light, I think so. I *know* so. We're back where we belong, Andrea, with the men we love. The more I thought about those weeks during my training, those few days on Eire and those here after Ryker's real death, the more I realized he really does love me and want me. He wouldn't have suffered so much when I disappeared if that weren't true. I see it in the way he looks at me, like he did today when he rescued us. I hear it in his voice. I feel it in his touch and kiss. Because he did his duty, what he truly believed was right, doesn't mean I'm not just as important to him. If he had done any less, he wouldn't be Varian Saar, the man I came to love. What he did to save his world and ours was unselfish. My mind is no longer dazed by stardust and I'm no longer walking in shadows. I know who and what I want: Varian Saar and our child, and a bright future together on Altair.''

Andrea sat up and embraced Jana. ''You're as smart as ever. No, smarter. I'm proud of you, Jana. Just think, we'll be married soon.''

Jana made a comical face and wriggled her fingers as she hummed part of the *Twilight Zone* theme. ''To aliens,'' she whispered. ''But such handsome and virile and nice aliens.''

Andrea giggled. ''You're right about that, Doc.''

Jana fell to the bed on her back and laughed. ''I haven't heard that quip in a long time. It's music to my ears, Andrea

McKay, music to my ears. Mercy, I'm glad you're here with me. We never imagined we would ever share a wild and wonderful adventure like this one."

Andrea held out her hand and used their youthful phrase: "Like sisters now, like sisters forever. I love you, Jana, my best friend."

Jana grasped it and repeated the words with a glowing smile.

The communications blackout and persistent pursuit in the cloaked ship continued for hours as the *Wanderlust* steadily caught up with Canissia's stolen vessel. They hadn't moved fast enough to create waverings in the nebulous clouds in their path that might be seen and suspected by her. Jana and Andrea came to the bridge to observe the climax of the episode that had begun many days ago on Darkar.

Varian smiled at Jana before he ordered Jarre to bring them up beside her. "Nigel, you handle weapons. I want to fire a blast across her belly and take out the engineering section to disable her. As soon as we get off that shot, Jarre, put us in position to take out her shuttle bay to prevent an escape attempt. Ferris, you be ready to take charge of our prisoner. If I get near that flaming-haired vixen, I might wring her treacherous throat."

"We have a *Spacer* ready to pursue if she tries to use an escape pod."

"Thanks, Jarre. Steady as she goes and stay alert, men. That woman is a tricky and unpredictable bitch."

"If she fires on us when we drop our shield, how do I respond?"

"She'll get a warning to surrender after I take out the engineering section. If she battles us, Nigel, follow standard defense procedure."

"Yes, sir."

Jana leaned over to ask Braq the meaning of those words.

The officer met her gaze and replied, "If surrender is refused and an attack is launched, we defend first, then destroy if endangered."

Jana glanced at the large ship on the screen where she and Andrea had been held captive. She read the markings and symbols to realize Canissia had told the truth about them. She recalled the woman's words and actions during their time together. "I don't think Canissia Garthon will surrender," she told Braq. "She was like a madwoman. If she can't escape punishment, she'll turn and fight, to the death."

"We think so, too, but it's her choice. We can't let her damage us."

Jana and Andrea watched the drama unfold. Ferris Laus joined the two women.

"Steady at the helm, slow and easy," Varian murmured as if to himself. "Jarre, let Nigel know when we're in position for him to fire. Do it in one shot, old friend, then take out her weapons bank," he related the change in orders. "Afterward, we'll swing around fast and get the shuttle bay before she can reach it. Jarre, line up for weapons bank second."

"If the bay is disabled, how will you get her off?" Jana asked Ferris.

"Through the *jerri* hatch." Seeing Jana's look of confusion, he explained, "That's a hatch atop the bridge for emergency rescue when other means of escape are cut off. We can set down our shuttle and connect to the other ship's hatch so she can climb aboard. It saves time in not having to don pressure suits and headgear, and usually there aren't enough of them available if a crew is large. That's how we had to save the crew of the *Galactic Gem*. It was slow going and we cut it close, too close for comfort. We had three minutes of safety zone before the ship blew when the last crewman got out."

"You mean all of you were almost killed?"

"Could have been, but Varian's a smart commander."

"And he has a loyal and skilled crew."

"Thanks, Jana. I know he was worried about being out of contact with you."

"Why?" How much, she mused, did this friend know or suspect?

"Because Taemin's on the loose. He should have been executed for treason. I can't believe Jurad would honor his law under the circumstances."

"Taemin is his son, Ferris."

"What son plots to kill his father? Just before we reached Cenza, one of Jurad's most trusted men overheard Taemin planning to murder him and Taemin's wife, blame it on rebels or spies, and take over as ruler. He was under guard when we arrived and exposed more evil about him."

"Someone helped him escape. If I were Jurad, I wouldn't trust him not to return and make another attempt. Royal blood shouldn't exempt him from punishment. Have they found any trace of him?"

"Not yet. We were hoping he wasn't the one who abducted you."

"Canissia is just as bad."

"I know about some of her crimes, but the others are sealed, for the Council's eyes only."

"Your people don't mind them keeping secrets like that?"

"No. It's always been that way. We trust them. To do what's best for us, they must be able to make decisions and act without the public's permission and knowledge. We've never had a *kadim* or a councilman or assemblyman who abused or betrayed his power and rank."

Until Segall Garthon, Jana's mind refuted. *But that will remain a secret*. She doubted Ferris knew anything about that guarded situation. "What about her father? Does he know about this crime yet?"

"Councilman Garthon retired recently. He gave bad health and exhaustion as his reasons. Supreme Commander Breccia Sard is taking his seat next week. It's a surety that Varian will be offered Sard's place."

"That's a big honor and powerful rank."

"Yes, it is, and Varian deserves it and is more than qualified for it."

"I'm sure he is and he'll—"

"In position, sir," Jarre said, halting everyone's conversations.

"Engineering section on target," Nigel reported from his panel.

"Fire at will!" Varian ordered as suspense mounted.

Action was swift after their cloaking shield was lowered to attack. Exterior noise was loud as a bright and large beam flashed across the darkening sky and crashed into the belly of the other ship. A giant gap resulted and items were sucked outside to float in space until salvaged.

Jana saw smoke, fire, and spinning debris. She witnessed other explosions through the hole in the crippled vessel. She waited and listened.

While Jarre moved the starship with speed and ease into position to take out any counterattack ability, Varian hailed their target, "Canissia Garthon, this is Commander Saar in the *Wanderlust* demanding your immediate surrender. There is no escape. Yield, woman, it's over."

Behind the redhead's screams of fury and insult, warning bells and buzzers could be heard over the monitor. "You bastard! How did you find me? How did you get through my shield? How dare you attack me!"

"Your shuttle bay is next after . . ." He paused as Nigel took out the weapons banks to prevent Canissia from firing powerful shots at them. Varian finished, "Your weapons are disabled. Resistance is now impossible."

Canissia yelled over the noise on her wounded vessel, "If you don't break off this attack and get to the penal colony fast, you won't be able to rescue that slut of yours before those barbaric prisoners screw her into oblivion. I left her hours ago. She's in terrible danger, so you'd better hurry."

Jana flushed a bright red at the crude remarks made about her in front of the men. Ferris grasped her hand and squeezed it. They exchanged smiles.

Jarre had taken them to the rear of the injured craft during the woman's rantings, and Nigel demolished the shuttle area.

Varian sent Jana a wink and smile. "I've already rescued Mrs. Triloni and Miss McKay," he responded. "They're aboard, safe and alive, and totally unharmed. That was me who sent you running from there. You can't hide from my new sensors; you can't escape; and you can't fight back. You have nothing to exchange for your freedom. You'll pay for your crimes. We have a place waiting for you on the female penal colony, for life."

"You wouldn't dare! Have you forgotten who I am?"

"Your father retired from the Council, so you will get no special treatment there. Taemin is exiled, so that ally is gone. You have no friends left, Cass. Your treachery and greed and hatred have done you in. Surrender, now!"

"I'll kill you both! I swear it. I'll kill you both one day."

"There is no escape from penal colonies, ever."

"I'll be the first. You won't get a night's sleep worrying about when I'll strike next. You'll be afraid to leave her alone for a minute. I've gotten to her twice and I'll do it again. I'll keep trying until she's dead. I'll never let Jana have you, and I'll never let you have her. Would you like to hear what she told me about you and Ryker? She said—"

The monitor went silent. Everyone exchanged curious glances.

"What happened?" Varian asked. "Did we lose contact?"

"I cut her off, sir," Vaiden said. "She was about to become crude and I didn't think it was necessary for us to be subjected to that."

"You did fine, Vaiden; thanks. Open one-way communications." After Vaiden obeyed, Varian said, "You can hear me, Cass, but we can't hear you. We cut you off before you got started with your lies and insults. We refuse to listen to them. You have two minutes to surrender before your ship goes critical and we're forced to leave the area. When I give the signal, all you can say is yes or no. I leave your fate and survival in your hands."

"Will anyone go aboard to capture her?" Jana asked Ferris.

"No, it's too dangerous. She could shoot anyone climbing inside, and her ship will go on self-destruct in two minutes. We heard the warning given over her ravings. Once it begins, we have twenty minutes to get her out and clear the area. Two minutes is all she can and will receive."

The short time span seemed to last an hour as everyone waited to see how the treacherous female would respond. When it ended, Varian asked for her answer. The channel remained silent. He asked again. Nothing. Varian warned her they were leaving and couldn't return.

"Answer me, Cass! This is your last chance to reply. I mean it. If your communications are disabled, signal us through the bridge *transascreen*."

They looked at the large window but saw no one and heard nothing.

"Don't be a fool, Cass, surrender. Your ship is going to blow soon, so we have to pull out of range. Time is up, woman. Give me your answer."

Varian looked at Nigel. "Safety zone?" he asked.

"We can't stay longer than one more minute. Even if she yields now, we don't have time to shuttle over, get her, and clear the area."

"Jarre, take us out of impact range. Nigel, keep sensors on her. We don't want any guesswork about her being on the ship when it blows."

"Did you think she would surrender?" Andrea asked Jana.

Jana didn't take her eyes off the ship on the screen. "No, I didn't. Canissia would rather go out in a blaze of freedom than live out her life on a penal colony where she has no power or privileges."

A pathetic voice came over the communicator. "Please, Varian, don't leave me here alone to die. I love you. I'm sorry. Please save me."

In a tone filled with resignation, the Commander replied, "I'm sorry, too, Cass, but you've waited too long. There's no time left for a rescue."

"You can't let me explode and burn! Think of all our years together. Some were happy. Please, I'm begging you. Come after me. We'll hurry."

"How much time, Nigel, before minimum—"

"No!" Jana shouted, startling everyone and causing Varian to look her way. "It's a trick to make you die with her. Even if there was enough time left, she would entrap you there. It's a trick, Varian. Please don't go."

Varian pulled his troubled gaze from Jana's and asked Nigel the same question. "If there's any chance, I have to take it, no matter who she is or what she's done. She might be telling the truth."

Jana looked at Varian and said, "If you leave this ship, so will I. If it's safe for you to go over in the shuttle, you won't mind me tagging along. If I can't go along, then it's too dangerous for you to do so. Right?"

Others quickly protested their commander's seeming intention to imperil his life saving a woman's they didn't think deserved it.

Varian silenced everyone. "I'll test her honesty," he said, then told Canissia that he was sending a security team over. "Be at the hatch," he ordered. "You'll have less than a minute to climb—"

"Don't bother, you bastard! It's you or no one."

Varian glanced at Jana. "I'm not coming over, Cass, so you can trap me there to blow up with you. Use the escape pod and we'll recover it."

"No. I'm going to die and you're to blame. You're killing me. *You.*"

"You're killing yourself, Cass; you have been for a long time. If you want to live, get to the escape pod now and jettison it. Time's wasting."

"If you hadn't brought Jana to Maffei, we would still be together."

"We had called it off long before I met Jana and our time together was brief. I never deceived you, Cass, never. I always told you that you weren't the woman for me. Every time you came after me, I told you the truth again."

"You want that alien bitch for your wife, don't you?"

"Yes, Cass, I do. I can marry her now that she's free."

Canissia sent a stream of crazy laughter over the system. "You can't have her. She's bound to Ryker forever. She's—"

Varian halted her words; he was sure they were about the baby. "Goodbye, Cass." He looked at Jarre and ordered him to get them out of there.

Varian put on a headset and had Canissia's last words fed only to his ears. He kept his head lowered to conceal the warring emotions racing through his body as the woman cursed him and Jana, boasted of her crimes, and painted mental pictures of what she wished she could do to the couple.

Jana walked to Varian's side, pulled off the tormenting headset, and smiled at him. "Don't do this to yourself. You aren't responsible for her black fate. She never intended to surrender. You did your duty to the best of your ability; that's all anybody can ask for. Let it go, Varian."

Varian's hand reached out and caressed her cheek. "Having power and rank aren't always easy, Jana. Some decisions are painful."

"I know, but there are some you can't make for others, like Canissia."

"I wanted to bring her in alive for questioning."

"You can question me later; she talked a great deal to me."

"Commander Saar, we're in safety zone and on stand-by," Jarre informed him.

"Thanks, Jarre," Varian said, recalling how many times in days gone by he had heard those words from Tesla Rilke, a friend he still missed.

All eyes were on the monitor when the stolen Pyropean vessel exploded. Ship fragments and debris scattered in all directions at a high rate of speed. What appeared to be fire was quickly extinguished without oxygen. Smoke swirled like clouds in the fading light. Then, it was quiet and dark again, and the ship was destroyed.

"Are you picking up an escape pod anywhere?" Varian questioned Vaiden.

"None, sir. She didn't attempt to save herself."

"I want every piece of debris checked to make certain she

didn't pull the same trick . . . Ryker and Jana did when they fled Taemin's trap.''

Varian stood with Jana near the *transascreen*. ''It's over, love,'' he said in a voice too quiet to be overheard. ''She was the last step.''

''What about Taemin? He's still alive and free, perhaps a threat.''

''Not anymore. He's in the Baracavia Galaxy. While you were resting, I received a message from Jurad via Brec. Jurad took away Taemin's wealth, ship, and crew; he had his son dropped on one of Bara's planets, which is at about the same stage of advancement as Earth. He's stranded there until they can manage space travel, so he's no threat to us. It's better than he deserves, but it's their law. Even if he got off that planet, he can't return to Pyropea; he's been exposed and banished for life. His marriage was abolished and his wife sent home to her family; the Tarterrians would never give him aid or sanctuary. Everyone in the Tri-Galaxy will soon know not to trust him or befriend him.''

''That's better than nothing. If we can sneak a visit later, I need to tell you some of Canissia's secrets.''

''Is that the only reason you want to see me in private?''

''What other motive could I have, you lusty space pirate?''

''What other motive indeed?'' he murmured with a seductive grin.

''Remember the first time we stood at this window together? You were proving my new fate to me. You said, and I quote: 'I had counted on your superior intelligence and keen perception to convince you that I spoke the truth,' and I responded: 'You win, Commander.' You said: 'I never doubted for that victory for a single minute, Jana.' Well, you space rogue, you have won—my heart and my commitment—and you always knew you would. I'm glad you never gave up on me, on us.''

''We'll be happy, Jana, I promise.''

''I know we will, all three of us.'' Jana glanced at Nigel and Andrea and amended, ''All *five* of us.''

"Nothing but debris, sir," Vaiden reported. "No survivor or pod."

"Take us to Darkar, Jarre."

"Yes, sir. What speed, sir?"

"Starlight. This beautiful and special lady is eager to get home and get her new life in order. Right, Jana?"

Chapter Twenty-one

"Are you sure? *Avatar* Kael?" Varian asked Jana once they were settled in his quarters.

"Yes, but it wasn't his fault and he doesn't even know what he's been doing." Jana explained what Canissia had told her about the planetary ruler of Zandia. "Now you'll be able to end her spell over him. I don't know how the formula of *Anti-Ren* has remained hidden from me and Tris. We'll search the records again after I reach Trilabs. We certainly don't want that powerful secret to fall into the wrong hands."

"You've been a superb partner in all of this, Moonbeam. I knew you were special the first moment I saw you. The more I was with you, the more I realized that truth. I chose well, the best, Jana Greyson. I'm only sorry it took so long for us to find peace and happiness."

"We have endured a lot of trials and tribulations, my love, but they're over now. Besides, some of them were very stimulating and educational and strengthening. How many people can live on the edge and taste danger without actually getting hurt? All we've been through has brought us closer together. We do make an excellent team, Rogue Saar.''

''I wouldn't want to repeat any of those episodes. I almost lost you.''

''I almost lost you, too, during that *Galactic Gem* task.''

Varian related the stirring and perilous tale. ''It was my father's old ship, Jana, the place where he and Shara met, where she began her evil plot and selfish siege on him, and where she birthed a series of tragedies for many people. As soon as I read the ship's markings, I had a bad feeling. She was showing signs of age, but she was still a sturdy transport vessel. She was hauling highly volatile *Barine* for chemical lasers, Ryker's invention and products. The longer we took and the closer we came to mutual destruction, the more I could hear Shara and Ryker laughing and taunting me about missing my deadline with you. It was almost as if their evil spirits were determined to wreak revenge on me from the grave.''

''She's gone and can never harm us again. So is her misguided son.''

''It doesn't look as if I'll have to expose Shara's survival and the extent of Ryker's treachery to Maal and Jurad. In a way, I'm relieved. I think the past can finally die.''

''I'm glad, too. Maybe everyone involved can find peace now, even Maal. And Tirol, too; at last he knows your father was innocent of Shara's deceits and wasn't to blame in any way for the murder of his daughter. I realize now what drove you to such a desperate ruse to obtain peace. Losing your parents to Shara's wickedness and Ryker's constant provocation gave you good reasons to hate and battle for years.''

''That's over now. For the first time, I'm free of bitter conflicts, sacrifices, and ghosts.''

She knew from the serene look in his sapphire eyes that his statement was true. The wild and reckless roller coaster ride they had been on since meeting each other had ended tonight with Canissia's defeat. Yet, life with this irresistible alien would always be stimulating and exciting, never dull. And she wouldn't want it any other way.

"I'm happy you decided to give me a reprieve on my deadline and gave me this chance to prove myself to you. I won't disappoint you."

Jana rolled him to his back and mounted his body with agility. "I'm a smart woman, remember? You know what the real problem was?" That question got his full attention. "You were trying to convince me of the truth while wearing Ryker's face and using his identity. It was him I was resisting and doubting. I was drawn to you as Ryker because of your resemblance in looks, and your brilliant personality kept shining through, but I couldn't trust you or respond fully to you while you were him. But when you became yourself again," she murmured as she caressed his face, "I was lost. All the love and passion you created in me, then suppressed, surfaced again to assail me. So, you see, your battle to win me was easy as soon as Rogue Saar returned to life. It's you and only you I love and want."

Varian gazed at the woman straddling his hips on the bed. His fingers slipped under the filmy material of her gown to stroke the outer sides of her sleek thighs. "It wasn't easy at any point. I was worried and scared, and I didn't know how to deal with those emotions."

Jana peeled off her transparent robe and flung it to the floor. She leaned forward to trail her fingertips over his broad shoulders and masculine chest. "Well, you don't have to do it anymore. You have me enthralled for life, my handsome and virile captor."

"As if that would be long enough with a woman like you."

With seductive leisure, she placed her hands on either side of his neck. With a slow but stimulating pace, she drifted them down his chest and teased over the ridges of his rib cage. Her gaze admired what she viewed and her hands adored what they touched. "You are the most splendid male specimen in existence in any galaxy, my dashing space pirate. How could I possibly let you escape? I love you."

"I love you, too, Moonbeam, more than you know or can

nagine.'' He eased his thumbs beneath the thin straps of her ightgown and pulled them off her golden shoulders. With her ssistance, he slid them over her hands. He watched the silky arment snake down her torso to pool like green water around er naked hips. With the bottom of her gown hiked up, only er feminine region was concealed from his smoldering gaze. air a blend of sunshine and moonlight tumbled down her back nd spilled over her shoulders. The colors of her eyes seemed swirl into a fusion of blue sky, verdant grass, and violet ower. She reminded him of a goddess come to life. His hands noved ever so slowly and provocatively up her arms and over er collarbone; they stroked her neck and roamed to her breasts. le cupped them, quivering in anticipation and pleasure. ''You re exquisite, my priceless treasure.''

Jana flattened her palms against the backs of his muscled rms and locked gazes with him. ''Just make certain you do o more plundering abroad after you've laid claim to me.''

''How could I when you own my wits and heart and all my trength? It is you who are the captor and master and I, your bedient slave.''

Jana massaged his arms with her palms. She used an exaggerated southern accent and sultry mood as she murmured, ''I vill be your fountain of love; I will quench your great thirst. Drink from me as you will and become intoxicated.''

He chuckled. ''You're teasing me, but it's with the truth, voman.''

Jana pulled the bunched gown over her head and cast it side. ''You have created a bold and wanton hussy in me, 'arian Saar. With you, I want to explore everything, to taste very pleasure.'' For a moment, she remembered that their best riends were in a room not far away, also sneaking a night of assionate lovemaking. ''I hope no one comes checking on ny of us tonight or we'll have some tough explaining to do.''

''Soon, Moonbeam, that won't be necessary.''

''I can hardly wait. But we have a few tiny matters to omplete first.''

"Not tonight. This time belongs only to us." He clasp
her neck and drew her head down so their mouths could fus

Their unclad bodies pressed together as they kissed a
caressed, enflaming their desires to a higher and brighter pitc
His teeth nibbled at her neck, shoulder, and ear. His hot brea
caused her to tingle with suspense of what lay ahead. S
sighed in contentment and her heart pounded in fiery arousa
eager to meld their bodies into one.

Jana arched as she eased his manhood within her pleadi
core. She rocked back and forth and rotated side to side as s
gave them blissful sensations. If any doubts about him h
truly ever existed, they were gone, conquered by their mutu
powerful love and entwined destinies.

Tonight was a fusion of hearts, a forging of their enti
beings, a total commitment to each other.

Jana's fiery responses increased Varian's hunger. He grasp
her body and rolled her to her back, placing himself atop he
Her ardor and need, and his own, inspired him to hold nothi
back. Ecstasy's flames engulfed him in a blazing glow th
only fulfillment could extinguish and then, only for a sho
time because his need for her was perpetual. His deft han
roved her luscious body and his lips savored her delectab
mouth, bringing them both to uncontrolled tremors of deligh
She uttered moans of feverish excitement as she became breat
less and rigid with urgency for him, a need he was only to
happy to appease.

They rode the waves of rapture until sweet and potent releas
swept over them both. They spoke of love, shared love, an
became love itself. The strong currents carried them awa
washed them clean of all troubles, and put them ashore amon
the stars. As they relaxed and calmed in the languid aftergl
of their powerful experience, they nestled together and kisse

"I told you I would fight for you, woman," Varian reminde
her with a grin, "and my victory is beyond words to describe."

"If this is how to celebrate, I shall challenge you to a batt
every day and night, especially if this is the weapon you us

to fight with,'' she teased, brushing her hand over his softening manhood.

''You're right, Jana Greyson, I have created a brazen vixen in you.''

''You can't blame me for that, Sir Pirate. You captured me and molded me into the woman I should be, a woman who could win the greatest prize in the Universe. You blazed into my life like a fiery comet, seared me with your touch, and carried me away in your wake.''

''And I shall never release you from it, Moonbeam, never.''

They talked for a while about many things, then slept cuddled together.

When they reached Darkar, Tristan and Martella joined them to report that their work in Trilabs was finished and Tristan had located the formula for *Anti-Ren*. Jana and Varian were surprised to learn it came from the wormlike creature inside the orchid-type flower Varian had used during his attempts to dupe her. A relieved and shame-faced Kagan greeted them with open exuberance and sincere contrition.

''You don't have to apologize, my friend,'' Jana told him. ''It wasn't your fault. You should remember she got to me once before with her cunning and skills even though I was under the protection of the *kadim* himself. We also fell prey to Taemin's cunning trap. It's over and we're safe. Please don't chastise yourself again.''

''You are a kind and intelligent woman, Jana Triloni. Thank you.''

''Soon, that will become Jana Saar,'' Varian said with a smile.

''Maal wishes to speak with you the moment you return,'' Kagan revealed almost reluctantly. ''He's worried about you, too.''

''I'll talk to him now if you'll get him on the *telecom* for me.''

* * *

"How did the conversation with Maal go?" Varian asked when she returned to the house and met him in the bedroom.

"He was overjoyed to see me back safe and alive. He had nothing but praise for you for rescuing his late grandson's wife. I related news of the fate of Taemin and Canissia; he's relieved they won't be threats to me anymore. I told him you used Ryker's new systems to find me and save me, and that made him proud and happy. I realized afterward perhaps I shouldn't have mentioned them to him or anyone."

He embraced her. "It's all right, Moonbeam; he'll learn about our new technology soon enough from other sources. So will Pyropea. It will make them respect our powers and strengths even more, so they won't be tempted to break their treaties. You and I worked too hard to get them to see them destroyed." He looked down at her. "We have to decide how to reveal our revived romance to everyone. I want us to marry next week."

As they talked and planned, they didn't suspect that Maal Triloni would die peacefully in his sleep that same night and remove any potential problem when her pregnancy was revealed in a few months.

Varian and Jana's marriage was delayed by a quick trip to Androas to pay their final respects to ex-*Kadim* Maal. After they viewed the three Triloni bodies in glassed cases in a stately mausoleum built for that purpose, Varian announced to the new ruler of the Androasian Empire, *Effecta* Dakin Agular, his plans to marry Jana the following week.

The ruler congratulated them and seemed genuinely pleased with the news. He credited Jana and Varian with the changes in Ryker which had inspired the Trilabs owner to evoke peace from his grandfather. He also thanked Jana for making the last days of the two Trilonis happy ones.

It was no secret to Agular that Jana and Varian had been

lovers long before she met and married the Androasian prince. He assumed a terrible misunderstanding had parted them and a heroic rescue and reunion had reunited them. Being a man who believed each day should be lived and enjoyed to the fullest, he was pleased to see Jana so radiant and happy.

Jana and Varian celebrated and danced at the party following their marriage. All their friends and close crewmen were present to share in the glorious event. Even a smiling and genial Dr. Mirren was there with his family.

Jana whirled about the floor in an ivory gown designed and made by a beaming Andrea McKay. It was of beaded lace and delicate embroidery with a fitted bodice and Victorian-style neckline of soft and sheer mesh. It featured a keyhole back, full skirt, and semicathedral train that was draped over one arm for easy movement. Seeded pearls and small silk flowers were secured to her tawny hair, piled for the occasion in curls atop her head. Jana wished there was more to an alien wedding ceremony than agreeing to unite, signing a legal document, and having a bracelet snapped on her wrist. But she was in Maffei and must follow their customs and traditions. At least the reception helped make the event romantic and special.

Flowers gave off heady fragrances; music was dreamy; champagne flowed, and food was abundant. All the guests enjoyed themselves to the fullest.

As she danced with *Kadim* Tirol Trygue, the galactic ruler said, "You have made my beloved grandson the happiest and proudest man alive. Thank you, Jana, for coming into his life. I am glad you have forgiven us for the way in which you entered our world. I know times have been hard for you, but you have my sincere gratitude forever. I do not believe any woman anywhere could have accomplished what you and Varian did. I am pleased and honored to have you as part of my family. I look forward," he leaned closer and whispered, "to having another little loved one soon."

Jana beamed with joy. "So do we, sir. I want to thank you

for how generously you have accepted me and for having our wedding in your home today.''

"There are two more marriages coming soon: Tristan's to Martella and Nigel's to your best friend. It seems love and romance are in the air. Perhaps it is a contagious infection even I can catch again one day. Perhaps I should search your world for the perfect woman as Varian and Nigel did.''

They danced another time before an eager Varian claimed his radiant bride. "Every moment you are away from me is sheer torment, woman.''

"We certainly can't have my groom suffering. What can I do to help?''

"You've already done it, Jana, you love me and married me and you're carrying my child. You've helped me obtain peace in the Tri-Galaxy. No man could be more blessed or fortunate than I am.''

Jana gazed at the two items that exposed their bond to the world: a ring of gold on her left hand with *caritrary* stones that matched her eyes—as was Earth's custom—and a gold bracelet encrusted with matching gems to symbolize that of Maffei's. They were from two different and distant worlds but bound together by great love and respect. They had overcome every obstacle stubborn fate had placed in their path to obtain this blissful goal. True, they were perfect for each other. She sent him a mischievous smile and asked, "How about twice blessed, my love?''

He looked at the ivory-clad beauty in confusion. "What do you mean?''

Jana pretended to toy with the golden sunburst on his rich wine dress uniform. "When Tris did my examination yesterday to make certain all was well with me so my future husband wouldn't worry about all the celebrating, he made a surprising discovery.'' She locked her merry gaze with his inquisitive one. "Being an extremely fertile space pirate, you have deposited more than one seed in your adoring mate. We're expecting twins, a boy and a girl. What do you think about naming them Galen and Amaya?''

"Twins . . . A boy and a girl . . . That's wonderful news, Moonbeam," he responded in astonishment.

"I thought you'd feel that way, and carrying twins will give me a plausible excuse for getting so plump and so fast. We'll still have to confine me to Altair at the end of my pregnancy so we can conceal the babies' birth dates. It will be more work and time involved but twice the fun. Right, my love?"

"It was certainly fun planting their seeds in you that night on Luz."

Jana stroked his strong jawline and savored his expression of pride. "You lusty rake, whatever shall I do with you and two children at once?"

"Love us, Moonbeam, just love us."

"I do."

Nigel and Andrea danced by and sent the glowing couple smiles.

"I suggested a plan they can use so Andrea can see her parents and they can meet Nigel," Jana told her husband. "Once a year, they can visit the McKays under the cover story of being secret agents for our government, a perfect excuse for why Andrea can't reveal where they live and why she can't be reached by them. At least they can see she's alive and well and happy. Nigel thinks it will work and, of course, Andrea is delighted."

"What a cunning woman I've captured. You never cease to amaze me, Jana Saar. It's a perfect solution."

Tirol joined them for a short time. He was told about the twins and their chosen names, one for his deceased daughter, Varian's mother, and the other for Varian's father. The older man was thrilled by the news.

When the newlyweds were alone again, Jana whispered, "I can hardly wait to get home and have you all to myself. With babies on the way, my time alone with my husband is limited. I'll have to take advantage of it."

"Altair will never be the same, never be better. I'm glad you turned Darkar over to the Supreme Council. Grandfather was surprised and delighted. They would have purchased it, Moonbeam; it was yours."

"We don't need the money, and I wanted to break all ties to Trilabs and the past. I'm a Saar now and only want Saarian things around me."

As they enjoyed their last dance of the evening, Varian held Jana in his possessive embrace. All dark shadows had fled and he vowed he would never let her slip through his fingers again. Despite the people watching them, their lips met in a kiss that aroused their passions. They experienced a joy and contentment which both had feared lost for eternity not long ago. Peace ruled their lives and hearts and reigned in the Tri-Galaxy. Tonight, the gods and fates smiled on Jana and Varian Saar. As the newlyweds gazed into each other's eyes and smiled, time seemed to cease for the Earthling beauty and the alien starship commander as they were assailed by the intensity, magic, and power of a love which had reached beyond the planets and stars themselves to bind their destinies into one.

Varian repeated what he had told her on his ship months ago: "This is how it should be for us, Moonbeam, magic and rapture in each other's arms. It will be like this forever; I promise."

Jana smiled and said, "I'll hold you to that vow, my love."

Moondust Rapture

As the sated Gods gather to watch mortals below,
The happy Fates laugh joyfully, for only they know:
Two hearts joined by love, Aliens no more;
Light conquered darkness; fiery passions soar.
Stardust has settled, Shadows have fled;
Magic and Rapture now rule in their stead . . .

The End, or is it only a beginning for new adventures . . .

Author's Note

I hope you enjoyed this flight into fantasy with me in *Stardus And Shadows* and will also enjoy Book I in this science-fictio romance series: *Moondust And Madness*, to be reprinted b Pinnacle/Zebra Books in November '92 to see how it all began It was exciting to travel beyond the Milky Way with Jana an Varian once more and you, my loyal readers, made it possibl with your many requests; thank you.

If you would like a current Janelle Taylor newsletter, com plete booklist, and bookmark, send a long self-addressed stamped envelope to:

Janelle Taylor Newsletter
P.O. Box 211646
Martinez, Georgia 30917-1646

Until we meet again on the pages of my next novel, I wis you fun reading, great romance, and an exciting fantasy or tw of your own.